INSPIRED BY A TRUE STORY

FREEDOM'S EDGE

A TALE OF CRISES AND VICTORY

JAGDISH GOSWAMI

Lucky Bat Books

A Lucky Bat Book

Freedom's Edge
Copyright 2015 by Jagdish Goswami

Cover Artist: Brandon Swann
Maps by Brandon Swann
Cover photo of Paramaribo Harbor, Suriname, by William Stanhope

Published by Lucky Bat Books

ISBN: 978-1-943588-14-5
10 9 8 7 6 5 4 3 2 1

Also available in digital formats.

ACKNOWLEDGEMENTS

I have been richly blessed with friends all throughout my life, starting from my earliest school day at an international school in India. It would be difficult to express my deep and sincere gratitude to all of them; however, most distinguished of them were Bijan Adlparvar, Remy Rowhani, Faiezeh Alavi, and Faiezeh Taife, who were all instrumental in giving me the gift of faith and an understanding that all of us on earth are like one family and that all mankind are citizens of the home mother earth.

Undoubtedly, I'd like to acknowledge my brother and sisters and their families, all of whom have always been there in both rough times and good times. I deeply appreciate my brother, Mukund, and my two sisters, Kumud and Hansa, for all the love they have showered on me.

To my teachers Dr. Ray, Mrs. Johnson, Mr. Behi, and Rezwan-khanum, and Mr. Afshin in school … I thank them for their dedicated work in guiding me to become a worthy citizen of this planet.

To the friends I made during my time as a medical student in India, Dr. Jayesh Shah, Dr. Jitendra Jadav, Dr. Chandresh Batra, Dr. Govindlal Bhanusali, Dr. Lekhraj Patel, Dr. Narender Chawla, Dr. Sheela Bharani, and Dr Balvant Arora, and my friends from the faculty of Engineering and Technology at the Maharaja Sayajirao University of Baroda Dinesh, Rajni, and Jay Bachkaniwala … all of these friends have been sources of strength and support at various stages in my life. To Mr. Ambalani who throughout my medical college and beyond has always been there for me when I most need. To Dr. Alexander Reyzelman, who has been a mentor and guide in many aspects of life. To Mr. Ghalilli and his family, who have all provided me with encouragement.

Other people to whom I owe much gratitude are Keely Smith of Grass Valley, for her wholehearted support toward the success of this book. To my attorney and good friend Harry Roth, and to Dr. Kayvan Haddadan, and Dr. Venugopal Bellum. Also, to my very close friend in Australia, Kaywan

Akhtarkhaveri, who is like a brother to me and has been a source of great inspiration all throughout my life.

There are many whom I may have forgotten to mention, and I ask for their forgiveness.

While writing this book there have been friends such as David Sutton, who helped with the technical facts need to strengthen the story. David is a writer and editor in his own capacity, and I greatly appreciate his contribution.

Lastly, but certainly not least, heartfelt thanks to Jessica Santina, the editing wizard. You and the rest of the wonderful people at Lucky Bat Books have buttressed this novel and have turned a dream into a reality, and for that I cannot adequately express my heartfelt gratitude, however much I try.

DEDICATION

This book is dedicated to my dear dad and mom, who sacrificed their lives for the education and development of all four of their children, even though they themselves did not have the opportunity to be educated. If they were present, they would have been thrilled to witness the publication of this book. To my dear father-in-law, Mr. Alavi, may his soul continue to progress in all the worlds; he was a man whose depth of sincerity, love, and care were always showered on us. To my dear mother-in-law, Nayereh-khanum, who still continues to encourage us in all of our endeavors until her last breath on this earthly plane.

And to my dear and beloved wife, Tahereh. This work of writing was highly encouraged by her, and her presence is a source of joy and happiness under all circumstances. We have traveled together to many parts of the world, including Guyana and Suriname, where the birth of this story took place in my mind.

Waterlooplein Square, Amsterdam
(temporary home of Roseweig family)

Hoorn

Haarlem,
in the principality of
Haarlemmermeer

Home of
Mijnheer Anders

Amsterdam

Netherlands

Rotterdam

Antwerp

Ghent

Brussels

Port of Ghent

Belgium

Germany

HOLLAND AND WESTERN EUROPE, 1942. AREA WHERE THE NAZIS' PURSUIT
OF THE ROSEWEIGS AND ADELMANNS BEGINS.

SURINAME, SOUTH AMERICA, HOME AND BASE CAMP OF EXPATRIATE
MARINE CORPS COLONEL ED BELTRAN.

Paramaribo

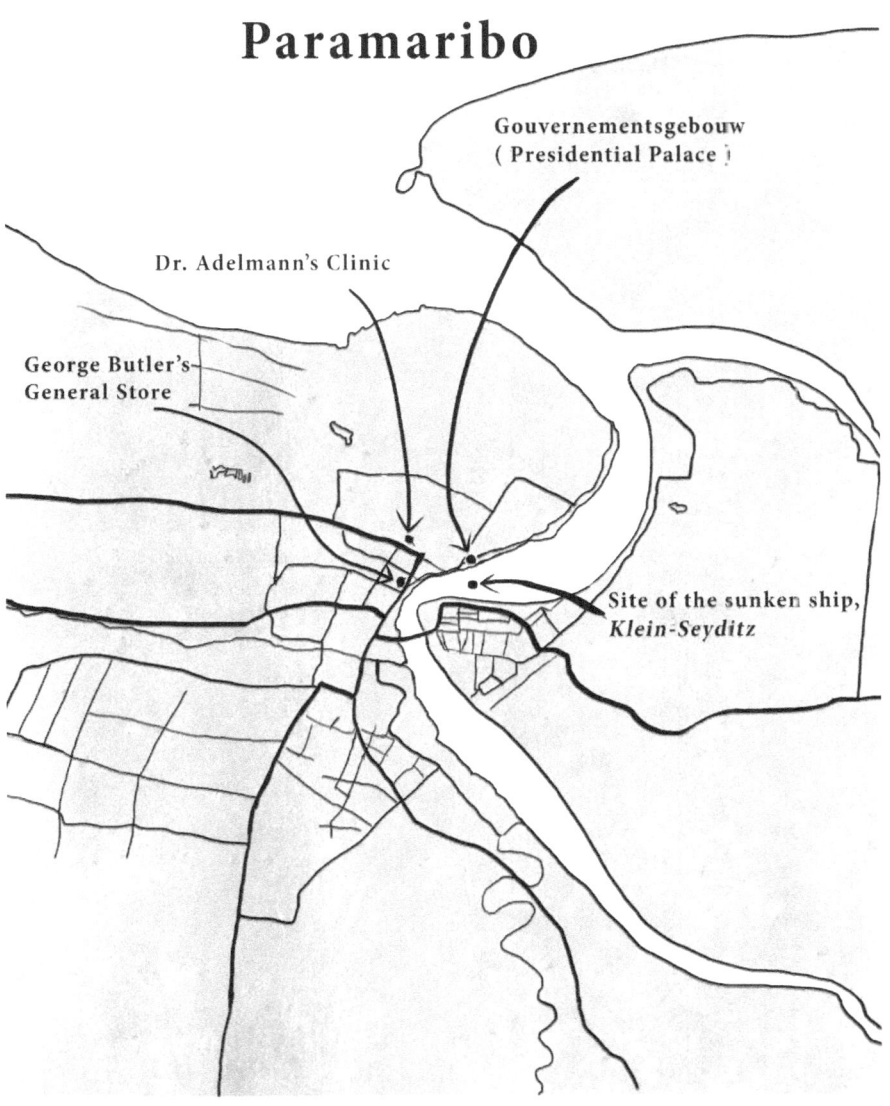

Gouvernementsgebouw
(Presidential Palace)

Dr. Adelmann's Clinic

George Butler's
General Store

Site of the sunken ship,
Klein-Seyditz

PARAMARIBO, SURINAME, AND SITES OF IMPORTANCE FOR REFUGEES IN
PLOT TO ESCAPE NAZIS.

Contents

PROLOGUE

It was going to be a bumpy flight. Hannah sighed deeply as she buckled herself into her compact little airplane seat and braced herself for the twenty-minute flight from Paramaribo, Suriname's relatively small capital city, due west to Nieuw Nickerie, the even smaller coastal city that her dear Aunt Sarah called home.

Hannah's perceptive 13-year-old granddaughter, Rachel, had heard the sigh. "What, Gran?" she asked, looking earnestly at her grandmother with big, dark eyes.

"Huh?" Hannah asked, pulled from her fatalistic imaginings of twisted metal—this tiny, single-engine puddle-jumper being carried out to sea. "Oh, nothing, darling. I'm just...you know. Tired. Anxious. I just hate these little planes." She patted Rachel's hand. The girl, so used to sleeping until midday now that she was a teenager, had been unable to sleep at all during the overnight trip that had taken her from New York to Paramaribo via Miami and Port of Spain. By now, she looked positively wan.

"How are *you* hanging in there? Are you excited to meet your family?" Hannah asked.

Rachel mustered enough energy to nod her head and smile weakly.

"I am!" came a high-spirited voice from the window seat across the aisle. Rachel's nine-year-old brother, Josh, appeared to be none the worse for wear after the more-than-twelve-hour travel day. His head, with its sprout of dark hair in a cowlick at the crown, was silhouetted against the strange gray-yellow light filtering in through the tiny airplane window. "When will we get there, Gran?"

"Joshie, I told you," said Hannah's daughter, Rose, disinterestedly, from the aisle seat next to Josh. She continued looking at her magazine as she spoke. "It's probably another half-hour. Just relax."

"Wow, look!" Josh cried, pointing out the window. "That wind is really blowing, Ma! Look!"

At this, Rose lifted her head to check on her mother. "You okay, Mom?" Hannah's knuckles were white from the vice grip her hands had on her arm rests.

Rose knew Hannah had never enjoyed flying anyway, even in the best of weather. In fact, except for the occasional train trip to upstate New York to visit her grandchildren, or to Atlantic City for a weekend with her girlfriends, Hannah rarely left the comforts of her Manhattan home. As lively and active as Hannah had always been, she'd never enjoyed travel—not surprising considering what it had always entailed when she'd been a child. Now, at 54, she found herself simply too far away from all she really wanted to see—her remaining family members. What was the point in going anywhere else? Plus, without Aunt Sarah to inspire her and make every outing feel like an adventure, travel simply held little appeal anymore. Rose cut her mother some slack; she figured her mother could hardly be blamed for this idiosyncrasy, considering what the woman had lived through.

But when Sarah had called while Hannah waited for the taxi that would take her to JFK Airport, it had been to warn her skittish niece about the unseasonably bad weather headed toward the coast of Suriname. Hannah's stomach lurched.

"I just wanted to prepare you, love," Sarah said. "They're predicting some storms."

Hannah knew that, in equatorial Suriname, rain was a daily occurrence for at least half the year. But what Sarah meant by "storms" was gale-force winds, tidal waves, and flooding. Despite being outside the hurricane zone, Suriname was no stranger to tropical storms. That's why Hannah, having long considered a return to Suriname with her grandchildren for a Diwali celebration, had thought a November trip, just outside the late-summer rainy season, would be nicely timed. So much for that plan.

She fidgeted with the mother-of-pearl buttons on her peach-colored silk shirt, then pretended to check her fingernails and appear cool and collected, but her show couldn't hide the gasps she made with each bobble of the little airplane as it made its ascent.

Nonetheless, if the plane could stay aloft for the next twenty minutes, Hannah would be reunited with her beloved Sarah, the aunt Hannah knew was still just as spirited, fiercely loyal, fun-loving, and beautiful at 65 as she had been forty years before, when Hannah herself had been a child of 14. Despite her fears, Hannah began to feel a different fluttering in her stomach: the butterflies of anticipation. She could almost feel her youth returning with each mile she drew closer to Sarah. She peered over at Josh, bouncing in his seat. *He's just like I was at his age,* thought Hannah.

"Hey, Gran!" Josh erupted, pointing excitedly out his window. "I think I see Auntie Sarah's house!"

⧗

NIEUW NICKERIE, SURINAME, SOUTH AMERICA

A pepper pot was just the thing to serve on a cool, stormy day like this, Sarah Beltran thought satisfactorily to herself. The warm fragrance of the stew's combination of beef, chili peppers, onions, and cloves emanated from the stew, which bubbled away on the stovetop.

Now that everything had been done in preparation for her family's arrival, Sarah was at a loss for what to do with all her nervous energy. She filled a kettle with water for tea but then thought twice and went to pour herself a shot of rum instead.

Among the many hobbies Ed had taken up in their forty years of marriage was a brief foray into distilling his own brand of spiced rum. Sarah had rolled her eyes and grudgingly gone along with the idea, thinking it silly but wanting to be a supportive wife. Then she'd tasted the heavenly stuff, and all qualms evaporated. She'd thought it a shame when Ed had abandoned the idea within a year's time, but a few cherished bottles still remained in the liquor cabinet, and Sarah thought that if any moment warranted cracking open a bottle, it was this one, on the precipice of seeing Hannah again and meeting her niece's family for the first time. It was Diwali, a Hindu festival celebrating the new moon that had become a holy time for this family, who were all coming together—for the first time since that fateful day forty years ago—to celebrate the hard-won freedom they had earned that day and which they all now enjoyed. But in the process, they would also be dredging up some difficult memories that Sarah had worked hard to bury.

Sarah knocked back the shot, gave the pepper pot another stir with the big wooden spoon, and looked out the window. Palm trees waved in the wind, but there sat Ed on the pier, still stubbornly fishing in the roiling sea.

"Well, hell, I might as well," she said, and poured herself another shot, keeping an eye on Ed to be sure she wouldn't be caught raiding their stash. She sighed with the relaxation she was already feeling from the sweet, spicy liquid warming her all the way to her belly.

She put the shot glass down on the counter, wiped her hands on her apron, and then looked down at herself. *Look at those wrinkled old hands,* she thought to herself. *I'm a far cry from the beauty I used to be when Hannah saw me last, that's for sure. God, what will she think of me!* She resolved to go put on another coat of lipstick.

Sarah bustled into the bathroom and took a good look at herself. She stared into her own eyes, evaluating whether they betrayed her full 65 years. Not a trace of the wateriness she so often saw in older people's eyes could be seen in her own; they were as richly brown and piercing as ever, not sunken or lined with wrinkles, as her sister Rebecca's eyes had been at 65. Rebecca's eyes had seen too much too soon…but then again, so had Sarah's.

Sarah had thought that 65 had seemed *so old* then. But she had been widowed at 24, so what did age really mean, anyhow? Here Sarah was now, 65, and she still felt as young as she had when she'd arrived in this tiny country by ship a little more than forty years ago. And if she was being honest with herself, although some gray streaks now mingled with the black of her long hair, which she now unfurled from its bun in order to scrutinize it carefully, she certainly didn't look *old*. Apparently, the coastal life had agreed with her and had kept her young. That and, of course, Ed.

She nodded once at herself in the mirror, satisfied, then wrapped her hair back into its bun and turned off the light. On her way back to the kitchen, she stopped to look appraisingly at the living room, the lay of the bungalow-by-the-sea that Ed's security business had enabled them to build years ago. It wasn't so much small as cozy. Ed hadn't wanted much, just a view of the sea, a pier for fishing, and her. Sarah blushed as she remembered him whispering this in her ear in their early days together. The house had been a lover's nest, and in every corner of the bungalow, from the framed snapshots of their honeymoon that hung above the couch to the hand-carved, four-poster bed where they had conceived Louise, their one and only child, 39 years ago. It extended to the oil paintings Sarah had done in the early years of their marriage, which depicted Rebecca, Jacob, and their children, as well as Ed, their darling daughter, and beloved scenes of her homeland, Germany.

The house still felt this way. Love lived here. She was proud to have helped create a home that she knew felt warm and inviting.

Still, nervous energy clawed at the edges of the nice buzz that the rum had given her. Sarah glanced at the clock, then calculated quickly. Hannah and her family would be hiring a car from the airport. They could arrive in twenty minutes, maybe even less. She picked up the phone and dialed her daughter's number.

Louise answered on the first ring with an exuberant, "Hi, Mom!"

She knew her mother so well, could envision the pacing that must be going on at her parents' house right now as they anxiously awaited their guests' arrival.

Sarah giggled at herself. "Am I that easy to read?"

"Mom, please," Louise playfully teased her. "You've called me three times a day for the last week. You need to *calm down*. She's your niece, for crying out loud."

"It's not just Hannah, love. It's…well, it's everyone. We've never met Hannah's grandkids, you know that. But also, it's Diwali. Yael's coming. And George and Dr. Ben… You're too young, you came along years afterward. You couldn't realize that it's because of them that we're here, that we're alive. We owe them *everything*."

Louise remained silent for a moment, taking that in. "I know, Mom. I may not have been around during that period of time, but I grew up hearing all those stories. I know them by heart. But is that why you're nervous?"

"I'm not really nervous, love, just excited," Sarah said, realizing that she did sound like a nervous Nellie. "Plus, we haven't all been together in decades. I just want it to go well. I want everyone to enjoy themselves."

"Well, I made the apple *kuchen* for dessert, and it came out beautifully," Louise offered, lightheartedly. "It may not be as good as Aunt Rebecca's or my cousin Hannah's, but I followed the recipe to the letter, and I'm feeling confident! What else is on the menu?"

"Pepper pot's bubbling away on the stove. George says he's bringing some sort of Indian dish, I can't remember what it was. At least we'll have something that's actually appropriate for Diwali, huh?" She laughed.

"What's Dad doing right now? Fishing?"

"What else?" Sarah said. "I'm going to have to drag him in any minute; it's looking like cats and dogs out there. I work out my nervous energy by calling you, and he does things his way." Sarah cast a glance out the side window to see the garden flowers whipping in the wind. A few fat rain drops began to fall. "Oh, it's raining now. Love, thanks for indulging me, but now I'd better go. When will you be here with the kids?"

"Around 5:30. Relax. Did you talk to Amos yet?"

"Oh, no, I forgot! I need to do that right now. Bye, love."

Sarah felt a swat at her bottom as she leaned down to hang up the phone. Ed, whistling a tune as he rubbed the rain out of his thick, gray hair, was still as flirtatious with Sarah as he had been when they'd met. "Hell of a storm brewing!" he called on his way to the bedroom.

"Ed, they'll be here soon," she called to his rain-soaked T-shirt. "For goodness sake, put on a nice shirt!"

She picked up the handset again and dialed Amos' number. Her nephew, older than his sister, Hannah, by four years, still resided in Paramaribo, where he had a thriving business as one of the city's most successful tour operators.

"'*ell*-o," called Amos cheerfully into the phone.

"It's me," said Sarah.

"I'll be there for dinner, I promise," Amos pleaded. Clearly, she'd over-played the nagging aunt this past week.

"No, I just remembered something. Did you get a hold of Dr. Ben, or George?"

"Uhhh…"

"Amos! I gave you *one* job!"

"No! That's not what I meant! Look, I called Dr. Ben, but it was a long time ago. I just haven't followed up. The man's in his eighties, Sarah. I don't think he understood what I was asking."

"Are you kidding? Dr. Ben's sharper than all of us. Good, he'll be here. What about George?"

"I called that number you gave me for his daughter's house and left a message. He hasn't called me back."

"How long ago was that?" Sarah pressed accusingly, as if Amos were still a teenager.

"I don't know…a few weeks?"

"Well, there's nothing we can do now. Hopefully Talia can be trusted to pass it along. Oh, Amos, you know better than anyone that they really *must* be here. How can we have such a celebration without the two men who made our lives what they are?"

"You're right, Sarah, I know. I've been a bit distracted with work I'll try them both again today."

"And call Yael, too," Sarah said. "Maybe she can bring Ben. Hannah's dying to see them all again, and meet their families."

"Okay, I'll do it when I hang up," Amos promised.

Sarah replaced the phone and looked out the window worriedly. The torrential rain seemed to be falling sideways. This year's Diwali festival would not be celebrated with the traditional lanterns on the streets of Paramaribo. What a shame.

It was a good thing Ed had tied the furniture down outside. Lightning lit up the sky, and an angry clap of thunder ripped from east to west over her head.

Oh, my Hannah. Be safe, love.

Sarah returned to the stove. As she gave the pepper pot another stir, she remembered another day forty years ago, when she had listened from inside a dark, terrifying place to another cruel storm raging around her. As she prepared for the joyful reunion ahead, she recalled that on that long-ago day, none of them had known whether they would ever see the sunshine again.

CHAPTER 1

JUNE 21, 1942
AFTERNOON

WATERLOOPLEIN SQUARE, AMSTERDAM, HOLLAND

Hannah huddled, trying to escape the rain that came bouncing in through the place in the wall that the bomb had shattered. She could hear her Papa and Mutter talking in low voices in the next room, where the tile stove still stood, its wounds patched with daubed mud. In exchange for the cooking it enabled them to do, they fed it bits of splintered furniture and scraps of coal, which Papa and Hannah's brother, Amos, found sometimes in the street when the Nazi supply trucks had passed. Ezekiel, Hannah's infant brother, clung to his mother despite the cloying heat of the humid, bombed-out building they now called home.

Hannah could not bear to be by the stove in this heat, and despite it being sunny until nearly ten o'clock, almost no light ever reached the stove room, so here she sat. The cool rain and its accompanying draft felt wonderful on her clammy skin, but she only had an hour or so to write Yael, her cousin, before the seaman who carried letters had to leave the square. It was a difficulty, despite Papa allowing her to use his fine fountain pen, because rain kept dampening the paper and draft made the edges of her nice paper flutter about on the splintery-edged wainscoting board she had to use as a desk. Hannah decided to do a draft and a final, despite having only her good birthday stationery to write on.

Dearest Yael,

I last wrote you before we had to leave Germany, when Papa finally decided it was too dangerous for God's People to stay there. I have no idea if that letter reached you.

I remember because of all the broken glass that it was the Kristallnacht when your father decided that your family had to leave Germany. Just before I sent you that last letter, the Brownshirts hurt many from the synagogue and broke all the windows everywhere in our neighborhood again. Even though he still had a business there, Papa was finally certain that we had to leave, and while we had to move at night and take rides in very dirty trucks and so on we managed to get here to Amsterdam. Still, the Nazis are here now too, and we must hide all the time. Several months ago, Aunt Sarah's husband Michael was taken to one of Hitler's camps. She came to live with us and helps Papa and Mutter with my new baby brother Ezekiel, but we take care of her too. We recently heard that Michael was dead. Sarah came with us to Amsterdam. In the daytime she is often cheerful and brave, but at night when everyone is asleep and she doesn't know I'm listening she cries.

Oh Yael, when will this terrible war end? When will we ever be safe walking the streets again? I hate this life of hiding indoors and running from one shattered hole in the wall to the next. One moment we're terrified as we run for our lives, but the next we're dreadfully bored and lonely as we sit around staring at each other for days at a time, or reading the same old books over and over. And we are always hungry. Because it is hard to get enough food and it is very cold, Papa and Mutter are always worried about little Ezekiel. I'm not sure why because from what I can see he seems to nurse all the time from Mutter's breast. I gather wood and sometimes at night I gather coal, but it is really too dangerous to be outside in daylight, so I stay inside reading my books and dreaming of the day when we can finally leave this place.

That is why I am writing this letter. Papa says many of our people have escaped to Suriname. He says our people are living safely there. Papa says that in addition to your family, Dr. Adelmann's family has gone there, too. Are you with him still? Papa says we must go there because there is no place in Europe where Jews can be safe now. I hope we leave soon because it is awful to keep running and hiding as we do, and Baruch HaShem, I will get to see you again. What is it like there?

All my love until I see you again, dear cousin.

Yours,

Hannah Roseweig

Then Hannah set about rendering a perfect copy, save only a smudge or two caused by a few errant drops of rain. She used one of the pretty envelopes that had come with the set, addressed the envelope to Yael Zeitweg in Paramaribo, Suriname, SOUTH AMERICA, but she did not put a stamp on it, of course. This letter would reach Yael by hand or not at all.

Outside, the storm was escalating. A treacherous gust of wind flipped the envelope over, smudging it unforgivably just as she finished the address, so Hannah had to start another, desperately careful despite her time running out.

Done at last, she licked the envelope containing the final draft to seal it. She escaped without notice—or so she believed—by her family, preoccupied as they were with Ezekiel, and quietly slipped out the door. She scurried like a rat between ruined buildings, and managed to catch the seaman as he emerged from what had been his family's cellar. She held her letter out in shaking hands.

"I didn't think you would make it, child," he said, taking the letter from her covertly. "Here. Let me get this in a nice safe sack." He smiled broadly at her as he slipped the letter in his bag.

Hannah noticed the seaman looked at her very closely, as men and boys were beginning to do, and ducked her head. She found it nice that all the boys were eager to show manners, but not altogether sure of what behavior would be proper with her new, big-girl status.

Sarah Lipinski had been preparing the family's meager dinner of stew made from tinned corned beef at the stove when Hannah sneaked out. Sarah had seen the letter in Hannah's hand. Sarah had observed Hannah closely in the last few months, and she could see that, despite the girl's young age, she was much more mature at age fourteen than her parents, Jacob and Rebecca, realized. Sarah saw that Rebecca, her much older sister, was far too consumed with worry about baby Ezekiel to keep a close eye on her two teenaged children. Eighteen now, Amos was a man and capable of taking care of himself and of being entrusted by Jacob with important "men's business." Just today, he had been out, running important and secret errands for his father. But Hannah... The girl's body was blossoming, and she had no idea what this meant. Hannah needed guidance. Sarah intended to provide it, whether it was welcomed or not.

At just 24, Sarah knew she was young, saw her own youth in every glance in the washroom's tiny, cracked mirror—the only one in the house. Her long black hair, much more striking in color than 38-year-old Rebecca's own dull mane, still shone lustrous and soft. But if she looked closely at the piercing dark eyes staring back at her in the mirror, she could read the sorrow in them. Only her eyes betrayed her.

She felt as if her entire life was now behind her. What was left for her? Widowed while still a newlywed, Sarah was sure that her one chance at happiness, the life she and Michael had set out on together, in which he would enter his family business and she would raise his children, was gone forever with him the moment he was taken to the work camps at Buchenwald. But as she stirred her stew, she considered that Hannah might be the closest thing she would ever have to a daughter of her own. The two were actually closer in age than Sarah and Rebecca were and enjoyed a sort of sisterly kinship that Sarah had never really had with her older sister.

She would keep silent and approach Hannah later about her covert escape. She would offer herself to Hannah as a trusted confidante. The idea provided something else to think about besides Michael, whose loss seemed a source of unending pain, even now, months after receiving word of his presumed death in the gas chamber. Each new morning, when she awakened and remembered that he was lost to her, she felt breathless, and it was as if he had died all over again. Worried for Sarah's well-being, as a single woman made frail with despair and misery, and desperate for her help with Ezekiel, their "surprise" child, Rebecca and Jacob had managed to coax her into living with them. Though grateful for her family, Sarah still awoke each morning feeling beaten and fought to keep from plunging into despair. But she wouldn't. She was needed. Living as refugees, eating rations, wearing all their clothes like human suitcases in order to travel from one bombed-out shack to the next, hiding in alleyways and foraging for food scraps ... it was no life for anyone but especially not these children, her niece and nephews.

Sarah was jolted from her reverie when the door opened, and a flushed, excited Hannah rushed in, as if blown in by the wind. Sarah looked up, startled, but said nothing when Hannah met her eyes, held one finger to her lips and silently pleaded with her aunt to say nothing of her outing. Sarah nodded once and continued stirring her sticky brown stew. With haste, Hannah tiptoed to the fire to join her family, none the wiser that she had ever left.

Sarah ladled the stew, with its potatoes and carrots and shreds of meat, into small bowls. Despite the family's lack of provisions, the young woman's culinary talents always managed to make something out of what seemed like nothing. Unfortunately, when divided among the five of them, it was never enough. How Rebecca managed to produce enough milk to feed her son, Sarah did not know, but the boy seemed to eat his fill.

"Blessed are You, *HaShem,* our God, King of the Universe, by whose word everything comes to be," said Jacob with bowed head at the hewn-wood table, around which the family gathered for their supper.

"Amen," responded each of them, one by one.

"*A sheynem dank* to Sarah, maker of this feast," Jacob addressed his sister-in-law, and with a twinkle in his eye gestured to his meager bowl. "We are blessed and grateful to have you among us to prepare such a delicious meal." Upon saying this, Jacob appeared immediately contrite. Of course, he knew Sarah would not be here at all were it not for her husband's death.

"It is nothing for me to do this," Sarah said, seeking to assure Jacob that she had taken no offense and modestly dismissing Jacob's praise with a wave. "It is the least I can do for you who have taken me in. I would be lost without you." At this, she looked her sister in the eye. Saying it aloud, Sarah knew it to be true. "*All* of you," she added, meeting eyes with each person at the table. Finally, her gaze rested on Hannah.

"May we eat now, Auntie?" Amos pressed. "I'm starving!"

"Oh, Amos, you are the very essence of gentility. Yes, eat!" laughed Sarah.

The tiny, surprisingly delicious bowls of stew warmed the Roseweigs' bellies and hearts but served as little more than a snack to keep ravenousness at bay. Sarah distinctly heard her strapping nephew's stomach gurgle and instantly felt guilty that she could not provide more food, was in fact taking it from the mouths of her sister's children simply by living here with them. A spoonful, maybe two, remained in her bowl, and she pushed it toward Amos.

"Take it. Please. I couldn't eat another bite," she said to him, making a show of patting her full stomach.

"Really?" he asked, clearly excited at the prospect of another bite.

"Don't let it go to waste, Amos," she added in a mock stern tone.

Greedily, he scraped his spoon along the bottom of her bowl, wrestling with his impulse to stick his face into the bowl and lick the bottom clean.

He can barely keep up with his growing bones, that boy, Sarah thought with some worry. *How can he still be growing at eighteen?* It was essential to keep the family's men strong and healthy, able to face the trials that lay ahead. Amos was continually showing himself to be a capable leader.

"The people are gathering tonight at Eli Rabin's home," Jacob said as he emptied his bowl and pushed himself from the table. "It is time to make our plans. The last of us will all be driven from our homes if we wait any longer. The Germans patrol the streets nightly looking for us."

"Oh, Jacob, shouldn't you wait? What if they see you in the streets?" Rebecca asked, shushing Ezekiel, who stirred sleepily in her arms.

"If not now, when, my love?" Jacob asked. "There is no more time. Amos, you'll come with me." The young man nodded, growing accustomed to such adult errands.

"But the storm! You hear the wind howling at our door!" Rebecca pressed.

"May *I* come with you, Jacob?" Sarah interrupted. The table fell silent as Jacob and Rebecca turned to face their sister.

"Absolutely not," Jacob said. "The Germans could find us at any moment. It is a terrible risk leaving this house. You must stay here with your sister to look after the children."

"Don't you see? That is exactly why I must go, Jacob. If something were to happen…" she stopped, caught her sister flinching in the candlelight, "Amos will be needed as the man of the house. What help would I, a poor widow, be to your family?"

Jacob looked from Sarah to Amos and then to his wife.

"I can be of help to you. I am clever and quick on my feet. *Please,* Jacob. I must … I must … *do* something. I simply cannot sit here any longer."

So it was decided.

⌛

Sensing the threat that the night's excursion would pose, Sarah, having dressed in her long underwear and warmest frock to protect against the rain, came to sit beside Hannah, who sat reading her worn copy of *Nesthäkchen* by the dim light of the fire in the stove room. She hoped to impart some sort of wisdom or exchange some fond words. It seemed a miracle that the girl was alone, but Rebecca had taken Ezekiel to say goodbye to Jacob, and Amos was taking his instructions as the "man of the house."

"Hannah, love, you cannot keep secrets from me. Where is it that you stole away to this evening before supper?"

"Please don't tell Papa, auntie," Hannah said, spreading her book on her lap and searching for possible eavesdroppers.

"Tell him what?"

Hannah watched her family closely to ensure they weren't listening. Then she turned to Sarah and whispered, with the hint of a smile on her lips, "I've sent a letter."

"A letter?"

"To my cousin, Yael, in Suriname."

"How did you send it, with Brownshirts on every street corner?"

"A ship carrying Dutch seamen leaves tonight for South America. My letter will be on it!" The girl was brimming with excitement and a clear sense of accomplishment. "Aunt Sarah, think of it! Freedom! Papa doesn't think I am old enough to understand, that I'm not grown up enough to help our family. But I *am*, Aunt Sarah! I know what must be done, and I can be of service!"

Sarah nodded her assent. It was true, she seemed the only one who saw that Hannah was growing up and how observant the girl was. "Yes, I know, love. That is why you must stay here with your mother. That keen mind of yours will surely be your family's saving grace."

Hannah beamed with the recognition, then looked down at her hands and grew serious.

"I wish Papa and Mutter could see it, too. I wish that I could attend tonight's meeting. I will go mad staying locked up in this drafty old house!"

Sarah patted the girl's shoulder. "Oh, my Hannah. *That* I truly understand. Listen, I will be your eyes and ears. Your papa may not share the details of tonight's meeting, but I will. I will tell you everything. I know that the women in this family are very strong and very smart, and one day we will have a chance to be the heroes and save the men in this family. You and I will be secret allies and confidantes. Okay?" She held out her pinky toward Hannah. The girl nodded satisfactorily and hooked her pinky finger with her aunt's.

"I have sent word to my dear cousin that we will soon come to see her in Suriname, the place Papa has spoken of. Wherever Suriname is, it must be a wonderful place to be home to so many dear ones we love. Don't you think so? Soon, perhaps we will be free to do as we please," Hannah mused dreamily.

Sarah thought for a moment and stared at the fire as she spoke. "But what if the Germans find us instead?"

CHAPTER 2

JUNE 21, 1942
EARLY MORNING

AMSTERDAM, HOLLAND

The face in the mirror still shocked him a bit, as it did every time light struck the scar that angled from near the top of his right ear to perilously near his nose. The straps of the dueling helmet had been a bit too loose, and it had been for a heavier-boned man in the first place. Still, at Heidelberg, the men dueled for their honor, and the scars, usually controlled by the long-used masks and guards, were seldom so blatant.

The first time Gunter Kramer had met the Führer, the man had commented on his scar and the courage it showed. Little did he know that Gunter had damned near lost control of his bladder when the hacking thing had sliced his face. Nonetheless, the scar probably had a lot to do with his being made an *oberst* at just 33 years of age. Being part of Luftwaffe Intelligence means a lowly rank unless someone noticed you, and scars were noticed.

Gunter dipped the coarse linen towel in the basin and wiped the remnants of lather off his face. He was caught off guard when a memory flooded his mind.

Little Emma, age five, her dark curls bent and knotted from sleep. Still in her nightgown, she sat on the wash basin, her sweet hand caressing his cheek, tears in her eyes.

"What is it, Mäuschen?

"You're bleeding, Papa!"

"Oh! That? That is nothing!" he assured her, wiping his face with a towel. "You see?"

Emma's hand gently, lightly touched the spot above her father's lip where faint dots of blood again formed.

"Does it hurt, Papa?"

"Not at all, my Mäuschen! I'm fit as a fiddle!"

Gunter leaned down to kiss his daughter and buried his nose into her neck, breathing in the lovely child scent of sleep. Her arms wrapped tightly around his neck, and she squealed with delight as he grabbed her around the waist and lifted her from the basin.

"Carry me, Papa! Carry me!" she cried as he slung her over his shoulder and hauled her like a sack of flour into the kitchen. "Gerta, my love, have you seen our darling Emma?"

The girl shrieked and giggled.

"No, I'm sorry, I haven't seen her!" Gerta said as she pounded the bread dough with her strong hands. "I hope she returns before her breakfast gets cold!"

Gunter shook his head to push the memory out of his mind. Such memories felt like cold steel in his gut. The next time he would see Emma, he was sure, she would be a young lady, not a little girl. He swallowed the lump that had formed in his throat and inhaled deeply to fortify himself.

He already wore his uniform jacket. Now he buttoned the elaborate thing, including the high collar, and squared his cap. He wiped the razor, rinsed the brush, and put both in their leather roll. There would be no valet for a soldier who had to hitchhike on everything from fighters to bombers and transports, so it served him well to remain self-reliant and aware of his kit. Then he backed away from the mirror and turned off the light.

Lastly, he drew the little automatic, a Sauer & Sohn Suhl 7.65 caliber, from its fitted leather holster. The lever on the side of the cleverly crafted air officer's *pistolen* meant he could cock and fire it one-handed, as that lever would cock the hammer without his having to work the slide. Still, *that* meant he must chamber a round, then lower the hammer gingerly in order to carry the ingenious thing in condition for one-handed operation. Following that ticklish operation, he dropped the magazine, topped it off with the round he carried in his pocket, then drew and checked the spare magazine, sheathed in the pouch integral to the holster. It was good German craftsmanship, but still Gunter wished it were made for something less anemic than the American .32 auto, which in his mind was nothing more than a lady's purse gun. Most officers who carried them did so purely for dress reasons, which didn't offer much reassurance or a sense of authority. The previous month, it had taken Gunter firing three rounds from it before an unruly member of the *maquis* would finally retreat.

Gunter grimaced, remembering the red-eyed, desperate man lunging at him, a stolen Mauser Kar98 held clumsily in his filthy hands. It was cold on the rocky hillside, and the shivering fellow fumbled a moment too long to work the toggle safety on the long, heavy Mauser's bolt end. Gunter's little auto had put three rounds across the top of a chest wrapped in layers of tattered fabric, probably above both the lungs and heart, but blood had gushed from the blue lips and the *maquisard* had sat down, sliding bumpily on the scree, so Gunter's aimed shot to his forehead and a short burst from the MP-42 of the escort trooper, who had been scrambling up the hill all the while, finished the resistant fighter before he ever succeeded in firing on the hated Germans.

But if I hadn't had this little fellow, he reminded himself, and he fondly patted the holster that was belted over his lean belly, *I'd be in a grave in France and would never see my Gerta and Emma again.* The promise of such a reunion was his sustenance, his only focus on these dark days when he had to pretend to care about his work or even his country.

This assignment was not what he had expected when he had become an intelligence officer. A degree with honors in engineering had gotten him into the Luftwaffe officer corps, but his height had meant that he would be too tall to fly a Messerschmidt, so he was relegated to Intelligence. But chasing *Juden* refugees in an occupied country? While Gunter honored the Führer, he believed that this campaign to eliminate the Jews would do far more harm than good to Germany. At least in France, he had been chasing resistance forces so the Luftwaffe and *Wehrmacht* could deal with them. Here, he was doing nothing but hunting scared people who wanted only to live outside the labor camps. Perhaps the Führer suspected his feelings, which was why Gunter had been relegated to this unsavory task. This was not an honorable occupation, he knew.

Gunter left the little W.C. quarters, his kit in hand, map case over his shoulder. It was not wise to let oneself get separated from one's baggage in this line of work. You never knew where the night would find you. Despite two weeks of returning to this same place, he did not intend to let down his guard.

CHAPTER 3

JUNE 21, 1942
AFTERNOON

HAARLEMMERMEER, HOLLAND

Oberst Gunter Kramer stood by the railroad tracks, concentrating on composing a tough expression on his face, which took as great an effort as he had ever exerted fighting with the saber. The SS troopers in his command would never understand an officer sympathizing with Juden, however miserable their plight. Fortunately, the wind and rain swirling in the air forced him to clench his jaw tightly, which conveyed a determination he didn't feel at heart.

Under foot crunched the gravel and cinders that had crumbled down from the exploded buildings near this spot. Gunter scoured the faces of the men assigned to him for any vestige of humanity. It helped to keep his eyes off the faces of the "baggage" as it shuffled into the already-reeking boxcar on the siding. Through the open sliding door he could see the streaked barrel with a single plank across it that had served as a toilet for the hundreds of people they had packed aboard on previous trips to hell and the reeking tracks on the floor that revealed where some had not reached the barrel in time.

This loading was getting harder to do. The captives had recently grown more active and resistant—like those in this lot—than had been the case when he had simply been herding starving refugees off the streets of this little town. While the Jews were not actively fighting back, just straining away from the horrid portal, the troopers were pricking with bayonets and clubbing ruthlessly to force frightened people into the stinking transport. There, a wife reacted to her husband being clubbed to his knees by weakly slapping at the grinning brute wielding the Mauser. Like swatting a fly, the trooper in turn slapped the feeble woman and her newborn wrapped in rags with a sweep of one hard hand.

Watching the exchange, Gunter bit down so hard to control his expression that he expected teeth to crack. This would have to be the last load. Tomorrow, he would have to order the steam generator and have the transport cars cleaned upon their return. Their choking smell was panicking the prisoners, making this horrible job even more difficult.

He strode forward, eyes locked on the brute who had just struck down a new mother.

"*Kleinfeldt!*" The trooper spun, coming to attention automatically. "*Ya, Herr …*"

"Don't turn your back on the prisoners, man!" Gunter strode in, ramrod straight, and using the icy lash of his voice to further confuse Kleinfeldt, who feared all officers as he had been taught and conditioned to do and now found himself ordered to have his back to an approaching and angry one.

Good, now you have a taste of it, Gunter thought satisfactorily. He stood elegantly and authoritatively beside the offending man, gloved hands clasped behind his back, leaning slightly forward at the hips, projecting contempt, and let his voice ring out for the edification of all. "And you are supposed to be putting *laborers for the Führer* on a train, professionally. This is neither the time nor place for bayonet or boxing training. If you want that sort of training, the front can use you. Does your desire for training surpass your desire to obey the Führer's orders, Kleinfeldt?"

Gunter could see the man's neck tremble. "If you make this wretched job any harder, and keep me standing in the rain any longer, I will assign you to guard this car from its roof on this trip." Despite having just threatened the man with a certain death, he glimpsed the flare of approval on a few troopers' faces. *Maybe they have not all lost their souls.*

As a surprising side effect of Gunter's speech, the refugees, almost all from Germany, took his words as an indication that they held some value, might have some hope. They began moving in a reluctant cooperation.

Striding back to his vantage point somewhat farther from the stench, Gunter inventoried the faces and body language of the gray-clad SS men he had been handed for this assignment. Their sub-lieutenant, or *Leutnant sur Zee,* was off with another detail, so he had here a *feldwebel,* a sergeant, and lower ranks only. While he had overseen command of these men for weeks now, he had never given them any reason to think he was kinder or less of a Hitler fanatic than their own lieutenant, a clone of Himmler who spouted astrology as if it were holy scripture and who barked his every word as if he were constantly being goosed by a poker.

The feldwebel, now given an excuse to force restraint on his men, did so efficiently and with quiet competence, and with a perceptible appreciativeness. He was the sort of man who had moved into the SS as a promotion, probably from the regular army, at the beginning of the war. Gunter thought that the man probably remembered the days in which the German military would have been appalled at its current work.

He consoled himself with the thought that at least they moved these poor bastards off to the labor camps without killing or beating them. At least. The Reich needed the labor, and these people could be enslaved because they were Jews and were therefore beneath contempt, but they needed not be beaten in the process.

"Papa, when will you come back to me?"

"When the war ends, my Mäuschen."

"When will this war ever end, Papa?"

When, indeed, Gunter thought miserably. He ached for his little girl. Against the wind driving rain into his back, he stood erect and watched the chattels pile onto the train.

CHAPTER 4

JUNE 21, 1942
LATE EVENING

AMSTERDAM, HOLLAND

Sarah walked with Jacob to the meeting with her head bowed forward, her long dark hair in wet hanks that clung to her face and neck. They had waited until the dark of night finally approach, and left Rebecca and her three children at home in the dark by the stove, bidding them goodnight, no one uttering the words all of them were thinking, which were, "I pray this will not be the last time I lay eyes on you."

The streets were inches deep in filthy water, and though she tiptoed as best she could around them, the black sludge crept mercilessly up her skirts.

As the two made their way gingerly across the narrow footbridge over the Oudeschans canal, then darted between buildings on Nieuwe Hoogstraat to avoid notice by the SS just a few blocks north at Nieuwmarkt, Sarah dragged her skirts along the filthy streets accumulated with the black slime of water ripe with excrement and coal dust mingled with vehicle exhaust. Then across the Geldersekade canal to Oude Hoogstraat and into a dark, narrow alleyway reeking of urine. The two tiptoed northward, finding refuge behind trash bins and in dark doorways when headlights threatened approach and then receded.

While the two rested in a doorway to calm their breath for the remaining fifty meters or so that Jacob indicated they had left to travel, Sarah finally broke her silence to inquire as to the object of this meeting. She had blindly followed him until now, believing it might be safest to remain ignorant should they become separated forcibly by the SS. Jacob explained to her that the old man, Herr Adelmann, recently arrived from their old home in Germany, had spoken to Jacob for hours the preceding night. As a result, her brother-in-law had been unwontedly quiet and anxious today, which she had noticed, and Amos had been absent most of the day. The Rabins' home just south of Bethaniënstraat was unfamiliar to her, but those present were long acquaintances of the Roseweigs.

An hour of stops and starts through Amsterdam's dirty, wet streets brought them to the unassuming black door on which Jacob knocked twice, waited a beat, and then knocked three times.

"Wie is er?"

"Twee dolende sterren," said Jacob. Two wandering stars, just like the stars Jews like them had been forced to wear while walking in their own neighborhood.

The door opened carefully, just a few feet, and then the sallow face of Choen Levin, the boy who teased Hannah mercilessly in *schul* by tickling her neck (clearly out of adoration for the blossoming girl), peered around the door. He recognized Jacob but started when he caught sight of Sarah.

"My wife's sister, Sarah Lipinski," Jacob introduced him.

The boy nodded once and then led them to the warmth of the fire-lit room where sat all the people who had come with the Roseweigs from Germany to Amsterdam months before.

Sarah's eyes adjusted to the light in the room, and she realized that all eyes were upon her. The only light came from the fireplace and a solitary candlestick upon the mantel. From right to left there was Eli Rabin, an accountant and partner of Jacob's, as well as Herr Adelmann, the special visitor whom they had all come to listen to, sitting closest to the fire in a blue upholstered chair, along with his son, young Levi Adelmann, who was a few years older than Hannah and who now sat on the floor, as close as he could to his father's feet. In the far right corner huddled Nathaniel Rabin, Amos's classmate and friend, in a ladder-backed chair, and his sister Aliza, who was just enough older than Hannah to sometimes be a bit impatient with her, cross-legged on the braided rug on the floor. In one of the few splintery chairs against the farthest wall from the fireplace sat Eli Rabin's widowed great aunt Gertrude. Albert Levin, Choen's father, stood uncomfortably against the doorframe, an unusually small one for Levin's Teutonic frame. The other fathers, the principal participants, stood in a tight circle in the middle of the room, occasionally eyeing Sarah, plainly surprised that she had come rather than Jacob's sensible son. All the others were there for support and witness. Fathers would be making the decisions, though Sarah knew her sister and the other mothers, most home with little ones tonight, would have their say later.

Aliza shifted and gestured to an empty spot near her where Sarah, standing awkwardly, could sit. Aliza patted her companionably on the shoulder as she settled. She seemed anxious to befriend Hannah's young aunt.

Jacob spoke quietly in the dim orange light, letting the intensity of his words serve for the volume they no longer dared use in this fugitive world. The only other sound was the crackle of the fire, the steady beat of the rain outside, and the occasional shuffling of shoes on the creaking wooden floor.

"Herr Adelmann has brought news of the Nazi camps. They are, at least some of them, killing many of the people sent to them."

A heavy weight lurched inside Sarah's stomach. *Michael.*

Many others around the room recoiled, too, Sarah could see. This fact had been rumored, and, of course, Sarah and many others had taken this for granted, but it had actually never been confirmed.

She closed her eyes and could still see, as if it were yesterday, the image that had greeted her the day of Michael's capture. Spurred by some unnamed feeling (Fear? Protectiveness?) in her gut, she had impulsively put on a nice dress, pulled her hair into her special barrette with the rhinestones, donned red lipstick, and taken the bus into the Würzburg city center to surprise Michael at the bank where he made his living and hopefully spirit him away for an early dinner.

Ironically, this gorgeously sunny afternoon would become host to the darkest moment of her life. Her heels clicked on the flagstones as she briskly, almost excitedly, approached the front steps of the bank. She lifted her eyes upward in anticipation and was brought to an abrupt halt by the sight of Michael, pressed forcibly against the front window that looked out from his tiny office.

Her breath caught as she took in the scene: two Gestapo officers, one with a gun to Michael's head and the other seemingly unfastening her husband's belt—likely to strike him with it. Michael's eyes stared directly into hers, and all in the span of seconds conveying his terror, his anger, his misery, and his recognition that this would be their last communication. *Turn back, my love. It's too late for me. It's all over. RUN. GO. NOW. I love you. I'm frightened.*

Sarah gasped, her hand flew to her mouth. She nodded understanding, blew him a kiss, and ran in the direction from which she'd come, madly, without thinking, letting the adrenaline course through her veins and the power of her steps exorcise the pain in her heart. Only after it felt like she'd been running for hours did she finally collapse somewhere along the bank of the Main River, bent over double and heaving for breath as flames burned in her chest, where it only just then hit her with blinding clarity her that her shoes had disappeared and her feet were bloody and her Michael was lost to her forever.

It was near a bend in this same river, miles away, where Michael and hundreds of other demoralized Jewish men were forced aboard a train at Kitzingen and led to their deaths.

Of course, while convinced reasonably that Michael had indeed been killed, Sarah realized that perhaps one tiny part of her had hoped, even believed, he might miraculously appear to her again when this horrific war on Jews was over. It's as if Michael dies another death each and every day. Tears filled Sarah's eyes, but in the firelight she discreetly could wipe her eyes without drawing attention to her misery. "There have been street sweeps and house searches for several weeks now in towns outlying Amsterdam, notably Haarlemmermeer and the farms around it. They have been sending people off on the trains from the station there. Inevitably, they will start here soon. We must leave." At this, Jacob turned to Herr Adelmann for confirmation and to encourage him to speak. The tired-looking gentleman, still bundled in his black trench coat and rumpled felt hat, sitting slumped in his chair as if under an enormous weight, looked at Jacob with watery, weary eyes, then reluctantly nodded at him.

There was a hubbub of speech, not just from the fathers. All wanted more detail, from Herr Adelmann first, and then from Jacob.

Herr Rabin was a learned, well-respected businessman with a thin mustache and long, pale fingers. He smoothed his deeply parted black hair, cleared his throat, and asked Jacob directly what they all asked internally but dreaded verbalizing.

"*Yakob*, there is nowhere to go. Vichy, in France, is untenable. We certainly can't go back to Germany, and the Nazis have heart friends all over Poland. I ask you, where do you propose we go?"

Jacob was used to running a counting house of more than a dozen men. Always somewhat taciturn and composed in matters of a serious nature, he remained calm, despite the frightened room full of his friends. His brown eyes looked straight into those of Herr Rabin. "Suriname."

A buzz of whispers spread around the small room.

"Why Suriname, *Yakob*? What is there for us?" came Sarah's flinty voice. She had no inhibitions speaking to the men, and there was an acerbic nature to her question. She had posed it in order to give Jacob and Herr Adelmann the floor again, to quiet the room. It was one way that she knew she could help, as she had promised him she could in order to be allowed to accompany him.

Though she had gotten wind—all the Roseweigs had—of Jacob's interest in Suriname, it was an unformed, lifeless plan with an air of the mysterious and dream-like, certainly nothing to pursue in earnest … was it?

The room grew silent, and she could feel the men's eyes on her, appraising her. She understood as a matter of fact that she was still beautiful despite their hard lives and her recent widowhood. Here, she would use it to her advantage.

"It is where Herr Adelmann's nephew, the *doktor,* is and where some of our neighbors from Germany have gone. It is in South America."

The reaction was disbelief and even anger from Herr Rabin. "We haven't a wheelbarrow, let alone a ship! Talk sense, *Yakob*, talk sense!"

Jacob drew himself up, donning dignity like a coat, a thing Sarah had seen him do with Hannah and Amos when he was being very serious with them, and Herr Rabin, sensing the shift, apologized instantly. "Forgive me, *Yakob*. I am just astonished …"

Jacob was really never one to be too formal, but he kept his "dignity coat" on for a moment and used the pause to quiet the room with his gaze before resuming. "I am speaking with the *utmost* sense, Eli. There is no safe place in Europe for us, short of England, and the sea between here and there is full of warships. It is being flown over by planes with Hitler's murderers flying them. Rommel is, if you believe even half of the German press…" several of the men snorted or laughed and Sarah chuckled, smiling and shaking her head, "about to conquer Cyrenaica, or Libya, if you will, and Mussolini is Hitler's kissing friend, so we cannot flee to Italy. The British are kissing the Arabs and blocking the way to Palestine. We *have* to go to the New World. What other choice do we have, I ask you?"

Herr Rabin nodded, reluctantly, but respectfully, and Jacob put a kind hand on his shoulder as he continued.

"I called you here tonight to ask you all to bring out and pool everything we have that has value," Jacob continued. *A-ha! That's where Amos was all day—rounding up attendees*, Sarah realized.

Jacob continued. "I have coins, and my wife has some jewelry, and all of us must have *something* for trade. From letters Herr Doctor Adelmann sent, we know the name of the policeman here who is responsible for the main docks. I will go speak to that man tomorrow and ask help finding a ship. We know that the party already there, my cousin among them, had help from that policeman more than two years ago when they came through Amsterdam and made their way to Suriname. The doctor tells me that he is a kind man, with a wife and daughter. At the time, my cousin wanted us to come to Suriname, too, and I wish now that I had listened and had gotten my family to safety. The Nazis weren't here, then."

Rueful comments drowned his speech for a few moments. But there was a worse interruption. The door flew open, and Otto Rabin, Nathaniel's older brother, stood panting and shuddering, his soaked legs revealing how heedlessly he had run through the puddled streets. "They are in Hoorn! Only an hour away! Already have captured hundreds of people!" He stooped with his hands on his knees, pausing to catch his breath and gulping air. His father moved to help him over to the wall and urged him to sit, pulling off his own jacket to wrap the boy's shaking legs.

Jacob knelt, added his coat to the elder Rabin's, and briskly rubbed Otto's wrist, asking urgently, "Who told you? And when were they there?"

Otto took a deep breath, with Jacob rubbing one wrist and his own father the other, his blood warmed enough that his voice had deepened and steadied when he spoke again. "I was at the telegraph office, I get messenger work there sometimes, and I look Dutch, sort of, so ..." Papa nodded. They all did whatever they could to feed themselves these days. Otto exhaled deeply. "The message was for the guard captain here, to let him know that a train would be coming through Amsterdam with prisoners, bound for Poland, a place called Sobibor. The message asked for guards along the rails through the main station, where they have to slow down and do track-switching."

Jacob stood, abruptly and made his voice stronger without shouting, a trick he had that compelled attention. "We need money, jewels, anything, so we can buy a way out. Everyone go back to your homes and then bring or send what you have to Herr Rabin. His family is in the center of our little *diaspora* here."

Many still wanted to talk, but Jacob pushed his hands down, like a man packing a basket of pillows. Everyone stilled. "We talk no more! Now we must *do*. The time for talk is over. Leave a few at a time, and *be careful*."

Otto struggled back to his feet, handing the older men their raincoats. He stamped his feet and moved toward his concerned younger brother, and Aliza rose, smiled, and patted Sarah once more, which Sarah found odd and somewhat patronizing, as she moved to embrace her brothers.

The trip back to their own bombed ruin was almost too quick for Sarah, considering how long it seemingly had taken them to make the trip here. Jacob was careful to assist her wherever he could over puddles and ruts in the road, but his paces were urgent, and she frequently stumbled. She watched him carefully. His face was a mask of consternation. He carried the weight of the world on his shoulders.

CHAPTER 5

JUNE 22, 1942
LATE AFTERNOON

WATERLOOPLEIN SQUARE, AMSTERDAM, HOLLAND

Jacob had paced the dusty floor in the stove room all morning and afternoon, nervously rehearsing his plan to meet with Mijnheer Anders, the policeman who seemed their only hope of escape. Herr Adelmann had sung this man's praises, insisting that Anders was a loyal friend to the Jews and had, almost single-handedly, ensured the safe passage of the good doctor, as well as Jacob's cousin, Saul, and his family. Yet the news that had come last night that the Nazis were bound for Amsterdam meant that the streets would be even less safe for travel. Brownshirts might be on every corner. Nothing, not one aspect of his visit to Anders' home, could go wrong.

Sarah looked up now and then from her sewing to observe Jacob. She saw that he felt an extraordinary, breathtaking weight bearing down on him—the weight of the hopes of everyone in Eli Rabin's home last night and of Jacob's own dear family, all of them looking to him for salvation—and it grew heavier by the minute. She saw his back hunching over with its burden as he paced around the tiny room.

Hannah, by contrast, who was bored to tears reading the same children's books over and over all day, had studied her father. He moved as a rat in a cage would—frantic, eyes darting, body twitching and jumpy. Sarah found herself in the extraordinary position of liaison, with feet in both the world of danger and secrets, the men's world, and the women's world, that of domestic life.

"Papa!" Hannah said in a harsh whisper so as not to wake Ezekiel, who was finally napping in Rebecca's arms, but to snap her father out of his reverie. The baby's shrieks had only served to push them all into near hysteria; it seemed certain that Hitler's men would burst in at any moment, alerted by the tiny screams.

Startled to hear his daughter's voice, Jacob's head jerked up. He looked at her with frenzied black eyes that frightened her with their intensity.

"Papa?" she repeated, meekly this time.

Sarah, Amos, and Rebecca, who gently rocked her baby on the other side of the room, knew the errand Jacob had to make tonight. Hannah, however, had not been apprised, and Sarah knew that the precocious girl didn't like being left out.

Upon hearing his daughter's voice, Jacob relaxed. "Yes, *Schätzchen?*"

"What's wrong, Papa? Has something happened?" Hannah probed.

"No, no, nothing. All is well."

As she watched Hannah's lovely face, Sarah felt a small sapling of an idea taking root in her mind.

"*Yakob,*" Sarah began, interrupting his thoughts. "Didn't Herr Adelmann say last night that the policeman has a daughter?"

"What?" Jacob said, startled out of his reverie to stop pacing and look questioningly at her.

Sarah continued slowly. "I was thinking … perhaps Hannah and I could serve as envoys, good luck charms for your expedition?"

Tall and lithe, Sarah didn't have the coloring of a Dutch woman, but she had recently learned that her feminine wiles allowed her to charm her way into situations. At just 24, a little over half Jacob's age, she saw that men found her alluring. With the right clothing and hair covering, she looked young enough to pose as Jacob's daughter. And though Hannah's build was slighter and her coloring was usually warm, speaking so strongly of her Jewish descent, just now, in the candlelight, it struck Sarah how very pale the girl had become in these months of only going outdoors at night. In fact, perhaps she was pale enough that, with Sarah's help, if her hair, too, were styled properly, if her clothes were just so, it might be possible …

It was instantly clear to Sarah that similar thoughts were occurring to Jacob. The frenzied look in his eyes changed, focusing intently now on the germ of an idea. Sarah watched his body shift as the idea seemed to wash over him.

"Papa, you're beginning to worry me!" Hannah said with a forced, nervous laugh as her father stood staring, not at her, but almost ... *through* her. She tugged self-consciously at the bottom of her brown dress, which was by now too small and threadbare, as she attempted to cover her knobby knees.

"*Yakob*, my love," pressed Rebecca in an urgent, hushed tone as she noticed the slow smile spreading across Sarah's face. "What is it, you two? Why do you stare so?"

So it was that Sarah, who was proving a valuable tool in Jacob's arsenal, and Hannah, thrilled to be given an opportunity to leave the house, were transformed into Annika and Esme, the two daughters of Godfried Jacobson—the Dutch names they would give to anyone who should show suspicion. And Hannah was granted her fondest wish: an important part to play in the evening's performance that would seal the fate of the Roseweig family. It was the role of a lifetime, and despite her excitement, Hannah wore an appropriately sober expression in order to reassure her father. The only thing that gave her away was the gleeful way in which she took the basket containing all her clothing in the world, folded to look like freshly cleaned laundry, from Sarah's hands, as if it had no weight at all. Rebecca's small, black eyes examined her daughter suspiciously, anxious about the danger involved in this plan for three of the most important people in her life.

Jacob and Sarah had made a convincing argument to Rebecca, helping her to quickly see the wisdom in this plan.

"Rebecca, a man walking the streets alone will only provoke the interest of any soldier, surely you can see that," Sarah had urged her sister, who sat terrified in her chair, clutching her baby to her breast for dear life. "But a Dutchman with his two daughters? Washer-women carrying laundry?"

Rebecca turned her attention to Jacob. "But, *Yakob*, you do not look at all Dutch!"

Sarah cut in. "Perhaps not, but Hannah ..." Sarah pointed to the girl, who was already excitedly bouncing in her seat. "Hannah is tall for her age and so fair now after months without seeing the sun. She could pass for a Dutch girl." Sarah envisioned the girl in her old blue-and-white checked dress that was by now too small for her. The dress, which ended just above Hannah's knees, had a very Dutch appearance, and if her light-brown hair were braided into two rows and tucked into Sarah's red scarf, the picture would be complete. Holding a basket of laundry, she could pass for a poor Dutch girl.

Rebecca had spoken the truth about Jacob—from his black eyes to his olive skin, dark hair, and short, stocky build, his appearance bespoke only pure German Jew, and they all knew it. But perhaps, Sarah thought, with his black overcoat buttoned to the neck, and with Amos' woolen cap from school pushed far down onto his head, Jacob could pass for Dutch. He, too, could carry his own basket on his shoulder, and use it to shield his dark eyes from the prying eyes of Nazis. Should he be stopped and questioned, he and Eli Rabin had, for months, worked together on their Dutch, practicing the unique cadence of their speech and the accuracy of a few key phrases, such as "pardon me" or "My name is Godfried Jacobson."

"Why will you not take Amos?" Rebecca proposed. Amos had nervously bustled about the house, restless with nervous energy, when Sarah and Jacob had gone to the previous night's meeting. The thought of him doing so again was enough to drive Rebecca mad.

"Amos must go with the Rabin boys. He is of best use to us with them," Jacob replied. He'd seen his son nearly reckless with nervous, teenaged energy and his fervent desire to be of use, a man now equal to his father. So when the boy had asked Jacob this morning whether he might join Nathaniel and Otto Rabin, who had appointed themselves "patrol guards," scanning the streets and reporting to their families and friends about each move the Nazis made, Jacob had consented. He had not liked sending his son into the fray, but he saw the usefulness of the endeavor, especially after Otto's brush with the Nazis last evening. Amos was fast, faster than any of the other boys, and long and lean, capable of moving quickly and easily in shadow, unseen.

"And you, sister?" Rebecca pressed, turning her attention accusatorially to Sarah, as if she believed Sarah an instigator of trouble. "Do you believe that *you*, with your black hair and dark eyes, could look Dutch? You, who have grown up a German Jew your whole life?"

"My dear sister," Sarah approached her sympathetically. *She must be out of her mind with worry.* Drawing on the small pool of confidence deep within her, she projected as much of it outwardly as she could. With a reassuring smile to Rebecca, she said, "With the right clothing, the right demeanor, I can be whatever I need to be." Then, with her hands on her hips and a toss of her hair for effect, she added, "Plus, I am what they call a 'diversionary tactic.'"

Hannah could see that her father was questioning the viability of this plan as the trio stepped quietly onto the main street. The enormity of his task became very clear to her as she studied his bearing and thought back to the sight of him pacing the floor all day. It was crucial to her that she not let him regret the decision to include her. She must show him that this was the only idea that made any sense or which stood a chance of working.

Sarah's brown shirt-dress with the tight-fitting bodice, along with the half-apron tied at the waist, showed off her figure attractively and were understated enough to look like something a Dutch girl would wear. Her long hair, tied in a knot on top of her head, was covered by a white Dutch bonnet, and on her feet were wooden shoes, both of which Sarah had purchased while vacationing in the northern city of Groningen with Michael several years ago, and which she could not bear to part with now that he was gone. Her inability to cast off these possessions had proven a blessing.

Jacob's eyes scoured the streets for Germans. He tried desperately to look casual, but Sarah could see him burrowing his hands deeply into his pockets so as not to reveal their uncontrollable shaking.

Hannah embraced her role with gusto, maintaining the poise and control of a film star. She knew Jacob was impressed by her when she caught him watching her. *See, Yakob?* Sarah thought as she watched Hannah carry herself so demurely and maturely. *Your little girl is not such a little girl anymore!* So excited was Hannah at the prospect of being useful in this endeavor that she veritably skipped through the streets with her basket, with the demeanor of a girl who had not a care or worry in the world—a Dutch girl.

Jacob had briefed the two of them about how to act upon arrival at Mijnheer Anders' home.

"You must be well-mannered, both of you perfect ladies. Be quiet and polite, let me do the talking," Jacob had instructed in a whisper as they'd stepped out into the streets. "The policeman has a daughter. Both of you, befriend her. Sarah, you and I will appeal to Mijnheer Anders." At that he looked pointedly into Sarah's eyes, conveying additional, unspoken wishes for her particular behavior.

"Hannah, my *Schätzen*," he continued, "Endear yourself to the girl. You must become a trusted companion to his daughter, and reveal your dear, affectionate nature to them both. This comes so naturally to you, my love, but it has never been more important."

Sarah understood his thinking. If the two of them couldn't appeal to the policeman's good will themselves, at least Anders might feel enough adoration for his sweet, precocious daughter that he would be moved to help them.

The small, prim, proper Dutch house looked a bit like one of Hannah's old dollhouses, with its clean brick, neat windows, cheerfully colored shutters, lace curtains, flower beds, and well-lit, welcoming front path. *Surely a home this friendly has equally friendly occupants,* Sarah hoped fervently as she, Jacob, and her niece slowly approached the front door. Jacob held his arm out in front of Sarah, restraining her. With the other arm, he put his hand on Hannah's shoulder, urging her forward, and said, "Hannah, knock and then stand in front of me." Perhaps the immediate sight of a sweet young girl would make them less likely to have the door slammed in their faces.

In seconds, the door opened wide, in a trusting, confident way that bespoke the residents' Dutch origins, and standing in the doorway was a girl of Hannah's age, with sparkling blue eyes, a swirl of nearly white blonde hair, and a starched, broadcloth apron stretched over a full red skirt and crisp white blouse. Sarah realized how poor the trio must appear, despite their best attempts to dress. *We must look like street rats. I hope she can't smell us,* Sarah thought to herself grimly, remembering that it had been weeks since any of them had bathed. The family had been settling for daily swipes with wet rags, and the humidity of the summer had made the air around them ripe with perspiration. Their best chance at securing help now would be appealing to Mijnheer Anders' pity.

"Yes?" said the young girl, presumably Anders' daughter, whose friendly, open face was questioning. After all, it was after eight o' clock, long past normal tradesman's hours. She looked from Hannah's face to Sarah's and finally to Jacob's. Jacob hastened to state their goal, keeping his voice reassuringly low.

"We need to speak with Mijnheer Nicolas Anders, if you please, *Fraulein*."

She stepped aside, bobbed her head with a dazzling smile and a courteous low wave, and urged them into the foyer. "Please, come in."

The girl smiled brightly at Hannah, and Hannah, in turn, smiled broadly back. The warmth of reassurance began to spread over Sarah's body as she saw the girls instantly forging a connection, in the way that young girls do. Though she knew the Dutch simply had not lived alongside the Nazis for long enough to become hard and suspicious, it was still astonishing to find this young girl so trusting and friendly to strangers. Especially strangers who looked as weather-beaten and poor as Sarah knew they appeared. After these months of hiding in shadows, it seemed so strange to find someone who wasn't jumpy, easily startled, or guarded at her front door.

Then, abruptly, Sarah felt another presence, that of a massively broad, square-shouldered, ruddy man with whitening hair that indicated he might be a decade or more older than Jacob. He wore woolen trousers and a matching vest over a white, button-down shirt, rolled at the cuffs. On his feet were leather slippers, and he wore no tie; it looked to Sarah as if he'd been enjoying a relaxing evening with a good book. He clutched a massive, curved, meerschaum pipe, from which curled fragrant, cherry-scented tobacco smoke. *He doesn't look like a policeman to me,* Sarah thought. *But that is probably a good thing.*

"Mijnheer Anders?" Jacob asked cautiously

"Yes, I am Nicolas Anders. And you are?" Anders asked, exhibiting a bit more caution than his daughter. Then again, Sarah realized, that must come with the job.

"I am *Yakob Roseweig,*" Jacob said, pronouncing it with full Yiddish emphasis and extending his hand openly to the man, in the standard Dutch greeting. Hannah watched Anders' face shift as he realized that these two people in his home were Jews and cautiously, hesitantly grasped Jacob's hand. Jacob seemed to apprehend the man's realization, and as if to insist that they posed no threat, he foisted Sarah and Hannah, one with each arm, in front of him, toward the policeman. "And this," he emphasized, pushing them ahead one by one, "Is Sarah Lipinski, my wife's sister, and my daughter, Hannah. I've left my wife at home with my two sons, Amos, who is 18, and Ezekiel, who was only recently born."

Sarah caught the man briefly surveying her then returning his eyes to Jacob's. He nodded curtly. It was clear that the man was confused by the two young ladies' presence, but he didn't ask, and Jacob didn't volunteer any further information.

"And the baskets?" Anders looked suspiciously, his head cocked. "Do you intend to wash those clothes?"

"Oh, no, forgive us," Jacob chortled, realizing how they must appear. "As with insects, Mijnheer, these are merely … protective coloration." Jacob maintained a joking tone, attempting to lighten the mood.

With his eyes still scrutinizing the three street rats who had landed unexpectedly in his parlor, Anders said to the blond girl, in Dutch-accented English, "Alexandra, please take Sarah and Hannah off and make some tea, and Mijnheer Roseweig and I will go talk in my office."

"Pardon me, Mijnheer Anders, but may I join you?" Sarah asked in a business-like tone that conveyed her maturity. "I assure you, I am well-acquainted with our errand and have made a promise to my sister that I will protect her wishes in this matter, as she was needed at home."

The man again nodded curtly. She took it as a good sign that he was willing to hear the two out, rather than abruptly ejecting them from his home or calling out for the nearest Nazi patrol. *If he would only listen, surely he will be moved by our plight to help us*, Sarah thought. *We will make him see.*

⧗

The room was as much den as office, with furniture covered in brass-nailed, plump, cushioned leather. An impressive rack of meerschaum pipes stood on the solid teak desk, and cases of worn books filled the cream-painted walls. The floor was a parquet of cherry wood—warm, red, and waxed to perfection.

Without wasting a moment, Jacob unburdened himself. "A man named Adelmann, a doctor, gave me your name. You helped him a year or so ago?"

Obviously startled, Anders' eyes widened. "Is he all right? Did you come from …?"

"Oh, no, he is fine," Jacob assured him. "He is in Suriname, safe. It was in a letter that he sent through his uncle, Herr Adelmann, a dear friend of mine, that your name was mentioned. Herr Adelmann and I, and several others …," he paused, preparing to ask his favor, "we … we would like to join him there, with your help."

The policeman's nod indicated acceptance and resignation. "It will not be so simple now. How many of you are there?"

"Four families, including my own. Fifteen, maybe twenty altogether, including, of course, our baby Ezekiel. Several children. The final number will be decided tomorrow; several are making their decisions now."

"That is a lot of *men* to get on board a ship with the Nazis looking at everybody on the docks. It is *impossible* to do with women and children, especially crying babies."

"I … we have thought of that. We men can pretend to be laborers or sailors, but the women and children …" Jacob trailed off, as he had no solution for this problem. He appeared disheartened to have come so far and be told no.

Anders' eyes lit on the basket Sarah had set down beside her chair. He grinned abruptly, revealing tobacco-yellowed teeth. "Ah, yes! Of course! We can send them aboard as bales of cloth!"

"Cloth?" Sarah piped up. She could only imagine going home to tell her sister that she and her baby boy would have to hide in laundry baskets.

"One of the few things Holland has to trade, or that we are permitted to trade, is cloth. Meanwhile, Suriname exports chocolate and coconuts, sometimes other things like coffee. So there are trades in and out. Not like in peacetime, of course. But, as you know, Suriname is Dutch, so it is somewhat easier. The Germans like to believe that they control all such trade and the countries engaging in it, of course, but, you see, the Americans have neutral relations with Suriname and engage in considerable trade there. They have troops stationed in Suriname to protect trade relations, and the Germans have no control in those coastal waters."

Sarah enjoyed hearing that there was any corner of the world in which the Germans did not have control. She grew excited as she began to follow the direction of Anders' explanation.

Suddenly, the two girls bustled in, chattering amiably in German as if they were old friends. Alexandra bore a tray of steaming tea, teacups, cream, and sugar; Hannah proudly carried the china plate of small cakes.

The heavenly aroma of the tea and cakes was the most delicious that any of them had encountered in at least four months. *Oh, I wish Rebecca could be here to share this,* Sarah thought hungrily. *I had forgotten the loveliness of these simple, civilized moments.*

Alexandra slowly, politely poured tea in the three teacups. Sarah watched the interminably long process and fought the urge to push the girls aside and shove every one of the tiny cakes down her throat and growl for more. She watched Hannah blush with pleasure to have been made part of this ritual so quickly … and, perhaps, at having quickly gobbled up a pilfered cake herself? Sarah then stole a glance at Jacob and saw his eyes welling with relief and, she thought, the same joy she herself took from such a tiny pleasure. Anders apparently saw it, too, because he abruptly turned his head away, put his pipe down in a clumsy, clattering way, and cleared his throat in mock irritation.

"You two go chatter *in the kitchen*," Anders said to his daughter, his emphasis a form of dismissal. "Please, make yourselves some more tea. Are there more cakes, Alexandra?"

"Yes, Papa, just a few," she replied as she gathered the tray to make an exit. "Shall I bring them?"

"Well, then, you two have them, and leave us to talk some more." Anders sat back in his chair with his tea and crossed his legs. The girls beamed their excitement for the treats and hustled out, their chatter barely pausing.

"*Danke*," said Jacob, his hand shaking slightly as it held the teacup poised to his lips.

Anders gestured as if to say, "Think nothing of it." The three sat in silence sipping their tea for a moment before Anders spoke up again. "How might you pay for passage?"

Sarah's stomach lurched with worry. *We can't pay. We have nothing.* And then, not for the first time, she considered whether her wedding ring might help, and whether she could ever bear to part with it.

"We don't yet know," Jacob said. "Last night we met and made the decision to go. We are all pooling any valuables and making a collection of what we have even as we speak. I will know in a day or two. It will be things other than money, for the most part."

The look the policeman gave to Jacob was both understanding and condescending. "It will have to pay a captain for a lot of risk. Already German U-boats are sinking trade ships all over the Atlantic, and adding four refugee families increases this risk a thousand fold. Not to mention the large quantity of food this will require. The Germans take everything they can to feed their army, and ships leaving these ports are usually on small rations, especially going home."

"Nursing mothers must be fully nourished, of course, but we are all used to going without, lately," Jacob said sadly. Sarah watched him working to control his shaking as he plucked a shortbread cake from the table and gave him a meaningful, reproachful glare. *Oh, Yakob, nothing is more repellant than naked hunger. Please control yourself; we need this man!*

The look Anders shot Jacob was shrewd. Abruptly, he whisked a linen napkin out of its ring, laid it on the table, and promptly dumped the remaining cakes into it. As he tightly wrapped the bundle and handed it over to Jacob, Anders said kindly, "I'm sure your wife would like some of these?"

Alexandra was wonderful. She was so careful and fast in the kitchen, Hannah could barely contain her admiration. And when the Dutch girl saw how careful Hannah was to capture every crumb of her cake, she ladled a generous bowl of soup from a great pot on the coal stove and insisted Hannah spoon up every drop. It was so good, after chilly night air and Hannah's too-short dress, and after having had no food since this morning's bread crusts. In fact, she had been feeling a little queasy from having gone so long without food. They had been eating stockfish soup and old dried bread for days now, and very little of that. Her mother got the most generous portions, because she had to make milk for little Ezekiel, but even she barely got half of what they used to eat at home in Germany.

Then they went to Alexandra's bedroom, and Alexandra showed her a music box with a little ceramic dancer in a tutu on it. To demonstrate for the captivated Hannah, she wound the tiny brass key on the bottom, and the tiny dancer twirled to the tiny bell music. Hannah was entranced.

She could recall having a little music box of her own once, a simple wooden box which played music when opened, on tiny little brass strings that were played by a small, rotating, brass cylinder covered in bumps that created music when a tiny brass needle bounced on them. A gift from her parents, it had been Hannah's favorite Christmas present as a child. But as boys are wont to do, Amos had broken it when he tried to make it go backward. Despite his being older, and a reckless boy, he had been so sorry, and both of them had been so afraid of what Papa would do if he found out what had happened to the special gift, that Hannah had placed the box in her little pine chest, where it had sat for years, silent. That chest and its contents had been left behind when the family finally abandoned Germany. Hannah was saddened by the memory of it and of all the special keepsakes left behind that she would never see again.

Alexandra's native tongue was Dutch, but she also spoke German and French as well as any native. She said she had some English, too, but that her papa discouraged her using it because he said her English "smelled of the docks." Hannah didn't quite understand the meaning of this expression but knew that anything smelling of the dank, dirty docks could not be good.

Hannah explained that she could speak German, Yiddish, and a bit of the Hebrew she'd learned at Yeshiva, but that wasn't good for anything in the outside world, as she had discovered. But no matter the language, the two communicated naturally, easily, with laughs, gestures, and facial expressions equal in importance to actual speech. Hannah reveled in the comfort of this home and the budding friendship with another girl, an unexpected gift to have found here and one that Hannah realized she had been desperately wanting.

When Jacob, Sarah, and Hannah had warmly thanked their gracious hosts, with Anders' kind assurance that arrangements would be made, the three carried that joy with them into the damp, dark night. It took only minutes, though, after rounding the corner and losing sight of the small, cheerful home, to realize the danger of their movements. *No one, even a dim-witted German guard, is going to believe we are hauling laundry about in the middle of the night,* Sarah thought ruefully as her feet hustled briskly across the gable stones.

She stole a glance at her niece, who still reflected a kind of glow from the evening's events, and who smiled persistently. Sarah's heart squeezed with love for Hannah, whose happiness alone, despite their current situation, seemed to light up even such a dark night as this.

CHAPTER 6

JUNE 23, 1942
MID-MORNING

HOORN, HOLLAND

"**K**leinfeldt!" Gunter shouted to his foolish subordinate. "I have no more time to waste teaching you how to do your work. Stand to attention!" Gunter focused his disgusted glare on Kleinfeldt and purposefully avoided glancing down at their feet, where the little *Juden* boy lay on the filthy loading platform behind the sooty warehouse they were raiding for *Juden* refugees. The boy was bleeding from a great scalp wound, which had been inflicted by the sadistic bastard. Gunter's heart clenched as he steadfastly ignored the wailing coming from the boy's mother, who was being held back ruthlessly by another trooper.

"I will not repeat an order. I have told you we are sending labor for the Führer's work. You have chosen, yet again, to utilize senseless violence for your own delight, thereby rendering the laborers useless."

Disgusted, Gunter snatched the Kar98 from Kleinfeldt's cross-chest holster. Kleinfeldt snapped to attention, and his hands reflexively snapped down to the seams of his trousers. Gunter turned, tossed the rifle to the feldwebel, who easily caught it. Then Gunter pulled Kleinfeldt's own ceremonial dagger, took the man's collar tips between his thumb and forefinger, and decisively sliced each one off. The SS designation badges dropped to the dirty floor. Kleinfeldt blanched and trembled.

"Now you are suitably uniformed for the labor battalion, which you will join immediately," Gunter said, relishing the opportunity to disgrace the cruel, stupid man. "Feldwebel! Bind this trash and put him on the truck."

Kleinfeldt stood in shock as Ermenthaller, the sergeant, slung over his shoulder what had, just moments before, been his own rifle. Then the sergeant pulled from his belt one of the binding cords all the troopers had looped through their belts to restrain prisoners and used it to tie Kleinfeldt's hands behind his back. The remainder of the SS detail stood frozen, surrounding their little band of prisoners, stunned by this ultimate act of degradation toward one of the toughest among their unit. Gunter scanned the faces of the remaining ten men, searching for … what? A trace of humanity? A conspiratorial nod or wink? He thought he detected looks of satisfaction on the faces of three of the men, and the sergeant's, too. *Three, perhaps four, who are glad to see this brute taken down,* thought Gunter, and he felt his lips draw up into a slight smile.

Feldwebel Ermenthaller marched Kleinfeldt to the transport truck and stolidly kicked the back of the man's knees with the edge of his jackboot. The former trooper crumpled. Ermenthaller knelt, silent and unmoved, and began trussing Kleinfeldt's ankles to his wrists, using another couple of lengths of the cord. Gunter watched, impressed, as the sergeant then matter-of-factly lifted the fellow with apparent ease and tossed him into the truck bed, which was at his own chest height, like a sack of grain. Ermenthaller was certainly a force to be reckoned with.

This made four weeks of filthy and degrading duty for Gunter. Worse, he had been charged with a difficult task: to capture one *particular* Jew. In doing so, he would have to speak individually with at least half of his frightened, dirty, and, often, sick captives. Gunter was extremely curious about what terrible deed this Doctor Adelmann must have done to have incited the Führer's particular rage. Of course, he realized, with the thousands already captured who had not yet been interrogated, it was entirely possible that the doctor was already in Sobibor.

"Line them up! As I finish with each man, put him on the truck," Gunter called to his men. The male prisoners' hands were already bound. Such precautions were not necessary with the children and women, of course, but with truck transport to the rail yard, they had to go to the extra trouble with the men, whose panic often made them unpredictable and difficult to deal with.

Gunter stopped the shuffling line as each downtrodden man was presented to him and asked the smattering of questions he had time for: Name? Origin? Occupation? Did you know Adelmann? His task was made harder by the frequently inaudible replies. He had tried questioning women on previous takes, but they often had sobbed so hard they were comprehensible, and often they had shrieking children clutched to them or hanging onto their skirts—a scene too ghastly to repeat. Now he only questioned the men.

The boy whom Kleinfeldt had decked stumbled past, hanging onto his mother, blood still pouring over his face. "Ermenthaller. Put a battle dressing on this one. He will be useless to the Führer dead."

With his usual impassiveness, the sergeant produced and applied the battle dressing from his belt pouch, binding it firmly but gently to the boy's head.

"It has bled clean," Ermenthaller addressed the mother in an emotionless voice. "Keep this on it until it scabs hard." The terrified mother nodded.

At last they were done with another futile interrogation session, the captives were loaded, and the troopers crowded in behind them, compressing the prisoners into the depths of the canvas-covered trucks.

Ermenthaller bent, groped about, and came up with Kleinfeldt's gear. He took the battle dressing from that and replaced his own. Gunter grinned at the practicality, and the sergeant, astonishingly, grinned back. "May as well shortcut the supply line, Sir."

Gunter climbed into the high cab of the lead truck, and they were off with a wave of his arm out the window.

Gunter began formulating a plan. He would requisition seven troopers from the Wehrmacht guard force, all privates. If he were to keep Ermenthaller (and he believed he would), and the other three men he had identified in tonight's proceedings, perhaps he would have a useful squad at his command.

CHAPTER 7

JUNE 23, 1942
MID-MORNING

WATERLOOPLEIN SQUARE, AMSTERDAM, HOLLAND

Sarah stared, astonished, at the immense pile, at least a pound, of diamonds, pearls, gold, silver, and precious gems that sat on the Roseweigs' modest, rough-hewn table. *We cannot even buy bread, and we have all this,* she thought ruefully.

It was the morning following their visit to the policeman's home, and Eli Rabin had, as promised, delivered what he had been able to collect from the families seeking passage to Suriname. All four families—the Rabins, Levins, Roseweigs, and the two Adelmanns still remaining in Amsterdam—had made the decision to go, realizing that there really were no other options for them. *This is all that remains of four families' lives. It's really not so very much,* Sarah thought.

But it was not only their jewels gleaming on the table. Abe Weismann, who had mentored Eli Rabin, was seventy-nine and was far too ill with diabetes and gangrene to make the journey. "This necklace," he had said, placing the item in Rabin's hand, "belonged to my mother. It is all I have left that belonged to her. I believe it has some value?"

Other families, too—the Levines, the Kravitzes, the Herschels, and even Eli's great aunt, Gertrude—had given items, some for delivery to family in America, some to ensure safe passage for loved ones, though they were unable, or unwilling, to leave their homes and make the journey.

She fingered her wedding ring, weighing whether or not to toss it onto the pile. She couldn't … not yet. If it was needed for passage, she would offer it, but not before. She had left her home and her country and was about to leave the continent altogether. She wasn't ready to leave Michael behind, too.

She absolved herself of guilt. She knew that Jacob and Rebecca had kept a few coins and treasures back, reserving them for their new life across the sea, and had expected everyone else to do the same. Still, this mound of wealth was more than any of them had reasonably expected, and it might actually buy them a future. Jacob's exhausted eyes stared disbelieving at the glimmering pile.

The three of them had returned from Anders' after midnight, following hours of hiding in shadows. They stumbled in, shaking and overly excited, waking Ezekiel, who had then cried all night. They had all slept fitfully, though Sarah doubted that Rebecca had slept at all.

"Do you think it will be enough, *Yakob*?" Rabin, Jacob's business partner, asked doubtfully.

"It will have to be. And realistically, the nature of this is more important than its quantity. It is small, so the captain can conceal it easily, trade or sell it anywhere." Jacob fingered a silver coin. "Even though the coinage is from many places, it is all pure metal coins, no debased Russian coin. The jewels are all *good*."

"When will you take it to the policeman?" Rabin asked, his mouth a thin line of tension.

Jacob sighed. "I cannot go today, not with Nazis crawling the streets, perhaps even in his office. We will sleep today and return this evening."

Jacob glanced at Sarah to confirm. She nodded her consent.

"Eli, you go home," Jacob turned his attention to his partner, patting him on the back. "You've done well, many thanks for your efforts in transporting these goods to us. They are in our safe hands now and will be guarded with our lives."

Rabin looked longingly at the pile one last time.

"Take another route than the one you took coming here," Jacob instructed. "I will send word to you when I know more."

"If you are stopped, everything is lost," Rabin said, a worrisome patriarch. "I found it hard to breathe on the way here, because I had it all in my coat! It is…a tremendous weight."

Jacob nodded, understanding the depth of the statement. "Sarah, Hannah, and I will divide it amongst ourselves. We traveled well last night. We are safer carrying 'laundry' together than I would be alone. Our sons are patrolling and will send word of any Nazi activity. I give you my word that we are taking every precaution."

Jacob sounded more assured than he felt, Sarah knew. But it was the only way to see that Rabin, an accountant to his bones, felt comfortable turning his back on all the valuables he had in the world and walking away without a guarantee of having purchased anything.

Sarah returned to the stove room, where Hannah had proceeded braiding her hair in preparation to become Esme for the journey, despite the hours that lay ahead before they would return to Anders' home. *We're as good as professional spies,* Sarah thought satisfactorily to herself and moved toward her bedroll to get some much-needed sleep before the long night ahead.

⧗

This evening, Nicolas Anders opened the door himself, again wearing his evening uniform of vest and slippers and smoking a pipe. He smiled and nodded upon seeing the familiar visitors. "Mijnheer Jacobson, welcome!" said Anders companionably and cheerily ushered them inside.

The smell of good food wafted past them. The thin soup of stockfish that Sarah had prepared for their supper had had a tiny bit of beet root in it, but they may as well have had nothing when the heavenly aroma of *apfelstrudel* and sausages hit Sarah like a blow. She turned her attention to Jacob, concerned once again that his unchecked hunger would betray him.

"Come in, come in, you are just in time for our supper! You will join us?"

Sarah's stomach lurched reflexively. She was at war with herself, desperate to eat, but ashamed to let down her guard and put herself into greater debt with Anders.

"We do not want to impose, Mijnheer," Jacob echoed her thoughts, though Hannah had moved toward the table enthusiastically, happy to partake in dinner with the family. Alexandra beckoned to the girl, but Sarah reached out to subtly restrain her.

"An imposition it is not, Herr Roseweig. Surely you have not had time to dine, as busy as you have been." His ruddy face was bland, betraying no pity.

Nonetheless, Jacob stood firm, which impressed Sarah. She had been close to relenting. "Mijnheer, it is very gracious of you to offer, but you see, my wife and sister-in-law prepared a delicious, hearty meal for us prior to our journey this evening."

Sarah lay down her laundry basket and removed from the top of the pile a small white square of linen. "Pardon me, Mijnheer Anders, but here is your fine napkin. We have laundered it for you. Thank you again for your great kindness last evening." Rebecca had insisted that Amos have one of the little cakes from Anders' home before she would eat the three remaining. Her milk had flowed well this morning.

Anders took the napkin from her. "Of course. If I cannot interest you in a meal, let us repair to the study. Please." He gestured for them to walk toward the familiar room to discuss business. "Hannah, why don't you sit with Alexandra? She has been anxious for your company today."

Hannah looked at her father for permission. He consented with a nod. No sense denying the poor girl a nice meal. She was discreet; she wouldn't express their deprivations to the Anders family. The girls chatted eagerly like old friends.

Once inside the leather-and-cherry-scented office, Jacob and Sarah extracted the jewelry and coinage from their various coat pockets, aprons, and laundry baskets. Once all pieces were assembled on the teak desk, Jacob pulled it together, as if trying to make the pile appear larger.

Anders opened a drawer, produced a scale and a rack of small weights, and placed them on the desk. He pulled a small pair of reading glasses from his shirt pocket and, methodically as an accountant, proceeded to weigh the items. Then he extracted a micrometer and measured the pearls. Jacob gaped, open-mouthed, at the thoroughness of the procedure. Anders grinned.

"I am a policeman in one of the great smuggling capitals of the world, Herr Roseweig. Of course I am an estimator of some experience!"

Jacob nodded.

"Please tell us, Mijnheer Anders," Sarah asserted herself, "Do you believe he have enough to secure passage?" She fingered her wedding ring again.

"This should allow me to negotiate passage," Anders said, still weighing and measuring. "Your families worked very hard for a very long time to put this together, *nein*?"

"That is true," Sarah said, relieved.

"Of course, we could not take our houses, our businesses, our furniture …" Jacob spoke, apropos of nothing, but clearly resentful and prideful.

Anders appeared not to have heard him. "Well, then!" he said, removing his reading glasses, putting them in his shirt pocket, and replacing the scale. "I have in my acquaintance several men engaged in foreign trade. These men are well acquainted with the sea captains whose ships come and go from the Port of Amsterdam. I will use these connections to secure passage for you and your families."

Sarah and Jacob exchanged relieved smiles, exhaling audibly.

"Mijnheer, pardon my ignorance, but might this cause you trouble? Draw attention to you?" Jacob asked, unwilling to relax until some greater assurance was offered.

"Herr Roseweig, you needn't worry. Do not forget, the Jews have friends in *Nederland*." Anders' eyes twinkled as he lit his pipe and put it in his mouth, drawing from it satisfactorily. "Now," he said, back to his business-like tone, "tomorrow I will speak with one of my acquaintances about ships that may embark from Amsterdam to Suriname, and we will begin making arrangements for your safe conveyance to that vessel. Come to see me tomorrow evening, after dark. Do not come here. Come to my office." With this, he looked pointedly at Sarah, then fixed his eyes on Jacob's. "Alone."

Sarah bridled at being excluded but reminded herself that her feelings were secondary to the plan. They were on a precipice, the very edge of the freedom that was, after all, the entire reason for all they had done, and she would do nothing to jeopardize it.

Jacob looked apologetically at Sarah and then confirmed with a nod to Anders, "Yes, I understand."

"I will see you tomorrow evening. I will have news." Anders spoke with a cursory tone, implying that the visit was at its end. There would be no promises, no overtures of hope or compassion for the helplessness and urgency that would ripple through the Roseweig family over the next twenty-four hours, the terror at leaving the only valuables they had in the world with a Dutch police officer.

Sarah had an impulse to run to the desk, slide all the jewels and coins into the front pocket of her apron, and run from the house. *How do we know it's not a trap?* she thought. *Could it all be an elaborate ruse to lure Jacob to the Nazis?*

But then she glanced through the office door, which Anders had just opened for them, and glimpsed Hannah and Alexandra, bosom mates, giggling and embracing each other like old friends, huddled together in the shared conspiracy of being young girls. Her mind was comforted. *No man who saw his daughter this way, so visibly delighted by new friendship, could be capable of destroying us like that. Surely no father could be so cruel.* She vowed to put her doubts aside and have faith that God had them safely in hand. She took a deep breath, exhaled with new confidence, and strode out Anders' door and into the dark night, as Annika once again.

The next twenty-four hours were an eternity. Sarah watched the small clock made of brass with the broken crystal face, which she had placed on the table so that it could be seen by all. It was only 7:30 in the morning.

They had all awakened with the sun this morning, before half past five, after another fitful night's sleep. Amos had left early in his patrol garb, but not before being warmly embraced by his family and handed a thick crust of bread, a canteen of water, and half a turnip by his aunt. *Perhaps the patrol will reveal some news to us today,* Sarah thought as she hugged him.

Now she paced the floor, scrubbed at the old kitchen counters as if intending to rub away its surface. She tapped her fingernails on the counter, musing to herself about life in faraway Suriname. She had a vision of herself, standing on a beach, watching the ship that had carried her to this safe, warm, new land sail into the sunset. *Tap tap tap* went her fingers on the counter. She glanced at her hands, worn with work. One nail was ragged. She put it to her lips, chewed off the ragged end. She paced toward the table, glanced at the clock.

It was 7:33.

Ezekiel mewed from the stove room, where Rebecca rocked him, and hummed a lullaby that did not sound familiar to Sarah. Perhaps Rebecca had made it up.

"Shhh, shhh," said Rebecca to Ezekiel, whose grunts and squirms became more agitated. Sarah was certain he could sense the tension in the room.

For his part, Jacob sighed. He paced, stopped, rocked from his heels to his toes, heaved heavy sighs, and proceeded to pace again. Occasionally, he checked his wrist for a watch he did not own anymore, then, seeming to remember for the first time that it had been left on the pile at the policemen's home, his agitation overcame him, and he heaved yet another sigh and paced once again.

"Please, *Yakob,* sit down!" urged Rebecca, agitated that another male in her home was in need of comfort. "There is nothing we can do, no place to go. We must be patient. *HaShem* is with us; he will not fail us. Be easy, my love."

If only it were so simple, thought Sarah, marveling at Rebecca's ability to remain calm and serene at such a time. She could not decide whether her older sister was short-sighted and ignorant of the crisis at hand or the wisest woman she knew.

Hannah read. She read voraciously, so deeply engaged in her copy of *Heidi,* which she had doubtless read at least a dozen times, that it was as if she were willing herself to be absorbed into the very page or as if scanning for clues. She didn't dare look up at the clock, didn't dare watch her father check his absent watch one more time or stare exasperatedly at Sarah as she scrubbed invisible spots from the kitchen sink. Because if she did, she believed she would go insane.

Jacob had apprised his daughter of Anders' instructions on their long walk home and offered reassurances to them both that he barely felt himself. It would all work out, he insisted. "Anders is a good man. I know this, I can see it. We can trust him." *He's trying to convince himself,* Hannah thought, and she looked at Sarah to see that her wise aunt seemed to be thinking the same thing.

Hannah glanced at the small clock. It was 7:42.

⧗

The day passed this way, with the Roseweig family balancing on a knife's edge, each of them bristling with palpable anxiety, veering wildly between fear and hope, despair and joy. Sarah made soup that, for once, none of them felt like eating, as nervous as their stomachs were.

Hannah finished *Heidi,* clapped the book shut, strode determinedly toward her bedroll where her small pile of books sat, and grabbed the top book off the pile. Then she marched right back to the stove room, resumed her place in her chair, and opened to page one.

Sarah had just one book, which she could not bring herself to read—Eugenie Marlitt's *Die zweite Frau*. But the trivialities of courtly romance could not gain her interest, and she had given up attempting to read this morning after rereading the same page at least six times and remembering nothing.

The brass clock read 4:10. At last, the light was waning through the tiny porthole window, meaning that it was beginning its slow descent behind their bombed-out shelter, and soon it would be nighttime.

Ezekiel, sensing that his family could do with no more irritations, blessedly did not fuss. He nursed from his starving mother all day, and Rebecca's already-gaunt cheeks showed new hollows today. Sarah was sure to give her sister extra soup today.

Amos had come home for soup, reporting that there had been no sightings of Brownshirts today, though a Nazi jeep had rattled down Mauritskade, near the harbor. This had only served to incite greater anxiety in his father, who stood up, paced the floor, and heaved a great sigh.

Then, at long last, darkness fell, and Jacob put on his jacket and woolen cap, gave his wife, daughter, and youngest son a heartfelt, parting kiss, meaningfully embraced his sister-in-law, and stepped into the night to learn of their fate.

Hannah had been heartily sad that she would not be allowed to return to visit with Alexandra. Last evening, Hannah's new friend had given her the music box containing the tiny ballerina, in a gesture of compassion for this family, which even that young Dutch girl could see had nothing. Afraid it would be ripped from her hands, Hannah had told no one of the gift, but every now and then, she stole away to her bedroll, where the music box was stowed under the pillow, and delicately fingered the tiny brass key on its bottom. And when she grew too tired to stay awake any longer, she climbed into the bed, blew out the candle at her bedside, and, in the safety of darkness, cuddled the music box close to her heart.

Jacob and Amos had both returned in the middle of the night. Sarah, who had been restless and unable to sleep at all, feigned sleep in the stove room when she heard father and son talking in whispers.

"… shipping carton? But how, Papa?" Amos was asking.

"We do not have a choice," Jacob said, taking off his hat and shoes wearily.

"Does my mother know?"

"No, I must tell her when she awakes. But she'll have time to get used to the idea."

"And Ezekiel?"

At this, Sarah heard Jacob rub his unshaven face and heave another great sigh. "I do not know, Amos. I must work all this out. Please, now, we must be quiet. Surely he is sleeping now."

Sarah had a sense of Jacob's meaning, remembering the meaningful way in which Anders had stared at the laundry basket the other night. And though the logistics of transport certainly concerned her, Sarah's hopes were bolstered so much by the tenor of the conversation that her heart soared, and the great ache of worry that had settled on her chest all day began unraveling. Soon, she was able to fall asleep.

CHAPTER 8

JULY 4, 1942
LATE AFTERNOON

HAARLEMMERMEER, HOLLAND

The corporal, clearly a courier, with his holstered luger and immense message pouch, stood respectfully by the door of Gunter's temporary quarters, his sidecar motorcycle at the curb. Alongside that stood his guard/passenger, a private first-class, wearing his Schmeisser submachine gun slung across his shoulder. Both were youngsters, regular Wehrmacht soldiers, fresh faced and well groomed.

Of course, they were also quite muddy from the motorcycle having kicked up mud from the still-wet roads. Gunter shivered when he saw them, thinking what a miserable duty it was to be a courier in Holland.

Their insignia showed they belonged to the garrison in Amsterdam, the unit through which Gunter's Luftwaffe superior communicated with him and through which he had been receiving pay for the last month.

The young man saluted. It was the same fascist gesture Gunter saw each day, but though it was executed precisely, as a courtesy, it somehow was without the body-trembling intensity the SS normally gave it.

"*Heil Hitler*," said the courier, business-like rather than with ferocious zeal.

"*Heil Hitler*," Gunter said dismissively.

"Oberst Kramer?"

"Yes," Gunter sighed. *Let's get on with it, shall we?* "What do you have for me, young man?"

But then Gunter caught the tiniest of glimmers of something in the courier's eyes. Anxiety? No. This was sympathy.

"Sir, it is bad news, I am afraid." He handed the envelope to Gunter.

Gerta and Emma. Gunter felt with immediate certainty that the item he held in his hand was of a personal nature. Any military business would be sealed from the view of an ordinary trooper, military courtesy and command privacy having been built into the system. An icy cold dread seized his heart.

The telegram, streaked with mud and starkly featuring the merest shred of news, read simply:

EMMA VERY ILL STOP

IN FRANZISKUS HOSPITAL STOP

STAYING WITH HER STOP

LOVE, GERTA STOP

"*Danke,*" Gunter said to the corporal, his eyes still scanning the paper as if more news might emerge from it. Then, thinking furiously, he called to the retreating back, "Wait! I will have to send a reply. Do you have the forms?"

"*Jawohl*, Herr Oberst," said the young man, reaching for his message pouch.

Gunter gestured for him to wait. "Come inside, both of you. You may leave the cycle. You can see where it sits from my window."

There was a little shock in the green eyes peering at him from under the mud-streaked helmet. Officers usually were not willing to have enlisted men in their quarters. The divide between officers and enlisted men in the German military was typically, emphatically upheld. The men cautiously looked at each other, obviously trying to determine whether to obey Wehrmacht convention or orders from an officer. The latter quickly won out.

Once they were inside, Gunter gestured for them to come in and then bounded up the stairs, barking to the orderly standing by the hall table, "Tea for three, sugar, and three meals!"

He went into the room he had been assigned just last week, when this Haarlemmermeer "exercise" began, tossed his cap and clipboard onto the bed, went to the commode, and splashed his face with water to clear his mind. If he could ever hope to see his darling Emma again, he must execute his steps perfectly. *Oh, Emma, my darling Emma.*

The realization that the troopers were still in the hall occurred to him in a flash. How long had he been upstairs?

He patted his face dry with a towel, and retreated down the steps, where the troopers stood stiffly and awkwardly in the small hallway.

"Come in, come in!" Gunter gestured to the parlor room. "*Sitzen!*" Before being seized for officer housing, this had been a midlevel hotel, so several comfortably upholstered chairs sat around the room. The troopers glanced at each other, in a bit of astonishment.

"You two are working out of Amsterdam, *nein*?" Gunter asked.

"*Jawohl*, Herr Oberst." The courier sat rigidly on the edge of the straightest chair.

"Please, be at ease," Gunter said to him. The young man's spine relaxed only marginally. "What are your names?"

"*Obergefreiter Kucher, Herr Oberst!*" said the courier, sitting up straight and saluting from his chair, clearly confused about the protocol of this situation.

"*Gefreiter Fruehauf, Herr Oberst!*" said the guard as he jumped from his seat, and Gunter realized that this was the first time the man had spoken.

Gunter gestured to the man that he was to sit. "Do you know why the telegram was not sent to the Haarlemmermeer outpost directly?"

"*Jawohl*, Herr Oberst," Kucher said. "The telegraph lines are down in several places because of this most recent storm. Our own oberst wanted you to have the message as quickly as possible."

"Tell him I am grateful for the courtesy." At this Kucher nodded. "How long did your trip take?"

"Three ... perhaps three and a half hours, Herr Oberst." He blushed, looking at Freuhauf. "Neither of us has a watch ..."

Outwardly, Gunter appeared calm and relaxed, but inwardly, his mind raced, performing calculations: *Mein Gott! If I send a query this very moment, it still will take eight hours to reach its destination and solicit a reply, at least. I should go to Amsterdam immediately, but I cannot leave this command without orders. And there is no one to give orders to me on this duty, short of Amsterdam, or maybe even Berlin...*

The orderly tapped at the door. Gunter's eyes had glazed, and he appeared not to have heard the knock.

"Herr Oberst?" the trooper tentatively asked.

Gunter was startled out of his reverie. "*Kommen!*"

The orderly entered with a tray, on which sat a pot, steaming nicely, as well as three chipped mugs, a bowl of sugar with a spoon, and, wondrously, a little pitcher of cream. Both the young troopers' eyes glistened. Gunter noted the troopers' yearnings and filed that away.

"*Danke.* When will food be ready?"

"It is ready now, Herr Oberst, but the mess is in another building, and it takes a few minutes to fetch. It should be on the way now. I telephoned immediately after you ordered it." The orderly stood to attention, studiously not looking at the remarkable guests seated in a senior officer's quarters.

"*Gut!* Bring some towels and hot water so these troopers can clean the mud off their faces and hands before they eat. And tell my driver, outside in the truck, to report here." *I cannot leave my command, but perhaps I can take my command with me,* he thought.

"*Jawohl*, Herr Oberst." The orderly departed briskly.

Minutes later, a meal of noodles and sausage, with a side of steaming cabbage, arrived. All three men attacked it hungrily, Gunter only slightly less urgently than the younger men. It had been another miserable day of driving desperate Jews out of depressing hiding places. The hot, solid food restored comfort to his body's core, contrasting with the cold fear that was clouding his mind.

He *had* to go home for a few days. He would have to get his unit into barracks, and even without this latest news, he was short-handed. Perhaps he could make the argument that Haarlemmermeer was hunted out? It wasn't far from true. Yesterday his unit had caught only forty, and today there had been fewer than a dozen …

There was another knock at the door, this time a robust trio of blows. The SS driver hadn't the subtlety of the orderly.

"*Kommen!*" Gunter called. Then without waiting even for the trooper to fully enter, let alone speak, he barked to the man, "Convey my orders to Feldwebel Ermenthaller!" The SS man braced to rigid attention. "All liberty is cancelled." *No one will have gotten loose yet. They will be just dismounting about now,* Gunter calculated.

"The unit is to eat a meal, then pack for unit relocation. The trucks are to be fully fueled, all equipment loaded, and the unit is to mount the trucks and report here."

Ermenthaller was actually the company sergeant, though he had been operating with Gunter's extended squad for weeks, whenever they were in the field.

"*Jawohl*, Herr Oberst." The driver turned as if to act on the orders.

"Where is Leutnant Eberhardt?" Gunter asked, stopping him in his tracks.

"Sir, I do not know exactly. He is likely at our quarters, because his squads were operating on the eastern side of the city today. Or perhaps he is on the way here. His room is on the ground floor of the other wing of this building."

Gunter had a moment of astonishment at learning this for the first time. He had never been so cavalier about a subordinate before. But he saw Eberhardt as a fascist's fascist, one who loved this foul work. He believed the detention of Jews would bring German salvation. Unchecked, Eberhardt would shoot them on sight. *The likes of that odious Kleinfeldt would never have gotten in trouble under his command*, Gunter thought with satisfaction.

"Check his quarters," Gunter said to the driver. "If he is there, ask him to report to me at his earliest convenience." He realized, as he spoke the words, that "at his earliest convenience" was something like "at a measured run" in the SS. "If he is not there, make sure the orderly on that floor is apprised to deliver the message immediately on his arrival. Dismissed!"

"*Jawohl,* Herr Oberst!" the driver said emphatically, with the zeal of being given an important mission. Then, compulsively, with a great heel click made subdued by muddy boots, he exclaimed, "*Heil Hitler!*" and exited the premises.

"*Heil Hitler!*" Gunter returned, thinking how, despite the Führer's many charms, it was tiresome exclaiming his name fifteen or twenty times a day.

Turning his attention back to his guests, silently eating, Gunter brought them into his newly formed plan. "I am ready for that form pad now, Obergefreiter Kucher."

Corporal Kucher, a baby-faced man, Gunter noted, fished it out of his pouch, handed it over to Gunter, and returned to his meal, appearing to have let down his guard a bit.

It occurred to Gunter, briefly, that he could have the men, their motorcycle, and the sidecar put onto a truck, which would kindly keep them out of the offensive mud. But the realization came immediately that on the bike, the men could be in Amsterdam hours faster than it would take his unit to transport them. They would have to go back the way they came.

Again came an SS-style knock. Gunter was growing quite annoyed at the repeated interruptions. He glanced at his own half-consumed meal, rapidly cooling, and forked half a sausage into his mouth, chewing mightily. The troopers grinned sympathetically as he chased down the last fragment of sausage and cabbage with tea.

"*Kommen!*"

Eberhardt took three confident, determined strides into the dining room. He stopped, with a heel click and "*Heil Hitler!*" before Gunter, who had risen to accept the guest. The small room suddenly seemed crowded.

Seeing the seated courier team, Eberhardt purpled and barked, "You! You do not stand to attention when an officer enters …"

Gunter interrupted him by simply waving the troopers down, in irritation, when she saw them snap to attention. "*Sitzen.*" They subsided, apprehensively. Eberhardt braced rigidly.

"*Heil Hitler.* Leutnant, we are relocating the unit to Amsterdam tonight. You are to take a meal, pack your belongings, and return here. I have ordered the unit to report here. Where are your squads?"

The lieutenant was indignant at having his authority undermined, which made it visibly hard for him to reply succinctly. "They are at the enlisted quarters now, Herr Oberst. I left them there and came here in the command car."

"Is that still here?"

"*Jawohl …*"

"*Gut!*" Gunter cut him off. "Have the driver take a meal here, as I have done for these tired couriers," he said pointedly, conveying his reprimand for the obstreperous lieutenant, "and then have him take the car to fuel and service before reporting back. I will use the half-armored truck, as I have been doing, and you will use the car to carry a road guard of three men so that cross roads will not slow us down. Use draperies, anything you may find, to make flags to stop traffic. And make sure your road guard has several lanterns with enough fuel or flashlights. I don't want them getting killed in the dark."

The lieutenant looked confused, skeptical of these new, strange orders. Gunter opted for flattery, which he knew Eberhardt was susceptible to. "You are our lead element, Leutnant. I am counting on you. Dismissed!"

Eberhardt stomped, saluted the Führer once more, turned on his heels, and yanked furiously at the door in a way that made Gunter fear the doorknob might come off in his hand. The door closed authoritatively, if not slammed.

"I thought I'd lose my doorknob, there…" Gunter said, then, startled that he'd spoken that out loud, turned to see Kucher and Freuhauf guffaw.

Gunter made his face mock solemn. "Shoddy Dutch fixtures, you know." He focused on Kucher.

"Obergefreiter Kucher."

The young man sprang to his feet, almost dropping his bowl.

"*Sitzen*. Drink another mug of tea. You are going to need it. When my unit gets here, they will have gas cans on board. Refuel your bike and put a spare can on the rack. I want you to take this to the telegraphy office tonight." The corporal gulped a bit.

"It is necessary to let command know we are moving the unit, so no train cars will be sent tomorrow. The Reich does not need to waste shipping capacity, and we will need barracks room for our unit when we arrive."

The men could not hide the expressions of dread on their faces. Gunter nodded sympathetically at them. "We, too, have been working all day, and my men will be almost as tired and miserable as you two when we arrive." They rewarded his comments with friendly and willing grins.

"Now, drink up. The commode is down the hall to the left. If you'll excuse me, I must write more messages."

"*Danke,* Herr Oberst," came the response, a duet.

The corporal waved his private out for first relief and poured tea, quietly, as instructed.

Gunter sat and began composing, cold food forgotten beside him. *Emma.*

CHAPTER 9

JULY 4, 1942
EVENING

PORT OF AMSTERDAM, HOLLAND

It was going to be even harder than they'd thought. Jacob frantically scanned the immense dock, its timbered surface of great, creosote-encrusted beams dense and echoing with the footfalls of the few people out here in the shadowy twilight hours. A few late-staying pelicans hung about, hoping for charity. The remnants of the day's fishing lined the edges—scraps of redolent bait, hunks of line, the occasional broken hook.

There was no cover here at all, and there were no crowds into which the family could disappear. Jacob and Nicolas would have to be utterly convincing as Dutch stevedores and the cargo cover for the women and children totally concealing. Their lives absolutely depended on it.

Nazi guards, their long deadly rifles slung, stood at every fifty-meter interval of the dock. There was no place here that was free from German eyes.

Convincing Rebecca of the viability of this plan had not been easy. Her terror of what it might mean for her beloved children, as always, was the basis for her reaction to hearing the news from Jacob on the morning after his solo trip to Anders' home. She, her sister, and her two youngest children—one of whom was a mere infant—were to climb inside sealed cargo crates, in which they would be packed like so much rubber tubing, aboard a great ship for weeks until they arrived in Suriname to face…what?

"I know it is hard to be still with the little one for a long time, *Liebchen*," Jacob empathized. "But the policeman has given us a few child's doses of laudanum, much as you'd use for flu, and when you must enter the bale, or the crate, you can drink it, and let Ezekiel have it through your milk, or you can just use an eyedropper and let him drink a little, enough to sleep with. It will be less than an hour, I assure you, and we will be very careful to make sure there is plenty of air."

Rebecca's eyes were rimmed with tears, sheer terror in their expression. Of course, Sarah could see that the terror was for Ezekiel, not herself.

"*Yakob*, what of Hannah and Amos?"

"Hannah will go aboard the same way as you, and Amos and Otto Rabin are big enough, and look enough like Dutch boys, that we can have them be stevedores like the men. Nicolas Anders has arranged it all. We can trust him, *Liebchen*, I am sure of it."

They huddled on the floor next to the barely warm patched stove, Ezekiel enveloped protectively in his mother's arms. Hannah and Sarah sat nearby, listening to Jacob's plan and sharing an understanding that this was, despite appearances, the best possible course of action. Amos, who had learned of the plan the previous night, was out on patrol with the Rabin boys.

"In eight days' time, all of the ladies in our travel party will go to the warehouse, in the early evening. You will go together with mops and brooms and buckets, dressed as cleaners. You will go into the office there then through an interior door to the warehouse. It will appear that you are a crew going to work at the end of the office day. We men will be stevedores, or deck hands, or even couriers or food vendors. We will go aboard the evening before, to make preparations for you all. Nicolas has many different kinds of clothing and tools from years of policing the docks. In truth, I believe he must have the soul of a frustrated playwright, because he is very good at this." He chuckled, looking for a sense of relief from his family. Only Sarah warmed.

"Nicolas is risking everything in this mission," Jacob said encouragingly. "He will be the one opening the warehouse office with his own inspection key and helping pack you ladies and all of our little ones with his own hands." Here, he looked pointedly into his daughter's eyes. "And Alexandra will be a cleaning woman, too, because they will have to have a guide."

Hannah beamed, proud of the kindness of her new, dear friend.

Jacob grinned, and, reluctantly, Rebecca smiled back in the dimness of their little nest, trying to put on a brave face for her husband. It was clear to all present that there was no alternative to this plan. Yet this seemed to do little to instill a sense of safety within her. Her hands seemed to shake uncontrollably as she diapered Ezekiel with the shoddy cotton that was cold when wet and had to be changed as soon as the infant wetted or soiled himself, causing a rash that would force unneeded wails from his lungs. Sarah nudged her niece, and the two tittered to see Jacob turn his head and fight the impulse to retch when the smell of his infant son's dirty diaper wafted toward him.

Rebecca heard the girls and turned to see the source. Despite her worry and the foulness of the task at hand, she giggled.

"Oh, *Yakob,* my big, strong man," she said it lovingly, as she brought the changed, dry, content baby back to her bosom. "My dear, you could never be a mother."

So, the plan fixed, the Roseweigs had nothing to do but bide their time quietly until the day when they would steal away on board ship. With a few rations supplied by Nicolas, to stop them leaving the house as much as possible, the family passed the slowest ten days of their lives.

Within twenty-four hours after receiving word from Anders that there would be a boat for them, Sarah and all members of the Roseweig family had gathered their most vital belongings together and had begun carrying them from room to room with them, in case it was determined that they needed to go into hiding elsewhere, hop aboard another boat, or simply hide from the Nazis that seemed to creep ever closer to them from all sides, like maggots on old meat. Sarah's pack contained only a few items of clothing, a small framed photograph of Michael, a hairbrush, a toothbrush, a pair of shoes, and all the money she possessed in the world, which amounted to only twenty-seven *Reichsmarks*—what remained of Michael's savings.

The first item Hannah had put into her old school bag, which she would take to Suriname, was the ballerina music box that Alexandra had given to her, along with her packet of stationery, a pen, a copy of *Heidi,* two dresses, a comb, a woolen scarf, a pack of cards, and the ties for her hair which she used to become Esme.

The bedrolls were wound tightly immediately upon waking each morning, like stout soldiers at the ready. Hannah had taken to chewing her nails, a nervous habit formed from sheer lack of occupation. That and shuffling her cards, which she did most days, when she and her mother and aunt weren't engaged in a game of Whist or Skat. The shuffling made a sound that drove Sarah to near madness, and many times she would join a game simply to force Hannah to stop shuffling, though the games helped the time to pass more quickly.

Remaining in their hovel at the height of summer was pure torture, and the craving for sunlight among all of them had become acute, not to mention the stifling, still, moist heat that kept the small room feeling like an oven almost continually.

"What do you imagine Suriname will be like?" Hannah mused during a game of Skat on the fourth evening. "In school, we read *Der Schweizerische Robinson,* about a family that were shipwrecked on an island in the Pacific. There were wild animals and terrible storms, and they were forced to live in a cave. Will we be forced to live that way?"

Sarah laughed at her niece's wild ideas. "Hannah, love, you have quite an imagination. Do you think Dr. Adelmann, or your papa, would expect us to live like savages?" Sarah caught Rebecca's worried glances, realizing that her sister very likely had the same fears, so she spoke in reassuring tones. "I think Suriname will be paradise. Palm trees, warm breezes, coconut shells…" She stretched her arms, arching her back and leaning her face up toward the ceiling, her hair falling down her back and nearly touching the floor. She extended her fingers outward as if she were a flower reaching toward the sky and exclaimed, "Oh! To stand in the sunshine again!"

Meanwhile, throughout the course of the ten days, Amos patrolled the streets with the Rabin boys and delivered messages between Jacob and the other families as they coordinated their plans. Often, Jacob and Rebecca sat listening to the wireless for news of the outside world—anything that might affect their plans. A great battle was taking place in the Atlantic, with German U-Boats torpedoing Allied subs and Navy ships. Jacob realized that successfully stealing aboard a ship was only the first leg of a dangerous journey and was by no means the only hurdle for his family to overcome. The journey would be considerably longer than it would otherwise, he understood, as the captain would be forced to traverse the eastern coast of Europe and skirt the conflict as much as possible.

The ten days felt interminable, and as day passed into weary day, each of them had wondered at some point whether this ambitious plan to escape to

South America were all some fantastic dream that actually would rot ever take place. On a page in his blank book, the one he had always carried with him for adding figures when he had worked as an accountant, a lifetime ago, Jacob had begun adding hash marks at nightfall in order to keep track of the passing days. He found himself checking it throughout the day, to be sure that time was indeed ticking by. With the summer sun shining until nearly ten o'clock, each day felt like at least two.

But indeed, miraculously, the time did pass, and on the tenth day, the family had gathered their belongings and come together at the door of the ruined building they had called home these past months and steeled themselves for the long journey ahead. Not one of them ventured a backward glance.

Their clothing reserve was small, just the two baskets Jacob, Sarah, and Hannah had been using as prop "laundry," but they had all taken care to wear several layers as they dressed that morning, despite the heat. They hoped that it would make them appear less wasted and hungry and thereby less likely to be refugees. They had persuaded Amos to wrap his middle in spare sweaters under his coat until he looked far better fed than he really was.

"Remember, we are going to be in a steel ship in the Atlantic," Jacob reminded them all. "It may be quite cold at times, and it is the season for tropical storms. You must all pray for warm weather and calm seas." They could only take what they could wear on their backs, and it was essential that they not appear to be wearing every stitch of clothing they owned, though they all were.

Ezekiel's baby things went into a bucket that would be part of Rebecca's cleaning-woman disguise; it was not unusual for women doing such work to take their infants with them, and that would solve the logistics of having mother and baby together for "packaging."

"*Yakob*, what will it be like in Suriname?" Rebecca asked. Sarah watched Jacob's face, knowing he himself honestly had no idea about what they would find in this place they would soon call home. Hannah looked anxiously to her father for confirmation that her fears would not be realized.

"I think you ladies will have to dress in grass skirts, like we saw in that American magazine…" Rebecca blushed scarlet. The young women in those photos had not worn *anything* above their waists.

Sunlight. They had fantasized about it in the months since coming to this wretched place and being forced to hide in darkness. *Suriname could scarcely be worse than this*, Sarah thought.

Hannah struggled not to cry. She and Aliza Rabin walked close to Alexandra, each of them with a bucket, mop, and broom in hand. They were at the front of the band of women, taking the most circumspect route to the warehouse district, next to the dock area. She quickly glanced at Rebecca, who wore little Ezekiel slung to her bosom with a blanket, walking alongside Sarah and the other mothers, Rachel Levin and Naomi Rabin. The men and older boys had all gone to the ships in their stevedore clothing to load "cargo" onto the ships.

Alexandra wore a bandana of white muslin, arranged to show her blonde bangs and pigtails. The rest of them, all dark-haired, wore bonnets and head-scarves carefully set to conceal their darkness.

"Alexa, *why* are you out here?" asked Hannah, who felt riddled with guilt about having her friend out on the German-infested streets.

"We have to look like we know where we are, and where we are going, and men never work in such cleaning crews." Alexandra's smile was as dazzling as usual, and her eyes gleamed with excitement. Hannah could see that Alexandra had some tricks up her sleeve so followed her friend loyally.

The patrol was on them without warning—four men, rifle-armed, with the armbands of the *Militarish Polizei*, the military police.

"*Halten Ze!*" called one, sternly.

They froze like a flock of hens threatened by a hawk. The unteroffizier, their corporal, leaned on his Mauser and grinned at Alexandra.

"Where are you going, Fraulein?" His expression was intent, but guilty a bit, using his duty to chat up a pretty girl.

Alexandra, used to men and their approaches now that she was a year and a half older than Hannah, smiled guilelessly and toyed with an escaping lock of hair. The men looked only at her, not at the tired and drab-looking older women, but although Sarah was following Mijnheer Anders' strict instructions to keep her head bowed so as not to attract attention, she nonetheless saw that one of the men glanced appreciatively at her own figure. They were bored young men, happy to have time speaking to an attractive girl. Sarah saw that Alexandra might use this to their advantage.

"We are to clean the offices of the Riferstrasse Warehouse, Mijnheer," said Alexandra, flirtatiously.

"Why does someone as pretty as you clean offices, Fraulein? You could make good money serving our *bier*, you know." They grinned like a pack of hungry wolves.

"*Ja*, and my uncle would beat me for being in such a place, and for talking with German soldiers when I didn't have to." Sarah inwardly congratulated the girl on her retort. Alexandra gave him a full glare, and the corporal visibly pulled into his shell, reminded that he was part of an invading and occupying force and that most of the Dutch openly despised them for the intrusion.

"Well, be on your way, Fraulein. And remember, the Reich is a friend of the Dutch people. If we, your good neighbors, had not come here, you would be hosting the *verdammt* English, and their forces are not nearly so well behaved."

Alexandra soothed him with a small smile, then almost whispered, in a babyish voice, "Perhaps that is true. The English sailors used such horrible language…"

The young man stepped back, waved them on, and they all eddied past Alexandra, who stood in place for a moment, freezing the squad's eyes.

"*Danke*, Unteroffizier …?"

"Kraus, Karl Kraus, Fraulein," he said, eagerly.

"Unteroffizier Kraus, *danke* for your courtesy, and good night." She slowly moved to catch up with the ladies. Sarah watched out of the corner of her eye as his gaze followed Alexandra, longing and hungry. As they went around the corner, Alexandra looked back and waved gently.

The encounter had been dealt with, Alexandra had done splendidly, and Hannah's heart had clenched. If only Alexa could come *with* them! The terrible Germans would be here forever, and not all of them would be polite.

"Alexa, how have you learned to deal so well with them?" Hannah asked as they hustled down yet another long boulevard and into an alley between the first of the warehouses.

"Papa has to deal with them every day, and while the older officers are not a trouble, their orderlies and messengers are just like that one—lonely young fellows who feel out of place in our country. Any of them with any training in manners can be kept in line."

Rebecca marched along shoulder to shoulder with Sarah, whose shining dark eyes, graceful lips, and elegantly boned face were not safe to show soldiers. Anders had been emphatic. Let Alexandra deal with any Germans, he had said. This had struck Sarah, his willingness to involve his daughter in this way, as odd and somewhat reckless. To Rebecca, Hannah, and Sarah, the most beauteous of the group, he had emphasized, "*Never* look at them. Keep your heads down, your hips slouched forward." With this he had demonstrated the slouch of a lowly drab, eliciting a smile from Sarah and a small giggle from Hannah. "Do this so that they cannot see the grace of your forms. They are under discipline, but it is thin discipline." The women nodded, solemnly.

At last they arrived at their warehouse, the offices located along one end of the immense structure with the rounded roof and low eaves. And there, the door opened, and Anders waved them in. Jacob and Amos were with him.

Jacob hugged his wife, then extended his arm and gestured for the women to enter. Anders urged them all through yet another door, into the warehouse proper.

At the far end of the great space, there was a wall of bales and beyond that an area where banding and lashing tools and materials lay, next to a great door that Sarah presumed must open to a loading dock. Overhead was a vaulted, cantilevered roof with its heavy intersecting planks, edges down, defining the arch. Great cross rafters held stark electric lights in downward facing hoods. Only one of the many lights was lit, just enough for a night watchman to make his way about.

"Here we are," Anders said grimly, which Sarah took to meant he was not impressed with the quarters they were about to occupy. "We will fit you each in and band the parts around your legs now, making sure the braces are set."

They look like coffins! Sarah thought, fighting to control her terror. She had been enthusiastic about this plan and had never wavered until now. Each bale held a structure that she realized was a heavy wire cage, rounded to a shape little more round than a woman's body, or in some cases, two kegs and some barrel hoops. Each had a tube, a tin can without ends, securely wired to it, and projecting almost to the outside of its bale. "You must understand, there will be one or two thicknesses of cloth over those ends," Anders continued, narrating her thoughts. "Breathing is not going to be like in the open air." Sarah felt fear seize her throat, and her breathing struggled for a moment, as though she were already in the constraints of her own cloth coffin.

"For most of this furniture, we have to thank our crab- and lobster-fishing friends, and for the rest, the cooper down the next lane," he grinned, "though they are unaware of having contributed. We did take leavings and rusty discards, so it should not raise any alarm."

He strode to the nearest of the bundles. "Let us get each of you fitted in now, and then we will have time to change the baby. Please use the convenience over there…."

He was indicating a neatly painted white door. Hannah and Aliza swooped toward it with hydraulic urgency, with the older women following. Inside the room, they found a neat toilet and basin behind it, with a small mirror in a wooden frame.

It took hours, in fact, with Jacob, Nicolas Anders, and Amos working almost nonstop to customize each female's hiding place. Finally, they were ready to begin putting on the final fastenings, to put the bales next to the door for the first loading in the rapidly approaching dawn.

"Jacob?" asked Naomi Rabin, timidly. "Where are Eli, and Aliza and my sons?" Sarah glanced at a very pregnant Rachel Levin, also eager to hear word of Albert and Choen.

"They went on board last night, with me. They are in a rope locker with some blankets. They are all right, sleeping the sleep of an opium den." Rachel and Naomi flinched briefly and then exhaled, relaxing when they realized the joke.

Jacob grinned and continued. "We are to sail on this evening's tide. You ladies, I am sorry, must stay in your fine new beds," he waved at the waiting, partly banded bales of cloth, from which, unfortunately, the odor of used crab traps was emanating, "until we are out of the bay and onto the high sea."

Sarah's mind reeled with the new knowledge that she would be forced to sit in darkness for nearly a full day. *Will we eat? How will we toilet? Are we to soil ourselves in these crates?*

Alexandra took Hannah aside, hugging the girl's dark head so that it was cheek to cheek with her own fair one. Tears rolled down both their cheeks.

"Here. This is for you," Alexa proffered a small bag. "Everyone is getting one, so you don't need to worry about sharing." The muslin bundle smelled of baked goods, but Hannah also heard sloshing.

"Biscuits with some butter, and beer in clamp-top bottles so you can open them in the bales, and so on."

Hannah was truly amazed, and simply stared at her friend, wide-eyed.

"Papa sent a box of these packets to the warehouse with one of his officers, yesterday," Alexandra explained, and drew out a little clamped flask, its ceramic and rubber stopper medical white. "And here is your laudanum. Do not take more than a sip at a time, and put the stopper back right away after each sip, because you will probably fall asleep without seeing it coming."

Hannah hugged Alexandra again, and over the Dutch girl's shoulder she saw that Nicolas and Jacob were handing out bundles and explaining similar flasks to the rest of the women. Sarah, she could see, was shaking her head, and as the girls rejoined the group, her objections became apparent.

"No one is going to make me into an addict! I have seen those creatures coming out of the opium houses in Austria!" As much as she dreaded the day ahead, the thought of spending it unconscious frightened her much more.

Nicolas waved a placatory hand. "No one will *make* you take any. But you will be in a smelly, tight place for many hours, and this is a way to stop cramping of the muscles, to induce sleep, and to help with the fear. Using it one day will not make you an addict. Believe me, I have dealt with sailors from all over the world for many years, and I know of what I speak."

His words helped comfort her somewhat. She would not be drinking the laudanum, though, she was sure. She'd rather be alert to any coming danger, to look out for the others as they slept. She worried most about the children. *Surely such a powerful drug cannot be safe for them.*

Then they all took turns in the water closet for the embarrassing process of removing undergarments and binding bundles of cloth to serve as diapers. "I had hoped you were out of diapers, *Liebchen*," Jacob smiled teasingly at Hannah, "but it is better to have the insurance."

Nicolas and Papa settled each woman into her bale, keeping the area around each one's face open or propped as long as possible, making certain that the air tube cans were close to the surface, and even piercing the cloths that covered them so that if the cloth were wetted it would not altogether stop the flow of air.

Hannah's body shook uncontrollably with fear as she slowly folded herself inside the crate. She had worried for so long about getting to the ship and about arriving in Suriname. But until now, she had not fully grasped the horrific nature of the time she would spend packed inside an airless crate. She shivered violently as she looked up and saw Jacob's face peering down worriedly at her.

"Oh my *Liebchen*… Your papa loves you." Hannah saw fear in her father's eyes and decided that she would put on a brave face for him.

"I love you too, Papa. I will see you tomorrow!" She smiled bravely up at him. A hovering Alexandra moved into her line of sight, and, after exchanging a momentary farewell glance with her new, dear friend, she tenderly closed the bale. Hannah could hear the banding going on, creaking slightly even through the muffling layers.

Then Papa's voice came through her can tunnel. "Do you have enough air, *Liebchen*?"

"*Ja*, Papa, it is good. Be careful. I love you."

"I love you, too, Daughter. Be brave, now."

The bale swung up, sickeningly, lifted by the winch arm of the dock cart, and Hannah knew Papa and Nicolas were cranking her up. She swung dizzily, the foot end of her bale scraping across the floor as the cart wheeled across it, and then her crate arrived with a muffled thump on the dock. They must have opened the great dock doors, but she had not heard it through her bale.

Only vibrations, she told herself reassuringly. *No noise, only vibrations.* Her thoughts tumbled, frantic as she began reacting to her helplessness. After a time, she thought, *It must have been at least an hour by now…*

"Hannah? Can you hear me? How is the air?"

Of course Papa would check on everyone. She realized he must be going on the truck with them, to make sure all the crates were put on board and weren't stacked too tightly.

"Fine, Papa? How is Mutter?"

"They are both good, but I can't be seen talking to a bale of cloth, *Liebchen*." Hannah chuckled, a moment of lightness in the dark.

⧗

When they went on board the truck, it was a shock, because obviously someone far less careful than Jacob was using the winch on the dock. Sarah hit the wall with a thump that hurt, the wire of her crab trap cocoon impacting the tender skin of her head.

I just hope they don't put anything over my air hole, Sarah prayed, but to no avail. They did, and though this did not cut off her air altogether, it was obvious that her air flow was now considerably less.

She was so very afraid to die and choked back the urge to scream—an impulse that would surely kill them all. She gripped the laudanum tightly and fought a battle in her mind over its use. She felt her bale shift as someone, probably Jacob, rearranged the way it lay.

She thought of her sister at that moment, tucked away even more tightly with her baby boy enfolded in her arms. *How terrified she must be! And with both of them sharing a small air tube like this!* A deep love, a childish longing for her older sister, welled up inside Sarah and brought tears to her eyes. Just as quickly, she wiped them away and vowed to remain calm and focus firmly on her sister's safety and the safety of her niece and nephews. She was a widow, a healthy woman without a child. It was Rebecca, she knew, who need all the strength and prayers she could muster.

She was now grateful for the tight confines of the wire mesh, because the truck obviously slipped in the slush, went in and out of potholes, and generally seemed to find every irregularity in the road surface. Her constriction was a blessing. Despite the jolts caused by the truck as it traveled, she was not thrown forcefully, controlled by her cage as she was.

The feel of progress changed, carrying with it a wooden vibration. *This must be the dock*, she realized. Now she understood what Jacob had explained to them earlier—that they had chosen the baled cloth instead of the crated cloth, because the bales would go on board directly from the trucks and into the hold right away, so as not to get wet in the slush. Crates, on the other hand, could even be strapped on deck, and left for hours more before their prisoners could get out.

Despite knowing in general what was happening, the sudden yank as her bale was seized and tossed, tumbling, made Sarah fear they had been discovered. Her mind raced frantically, reminding her of what Jacob had instructed them would happen. She realized that the bales were being put into a net, a sort of huge bag to winch aboard, like those they'd seen at a distance from shore. She remembered Rachel Levin's swollen belly, its precious contents certainly at peril in this situation. *Oh, Rebecca, I hope they haven't thrown you on top of Ezekiel!* she thought in horror.

Her own situation was far from comfortable, as she was now practically standing on her head as the piled bales filled their container and then tilted brutally as that constraint tightened and lifted. The wire cage she had come to trust had warped, bent, straining her backward at the waist, and she scrabbled to accommodate the bend. *I am too young to become a pretzel!* The thought of the twisted treat made her smile in the dark. *I must be losing my mind already.*

An interminable swoop made her feel as if her stomach was back on the dock, and then there was an immense swaying as their jumble swung out and over the hold. By the nature of this putative cargo, men would take the bales out and stack them to conserve space. Papa had intended to be already in the hold, working as a stevedore, and Sarah knew she would not be dumped out from a great height to plummet into the hold like some loading she had seen in pictures. Still, she winced as she considered the bruises she would endure. *Oh, Rebecca! Oh, Ezekiel!*

The settling of the bales into the hold was far from gentle. Warned, Sarah carefully kept her mouth closed, her teeth firmly together. Her bale toppled so she was facedown, her air tube under her face, still with access to air but worrisome nonetheless. After an eternity spent in this position, she was lifted, with gentle force.

Then came a familiar voice in a strained whisper. "Hello?" It was Jacob. Her heart soared at the sound of his voice.

"*Yakob!* Hello!"

"*Baruch HaShem!* Now we are all safe! Now wait and be quiet. You and the other breathing bales are going to be on top of stacks, but we can't talk, because the Germans are sure to inspect again during loading. Hush now."

Another interminable wait, her bale moving now with the movement of the ship at dock, a quiet, almost soothing rocking motion. The air was still good, if smelling too much of crab trap and musty hold, and Sarah tried to quiet her trembling. Feeling wetness, she found where a thick, rusted, broken wire of the trap had penetrated three skirts and a slip to poke into her bottom. Pulling herself off of the offending stub of wire was serious pain, and pressing the nasty projection flat scraped her fingers, but she folded her multiple clothing over the puncture as a pad to stop the bleeding. *I wonder if crabs carry tetanus,* she thought. She was shaking again before the bale moved, lifted, settled, and was scooted sideways, obviously being added to a stack.

Still at last, her stomach quivering, the tears came in a flood. *Safe for now. And alive.*

Sarah fumbled and found her little flask. Forgetting her earlier protestations, the terror—of being discovered, of being suffocated and left to die here—overcame her and as the tears poured down her checks, her trembling became violent. She had to calm herself. With shaking hands, she took two sips before she stoppered it, carefully, and closed the eyes that had been staring into the dark for hours. Sleep indeed came without her seeing it coming.

CHAPTER 10

JULY 4, 1942
EVENING

PORT OF AMSTERDAM, HOLLAND

"They are here, *Yakob*. Let us give them smiles," Nicolas had instructed them that evening before taking a couple of deep breaths himself, both of them having labored to construct the hiding bales for several hours, after an equally strenuous day.

When Jacob had watched the rest of his family approach, he looked closely for signs of…what? Terror? Excitement? Rebecca's eyes betrayed the former, as she clung tightly to their infant son and looked to her husband for reassurance. She understood the risks fully and was hard put not to cry. But Jacob noted that both Hannah and Sarah looked more excited than scared. Their familiar resilience bucked up Jacob's hope, despite his knot of worries. He hoped fervently that Rebecca too would benefit from their influence.

Fitting the mothers and daughters into their bales was painstaking, and Jacob felt his ribs cramp with all the bending and tugging. He hadn't much strength left after months of poor food and broken sleep, but he told himself to be strong for his family. This was hard. An accountant did not develop a lot of muscle, and now this painstaking physical task, on which his family's lives and the lives of the women and children of all the families depended, taxed his last reserves.

Finally, all cocooned, all checked for their ability to breathe, and all slid, with the help of the cart, into a long row inside the rolling loading dock door, the hidden women and children were ready for the outside world.

Alexandra shook his hand solemnly, glanced anxiously at the row of bales, and retreated to the office to wait for Nicolas.

With the door up, gray predawn lit the warehouse better than had the lone, high ceiling bulb. Nicolas and Jacob began sliding the bales out to the edge of the dock, making it so that the loading crew had to move the bales as little as possible. He hoped that the truckers would not have any loaders with them, so that he and his fellow stowaways could do all of the moving themselves.

But it was not to be. The lorries, with their stake sides and canvas hooped tops, lumbered between the giant warehouses, looking at first like tiny beetles between bricks, and then like the mechanized colossi that they were.

Nicolas, seeing the sheer size of the truck that first backed to the dock, jumped heavily down to speak to the driver. Jacob could hear him, as the engine switched off.

"...on top, because these are the bales with the lading tickets," he heard Nicolas telling the driver in Dutch, a language he had come to learn almost as well as German. "We'll pull most of the load from the stacks inside."

Then, with horror, Jacob saw the hay hooks in the hands and belts of the loaders who dismounted from the cab and the cargo bed. He gestured as inconspicuously and as urgently as he could manage to call Nicolas over.

The policeman, in vest and work shirt as befitted his role as a warehouse man, trotted over, purpling a bit with the effort. Jacob considered that this is not the man's usual endeavor, and those beloved pipes of his certainly did not help. Jacob bent, seized Nicolas' wrist in an acrobat's grip, and heaved back desperately to help the heavier man regain the dock.

"They have hooks!" Jacob shouted in a whisper into Nicolas' ear. The policeman immediately understood the danger and turned to shout at the driver, who appeared to be in charge and of a different status than the loaders, because now he was leaning against his cab and lighting a cigarette.

"No hooks today, boys, this is finished cloth. Every hook set costs yards of cloth, and the inspector on the other side of the pond can slash our payables!" At the same time, he waved the workmen over to him and cocked his head at the driver—all courtesy to the team leader. Jacob held his breath.

"He's right, *rooinecks*, this isn't a load of rags," the driver called, quick to establish that he was in charge. "Put them in the cab."

There was grumbling, but the driver, happy to use his authority, was persistent. "You have no idea how it feels to open a cargo from Europe and find some lazy stupid has ruined something you've paid well for. Put 'em in the cab. And, Ernst, no smoking in the warehouse!" This last was directed at a sullen fellow in overalls who was on the verge of striking a big lucifer match.

One leaped down, the others passed him their hooks, and this first peril was mastered.

Jacob aided as Nicolas directed the loaders to the appropriate stacks inside, helping put normal bales on the platform of the steel wheeled cart, then leaning into the load as if helping to push, though the real reason was that if he didn't lean on something, he would fall down from exhaustion. There was nothing left in him. He could barely breathe. His chest heaved, his limbs felt like straws, and dizziness almost felled him. He followed the cart to the dock, grateful for the restful ruse.

Fortunately, one of the loaders who had come with the truck leaped automatically into the cargo bed, and the cart was manhandled down a stout timber ramp he deployed from where it had been lashed inside the bed. After that, there was only room alongside the cart for the two who had come with the truck, and Jacob was able to busy himself fussing about the bales that were so precious. He spoke first to Hannah, then Rebecca, and then Sarah. All were safe. He tried to speak words of comfort to them but had to stop his anxious inspecting as workmen and the cart reemerged onto the dock.

Four more carts were loaded, and Jacob was able to participate as before. Just in time for the cargo that mattered.

A dreadful realization occurred to him: They were going to be *stacked*. At the very back of the truck, but stacked. The horror made his throat feel like an iron pipe being crushed. It took agonizing time to resume breathing.

Against the outer wall of the warehouse, there was a bit of lumber and chock clutter, sorted with Dutch neatness by thickness and length. Jacob sidled over to where Nicolas stood and spoke urgently to the men.

"Boys, I want to be able to reach the label tags from the open tailgate," Jacob instructed in Dutch, sounding more firm than he felt as the idea sprang to him. "So as we get each layer on, I want to put in a chock or a block, so we can reach in for the inspector." He turned to Nicolas, who nodded appreciatively at him for the invention.

This was not usual, but then, mercifully, these were not the most gifted or analytical of workmen, either.

Nicolas was now at the culmination of his act here, and he made a fine climax.

"Mijnheer Driver, I would appreciate your taking my accountant here with you, because I want him there for the loading count, and I don't want to lose track of the manifested stuff."

The driver grinned at Jacob and laughed a bit. "Didn't think he was a workman. Pencil pusher can't even lift a bale!" But he genially waved Jacob to the cab, offering him the wide seat as befitted someone of better status than stevedore.

Nicolas came to the driver's window, patted his arm, and tendered an envelope. "*Danke*. Give your boys what is fair and the rest for you, Mijnheer." Jacob tried to convey all his gratitude with the look he gave Nicolas as the Dutch policeman waved them on.

The driver thumbed open his envelope as he slowly pulled away from the dock and let out a gratified grunt.

As they lumbered out of the warehouse lane and turned to head downward to the docks, the driver leaned confidingly toward Jacob. "Good of you to try to help, but don't kill yourself on the unload. Just tell my boys where you want what. They'll do the lifting."

Jacob nodded at him appreciatively, thinking to himself that Nicolas was so good at crooked things, he must have been a very good policeman.

⧗

Nazis. They were everywhere on the docks, as they had been on the day Nicolas had shown him the dock the first time, and as they had been yesterday, as they had smuggled men and boys aboard in work party roles. Even expected, they chilled Jacob, associated so closely with death as they were, and alien as they had become, despite their having been countrymen for most of his life. The gray uniforms represented the death of not only his family's way of life and home but also of all the people he held dear. Their sight had become nauseating, not unlike what one felt seeing vultures tear slain flesh along the roadway.

The creatures would want to strut and look important, he knew, and he had to let them speak to the driver, because he could not speak German in such a way as to sound like a Dutchman, and he didn't have papers. The clipboard he clutched was accurate as to the load; the tags on the human-bearing bales, those that bore tags, were accurate as to type of cloth but could not be with regard to weight. They had entered only bale dimensions and count, hoping to avoid any chance of a weighing.

Jacob climbed down from the cab, trying to move like a decently fed Dutchman rather than a near-starving Jewish refugee. As the slower loaders climbed down from the truck bed, he indicated the rearmost bales, and a place a bit off to the side. The first bale came down with a velocity that nearly made him scream, and impacted the dock timbers with a flat *whumph*!

Who was that? He couldn't let that happen. Necks could be broken; one mother was seven months along in a pregnancy, not to mention his own little one in with Rebecca.

"None of that, now! If you break a band, we don't have the tools to refasten, and the bale could come apart," he told the men, attempting to sound like a man nervous about the mistreatment of bales of cloth, not his family. "*Two* of you. Lift them down, place them there, and labels up!" Used to giving directions in his own accounting business, and urgent with the responsibility he bore, Jacob spoke with, to his own astonishment, crisp authority.

And to his further astonishment, the workmen meekly complied. Jacob stood by with his clipboard of authority, visually ensuring that the little slits that revealed breathing tubes were upright or outboard on all the important bales. He pulled part of each tag off then made the relevant tic marks on his loading sheet.

The driver stood leaning again against his truck, smoking another cigarette. "Told you they'd do what you tell them."

"So you did. Can you have them load the net there with the other bales first?" Jacob's father had taught him that it was always better to work through the supervisor—it made them feel important and happy to please. Clearly, his father had known what he was talking about. After all, his people had been eliciting cooperation in potentially hostile populations for a long time.

At the last, so intent had he been to make sure that the populated bales wound up on the top, or at least the outside of the great cargo net, Jacob was seized with abject fear as he glanced up from his ritual clipboard to see, standing impatiently in front of him, a German feldwebel, holding out his gloved hand. He almost froze, but extended the board with trepidation that must have looked like the deference the beasts demanded, because the man just glanced down the columns and noted numbers, flipped cursorily through the lading tag ends held under the clip, then scrawled a signature at the bottom of the sheet. Then, flipping that up, tore off the carbon copy Jacob had not even been conscious he was making. He was obviously carrying out a many times repeated task.

Thrusting the thing back at Jacob, the feldwebel nodded crisply. Jacob croaked, "*Danke*" in so congested a voice there was no danger of accent recognition, and the moment of greatest danger was over.

The net was going up!

Two quick strides took him to the driver, who took the clipboard with a questioning look.

"I'm going on board to make sure of stowage. We lost some bales last trip," said Jacob breathlessly.

The driver's eyes widened a moment. Had he caught on? Then came the man's bemused, "Good luck, little man." He waved and turned to his truck as Jacob skittered over to the net and seized upon it, kicking his feet in to secure bracing for his legs. The net contracted, lurched, skidded a bit, and then was aloft, swaying as the windlass drew it up and the boom began to swing out.

As the net reached the apogee of its upward trajectory, the boom swung it over the gaping mouth of the hold, as was supposed to happen. *I just didn't realize it would be swinging so and that I would be so sick.* He was gripping the cabled rope of the net so hard his hands had lost feeling.

Jacob realized, as the net paused at the top of the hold, that the boom operator expected him to jump to the deck. He freed one hand with as great an act of will as he had ever exerted, shook his head, and gestured a thumbs down signal to be loaded into the hold with the net. The operator shrugged, reengaged the gears, and they sank beneath the deck.

Fortunately, the boom operator lowered the net with greater care than was normally given to cloth bales. They all landed promptly, gently aboard, and figures sprang out from shadows to release the hook that held the net. Jacob recognized Otto and supposed the other was one of the sailors, a dusky fellow whose teeth gleamed against his skin. And there was Amos!

They hugged, fast and hard.

The next minutes were scrambling, frantic, as they located and oriented all of their concealed people, then manhandled those bales to upper positions of stability and spoke to each occupant. Several just mumbled, obviously having used their flasks already. Once again, Jacob silently sent his thanks to Nicolas for having provided those. These women had had enough of terror.

It was only as he was being laid on the deck of the hold, gently, that the days of hunger, exhaustion, and physical and emotional strain got the better of him, and he abruptly fainted.

CHAPTER 11

JULY 5, 1942
11:50 P.M.

PARAMARIBO, SURINAME

George Butler startled awake to the urgent sound of tapping. He looked at the alarm clock next to the bed and saw that it was just before midnight.

His wife, Lijsbet, stirred, mumbling, insulated from the noise in her nest on the other side of the bed. She always burrowed deep under covers, gathering them in while she burrowed, as soon as she fell asleep. George called her his own "rare bird, the Gold Crested Burrowing Coversnitch." Her English and education were as fine as his, and the affectionate name always made her smile.

George was sure to avoid waking her. Midway through another pregnancy, she was more beautiful than ever, but she needed her sleep.

Robed, he shuffled barefooted out of the bedroom, closing the door softly behind him, and then made his way to the kitchen door, where the tapping was beginning again. Who could be knocking at this hour?

He opened the door to find a boy shuffling foot to foot outside. It was the oldest son of Hendrick, the night telegrapher and radio operator at the port.

"Mijnheer, my father says this is a code you said would come, that it was to be delivered immediately?" He was clearly apologetic for waking the important trader and general store proprietor and diffidently held out a waxed envelope.

Whispering, holding finger to lips to urge the boy to speak softly, too, George said, "I will ask you to wait out here while I see if I must send a reply. I would ask you in, but my wife and son are asleep."

The boy nodded. Pushing the door to, George went immediately to the bowl where coinage waited for just this sort of thing. His livelihood depended on fast and reliable communication. Scooping a generous handful, he tossed the envelope to the table, cracked open the door again, and filled the boy's hands. "This is for *you*. I will thank your father later. Just wait a bit."

Seated at the table, he lit one of the candles in the holder there. He opened the envelope and read the refugee code that he had worked out with that Dutch cop the previous year. This one had been sent from the French-flagged ship *Bon Chance*, and there were seventeen of them! Families, obviously.

He opened the door again, to see the youngster's enthusiastic smile. George had just given him more than most men made for a day's work.

"*Jong*, here is the envelope back, and I don't need to send a return Thank you and good night."

"You too, Mijnheer," the boy said with a gleaming grin that receded into the night.

He would have to wake up Dr. Adelmann, he thought, then remembered the hour and decided to tell him first thing in the morning. Then he thought better of it. Adelmann had been worried sick for months, his own nephew being one of the refugees. Before changing his mind again, George put on his shoes and decided to walk over to Adelmann's house right away and disturb his night, too. After all, the good doctor had to do a lot of planning with seventeen people headed their way for good.

Maybe he will break out a bottle of good wine, George thought to himself as he pulled on his overcoat, careful to close the door behind him quietly so as not to wake his family. If even a couple of the refugees were half as useful as Dr. Adelmann had been to Paramaribo, these people would enrich them all.

CHAPTER 12

JULY 6, 1942
3:25 A.M.

ABOARD THE VESSEL *BON CHANCE*

It's so dark! The thought sprang instantly to Hannah's mind as she started awake, her face smashed into the heavy wire cage. Reminded of her circumstances, she stilled. Her mouth felt like dusty flannel, and the smell of her cocoon was terrible, a mix of old crab and rust from the crab traps, the dusty-smelling cloth, and…*I have used my diaper.* She hadn't wet the bed since she had been four!

She sneezed, several times, explosively, and felt urine squirt into her already wet pads as her stomach clenched with the convulsions. Resigned, and fortified with a practical perspective that came from being an older sister who frequently cared for her infant brother, she sighed heavily, closed her eyes, and finished emptying her full bladder. *At least I am flat, and not head down,* reminded herself, and chuckled lightly at the thought. She had relieved the usual morning pressure on her bladder, but now the rags that had formed a measure of insurance against soggy bedding were swollen and leaking, and the skin noticeably irritated from having lay in her own filth for hours.

Freed of the immediacy of a full bladder, Hannah realized that she was swaying and rocking, impacting the cage with her shoulder on the left and the length of her leg on the right. It was like being rocked in a cheese grater. *Of course,* she realized with a glimmer of joy, *we are on the ocean.* A frenzy of crashing sounds surrounded her—the sound of a violent storm raging at sea. Fear seized her throat as she envisioned being overcome by giant waves, pulling her under.

With just inches enough to move her arms, Hannah reached down and freed her legs of her skirt, untied the wet mass, and worked it down to below her feet. She lay reeking, and terribly thirsty. *More laudanum?* Groping within her tight confines for the little flask, she encountered instead the parcel of bottles and food Alexandra had gifted her with. One of the seals had been pushed aside during her trip on board, and Hannah realized that the pungent odor of beer was part of the horrible stew of smells. Most of the biscuits in the bundle were sodden mush. The bottle still held a bit, and because there was barely room to get her hands to her face, some of that went over her chin and cheek as she tried to get it to her mouth. Relief was immediate and blissful from the few spoonfuls she managed. She was surprised to realize that good Dutch beer cut her thirst better than water.

She considered drinking the other bottle but thought better of it. She had no idea how long she would be confined in this place, and with her diaper now gone, the results of drinking more might actually worsen her uncomfortable circumstances. She shivered, chilled from lying in dampness. *Of course, I am wrapped in a lot of cloth, and it can't smell any worse in here, I may as well drink it,* she debated, then realized with a twinge that, indeed, it *could* smell worse in here. Hannah held very still. She fumbled the bundle up by her face, and lipped out some of the beer-soaked biscuit pap. She could learn to like beer.

The rocking became more violent, tossing her head against the rough wire, coating her cheek with mushy biscuit, and scraping her leg even through the heavy skirt. Under her head, she had bundled the heavy woolen winter bloomers she had worn under her skirts as a pillow when they had put her in the bale. The problem was that she could not get her hand above her head to reposition them for padding where she was hitting.

In a flash of genius, Hannah managed to seize the garment with her teeth, dog-like, with some twisting and at the expense of her cheek as it scraped against the cage when she slammed into her surrounds yet again. Levering with her head, she finally worked the cloth under her head to cushion her.

She sought the laudanum, then stopped. If the ship were to change course, this pillow to slip, or the wind to change direction, she could get torn to pieces while drugged and unconscious. She didn't dare use it. It was a terrible realization. Her bowel knotted, the swollen wire puncture in her lower cheek ached, and she realized that the ache in her lower abdomen was more than just hunger or discomfort from her position.

What if the Nazis took Papa and the others before the ship left the dock? This thought occurred all in a rush to Hannah and froze her with fear. *What if we are alone here?* Even if none of them had let slip to the Nazis where they were, who among the sailors would know which bales they were in? What if no one let them out?

Alone in darkness, Hannah began to cry.

⧗

Jacob lurched through the black, wet night, groping and clutching along the rail, clinging with frozen hands to the rough, rusted cable as the ship heaved and swayed on the stormy sea, somewhere, Jacob guessed, off the Belgian Coast. He paused every few feet to spew fruitlessly over the side. All that emerged by now was a tiny bit of acid bile. How could his stomach be any emptier?

The bridge was welcome shelter from the wet wind sweeping across the heaving deck. Jacob knocked, to be polite, unsure whether he could be heard. Then he opened the great metal hatch and stumbled through it, almost losing it to the wind but succeeding in slamming it against the freezing night.

The captain looked up from a charting table and grinned an evil grin that lit his dark face.

"You do not look like you are enjoying the voyage, *Mon Ami*," said the captain in surprisingly unaccented English.

Jacob tried, futilely, to smile. In his own halting and heavily accented English, he replied, "This is the first time any of us have been on water bigger than a lake, Captain. It is very… startling."

"You will get used to it, or you will be very, very thin before we get to shore." Looking Jacob up and down in an appraising inventory, the captain half turned. "Here." He gestured to the other man in the room, a seaman who was on a stool by the bound wheel. He spoke a one-word command: "*Kaff.*"

A hanging alcohol stove swung in the corner of the crowded room, and clamped to its upper surface was a huge percolator. The sailor, balancing adroitly, poured jet black liquid into an immense mug, careful to fill it only halfway. Raising an inquiring eyebrow, he offered the cup to Jacob and gestured to an open sack of sugar and a crusted can of condensed milk in a railed cubby in the corner of the room.

"It may be wasted on me, but thank you very much," Jacob said, urging his body to keep at least this small nourishment down. He'd had nothing to eat in more than a full day. He gratefully wrapped his cold-stiffened hands around the warm ceramic and moved to the corner to pour in the thick milk and two big spoons of sugar, then stirred and gulped. Astonishingly, he felt his stomach settle immediately. In fact, his vision, which had been blurring badly, sharpened. Surely, he must be on the edge of starvation.

With a sigh of relief for the comfort of the coffee, Jacob brought himself back to the task at hand. "Captain, I am the…spokesperson for the people who are in your hold. I am *Yakob* Roseweig."

"I am Ramon Cervantes. You can call me Captain," said Cervantes with a grin, which matched that of the seaman. Jacob sensed that Cervantes held his authority dear.

"Well, Captain, I need to know whether it is safe for us to extract our wives and children now? Where are we?" His eyes darted around, uncertain, and then, taking a deep breath, Jacob added, "And we will need some food for them soon…"

"I knew you'd be trouble, but I owe Old Nicholas more than one favor. Sorry, but the only hot food on board is that coffee pot until we clear the storm. I can send in some canned milk. We have some bread from shore and some canned meat."

The captain's voice made it clear that he thought the offerings meager, but to Jacob, they sounded like manna from heaven.

"You are going to have to set up some buckets for toilets and take care of those yourselves," Cervantes continued. "It's not safe for women and kids to go on deck. Actually, not for you men, either, with no sea legs. After we get into calmer waters or weather—*if* we get them—I'll have someone show you how to use a Marine head."

Jacob felt his head spinning. "Kids" he knew was an English word for children, but…

"Pardon me? Head?"

The captain and his crewman roared with laughter.

"On the old sailing ships, the toilet boards were located at the front of the ship—that is, downwind. That part of the ship was called the forecastle. So at the head, the leading edge, of the forecastle. Head."

"Ah! Thank you. I would not have understood that in a thousand years." Jacob rubbed his head, embarrassed and realizing how many great and tiny things he would learn in the coming weeks.

As if reading his mind, Cervantes said, "You *will* learn. You will have to, because not only will you need to understand orders in a hurry, you will need to help on board. I don't have a single extra sailor, and they all have full workloads already."

"We would be glad to be of any help we can, but first we must have some food and rest, Captain. It has been very difficult for us for a long time. We grown men and the older boys will be available as soon—"

"Be aware, Mr. Roseweig," the captain cut him off, "I will *tell* you when you are available. That is how it works on shipboard." The captain was very intent. Jacob gulped.

"Of course. You are the captain." Jacob saw the intensity fade. This had been the right thing to say. He continued. "Among us are an expectant mother and my own wife, who is aboard with our infant son. But I am sure some of the ladies would be glad to help cook, for example."

Now the captain and the seaman looked at each other and grinned again. "If you can get our cook out of his galley, you are welcome. He is a very bad cook. And they will *want* to kick him out, because he smells really badly."

In a flash, Jacob was reminded of his chief reason for having entered the hold in the first place. "Can we free our women and children?"

"Yes. No one could board us in this weather in any case, and we will be off the Belgian coast in no more than another hour. By tomorrow we will be off France, going through the channel. *Bon Chance*," he said proudly, "makes almost four knots!"

Jacob worked numbers reflexively. At this rate, they would be aboard this floating prison another three weeks.

The captain was all business. "I'll have Rafael here roust out someone to get you tools to get your people out, and some buckets, and something to eat and drink. Fresh water is for drinking. If you want to wash, use sea water. Our distiller is ancient and has arthritis. Drink what you need, just don't waste any."

Returning to the hold was as desperately frightening as had been his trip to the bridge. The only improvement Jacob noticed was that his vomiting had stopped, as the warmth in his stomach persisted despite the freezing spray.

A detour to the chained-down crate that held Herr Adelmann and Levi nearly got him washed overboard. He pulled spry young Levi out of the crate first, and he managed a few windblown words with Herr Adelmann as the two pulled him out, then made his shivering way back to the hold that held the precious bales.

A work light, shielded with a mesh cover, lit the hold dimly. Levin and the other men were moving about the bales, speaking into them, some very urgently.

"We can take them out! The captain, Cervantes, is sending a seaman with tools. And remember that we must all call him 'Captain' when we speak to him!" The men and boys nodded their understanding. "But here," Jacob added, fumbling out his beloved old penknife, "we can cut the cloth away from over the breathing tubes."

Jacob scrambled to do just that and found himself trembling and shaking with the cold. He dropped the little knife, and Otto lunged for it as it skittered across the steel floor, or deck, as the captain had called it. And the walls were "bulkheads," the stairs "ladders," the toilet a "head." Jacob slumped, exhausted, onto a bale as Otto flashed him a grin and swooped for the knife. The deck heaved as the boy bent, sending him somersaulting into a pile of bales. Amos, moving carefully, recovered his Father's bone-handled little treasure and began removing patches of cloth where slits revealed covered breathing tubes. Jacob, unable to walk the length of the ship without collapsing, felt worthless as he looked on.

Minutes were consumed with trying to speak to the captive women and children, and then the hatch heaved open in the forward partition, and a short, fat man in a watchcap and peacoat backed in, arms full of tools. An amusing few minutes passed as the stowaways realized that the seaman had no German or English, and that they had no idea how to use the tools. The looks they received from the seaman were incredulous, until he finally resorted to demonstration, as Albert Levin fumbled to cut bands.

Bands snapped under bolt cutters, eager hands stripped away cloth, and several men and boys recoiled at the stench that emerged. Levin bent and lifted away a section of the steel mesh that encased a mother and infant. He lifted Jacob's son, Ezekiel, gingerly from Rebecca's saturated and smeared bosom, walked with the utmost care to Jacob, and put the unconscious and odorous burden into his friend's shaking arms. Still in drugged sleep, the tiniest Roseweig was breathing.

At that moment, a paroxysm of nausea overcame Jacob, and he discovered that he could vomit while grinning from ear to ear.

The seaman almost fled, but then he looked at Rebecca's beautiful, if besmirched, face as solicitous hands brought her out of her bale and gestured about at other bales. "*Mas mujeres*?" he inquired.

Jacob knew *one* word of Spanish. The sailor's words meant nothing to him, but the question was obvious. He employed his one Spanish word, "*Si*," as he gazed fondly at his wife.

He almost chuckled at the eagerness with which the rotund man began opening bales, like a man seeking treasure, but was forestalled by his own gagging as a wave of odor wafted up from his youngest child. He snagged unbaled cloth to wipe Ezekiel dry, if not really clean, and bound a piece of it to serve as diaper, wrapping the boy against the chill of the hold. Rebecca slumped, trying to stand, tears streaming down her face as much from relief as from the methane-laden atmosphere she was leaving. Her skirt and blouse were a sodden mess, and her stained blouse gaped open as one milk-dripping breast bounced gently out. Amos reached gingerly to close the cloth over his dazed mother and assisted her in staggering to a seat on one of the ubiquitous bales.

None of the others had a child as young as Ezekiel, though all held their breath as a pregnant and seemingly unharmed Rachel Levin emerged awkwardly from her bale. All had similarly disastrous issues of soiling, and Sarah, emerging almost serene, directed the stringing of cloth to create a curtain, making a privacy corner in the hold. The women all retreated there one by one to attempt to clean themselves. Hannah emerged, face smeared with the paste of biscuits soaked in beer, and positively slunk into the privacy corner as soon as she could. The hold had quickly become filled with every human odor imaginable, and the seaman hustled out, slamming the hatch behind him.

He returned surprisingly quickly, bearing buckets, one of which brimmed with icy cold seawater. A feminine arm emerged from the privacy corner and the seawater was whisked within. Other trips produced a mop, more seawater, and, finally, a great ridged metal canister with a water spout at the bottom that operated with a button, and several metal cups with wire handles for drinking the fresh water.

Sarah was emphatic as she set to work, energized by a purpose and their newfound freedom. "Everyone wash their hands first. Then wash faces, and we must pull all the soiled clothing and material into one place so we can keep from touching it." She began to draw water and dip a cloth scrap in it, and the seaman gestured urgently.

Jacob remembered. "We can only use seawater for washing. Fresh water is limited to drinking." Sarah gaped at him, but complied.

The round little seaman could not take his eyes off of Sarah's face, beautiful despite recent events. She graced him with a smile and saw that it almost visibly warmed him. She smiled inwardly. "Blankets?" He held up his hands in incomprehension. Sarah made gestures of wrapping herself in a blanket for warmth. The little fellow shrugged ignorance and gestured with two fingers at his eyes, conveying that he would look for them, then trotted out again.

While he was gone, another seaman, the same one who had been on the bridge with the captain, arrived with a canvas sack that held canned beef, canned milk, and several loaves of crusty bread. He took in the scene—the malodorous women, the tiny baby in Jacob's arms, the buckets, the obvious attempts at clean-up and organization—and nodded. Then he hefted the water container left by his cohort, drained its remaining contents into the cups about it, and toted it away, gesturing Amos to come with him. Amos looked to Jacob, who gestured him along. "Does anyone else want to go help carry?" Jacob asked, scanning the room. Otto sprang to join the water party.

Sarah emerged from the privacy hold and stood, scanning her environs. She nodded once, satisfied. They had escaped. They had food and water, and, even if they were utterly poor and very much in need of bathing, they were alive. She fingered the ring on her finger—she had managed to escape Holland with it—and sent a prayer up to God in heaven. *Please watch over us and guide our safe passage.*

She thought then of Michael. She had known he was dead, had been told as much. Yet the fact that she was now on board a ship that was taking her away from Europe forever seemed to further cement his loss in her mind. *Oh, Michael, my love, how I miss you and wish you were with me. We are on the very edge of freedom. I can almost taste it!*

There were no plates, but there were pocketknives, and almost everyone had a spoon. Men each carried a razor in one pocket, a bar of soap in another, a spoon, and usually a pocketknife. Belts served as strops. This had become their habit over months of fleeing.

The corned beef was thick with salt and fat and spread lumpily over bread sliced raggedly with pocket knives. The little cans of milk went hand to hand after being punctured. Each poured a sip at a time without touching lips to the can. They were intent, eager. This was better fare than they had had for months. No one even lifted an eyebrow at meat and milk at one meal. No one was even near orthodox, but at home they would never have even thought of the combination. Now, no one cared.

While they were eating, almost reverently, the little round man came back, a stack of woolen blankets in his arms. Jacob made their thanks obvious, but only when Sarah added one of her wide open smiles and patted his shoulder did the little man seem compensated. She felt a twinge of guilt over the manipulation but quickly shook it off. It had harmed no one and had even seemed to please the short, pudgy man.

After he had again gone, to a chorus of thanks from all, Albert Levin turned to Sarah and grinned. "With the effect your smile has on men, we may not need money where we are going!"

Sarah looked haughtily at him, but her eyes twinkled. "I was just being courteous."

"With cloth under us, and blankets over, and sleeping a bit closer than families usually do, I think we can keep warm." Jacob straightened from a blanket count, aware that "closer" meant "huddled like sheep," but trying to be cheerful.

"*Yakob*, I think we had better make a room of these bales, and make a floor of them, too, and maybe that way we can keep warmer." Levin had said this as he looked thoughtfully at the steel floor. "This is not a good mattress here, and this place is so big, it seems to have its own weather."

So after filling their bellies, everyone in the group stood and began working together to create a nest of blankets and discarded cloth. Then, despite having spent nearly twenty-four hours lying still, they collapsed in an exhausted heap and fell into a long, deep sleep.

"All right! Everyone up!" The clang of the opening hatch and the captain's bellow came almost together.

Jacob sprang to his feet and promptly fell as the ship rolled. He stood again, cautiously, and peered blearily at the glaring man in the hatchway.

"I send you food and water and treat you with courtesy, and you *steal*?"

"Captain, what do…?"

Cervantes strode to their nest of bales, then reached and flicked away one of the blankets that had just moments before kept his wife and Ezekiel warm. "These. One from every one of our bunks and all of our spares."

Jacob crossed to the captain unthinkingly, acting on a defensive instinct. Without the cowardice he'd displayed earlier, he now stood only inches from the man's face, talking with such intensity that the man stepped backward, color draining from his face.

"Those were brought us by *your* seaman, who apparently thought that mothers and infants should have some way to keep warm!" Jacob shouted, energy growing as he spoke. "And the woman you have taken that from is my wife, and that is my son, and if you ever offer my family insult again, I will retaliate. Is that clear, Captain?"

Jacob was shaking with rage, months of outrage and fear and anxiety having reached the breaking point. It was too late to rein in now; it might risk all of their lives, but he had had enough. It was enough.

He continued. "And none of us has been out of this…" he fumbled, looking around, as if to see the word, "hold since I came back to it last night."

The captain, astonishingly, grinned. "And was the seaman who stole my blankets a fat little man named Raoul?"

Jacob was brought up short and cocked his head. The captain seemed to value insistence, self-respect. "His name I do not know, but we asked him for blankets, and he brought these."

"You speak Spanish?" There was suspicion in the captain's voice.

Sarah emerged from her segment of the nest, stretched, and said, caustically, in very slow English, "None of us has more than a few words of Spanish, Captain; I just did this." She pantomimed warming herself with a blanket. "And he brought these."

Jacob had never seen a man's jaw drop so literally.

The captain half bowed to Sarah, but spoke to Jacob. "I apologize for insulting your wife. I thought you were taking liberties on my ship on your first night aboard, after I had taken great risks for you."

And for all of our coins and gold and jewels, Sarah thought ruefully.

Looking at Sarah in open admiration, the captain continued, "And I can see that Raoul was powerless in the face of superior force." A grin spread across his face. "Keep the blankets. I will send in some tarps that you can use to roof over this bunking space. We can't have so much as a kerosene lantern in here because of the fire danger."

He looked about at the people fumbling with clothing and drinking water, and generally trying to be alert after very few hours of sleep. "These are all the blankets on board, however. I have only four crewmen, and we will all be chilly on this voyage. *We* do not have warm people to sleep with. We are not a passenger vessel. Use cloth for bedding. It can always be laundered ashore. Don't," he glared about, seeing diapers obviously torn from cargo, "cut up any more of it. The cloth in the 'bales' your ladies were in was donated by the policeman. Do what you want with that. Usually, we tie clothing to a rope and trail it in the wake, which makes it very clean after an hour or so. Then we wring it out and dry it in the engine room, and shake out the salt. Do try to keep the area here clean."

And with that, he turned on his heels and left the hold just as quickly as he'd arrived.

Herr Adelmann squinted in the gray dawn light and staggered among the small folk lying scattered about him. The lids were finally being pried off the crates to release those imprisoned inside. As a lid came reluctantly off, he was met with a gust of warm air—vastly warmer than the hold was, he did not fail to notice, and smelling almost as bad. Nearby, Jacob bent, took up a little one who was still sleeping a drugged sleep, and led the procession of child-carrying fathers and boys back to the hold. A damp grayness hung about in the early morning, and the sea was still in swells, but at least there was no rain just now, and the swells were smooth immensities, with only occasional whitecaps.

For a day they labored to launder and mop and swab down small people, who protested vociferously about the frigid sea water. Soiled and soaked cloth from their bales was tied up in ropes and cast off the stern for a sort of cleaning. All of them, both men and women, took brief turns wringing; Jacob was convinced that the only reason the sea water had not turned to ice was because it had salt in it. After a few wring-outs, numb hands had to be tucked into armpits for excruciating rewarming.

Clothes were then hung to dry all about the engine room, which was welcome work because it was the only place that was at all warm on board the *Bon Chance*—warmer even than the bridge, a place to which none of them had yet been invited.

When the captain entered the scrupulously neatened hold that afternoon, he looked about approvingly before turning his attention to Jacob. "Mijnheer Roseweig, today I require four men to do scraping and painting And if some ladies could look at the galley, I would appreciate it. I have told the cook to show them where things are and to stay out of their way."

Jacob smiled, proud that he seemed to be pleased, and glad to be able to help. This was a reasonable request from the captain, especially as he had given them a day's recovery time. "We could, all six men and two well-grown boys, probably do the job faster," Jacob offered. Now that they all had a few meals in their bellies, he felt all the men in their party would welcome the chance to move about the ship.

The captain's grin was evil, again. "The job of scraping and painting is *never* done on a metal ship, and since I usually don't have enough hands to see to necessary work, let alone maintenance, and the owners are too cheap to supply port labor, I intend to take advantage of the extra hands on board this entire voyage. But it would be good if all of you did the work the first day, and I will have a seaman show you how it is done." He turned and strode away, whistling happily. Despite the realization that they had paid to do free labor, Jacob felt no irritation. He turned and headed out to notify the new work crew.

By the next day, those who comprised the work party had learned to make knee pads and wrap newly sore hands in cloth to stave off blisters. But the work was self-paced and not abusive. They had all simply been without adequate food and exercise for so long that it was at the limit of their physical abilities.

Meanwhile, Sarah and Hannah had taken charge of the little galley and managed to feed everyone hot food and abundant coffee throughout that day.

All the while, they scrubbed and muttered, scandalized by the sheer volume of work to do to whip the filthy galley into shape, even as things simmered and fried and boiled, and good smells wafted about the frigid decks.

"Papa, I don't think that man has ever so much as *washed* a pot," Hannah said to Jacob as he came to see them that evening. "Some of these things are so crusted you can't see the metal." The two young women wore clothes that were soaked from scrubbing and splashing about, and small pieces of their hair, which had been tied up with rags, hung damp and wild around their warm, glistening faces. Jacob worked to keep the amusement off his face, so gratified was he that their lives had been infused with positive purpose. A glance at Sarah's bitter scowl tempered his mood. He nodded sympathetically and quietly took his plate of fried eggs chopped into corned beef hash before retreating. He knew this was the last of the eggs, and only one day's worth of bread remained in their stores. Deprivation was no stranger, but he regretted the loss just the same. Of course, extra food stores would have attracted attention on this ship meant for only a handful of seamen. He counted his blessings for the few old cases of Argentinian beef they had left and that they had been able to buy so many potatoes, beets, and carrots—all of it would be essential staples over the coming weeks.

By the third day of the new galley regimen, the captain and crew were obviously delighted with the progress of work that had come about on board the *Bon Chance*—all, that is, except for the exiled cook, who had become almost mutinous, demanding that he be allowed once again in the galley. The captain was enjoying the process of demoting the cook to metal scraper when Rebecca intervened.

She, too, was enjoying a renewed sense of purpose and delighted in the maternal tasks of feeding a crew of hard-working, hungry men. It had been a long time since she had put to use her once-celebrated cooking talents; she believed it had been before Ezekiel was born when she had last prepared a proper meal. With one arm she cradled her sleeping baby boy, and with the other she stirred a great pot of food with a large wooden spoon. She was doing a borscht of sorts today, using beets that had been hung in nets outside and corned beef, whipping up a sort of sour cream with condensed milk and a drizzle of vinegar. "Captain, let us *train* him," she urged Cervantes. "He just hasn't been taught how to keep a kitchen." She blushed, realizing her error. "I mean, a galley."

"Antonio, you hear that? You learn how to keep a galley the way these ladies keep it and you can sail with me again. But I am never going back to the way you have been destroying our food for the last few years."

Reduced nearly to tears in his shame, Antonio could not meet the captain's eyes. He nodded, lowered his head, and slowly plodded away.

⧖

Captain Cervantes summoned Jacob to the bridge the next day. He poured coffee with his own hand and gestured to a stool for his guest to sit. "I was chatting with your wife," he held up a placatory hand, as Jacob's gaze sharpened. "Not to worry, it was with the *utmost* respect, while she was doing that wonderful strudel with the dried apples yesterday. She tells me that you are an accountant."

"This is true."

"I am a good sailor. I am good with charts and handling men and knowing currents and courses. I am a terrible accountant. I have accounts payable books and fuel records and receipts and bills of lading, and I have almost no way to organize them. I am always in trouble with my owners about records. I don't suppose you could help?"

"Do you have ledger books, envelopes, writing paper? Pens?"

Cervantes opened a metal cabinet. There were shelves of such supplies. Other shelves held clipped bundles of dog-eared receipts, loose sheets with scrawled notes, bills of lading. Those shelves were stuffed full. He could easily see the magnitude of the problem.

"It is likely I would ask you many questions during the day about particular forms, or ways of recording, while I learn the ways of your trading. Would that be acceptable to you?" Jacob saw the captain's eagerness surface as he nodded enthusiastically. Inwardly, Jacob was thrilled by the prospect of practicing his profession rather than the awful scraping and painting, to be valued for his expertise. He read desperation on the captain's face and saw an opportunity for leverage. "And could you, perhaps, spare Herr Levin from the scraping, should I need another accountant to help?" The captain's face assumed the expression of a fisherman who has pulled in his line to find two fish upon it rather than one.

And thereafter, as the women created a revolution of cleanliness and culinary improvement on board the ship steaming its way rapidly to his family's freedom, Jacob labored at the chart table on the bridge between course-plotting sessions, storm or fair. Antonio began to cook again, and even, upon Sarah's insistence to the captain that a cook simply must be clean at all times, began washing regularly and shaving often. After Sarah threw him out of the galley for smoking over an open pot, terrifying him with her ire, he stopped smoking in there altogether. She had thrown him out wielding a steaming spoon like a short sword.

One day, as he and Levin shuffled stacks of completed calculations and began a serious ledger entry, it occurred to Jacob that he had become surprisingly competent in international shipping and the requisite forms in four countries. He smiled, satisfied by the hard work. Soon the two accountants would have the system so simplified that even Captain Cervantes could maintain it.

CHAPTER 13

JULY 10, 1942
7:40 A.M.

PARAMARIBO, SURINAME

George gulped down Lijsbet's proffered coffee gratefully. He heartily regretted the third bottle of wine that Dr. Adelmann had offered him last night. But it sure had been nice while they were drinking it. He was paying for it this morning, though. He gulped the strong brew and tried to look alert. Morning light flooded their kitchen. Carmina, Lijsbet's housekeeper, busied herself with cast-iron cookware at the big wood stove, making good smells of refried beans simmering in sweet lard, eggs frying in butter, and bacon. George felt his stomach churn a bit in anticipation, even as he winced at the unpleasant wailing sounds coming from their son, John, who was receiving a diaper change from his nanny in the nursery.

"*Schatze*, why were you out drinking last night? Are you seeing a slimmer woman?" Lijsbet was joking, but her curiosity was real. Despite his attempt not to wake her, she had noticed his absence.

"A message came last night that there is another party of refugees coming from Amsterdam. *Twenty-six* of Dr. Adelmann's people! He insisted on the wine. My dear, it is all his fault," he told her in a mock tone of righteousness.

Lijsbet smiled archly. "Well, as long as it was with a man," she said, reaching across him to take a piece of bacon from the platter. "But you should get some sleep before you go out. Your eyes are red like a rabbit's." She caressed his neck gently as she maneuvered awkwardly to sit beside him, her swollen belly making it difficulty. George patted it gently as he savored the rubbing.

"I can't. The doctor is renting my new storage building for temporary housing. None of his folks has a lot of room, and we have to get the carpenters to work on it. He wants private rooms and cots and to have jakes dug. Of course, there is not a spare toilet in this country until we can trade with the Yankees freely again, so instead it must be neatly painted outhouses and sacks of quicklime. And then I have to see to the plumbers to set up a pair of shower buildings. I'm going to do the modifications at cost, but as the place has been empty for the six months since I had it built, I'm glad to rent it. This war is playing hell with shipping. Making rooms in it will make it more efficient for small lots of goods, and with locks on the doors, it will be handy for higher value shipments, so it will be better for us when we get it back."

"You always make good decisions, *Schatze*. But how can Dr. Adelmann do all of that? He barely had two shirts when he came here."

"He says all of the Jewish folk here will help. He called it an opportunity for doing a *mitzvah*, a good act before God. And the doctor has become very successful here. He is now personal physician to the president and to several of the legislature." Lijsbet appeared impressed and nodded approvingly. "And though he charges little at his clinic, many people go there," George continued. "To add to that, though I didn't tell you before…" George grinned and hesitated before continuing.

Lijsbet, searching for a comfortable position in her chair and making a tiny suppressed grunt, looked up. "Didn't tell me *what*?"

"The doctor had *some* money when he came here, as well as his diplomas and instruments. And his money has been keeping company with our money in stocking the store, trucking coffee here to the port, and so on. I've been able to move more quickly on deals, he has made a good profit, and the good doctor is *not* poor."

"*Schatze*, you have always said you wouldn't take a partner…" She was alarmed and concerned.

"I haven't," he insisted. "I do business as I always have, making my own decisions, but sometimes I reach for the doctor's cash in a hurry, and pay interest to use it. And sometimes he puts his money with mine and shares risks and profits. So far neither of us has lost any money, though a couple of times we've been lucky to break even with this shipping mess."

"Yes, I know. But at least the coastal shipping is good, and the inland trade," she smiled. "That Brazilian lace is beautiful! Carmina and I will have the curtains finished today." Lijsbet would have lived in a hut with George, but she did enjoy having security and nice things.

"Plus," George added as he downed the last of his coffee and rose to start his day, "since the doctor started attending to the president and his family, I get a lot more government business than I used to. Now, my dear, I am off to set up a hotel for refugees." He leaned down and kissed her gently on her cheek, patted her belly one more time for good measure, and strode out into the sunshine.

CHAPTER 14

JULY 11, 1942
4:10 P.M.

AMSTERDAM, HOLLAND

Wehrmacht Headquarters was a place of orderly confusion. Gunter Kramer had been there for twenty hours and had yet to get a telegram from his own headquarters. It was ridiculous, even in the middle of a war. They had so many clerks in Berlin, they practically outnumbered the civilians.

Gunter strode to the desk of the on-duty communications officer, the one who had been there when he had sent his urgent leave request a week ago, for once not needing to think consciously to affect the imperious and out-of-my-way stride of a high-ranking officer.

"*Heil Hitler!*" Radiating murderous menace, Gunter's grim and tight-jawed demeanor removed any idea the lieutenant might have had of saluting from the seated position. His straight wooden chair crashed over backward as he rocketed to his feet in an effort to pretend he had never even *considered* not standing to attention.

"Nothing yet, Herr Oberst." The slickly groomed officer-clerk found it hard to maintain eye contact with the man in front of him. It was particularly hard to keep his hands at his sides, as he felt a great urge to protect his throat.

"Take a follow-up message."

And while the fellow hesitated to break attention, Gunter barked, "*Sitzen!* Message follows." He continued to glare while the lieutenant fumbled for his dropped chair and then for the pen he immediately dropped as well. The aborted reflex to refer the oberst to the feldwebel clerk on the other side of the office died in his throat, and he poised the pen to take the message.

To: ReichsMinister Joseph Goebbels.

From: Oberst Gunter Kramer

Subject: Compassionate leave 72 hours duration.

Message: My previous communication on this sue-
ject has apparently gone astray STOP My wife has
notified me of the serious illness of my daughter
Emma, whom you may recall STOP My unit is now
in Amsterdam, the quarry in Hoorn being exhausted
STOP I have a responsible officer to leave in charge
during my absence STOP I request your urgent attention to this matter END.

Gunter's delivery had been deliberately slow. The lieutenant had what was obviously a complete copy, yet he hesitated, looking behind Gunter rather than rising to hurry the message to the sending key. Gunter felt his face redden and his neck swell. "What delays you, Leutnant?" The unspoken message was effective, as the smarmy fellow turned pale and looked faint, but instead of sprinting for the telegraphy key, he pointed behind Gunter, who was in a spread-legged position in front of his desk.

Gunter spun to confront the feldwebel clerk, who held out a telegraphy form, apologetically, while bracing to attention. His face was frozen, but he blurted out, "So sorry, Sir."

Gunter snatched the yellow sheet and read:

To: Oberst Gunter Kramer

From: Gerta Kramer

Subject: Emma

Message: Emma has died STOP I am very ill STOP
Please come END

Despite the shock, which left his knees feeling loose and his stomach as if it were full of iron, Gunter acknowledged the honest sympathy in the feldwebel's eyes. "Thank you."

He executed a precise about-face.

"Modify the message. Write the following: My previous message has obviously gone astray STOP. I was requesting urgent compassionate leave because my daughter Emma was seriously ill STOP. I have just been informed she is now dead, and my wife Gerta is very ill STOP. You met both of them when you visited our home last year STOP. I repeat my request STOP. I have a responsible officer to leave in command during my absence END.

"Send. That. Now."

⧗

Gunter staggered to the straight chair he had occupied for hours, collapsing rather than sitting.

Little Emma. Just old enough that her mind had been beginning to awaken. She had just been able to hold conversations, ask questions, or offer spontaneous affection. Gunter remembered her in her white jumper at Easter, so proud of her sprig of peonies. *She was so warm, clinging to my leg...*

Gunter was unaware of the tears flooding his face, streaming down to soak his collar. He sat rigid, not acknowledging those around him or the visibility of his wrenching pain. None dared approach him. He gazed, open-eyed but blind to all but the shattered ruin of his own heart.

He became aware that the feldwebel was standing, braced, in front of him. Astonishingly, the lieutenant stood behind him, similarly braced, but standing behind his man, a decency with which Gunter would not have previously credited the fellow. Finally, he focused on the form the feldwebel held in a trembling hand.

To: OBERST GUNTER KRAMER

FROM: REICHSMINISTER JOSEPH GOEBBELS

SUBJECT: COMPASSIONATE LEAVE

MESSAGE: LEAVE IS DENIED STOP SYMPATHY FOR YOUR LOSS STOP AS YOU ARE AWARE, STRICT URGENCY IN TRACKING ADELMANN STOP FUHRER VERY UNHAPPY WITH YOUR FAILURE TO APPREHEND HIM STOP RETURN TO YOUR DUTIES IMMEDIATELY END

When the lieutenant hesitantly held out a brimming water glass of schnapps, Gunter swallowed all of it without tasting or feeling the burn. He put the glass back in the lieutenant's hand, said, "*Danke*," and marched out of the headquarters building.

⧗

Still drunk, ambulatory only by habit, Gunter was loading his troops onto their trucks the next morning when a courier arrived at the barracks with a telegram.

To: OBERST GUNTER KRAMER

FROM: DIRECTOR, FRANZISKUS HOSPITAL

SUBJECT: GERTA KRAMER

MESSAGE: DEEPEST SYMPATHY STOP YOUR WIFE HAS DIED STOP QUERY INSTRUCTIONS FOR FUNERALS FOR GERTA AND EMMA KRAMER STOP

CHAPTER 15

JULY 11, 1942
2:00 P.M.

DEEP IN THE ATLANTIC, ON BOARD THE *BON CHANCE*

Ezekiel's thin wail filled the hold. Rebecca could not rock him as she usually did, because the *Bon Chance* was rocking all of them. Wildly. Occasionally, one of the giant swells became an equally huge wave and the ship slammed off a crest into a trough like a pot hitting a floor. It was all Rebecca could do to cushion him against the slams. The freighter that had seemed so large when they first moved about her felt tiny in this storm's grip.

Today, none of the boys and men were working, except for Jacob, who had faithfully made his way to the bridge hours ago.

The galley simply could not operate in these conditions, Sarah had insisted as she and a decidedly green Hannah stumbled on deck. Besides, Rebecca had been far too distracted by Ezekiel, who had grown worse with each passing day. Thus, their only food was what could be found in cans and the last of the bread they had succeeded in baking before the storm, when they had managed to clean and use the galley oven. It was infinitely better than the way they had been eating ashore, but a comedown from the magnificent, hot, and properly cooked food they had succeeded in coaxing out of the rescued galley.

Hannah nestled next her mother, helping to cocoon Ezekiel. It did no good, for the tiny boy wailed unceasingly and dribbled vomit. "I don't know what is wrong, Sarah. We have had more food this week than we have had since he was born, and I am being a good dairy. He just … isn't taking enough." In fact, her full breasts were leaking through the pads she had had to resort to this morning. Every time she tried to nurse, Ezekiel would decline to latch on, or would suck briefly and immediately throw it up. His skin was looking tighter, and she feared he was becoming dehydrated. Still, when she tried gently pouring water into the wailing mouth, it simply dribbled out. Her head ached with the incessant noise, her swollen breasts hurt, and the baby sound only provoked them to grow fuller.

Sarah knelt opposite them, bracing against cloth bales, struggling to organize the baby "blankets" and "diapers" they had made of their cloth bales, and slapping salt powder out of ocean-laundered fiber. If it wasn't beaten out, the salt abraded the baby's tender skin.

Sarah fought to conceal her worry for the child, whom most of the women on board were increasingly convinced was in a dire way. "I don't know what to tell you, love, as I've never had one of my own. And none of the other mothers has had one like this for so long." Sarah could not help but wince as Ezekiel's cry became an enraged and frustrated scream that lanced ear drums. Her heart broke for her poor distraught sister, who was utterly at a loss for what to do.

The others in their party had given Rebecca and Ezekiel a small bale cubicle to themselves, since Ezekiel's wailing and vomiting had now been non-stop for twenty-four hours. All the men and boys had erected the separate nest for the Roseweig family with considerable energy after Ezekiel had deafened everyone for several hours. Even Amos had removed himself to talk with his friends in the main cubicle. Only Rebecca and Hannah remained, and Sarah had been with them, helping, since waking this dark morning.

The interior hatch slammed open, ripping itself out of Jacob's hand as the ship heeled dramatically. He took a blow from it on its return swing and, with the help of two other men who leaped up, secured it. He had with him one of the sheet-metal water cans and a sack of food cans. Gesturing to the other fathers to distribute the items, Jacob crabbed his way to his family's nest, scuttling on all fours but still skidding about. He fumbled in his coat.

"Here is a gift from the captain for Ezekiel." He held out a little glass flask, closed by a cork. "It is a liquor called rum. He says it sometimes relaxes crying babies or babies who are getting teeth."

Rebecca looked doubtful. "I used beer on pacifiers for Amos and Hannah, remember. I just don't know if we can get any in him. And he is *not* teething."

They succeeded only in getting some of the pungent stuff to lay in Ezekiel's mouth a few moments, and he spit, vomiting on top of it, coughing violently.

Sarah crouched close. "Here, *Yakob*. Take this kerchief. It is clean. Put the tip in the water cup, there…" Jacob handed the dripping thing back to Sarah. She flipped it to double the fabric, poured some of the rum into the cloth fold, and gently swabbed Ezekiel's mouth. She squeezed just a few drops onto his tongue, and all held breath. Ezekiel mouthed fitfully, made a swallowing spasm. Sarah hurriedly folded another corner of the kerchief, they repeated the dunking and rum application, and Sarah this time put the wetted corner into the infant's mouth with her finger, pressed it against his tongue, and then squeezed a few more drops onto his tongue before withdrawing. Ezekiel smacked his lips, made an abortive sucking motion with them. A third application, almost a tablespoon of water swallowed, and Rebecca tried again to get him to nurse. He would not but was not screaming.

Jacob put rum into the water that remained in the cup, just a few spoonfuls, and Rebecca poured tiny dribbles into Ezekiel's mouth, waiting after each dribble for the smacking motion. Jacob, Sarah, and Hannah surrounded mother and child, bracing her, trying to give her the steadiness to minister to him.

All of a sudden, Hannah gave a start and exclaimed "Oh!" All turned to look at her. "Papa, I still have a little bit of that laudanum, and maybe others do, too?"

Rebecca looked down at the fussing but quiet boy, shaking her head. "I used that on him to put him in the bale, and when he woke he was not able to nurse for almost three hours. We need to get water in him now, while he is awake. Maybe later we can use just a little drop of the laudanum so he will sleep. He hasn't slept all night and half a day."

They were thrown almost out of the nest space with a violent forward pitch of the vessel. "If anyone can sleep in this, it will be a miracle," Jacob said wryly. "The captain appeared quite amused by my worry. He said this is the middle of the Atlantic Ocean, and storms like this are one of the reasons to make ships of steel. He also said that no one is to go on deck *for any reason* until the storm is over." They all glanced darkly at the screened corner where the toilet buckets reeked.

Sarah gave a snort. "All I can say, *Yakob*, is that Suriname had better be a very nice place." Despite the circumstances, they all chuckled.

⧗

It was a very long day and night. Ezekiel would not—or could not—nurse, and though they managed to get water with a hint of rum into him several times, he slept only fitfully, resuming his tired wail each time he woke. As night deepened, they gave him rum and water and two drops of laudanum, whereupon he finally slept.

Toward morning the swells, still massive, became regular, and while rain and hail still cascaded across the decks, resounding in the steel box in which they dwelt, the waves no longer crashed over the ship. Tented in the single blanket they shared, Rebecca and Jacob, keeping him between them against the cold, tried to get Ezekiel to nurse again. He struggled, spasmed, choked, and was limp in their arms.

⧗

Rebecca's scream snapped everyone in the hold awake. She bent over her baby, rocking him and shaking him gently. Jacob put his hands around the tiny chest and tried to get his son to breathe, but Ezekiel was utterly flaccid, head hanging loosely, eyelids half open on already dulling orbs. Sarah slid into their nest, already falling to her knees, took in the situation in a glance despite the dimness, and scooped Ezekiel from Rebecca's arms. She determinedly inserted her little finger into the slack mouth and groped, but unable to resuscitate him or provoke a response, she sagged. She gently lay the little body back in the kneeling, keening Rebecca's arms.

She cast about for words of comfort, but her voice only sounded clinical and matter-of-fact as she reported, "Not an obstruction. And we checked for that yesterday." Sarah berated herself the moment the words had left her mouth. She knew she was utterly useless in such moments of emotional pain. She was a woman of action. But this, she could do nothing to fix. She could think of only one thing that might be of some help to the sorrowful family. "Rebecca, *Yakob*, let us make the *tachrichim*."

Rebecca's eyes snapped up. "Not bale cloth, Sarah. He will not go to *HaShem* in bale cloth."

Sarah nodded. "No, love, not bale cloth."

Through all of this, Amos and Hannah had sat up on opposite sides of the nest in their own cloth coverings, and now they scuttled on their knees in the low space, closed wordlessly upon their mother as she held their brother's tiny body, and embraced her through their tears.

⧗

By holy law, the burial must take place within a day. There was no way to know how long they would be able to safely go on deck, which added another element of urgency to the proceedings. The fathers met, Adelmann helping to support the weeping Jacob. "We have no rabbi. We have no one who has ever been a member of *chevra kadisha*. So without rabbi or burial society, we must do it all. I will go to the captain and ask for a reduction in speed during the burial."

The women who were mothers would all perform the *taharah*, in which the body would be prepared for burial. Before they entered the Roseweigs' nest for the cleansing, all covered their heads. Only Sarah remained in her own place, sewing upon a beautiful, treasured lace shawl of their mother's. It was the only pristine piece of white cloth in the possession of the party.

Adelmann returned, the captain with him, and found that, astonishingly, every grown man in the group had retained a *tallith*. He sought his own prayer shawl. As the tiny figure lay on a cradle sling of the common cloth, the fine lace of its shroud almost glowed in the dim work light. Hannah and Amos stood behind their parents, Amos without a tallith, but wearing the *yarmulke* he had been given at his Bar Mitzvah in the awful days just before they had fled Germany.

The captain whispered, cap in hand, to Adelmann, "I can have my mate, who plays the accordion, make it sound like an organ." Adelmann had to smile at the misplaced generosity.

"Our funerals do not involve any music or flowers. And Captain, you should put your hat back *on* … thank you for the generous offer. It is enough you have slowed the ship for us."

Jacob had to use his penknife to start the *k'riah* tear in his lapel. Rebecca's coat was equally resistant and he helped her. Amos emulated him and aided Hannah in the rending of garments.

Then the fathers began the carry, Adelmann performing the count of the seven stops, bringing them all, now drenched, to the railing on deck. Jacob and Rebecca stood briefly at Ezekiel's head, the sling tipped, and the tiny bundle disappeared into the foaming sea.

All the women retreated to the bulkhead inboard, and the men folded the sling, adjusted their talliths, and said *kaddish*, their mourning prayers accompanied by cold rain.

They returned to their own steel coffin, and the voyage resumed speed.

CHAPTER 16

JULY 16, 1942
10:30 A.M.

ABOARD THE *BON CHANCE*

"Amos, your mother is not well," Jacob quietly said to his only remaining son as his eyes remained fixed on Rebecca from some distance away. Amos' concern was also apparent, and Jacob sensed that the boy craved an opportunity to be of service to his mother. "I must leave her in order to take care of necessities. But I don't want her alone. I particularly don't want her alone on deck. If she is on deck, she must have both you and Hannah with her." He nodded to his pale-faced daughter, who sat upon the deck, her back against the bulkhead, hugging her knees to her chest. He noted that the girl's eyes were as red and swollen as her mother's. "She is to have you holding her arm when she goes anywhere *near* the rail. I am afraid she might try to join Ezekiel." Jacob's low voice vibrated with intensity. Both teens nodded earnestly, shock showing on their faces.

Jacob regretted having to share this further piece of distressing information with his children, but it was the only thing he could do to stem the growing panic about what Rebecca might do in her grief. Just yesterday, he had found her standing at the rail, leaning over to peer at the water. She had not been holding on, and had not appeared to care that the ship was rolling or that it was raining. He was terrified.

"The captain does not expect me to come to the bridge. Herr Adelmann has told him of our sitting *shiva*. But when the seven days are accomplished, I must continue work on the ship records, and then, one of you, or perhaps Sarah, must be with her *every moment*." He gazed earnestly at his surviving children, thinking how they were too young to have so much responsibility thrust upon them, but how proud he was of the strength they had already shown thus far. Their faces reflected obvious fear, and Jacob felt both guilty and relieved—it was awful, but at least if they were scared, they would be more careful.

"Mothers always suffer when a child dies, and when one dies so young, sometimes it takes more time to recover. Sitting shiva helps, and the cleansing thereafter." Even as he said this, Jacob wondered how they would have a proper cleansing on board this steel shell. There would be no sacred bath, only buckets and seawater.

Hannah almost stammered, sounding very small and young. "Will Mutter be better after sitting shiva?"

"*Liebchen*, I hope so. But we must be very careful of her."

Across the hold, Rebecca turned away from the small packs of child's things she had been making to pass on to other mothers. Such things as diapers and pins were precious—so precious and scarce that she was doing this task of redistribution during shiva, a time in which work is forbidden. But she found she could not remain still in the hold. She moved toward the outer deck hatch ladder, fumbling, stepping on her own stained skirt as she endeavored the first rung. Jacob sprinted to her, Amos beside him.

"Love, let Amos go first to swing that heavy latch, and I will go behind you to keep your skirt out from under your shoes." Rebecca, her face still and white, stood listlessly aside as Amos started up, then seemed to instantly lose any sense of what she had been about. Jacob waited, wordless, knowing that putting an arm around her would no more help now than it had in the many hours he had already held her. It was as if she could no longer feel the gestures of love.

Finally, she turned and lifted her foot to mount the ladder. Jacob dealt with the skirt, and they ascended, Amos reaching down from the deck to aid his mother.

When Jacob emerged, he saw with approval that Amos had his mother's arm, as much to help her stand on the deck of the undulating ship as to comply with Jacob's instructions. He managed to do it casually, so that putting himself between her and the rail appeared totally natural. Jacob closed the hatch and joined them.

Rebecca had stood out here, staring at the water where Ezekiel's tiny shroud had vanished, for many hours every day since his passing—sometimes at night, seeming not even to notice when the cold started her shuddering convulsively. So she stood now. She knew that the water into which her little boy had fallen was now many hundreds of miles behind them, but she felt that as long as she continued looking at the water over the rail, it felt to her heart that it was the very same water, and that she could remain close to him. To tear her eyes away meant resolving to move on, and that she could not imagine ever being able to do.

So she stood, silent and resolute, with Jacob and Amos flanking her to lend her their warmth in the light drizzle and low wind. Waves peaked in small whitecaps over the windward sides of the swells, like flecks of lint on great green bolsters. The time stretched to hours, boy and man shifting to relieve calves and thighs that worked to maintain balance. Never locking, always swaying, the simple act of standing cost extraordinary energy. Finally, Jacob turned inward to Rebecca. "Love, Amos is becoming cold."

Rebecca did not even glance aside from her obsession with the sea rushing past the hull. "Tell him to go inside. You go too. I am fine."

This was as far from the truth as it could be. Jacob had never seen anyone less fine in his life. "Amos, go see if Hannah would like some air." Amos scuttled to the hatch, moving as stiffly as if he were an aged man. It was only then that Jacob realized how chilled his own windward side was.

Rebecca turned to him and said, "Husband, I am not going to kill myself. I may die of this grief, but it will not be my choice." Jacob's heart seized for her. He took her hand and then tugged it as a gust of cold wind nearly knocked him off his feet.

"My dear, it is not good to be in this cold for so long. You need warmth and…"

"I need to say goodbye to Ezekiel. Let me do that."

Jacob reluctantly nodded consent. "As long as you need, dear."

The hatch reopened to reveal Hannah, bearing the family's one blanket, folded over her coated arm. She made her way to her parents, staggering as the increasing roll made controlled walking more difficult, and she and Jacob draped the woolen thing about Rebecca, so she could remain tented on the icy deck. They stood there until the dark of night and slicing rain drove them to guide Rebecca back to the hatch. Jacob was sure that if they were not with her, Rebecca might have stood there until morning, could she stay alive that long. This had gone far past sitting *Shiva*, but what else could he do but stand beside her?

Back in the common sleeping room, their family nest now disassembled at the quiet rest of Jacob to the other fathers, Sarah brought a thermos from the bridge, poured steaming broth into the screw-off cup, and held it to Rebecca's lips. She sat motionless, gazing into a distance only she could see. She started, glanced down, opened her lips, sipped, and swallowed. "*Danke.* That is enough."

"Love, you must take more. You have not eaten in two days." Sarah saw desperation on Jacob's face, and with a renewed sense of purpose, she set about waking her sister from her stupor. She spoke practically, no hesitation in her voice, and Rebecca dutifully sipped and swallowed, taking half of the cup before grimacing and waving it away. "I cannot take more. *Danke.*"

Dampened though it was, the blanket was better than the frigid air of the hold. Jacob settled Rebecca in their little cloth nestling place, lay down behind her, and put the blanket over them. Hannah, meeting his eyes, lay in front of her mother, another spoon. Jacob lay awake, listening to Hannah's breathing change to the sweet rhythm of a child's sleep, and waiting, futilely, for the sound of Rebecca's breath to change. It did not, and after hours of holding still, lest he interrupt the advance of sleep for his wife, Jacob slept.

Waking was abrupt; fear shot through him. But Rebecca still lay in his arms, still warmed between his body and Hannah's. Her breathing, even and passionless, was the same as when sleep had claimed him. She felt thinner, less attached to the world, and Jacob had to nuzzle his mouth into her neck, laying her dense fall of hair aside with side strokes of his face, to kiss her skin where the great artery still pulsed, so slowly and lightly.

Seven days after Ezekiel's death, shiva ended. Jacob bathed himself with seawater, standing on the deck abaft the hold, treasuring the rare sunlight even as the icy seawater stole his breath. He scrubbed hair and beard with strong lye soap and scrubbed at the hidden places of his body, fetid after shiva's abstinence from washing. He put on the change of clothing that was all he had left, a threadbare shirt and an old pair of suit trousers. He wished that he could send the old clothing into the sea, but as he would certainly need them again, he instead tied a rope around the bundle and tossed them in for a cleansing beating in the ocean.

On the other side of the afterdeck, Sarah assisted Rebecca in her own cleansing and clothing change. As she gently washed her listless sister, Sarah imagined that she was washing away her sadness.

Captain Cervantes smiled with real sincerity when Jacob reentered his bridge on the following morning. "*Buenos dias!* I feared my records would go back to their old ways without you!" He slapped Jacob on the back, then adjusted to a more serious tone. "How is your wife?"

Jacob noted that the welcome was sincere. He was glad of this and hoped that it might mean potential future business with this man or his ship owners on another, less unbalanced, occasion. "She is very sad and very tired. We must keep her from too much sorrowing time. Can you make a request for *apfelstrudel* or something of the sort?"

Cervantes grinned. "I would never have intruded on her without your asking, but it would greatly help the morale of my overworked crew if she did make another of those magnificent things! However, food is something we must talk about in any case." He was suddenly somber. "I know all of you have been hungry for too long. Nicolas took care to tell me, you know."

Jacob actually had not known but felt another surge of gratitude for the kind man who had saved all of their lives.

"So we have used food freely so far. But all the fresh eggs, the butter, the bread, the vegetables, all are gone. We have cases of bully beef, nets of beets and carrots, and a lot of flour, though most of that is full of weevils. But the nets of beets and carrots are much smaller, and there are only four cases of the meat left. And so…" His voice trailed off, though Jacob's experience and rumbling stomach told him that severe rationing was in store. He nodded in understanding.

"We are going to be short of food very soon," Cervantes continued. "We usually bring food *to* Amsterdam, not take it away, since the start of the German occupation. And we did not dare to lay in much more than our usual stores, for fear the Nazi turds would suspect passengers."

"How bad, Captain?" Jacob had gone hungry before and knew he could again, but Rebecca was already so thin that a strong wind might blow her away. Surely she could eat no less. And Hannah and Amos had just started to look rosy again.

"With the flour and the bully beef, we would not starve. But there is very little fresh food, and we could have the beginnings of scurvy, and none of your party can really take much more food restriction."

Baruch HaShem, Jacob thought.

"So I have changed course a bit, and instead of angling off for South America, we are curving south, headed for Lisboa."

"Lisboa?"

"Oh. Lisbon, in Portugal. It is a trading port we seldom visit, and it will stretch our fuel, if there is not enough diesel there to top our tanks."

"We have no more money…" Jacob said.

The captain waved that away with a great paw. "I have had a radio message. From Suriname. Extra costs of a restocking port call are covered. In fact, I have," he grinned widely, "an order for sherry as good as the whole cloth cargo! Who in Suriname likes you so much?"

"We know a few people there, who were refugees like us only a year or so ago. No one in a position to order fine wine."

"Well, we will be entering port in another day; we still have dried apples, which I have threatened my crew with death for touching since I tasted your wife's *apfelstrudel* the first time; and my once-useless cook needs to learn how to make that to avoid a life ashore."

Jacob waved just once before diving out of the bridge hatch to convey "captain's orders" to Rebecca, Sarah, and Hannah.

Lisbon held the dregs of the wartime world. There were two impounded German freighters, wooden *dhows* from Africa, and an American vessel that looked as ragged as the *Bon Chance.*

The Roseweigs, the Levins, the Rabins, and the Adelmanns had gotten only a brief glimpse from the bridge. They would all have to hide in the hold while in port, and for several hours before entering the channel. They had all worked, along with two of the seamen, to reconfigure the cloth bales in order to make a sort of wall in the hold behind which they could hide. After the quick look at the port that Captain Cervantes had allowed them to take, they were hustled down the central passageway, through the inner hatch to the hold, and into the congested space behind the cloth. The seamen finished the wall with the last bales. There was just room for everyone to lie down, with the only blankets folded up to make a soft nest for Rachel Levin and her burgeoning pregnant belly. There was only a little space for the necessary buckets, mercifully empty and clean for now, though all knew this would not last and dreaded the hours to come.

It was a tense return to the terrifying time of their embarkation. Rebecca shivered in Jacob's arm and whispered, "It was dark like this and smelled like this when…" She choked.

"I know, love, but here we have food and water and friends and plenty of air," Jacob said soothingly.

"It is still a coffin of cloth."

"Hush, my love," Jacob shushed her. "Here is your son and your daughter, and your sister, and I, who love you forever. Come back to us. Ezekiel had the dignity of ceremony, and we will always remember him and the love we had for him. You need to come back to us now. You must live for us. Amos and Hannah are still children who need their mother. Come back to us. Shiva is over."

She stiffened. Rebecca did not speak again, and none of the others dared speak to her. All he could do was hold her and hope.

They were in port two days and a night, and the families remained in their hovel all that time. Nothing entered the world of their hiding place save the occasional gonging echo through the hull. The boredom that set in as they all lay there in the dark, unable to do anything to pass the time and reluctant to speak above a whisper for fear of being caught, was excruciating and made the two days feel like forty. Of course, matters were worsened when the buckets inevitably became full; the air became foul, despite the seawater that had filled a third of each bucket to start.

Groans came from all, as the inactivity set up cramps and tensions. Albert Levin could frequently be seen rubbing his wife's aching back and shoulders, and the boys—Amos, Nathaniel, Otto, Choen, and Levi—found their adolescent hormones difficult to suppress. They all struggled to remain still and wound up bouncing their legs, cracking their knuckles, and generally fidgeting to everyone's great annoyance.

In her grief and irritation at Jacob, Rebecca's method of escape was through spending much of the approximately thirty-six hours asleep.

Sarah marveled at her sister's ability to sleep in such conditions. Despite the many months she had been a refugee with the Roseweigs, she had never been able to overcome her tendency toward light sleep and frequent waking, even in the best of conditions. The loud, guttural snoring emitted from Jacob and Eli Rabin, alternately, in addition to the fetid smell and the cramped conditions, made sleep an impossibility. She accepted this fact and resolved instead that if she couldn't sleep, she would sink instead into a restful, meditative state, daydreaming of Michael and of joyful days gone by.

"Sarah? Are you awake?" Hannah's small voice came in the quiet. It was impossible to tell what time it was in the dark hold, but the other residents had been quiet for a long time, save Jacob's whistling snore.

"Yes, love. I can't sleep. How are you?"

"We are so close to having our freedom, and yet we are so far away. I feel as if I might burst if I have to stay here much longer!" Hannah's voice increased in volume, and Sarah quietly shushed her.

"Have you heard the tale of the donkeys?" Sarah asked quietly?

"I don't think so," Hannah said.

"Once upon a time, the donkeys complained to their Creator that they were treated cruelly by man. They said to him, 'We are forced to carry burdens that all other animals, and even Man himself, would sink under. And to make matters worse, they beat us to make us go faster, even when it is impossible given our bodies and the impossible weight of their loads.' The donkeys asked the Creator to make it impossible for Man to ever beat them again.

"The Creator sympathized with their plight but knew it would be impossible to forbid men from beating them, but he came up with another idea. He would dull the donkeys' senses, so that their skins would be tough enough to resist the blows, and to fatigue the arms of he who should whip the donkeys. 'Oh, thank you, *HaShem*,' the donkeys cried, and they rejoiced."

Sarah concluded her tale, and Hannah remained quiet in the dark—so quiet that Sarah began to believe her niece was asleep. At last Hannah spoke.

"Our skins will be very tough indeed, won't they, Aunt Sarah?"

At last, late on the second day, a hole opened in the bale wall as one bale in the puzzle of a wall was removed, and in came the welcome, booming voice of Captain Cervantes bellowing into their chamber. "All out! Back to work, lazy bones!" To his credit, Cervantes only winced a bit at the smells emanating from the opening. The filthy denizens of the odorous chamber all slammed eyelids shut against the rush of light.

"The hatch above is open!" exclaimed Amos. "That is sunlight!"

Suddenly energized, Hannah sprang up and immediately began clambering to climb out through the hole, unwilling to wait another moment. Sarah stood and stretched her arms high above her head, bending her back slightly and feeling it crack. Jacob jostled Rebecca to wake her, and she sat up, rubbing her eyes against the light. Cervantes and two of his crew began pulling bales away to clear a path out of the tiny compartment. Several people stumbled as they clambered out, tears streaming in the radiance. Rachel Levin required help from her husband and son to reach a standing position, but she seemed no worse for wear.

"Ladies to starboard, gentlemen to port," instructed the captain, pointing up toward the deck. "There is *paella* to eat, as soon as you have washed up."

Rebecca, to Jacob's astonishment, yawned a great yawn and, with a gleam in her eye, smiled at the captain. "What is paella, Captain, and did Antonio cook it?" She sounded humorously suspicious. Sarah couldn't help emitting a small chuckle, and she felt pride for her sister swell in her chest. Rebecca seemed to have recovered her good humor in her sleep.

Cervantes bowed, regarding her with great solemnity. "Absolutely not! There are buckets of paella, which is a seafood stew, from a fine cooking establishment ashore. It is a beloved dish of the Portuguese, which contains mussels, clams, fish, peppers, corn, okra…"

The Roseweigs, actually drooling, did not remain long enough to hear the captain finish his description.

After the paella, everyone had to wash again. It had been the most wonderfully engaging of meals, requiring the stowaways to wrestle with shells and crab claws, to gasp at the peppery broth, and, eaten as it was on a sunny deck, say a fond farewell to the gloom and fetor of the hidden room for good.

Jacob waved a dripping crab claw magnanimously and stifled a belch. At this, Rebecca met eyes with her sister and the two suppressed a conspiratorial giggle at his expense. Sarah was coming to believe that Rebecca's heart was truly on the mend. "Captain," Jacob called to the other end of the large table, "would you like me to regularize the records of another ship in gratitude for this meal?"

"Not necessary," Cervantes waved him off, enjoying being magnanimous. "And we have apples, flour *without* weevils, cabbages, turnips, beets," and addressing Rebecca and Sarah under his breath, "all I could find still for sale in winter. There's also butter, olive oil, two sides of beef that we must eat within a week, and there are big cages of chickens just forward of the taffrail. Also, we have the forward hold half full of sherry. And here," he reached down for a bottle that had lurked unnoticed by his boot, "is a sample of our cargo. More there." He indicated a crate next to the bridge hatch, from which straw protruded, and indicated to a nearby crew member with an expressive wave that the seaman was to crack open the case and serve the contents to all.

"And now, if you and your wife would join me on the bridge..." Jacob immediately understood, and his chest visibly puffed. He took Rebecca's arm, and, smiling, they followed the captain into his cluttered realm.

Cervantes poured the golden fluid into bridge cups, diluting their long-established veneer of coffee oils. Rebecca's face subtly betrayed her apprehension, this being her first alcohol since before she had become pregnant with Ezekiel, and perhaps even before that. But she took her mug with a gracious smile. She sipped from her cup, and although it burned the back of her throat, she was surprised to discover that the stuff was rich and delicious, and it instantly warmed and soothed her aching, tired body. This first drink in months seemed to visibly melt all the tension out of Jacob's muscles in moments. A satisfied sigh escaped from his throat as he relaxed and quaffed again from his cup.

"I have had another radio talk with the port in Suriname," the captain began, his tone more serious now that it was just the three of them. "I was given no names, but 'the Doctor' is putting together a place for you all to stay. I am told there is work to be had for many of you, and I am assured there will be 'appropriate help' for all."

Jacob and Rebecca exchanged excited glances. This was really happening. They were truly saved!

"Also, the message authorized the extra food purchases, such as the beef, the butter, and the extra sherry. The message I was given stated, that I was to 'fatten stock well,' as there will be evaluations performed on each arriving passenger's condition upon arrival." With this, the captain's face spread into a wide, ferocious grin. "Therefore, I would appreciate it if you all ate a little too much and slept an extra hour each day until our arrival."

Jacob could not help it. He collapsed off his stool, roaring with laughter. Only through some adroit juggling did he manage to avoid spilling the wonderful sherry. And, miracle of miracles, he heard Rebecca giggle.

All would be well. They were saved.

⌛

Once off the coast of Portugal, the storms returned, though they were not accompanied by the whistling chill of death that those on board had experienced in the Channel. The popular galley shut down for heavy storms, but there were sturdy male volunteers to make braces for pots, to carry fresh water from the distillery, and to peel and clean vegetables. One and all, refugees and crew, wanted the galley to operate efficiently.

"I would not have believed it if I had not seen. Seamen *volunteering* to scrub pots," said a sincerely disbelieving Cervantes, head hanging out the portside bridge hatch, craning back to see the galley twenty feet astern. Jacob just smiled. He had seen the seamen in question, each of them with pots hanging from one hand, the other clutching apple tarts powdered with cinnamon. He himself had been inveigled into household repairs by the same form of bribery many times.

"You know what they are being bribed with?" the captain asked.

"The usual currency is apple tarts, I believe."

"Do you think we could get a few for the hardworking bridge crew, too?"

Jacob smiled, nodded, and went out to solicit help from Rebecca and Sarah.

Good food (at least between storms), the opportunity to wash and dry clothing, adequate (if primitive) sanitation, and a crew that increasingly valued their passengers—all of it seemed ideal, but Jacob had overheard the radio traffic from the bridge and knew how on edge the captain and his men truly were, and how vigilantly they watched the horizon for steam plumes or periscopes. This was a wartime sea, and sturdy as the rusty old *Bon Chance* was, it hadn't a chance against even the least of naval assailants.

While Rebecca's first giggle had not exactly been a floodgate of mirth, it had heralded a gradual lightening of mood.

"Captain?" Almost two weeks out of Lisbon, Sarah and Rebecca stuck their heads into the open bridge hatch, timidly. Hannah hovered behind them. Jacob could see they were all bursting with something funny.

Cervantes knew the formidable team of Hannah and Sarah well enough to be a bit apprehensive by now. Their mischief was a grace note on board, but after one seaman had commented on the dire effects of cabbage in some form at almost every meal, and then had, during his next shave, unwittingly dyed his own face with green food coloring with a strategically planted wash cloth as peals of laughter emitted from a fleeing Hannah and Sarah, the captain had been a bit more wary.

"Yes?" he asked cautiously.

"Did you enjoy lunch?" Sarah was earnestly inquiring.

"Of course. All lunches are enjoyable since you fine ladies rescued my galley."

Rebecca and Sarah shared a satisfied glance. It was Rebecca's turn. "Antonio cooked it." Cervantes was always gallant to Sarah, devouring her with his eyes, though, devout Catholic husband that he was, he had made no overt advances. They teased each other a bit, but when Rebecca spoke to the captain, it was always simple truth.

Cervantes reeled, almost losing perch on his stool and asked, incredulous, "The *apfelstrudel*?"

They nodded solemnly, though Hannah's giggle spoiled the solemnity a bit as she chortled, "Crust *and* filling!"

"The potatoes au gratin?"

Again, three smug nods.

"The breaded strip steak?"

More nods.

"The cabbage with vinegar?"

A chorus of three voices sang, "Every bite!"

"Antonio!" Three feminine forms recoiled at the captain's bellowing command.

Shaven, cleanly dressed, and obviously very apprehensive, Antonio popped into view from the direction of the galley. "*Si, Capitan*?"

"Antonio, if you continue to cook this way, and continue to learn from these wonderful women, your pay is now that of a full, able-bodied seaman, and you will be listed on the ship's roster as Chef. Well done!"

All could see the cook's—chef's—face begin to crumple with emotion as the full weight of the captain's speech penetrated. "*Gracias, mi Capitan!*"

"Now, learn how to make the *borscht*, and the sauce Hollandaise, and the poached eggs … and how to bake bread the way these ladies do," the captain instructed. As he did so, Antonio's face lost its enthusiasm. "You have another week and a half. Dismissed!"

Antonio nodded once, saluted his captain, and bustled out quickly with his head down.

Cervantes uncoiled from his tall stool, and without his broad frame seeming at all affected by the swaying deck, bowed profoundly to the trio of women in his hatchway.

"You are miracle workers. That man was due to be cast off on the beach as an incompetent poisoner, and you have saved him. And our stomachs."

CHAPTER 17

JULY 17, 1942
EARLY AFTERNOON

PARAMARIBO, SURINAME

George was busy. *Too* busy, perhaps. Between rounding up and keeping plasterers, carpenters, and plumbers busy, keeping Lijsbet's back rubbed, preparing barracks for those on board the approaching ship, and trying to maintain a profit from the thin-yet-surviving coastal and inland trade, it seemed he had to always be in three places at once. Now Dr. Adelmann had another project.

"A synagogue? You want to rebuild a *synagogue*?" George asked incredulously. "How big? And what will the authorities say? There are Catholic priests attached to this government like starfish on mussels!"

"The president has promised me personally that there will be no problem with the authorities, and his confessor, Father Bartolo, has asked if he may attend the first service after the renovation," the doctor replied in his usual, comforting tones. *This man could sell water to the fish,* George thought, already reconciled to meeting the request.

Ben Adelmann was an excellent doctor. He had attended every member of George's family, as well as the president and several of the legislature. His modern European education and methods made the local "physicians" look like shamanic practitioners. In fact, a couple of those had left their solo practices to work under Adelmann's direction at his clinic, reentering an educational phase in an honest acknowledgment of what this quietly brilliant Jewish doctor had to teach them. Still, this was an astonishing development. Adelmann, his family, and a few friends had been here less than two years, and while all were hardworking folk, they had been busy establishing lives in their new home. None of the others had Adelmann's sheer charm and intelligence, and, for a few of the adults, the new language was proving a great barrier. George was banker to all of them, the doctor included, and knew how close to the bone they were from time to time. Adelmann had raised seed money and had worked it, as George had explained to Lijsbet, but was by no means wealthy … yet.

"Forgive me, but I know something of your finances, since you not only trade as my partner, but you *bank* with me. Between the warehouse and your half share of that sherry cargo, your pockets are almost empty. Where is all of this going to come from?"

"New York." The doctor kept a straight face as he poured a top-up for each of their wine glasses. The crimson fluid glowed richly in the sunlight slanting through the deep-set window of the adobe. Adelmann had adopted and refined one of the older homes in the city.

"*New York*?" George was taken aback. There was almost no outgoing trade from the States since they had entered into an alliance with Russia and the British and were now unwilling to do business with Germany, which occupied Holland and kept claiming control of its satellite, Suriname.

George was scouring Brazil for pre-war American plumbing fixtures. Light bulbs were as precious as gold. He would have swum out personally to greet an American trading vessel other than Alcoa's bauxite freighters. Adelmann would have, too, he knew, for a fresh supply of penicillin.

"Many Jewish people live and trade in New York, in things like diamonds. Some of them wish to perform a *mitzvah*, even though we here are not as … traditional as they are," Adelmann explained. "A small synagogue, an old one, a self-filling sacred bath, just the minimums to follow our way with respect and modern sanitation."

What in hell is a sacred bath? George wondered and then asked, "How?"

Adelmann looked smug. "The money has come through, oddly enough, both Uruguay and Brazil. It is in gold, and it is enough to hire all the workers you are using on the warehouse conversion and several more. I *do* need to get it into your big safe at the bank as soon as possible."

"Tomorrow morning. The tellers have gone home already, and the night guard tends to be hard to wake. And you are using *me* because…?"

"Because you are honest, you know every workman in the area, and you know where every board and pipe in the country is to be had. Plus, I would have no idea of how to go about building so much as a shed, myself. Of course, there is not a Jewish contractor in this country. We would like this building, these buildings, to be of traditional adobe—thick, solid, cool, and quiet. Wood fixtures are to be finely finished."

George was skeptical. "It will have to wait until the warehouse work is done. There are only two plumbers in this city, and it is hard to keep either of them working once they have enough money for wine."

Adelmann grinned. "We can wait. On another subject, I have very little information as to who is coming. There are several families, as I understand, but aside from my uncle and cousin, just one family is known to us. This family, the Roseweigs, have a daughter, Hannah. This girl has written a letter to her cousin, Yael, daughter to one of my friends, named Zeitweig, who came to Suriname last year from Germany. This is how I learned that that Roseweigs were on board this ship. That family's head, *Yakob* Roseweig, is the former proprietor of an accounting house in Munich. He speaks English as well as German, is thoroughly well thought of, and I was wondering if you might have a job for him?"

Up until this moment, George had been a reluctant participant in this conversation that would mean even more work. But at this latest news, George perked up. His eyes opened wide, and his back became ramrod straight. "An accountant? A *trained* accountant? Do not joke with me, doctor!"

Adelmann's expression grew even more smug and satisfied. "Oh, believe me, I would not joke about this."

"That is something I had never hoped for, a dream come true!" George beamed. He had his big store, the bank, a small trucking fleet, and deals over three countries, which made for stacks of bills, invoices, bills of lading, contracts in four languages, and a mountain of filing. He needed to establish a garage, set up stores in outlying communities... The list was endless and had become a source of great tension for George. "For an accountant, I will pay not only money but a *house*! Do you have any idea how much of my life is tied up crouched over a desk?"

Adelmann grinned again, leaned back, and quaffed wine. "What else do you bitch about every time we speak?"

George grinned back. It was true. His records time was eating up his life, and with Lijsbet expecting again, his time would only shrink. For a real accountant, he was willing to give Adelmann whatever he wanted.

"You have plans for this synagogue?"

"Not yet. There are some requirements, just as there would be for a Christian church, but with a few differences, of course. We will have general plans in a few weeks, and at that time we'll talk with you about what is or is not feasible, what may have to wait for more time or better trade, and so on ..."

George was no longer listening. His head was spinning with glorious possibilities.

His head was still spinning—partly due to the wine—as he walked home to his back-rubbing responsibilities. He always drank too much with Adelmann, largely because the doctor bought the best wine he could find. That exquisite Petit Syrah had found its way to Adelmann's cellar from Argentina.

He was so lost in thought about the prospect of having an accountant, and of wine, and of the cargo of sherry he had received that he could sell in Brazil or give as gifts, that he completely failed to notice the immense clouds piling up over the sea.

CHAPTER 18

JULY 17, 1942
3:30 P.M.

AMSTERDAM, HOLLAND

Alcohol did not help. Immersing one's self in the mind-numbing, sordid task of pursuing terrified people through slums, attics, and sewers, then loading them on trucks and trains for transport, did not help, either. All day, all Gunter Kramer saw on the faces of the sobbing children of the refugees was little Emma's face; in the lined, worried mothers' faces was his dear Greta. Increasingly, his work tore at his heart, strengthened his anger and despair, and felt utterly without purpose. More, daily, he had to drink to get through the day. He would shovel down whatever was presented for food, then add schnapps or the vile grappa that came from the useless Italian ally. He took to carrying a flask, an affectation common among officers and which he had at one time despised. Gunter was sick to his soul and had stopped caring about anything.

Vaguely, he understood that the news from North Africa was not what it seemed to be. The same places kept recurring in the reports. Rommel seemed to be bouncing back and forth, up and down the coast like a ball.

Gunter's one personal project, to exchange as many of his SS brutes for regular Wehrmacht as he could, had gone surprisingly well. There was, it seemed, a demand for the SS on the veiled Eastern Front. Just what that was, however, was an ongoing mystery; the Poles were decisively defeated, Russia an ally. What little contact he had with other officers outside the refugee-hunting cadre yielded subtle warning about what was happening in Poland. Insurgents were taking a toll on the unstoppable Reich, but not enough, surely, to account for the dearth of materiel throughout the Reich.

At Wehrmacht headquarters one morning, he saw the unteroffizier Kucher and his sidecar rider sprawled wearily in chairs just outside the entrance. They looked harshly used.

"Unteroffizier," Kucher lurched up, blearily. "*Sitzen*, Kucher." The corporal looked up, startled, and recognized the oberst who had been so decent a few weeks back.

"Herr Oberst. Did you get to see your family?" He asked this with a smile, obviously expecting to hear that their long night of effort had yielded relief for this decent man.

Gunter sagged. He had not had to speak his new reality up until now, and somehow that process of speaking made it more final, more rending.

"*Nein*. They … they died," he said, barely above a whisper, and then paused to avoid a sob. "But," he gulped, "thank you for remembering, Unteroffizier."

The boy's eyes showed shock, as did his companion's. "I am so sorry, Herr Oberst."

"Nothing to do about it, just another despicable result of this senseless war," Gunter said, and Kucher's face registered some surprise at the oberst's outspokenness. Gunter shifted to a more appropriate tone. "Are you two flyabouts attached here?"

"*Ya*, Herr Oberst, we are attached here, but we are frequently sent to France, sometimes back to Germany—long trips with items too valuable to wait for trains."

"Would you like to work shorter trips for a while?"

Both youngsters, obviously at the edge of even their young strength, nodded earnestly.

"*Gut*. I will request that you and your motorcycle be attached to my unit. We are rousting out *Juden* labor, and we are often miles apart—a squad here, a squad there. We need to coordinate. Better to sleep in a bed after a hot meal every night, eh?"

Again, earnest nods, and the boys struggled erect to proffer a Wehrmacht salute, gratitude in their eyes.

I can send away two more of those SS swine, Gunter thought satisfactorily as he extracted his moleskine notebook and a pencil from the worn map case that hung, as ever, at his side. "Give me paybook numbers, so I can do the forms. And *try* to get your cycle serviced before you report to me."

That would leave him with only Feldwebel Ermenthaller and just two other SS, the least offensive of the bunch, but he wished he could get rid of them, too. Ermenthaller was the only reason, Gunter knew, why the unit functioned on a daily basis. Over the last month, Gunter had come to trust the feldwebel, and what was more, to like him—no small thing in this dismal setting, in this situation. Gunter saw Ermenthaller as a man who could be trusted, who could be counted on to keep confidences. An ally.

The odious Eberhardt had left gleefully for Poland, where the SS seemed to be very active, a week before. His absence was a tiny relief in a world of gray hopelessness.

CHAPTER 19

JULY 20, 1942
MID-MORNING
ON BOARD THE *BON CHANCE*

Hannah rocketed down the deck, so used to its rolling by now that she no longer noticed the sway. "Papa! Papa! Papa! There are fish in the air! There are fish flying!" She skidded to a halt by the bridge, grabbed the edge of the hatchway, and shoved her head in to see the captain, who was roaring with laughter, poke a thumb into the steering crewman's ribs.

"What do you think about that?" he asked the crewman with a grin. "You think this young lady has been into that sherry hold?" Jacob was just swiveling around on his stool, taking the glasses from his eyes, and he too was grinning, enjoying the sight of his daughter's pure pleasure.

"But there really are, and there are a lot of them!" Hannah insisted, not getting the joke.

The captain held his hands out, indicating a length of about a foot or a little more. "Like this?" He then made another, wider two-handed gesture. "And they have fins like wings, about this wide?"

"Yes, yes! And two of them landed on deck and bounced around until they fell back into the water!"

The captain looked jovial. "If any more of them come on board, you must catch them! They are delicious!" The crewman looked around and nodded earnestly. Hannah was appalled. How could you *eat* such a beautiful, unique creature?

"It *would* be very nice to have some fresh fish, *Liebchen*." She was disappointed to hear this from her papa, too.

The captain continued, "When we get to shore, you will see flying fish for sale in the marketplace. Everyone likes to eat them, and I think that's why they learned how to fly; everything in the ocean likes to eat them, too!" The men all laughed, and Hannah left in disgust.

Hannah's mother was no better. In fact, *she* went so far as to send all the children to the deck to watch for flying fish coming aboard. She and Sarah began chatting animatedly over what they could do with some fresh fish for dinner. The two of them had begun to take the excellence of the *Bon Chance*'s galley very personally.

Hannah tried to remain aloof, but when the next school of glittering shapes began arcing out of the azure water and a few landed on deck, she found herself scrambling gleefully with the others to catch the wriggling things. Once she had one in hand, it nearly escaped because Hannah had never had a live fish in her hands before, and its coolness and strength, not to mention its slippery scales, were very startling. Sarah demonstrated how to smack the back of a fish's head on the deck to stun it. Hannah looked at her aunt as if she had never seen her before. But finally she thumped her own fish clumsily on the wooden deck, lost her grip, and was disgraced when Aliza Rabin seized upon the released prey and executed it enthusiastically.

Within several minutes, the group had gathered half a dozen gleaming carcasses. But though they waited hopefully for another hour for more, none of the entrancing aerialists landed on board again.

Rebecca and Sarah reluctantly gave up the wait and took the fish away to the galley and began discussing how they would prepare the fish for that evening's dinner. "There will be enough for everyone to have a taste!" Sarah called over her shoulder as they disappeared.

Hannah was pleased to see her mother happy about something. They had all missed sweet little Ezekiel—as his big sister and a constant caregiver to him, she felt his loss keenly. But she had not indulged openly in her grief, in an attempt to be strong for her mother, who seemed utterly incapable of bearing the loss. Over the last several weeks, Rebecca had clearly enjoyed the game of training Antonio to be a chef, as had Hannah and Sarah, but she had too often worn an expression of sorrow, and it seemed permanently etched on her face, despite the joy of sailing the calm seas and chasing fish under a blue sky.

They had all eaten more food, delicious food, on this old ship than they had eaten in the many months they had been in Holland, and every refugee aboard now looked far healthier than they had just a few weeks before. The crew had become their friends, and the day-to-day realities of shipboard life, despite the necessary buckets and having to sleep in a metal box on musty cloth, were now automatic and almost effortless. In fact, Hannah had begun recently to feel as if the *Bon Chance* was her home.

She had started to consider what life in Suriname would entail. She couldn't imagine the place or its people. All the cooking she and her mother and aunt had been doing had opened her mind to the idea of opening a restaurant—eating well any time they wanted while earning a living doing something they truly enjoyed.

Then again, what did they have? Nothing. No home. No knives. No shoes. Every sock had a hole in it, and each of them had only three or four items of clothing. Her papa, she knew, had his glasses, a fountain pen, and the family's *mezusah* in his pocket. That was all they had of their home.

Hannah found herself musing sadly, leaning on the rail, and it took her several minutes to realize that the line on the far horizon where the ocean curved around the world was the edge of land.

CHAPTER 20

JULY 25, 1942
4:50 P.M.

PORT OF PARAMARIBO, SURINAME

It was a blue-sky day, but the humid air was stiflingly hot as the *Bon Chance* dropped anchor at the Port of Paramaribo. Palm trees, a sight the refugees had never seen, dotted the coastline as far as the eye could see in either direction. Seagulls swarmed overhead, and it struck Hannah that Suriname looked exactly like pictures she had seen in school books.

Yet despite the foreignness of this equatorial land, she also noted that the buildings bore a striking resemblance to those lining the streets of Holland, with their jaunty, upright postures and colorful exteriors. Although here, columns and large, welcoming front porches suggested an expansive freedom, somehow, unlike the closed-off wrecks they had left behind in Amsterdam.

The Roseweigs, Sarah, and their fellow stowaways all staggered when they stepped onto the dock. Poor Rachel Levin, who had been as stoic an expectant mother as one could hope to be, promptly vomited within a minute of standing on dry land. Hannah giggled. This was even worse than their first days on board the ship.

Deep laughter drew their eyes as the captain leaned out of the bridge house and called, good-naturedly, "Nothing a day ashore won't cure!"

Sarah exited last, having lingered a minute for a goodbye to Cervantes.

"Good luck to you, my dear," he had said, removing his hat and giving her a chivalrous bow, all pretense at his stern authority gone.

"Thanks to you, from the bottom of my heart, for all you have done for us. Bless you." She stood on her tiptoes and kissed his cheek. A blush spread up his neck and into his cheeks. He nodded silently, and with a broad sweep of his arm bid her carefully leave the ship.

The disembarking refugees held to the railing of the dock, ignoring sticky bits of mussels, scales, broken-off hooks, and the white signatures of seagulls encrusted on it.

A man with a white linen suit and a flat white hat hurried down the dock. *This must be the famous Doktor Adelmann!* thought Sarah as she cautiously sidled down the ramp. *He looks so much like Herr Adelmann and Levi!*

Hurrying ahead of a small group of people, the doctor fairly trotted to embrace his uncle and cousin. "*Baruch HaShem!* Come, there are some people to meet, and we have a place for you to stay!"

"Hannah!" came a shriek from the ramp. Hannah sought the source of the voice and felt tears sting her eyes when she saw it was Yael approaching. Her beloved cousin was more beautiful that Hannah remembered. The girl wore a sunny yellow, embroidered linen dress, finely tailored with no torn seams or dirty hems, which had become part of the uniform for Hannah and her fellow female passengers. What was more, though, was the healthy glow Yael wore, the pink cheeks and sparkling brown eyes, the figure that featured healthy curves and a more womanly shape that Hannah had seen on her before. Hannah's pace picked up, and she staggered toward her cousin, arms outstretched. Their hug felt like a magic balm, better than she had imagined a hug could. Hannah squeezed, never wanting to let go, and looked up to see Yael's parents, her *Onkel* Caleb and *Tante* Deborah, wearing huge smiles and warmly embracing Jacob and Rebecca.

After the initial greetings, Dr. Adelmann began talking loudly, giving instructions to the arrival party, all the while with one arm around his uncle and the other around Levi. "You and Levi will stay with us, Else insists, and we have room. Everyone else has beds and showers… and who is *Yakob*?"

All heads turned to seek out Jacob, who held Rebecca's elbow to steady her sea legs and had been making his anxious way to the good doctor who had secured all their futures. When the doctor saw him, a broad smile spread across his face, and he doffed his hat and warmly shook Jacob's hand, then turned to gesture to an older man with thick, graying hair who was trailing the greeters onto the dock, walking with a confident stroll not often seen in Jewish men.

Introductions were a continuing flurry, with the meeting people embracing and carrying bundles that contained all the *Bon Chance*'s passengers owned. The gentleman negotiated the crowd carefully as he approached Jacob, hand outstretched.

"Herr Roseweig, this is George Butler," Dr. Adelmann said, clapping both men on the back jovially.

George Butler was a tall, broad-shouldered Englishman who moved, Sarah thought, like a big, happy tomcat. He reminded her, just a bit, of a handsomer Mijnheer Anders, which immediately put her at ease. She liked him instantly.

"Captain Cervantes tells me you are an accountant," he said in English to Jacob while shaking his hand. "How good is your English?"

Jacob's eyes shot wide open. "Good. Not fully fluent but good. We had … English customers at home."

"The captain also tells me you saved his job. Or at least his sanity," George said approvingly.

Jacob chuckled. "The captain does exaggerate. He simply hates to keep accounts."

"So do I," George grinned broadly, displaying beautiful teeth.

Papa gestured the family over. "Mr. Butler, my wife Rebecca, my son Amos, my daughter Hannah, and my wife's sister, Sarah Lipinski." Hannah noticed the intense look Mr. Butler gave Sarah, like most men seemed to do with her raven-haired aunt. Sarah's hair was lustrous in the bright sun and soft breeze. Hannah looked down at herself, hoping she would grow to look more like her aunt.

"Honored, honored," George said, bowing cordially to each. Sarah noted the enormous size of his clean, beautiful hands.

George turned his attention back to Jacob, and his face grew serious. "Herr Roseweig, I have several businesses. I need an accountant, and Dr. Ben here tells me you are the man for the job. Are you interested?"

Jacob seemed physically taken aback and actually stammered a little bit as he formed his reply. "Of course. Just … let me get my family settled…"

He's gone too long without good fortune, Sarah thought.

"Well, if you are interested, you should bring them."

At this, Jacob looked puzzled, and George quickly explained. "You see, while the dormitory that your fellow travelers will call home is nice—and I should know because I built it myself—this job comes with a *house.*"

Jacob's face went white with astonishment. Hannah began to jump up and down, and Rebecca's hand flew to her throat.

George led them by foot along the well-manicured streets of Paramaribo, past enormous, cheerfully green lawns and blindingly white residences, interspersed with structures resembling pictures Hannah had seen of India—mosques topped with ornate, gold minarets and decorated with hand painted tiles.

The walk was not far, and their burdens were light, so within minutes they arrived at the house George had told them about, which was to be their new home. It was tiled adobe, and bigger than their old home in Germany had been. Purple blooming jacarandas lined the street, and two of them framed the door. The house had a water pump in the kitchen and a wood jakes in the depths of the big, walled backyard, like most of the houses they had seen on the way here. All noted, approvingly, that the roof was composed of tile, not thatch—a good thing considering Sarah had seen a few shining rats' eyes regarding them from some of the roofs they'd passed on the way here.

"I had a lady clean this house when I knew you were close. Put your things inside and come to the store. Credit comes with the job, too. I suppose you could use clothes, food, house things?" He looked extraordinarily casual as he spoke of purchasing things they had spent months desperately scrounging for.

Jacob's jaw dropped, and he fixed George with a real stare. Rebecca's eyes filled with tears.

"What kind of accounting job *is* this?"

Mr. Butler grinned an evil grin. "You can have no idea."

CHAPTER 21

AUGUST 15, 1942
7:30 P.M.

AMSTERDAM, HOLLAND

Gunter paused before the barracks, doffed his broad-crowned officer's cap and swiped his filthy brow with his sleeve before replacing the cap crookedly on his head. Then he shook the soaking wet cap in a futile attempt to remove some of the water, and clapped his gloves together to free some of the mud that had become encrusted on them during the week's rains, though it did little to neaten the gloves. He stomped his boots to dislodge some of the mud there, which was no help, and he ended up resorting to the stick leaning against the door frame to prod at the mess. They weighed less when he was done, but they looked as bad as the rest of him.

His condition was his own fault. For many weeks now the task of chasing down innocent people had been almost more than he could bear. Having no recourse and having been denied repeated requests for a combat post, he had resorted to walking the next day's target area alone, armed only with the little pistol, thereby giving warning of an incipient sweep. As a result, the unit's takings had become very slim indeed. And while Gunter was doing this to salve his own conscience and to exact his own sort of revenge, he hoped that it would result ultimately in their being given something honorable to do.

Today, he had walked not only the next day's intended target area, but all the way back to his unit's barracks, all in the driving rain.

Having barracks space at all was unusual for his unit, as they had to change location every few days in order to carry out their disgusting duties. Gunter had scheduled the previous week's activities in such a way that they had been able to move each day's pursuit of refugees in a miles-wide circle around this barracks space. For once, his men now had an opportunity to clean their uniforms and their weapons, bathe their bodies, and have light at night to write letters. The days were rapidly growing shorter.

Despite the repetitious and dehumanizing nature of their work, there had been a marked improvement in morale. Ermenthaller had seen to it that this opportunity was not wasted, and he had taken advantage of the nearby motor pool to have all of their vehicles serviced.

It was really too wet and muddy for the men to work in the open when there was an active storm as there had been that day, and the standing water and slick mud made it dangerous to walk, let alone drive, the cobbled streets. So today the unit had been allowed a holiday of sorts, and as Gunter stepped inside the barracks, he could smell the mouthwatering odor of sauerkraut and sausages simmering on the coal stove. He briefly considered asking for a complimentary plate of it but then caught himself: Of course he *could* get one, but he shouldn't. There would be just enough ration for each man in that pot. He could wait.

For once he was sober. Not because he chose to be but because there was no liquor to be had in this damned city. Supplies had become scarce, rations had been tightened, and everything necessary was in scant supply. The disastrous and mysterious drawdown of supplies was eating everything, not just from Germany but from all of the occupied countries and territories of Europe. And to top off his unwelcome sobriety, Kucher had just intercepted his muddy trudge with a missive from Luftwaffe headquarters in Berlin, routed through the Wehrmacht headquarters here in Amsterdam. Gunter had to go fawn obsequiously over Reichsminister Goebbels, at the Reichstag.

Gunter had already issued orders for the following morning, and because he had motor pool transport trucks coming to his designated area, he knew he must continue with at least one day's operation before he could free himself to ride the rails into Germany at the bidding of his boss.

It was infuriating to realize that for what was probably a purely social encounter, he would be able to reenter his home country, but to attend the final illnesses of his daughter and his wife, he had not been allowed to do so. If the means had been available, Gunter would have drunk himself senseless hours ago.

In a way, it was puzzling how he could objectively see the poisonous reality of the "court" environment in Berlin now, and just a few months ago he had felt admiration and warmth for not only Goebbels but for *Der Fuhrer*. Now the probable failure of Rommel's work in North Africa had become obvious to the entire officer corps of Germany, due to the ridiculous joint command situation and the precariousness of supply. The incestuous and murderous nature of Reich headquarters was well known. Hitler's strutting still paraded across every screen in every theater, and his bombastic speeches echoed from every radio, but for Gunter, along with the loss of his family, he had lost the mask of *belonging* that had obscured the nature of the Reich for him. He still loved Germany and felt she deserved more land, and better treatment for her dispersed folk in the Russian fringes, in Alsace, elsewhere. He felt German *kultur* was superior to that of any other *volk*.

This process of hunting down Jews and other refugees here in Amsterdam had become a grinding horror for the pursuers as well. There were very, very few left, and those had become adept at concealment and subterfuge and had achieved an alertness like frequently hunted animals in a forest. Here, however, the trees were ruined buildings and the forest bombed neighborhoods that impeded pursuers and sheltered the prey. Gunter's solo tours of areas targeted for sweeps simply exaggerated a trend.

Their unit had actually taken casualties over the last few weeks. Once, a desperate husband had managed to strike one of the troopers with an axe as they entered the cellar where that man's family had been hiding. The trooper had screamed and died, thrashing, the axe transecting his eye socket and lodging deep in his brain. They had killed the Jew immediately, of course. The wife and daughters he had been trying so desperately to defend went on one of the stinking train cars to Sobibor. Ermenthaller had clubbed down the SS trooper who had begun lifting the woman's skirts to take a more personal revenge for his SS comrade.

When boots were soaked, the leather softened and easily stretched; there was no support, and persistently soaked, cold boots had caused at least two men to have trenchfoot as well. He made a mental note to find wax or oil, as the better part of his squad was already useless. It felt odd, the contrast between his natural concern for his men and his growing revulsion at the work he must use them for. While his prey had gained human faces, his troopers had retained theirs. It made for a lot of drunkenness for Gunter. And lacking liquor, it made for a lot of angst.

"Ermenthaller." The big feldwebel, used now to his informal oberst, did not spring to attention but remained poised artistically over the kettle, which he was stirring with a long spoon. "*Ja,* Herr Oberst."

"We will be working sector seven tomorrow morning, and I will have to leave for Berlin tomorrow in the late afternoon. Accordingly, I would like you to give everyone liberty the day after tomorrow for a day and night, and then to improve this barracks for the remainder of the time I have to be away. There are drafts, the sinks have forgotten how to be white, and the walls need whitewash desperately."

Ermenthaller could not suppress an ecstatic grin. Gunter strongly suspected that his feldwebel was in as uncomfortable an ethical situation as he found himself.

Gunter turned on his heel but stopped abruptly when Ermenthaller said, "Herr Oberst?"

"Yes?"

"I … My condolences … on the loss of your family, Herr Oberst." His eyes, for the first time, met Gunter's squarely. "Might you … find an opportunity to put their affairs in order while you are in Germany, Sir?"

He must trust me, too, to speak to me in this familiar way, Gunter thought. The prospect of unburdening his soul made him feel light.

"I am afraid that I seem to have fallen out of favor with *Der Fuhrer.* I do not believe I will be given leave to do so, Feldwebel. Not until my assignment is complete."

Ermenthaller's face took on a puzzled expression. "Pardon me, Herr Oberst, but is there no way in which you can get back into his good graces?"

"This is useless." Gunter made his voice sound as disgusted as he could. These bombed homes next to the old trading square were empty of everything but human scat, discarded rags, and rot. When he had walked this area of Waterlooplein Square yesterday, he had seen glimpses of frightened faces, but today, another cold, gray, miserable afternoon, no one was here.

Gunter followed his squad into a pierced shell that had once been a human living place. One of the good Dutch tile stoves in the dark central room of the house had been patched with mud, obviously by hand because of the prints in the patches. *Again, nothing.* He turned to leave, and as he traversed the room with a bomb-pierced exterior wall that had let in rain that had formed a small puddle, something incongruous caught his eye. Tucked into the crack in the wall was a crumple of delicate pink paper. It looked like the kind of thing his wife had loved. He gathered in the little scraps and, pulling off one of his gloves, smoothed them. His heart froze as he read the scrawl, with its exquisite curlicues and swirls:

> Oh Yael, when will this terrible war end? When will we ever be safe walking the streets again? I hate this life of hiding indoors and running from one shattered hole in the wall to the next. One moment we're terrified as we run for our lives, but the next we're dreadfully bored and lonely as we sit around staring at each other for days at a time, or reading the same old books over and over. And we are always hungry…

An enormous lump filled Gunter's throat, and his five-year-old's small voice came back to him, as clearly as if she were standing beside him *"Papa, when will you come back to me?"*

"When the war ends, my Mäuschen."

"When will this war ever end, Papa?"

It was obvious that this letter had been written by a young girl. A Jewish girl. He tenderly smoothed the flowered pink paper and blinked to clear the tears that had begun to well in his eyes. The pain in his heart was unbearable. Then his eyes hit upon the words that made Gunter's blood run cold:

> Papa says many of our people have escaped to Suriname. He says our people are living safely there. Papa says that in addition to your family, Dr. Adelmann's family has gone there, too. Are you with him still? Papa says we must go there because there is no place in Europe where Jews can be safe now…

Suriname. *Adelmann and his people are in Suriname.*

Here was what he had been seeking all these months. Here is what the Führer had made Gunter's singular mission, the task that held the utmost priority, above all else. Here, the words in a child's letter, was what had prevented him from being allowed to return home to see his wife and child one last time.

This girl, this innocent, hungry child, whose words had struck a chord in his heart by reminding him of Emma, was what he and his men had been packing up cruelly onto rail cars and sending off to a life of hard labor.

Bile rose in his throat, and a white hot fury blinded him for a moment. He folded the paper, stuck it back inside its envelope, and tucked it securely into his battered map case. Hannah was her name. And when he tried to picture her, he saw only Emma's face.

⌛

Berlin looked alien now. There were no longer flower vendors on the streets; no one hawked sausages or peonies or cream-filled pastries to pass-ersby. At least half of the people he could see were in one or another of the wonderful variety of Nazi uniforms. And many of those looked thread-bare. Gunter shifted his duffel from one hand to the other, repositioned his now-precious map case and pistol, and strode along a sidewalk that seemed to be located on a planet he had never visited before. Ahead was one of Albert Speer's masterpieces of overkill. This one housed the *persona grata* of the currently frustrated German Empire. In front of the entrance to Luftwaffe Headquarters stood goose-stepped sentries, crossing and re-crossing in an absurd parody of alertness.

"*Heil Hitler!*"

"*Heil Hitler!*" Gunter's Nazi salute was somewhat hampered by the duffel coat he wore over his sole surviving dress uniform. He heard stitches in the shoulder seam rip. In fact, he had traded his own good overcoat for a big jug of grappa just a week previous. The shoddy thing he wore now was all that had been available in the almost exhausted supply store in Amsterdam that he'd visited the day before. He handed it off to the door attendant as he entered, in any case. The uniform he wore under it was still in good shape and clean, having been in his clothing bag for months. Gunter strode down the hallway and made his way into the suite Goebbels occupied.

The Reichsminister, as it transpired, was not in. But the aide-de-camp on duty had a neat little cream-colored envelope for Gunter. Inside was an invitation to a reception at the Reichstag this very evening.

"Herr Oberst, would you care to take luncheon in the cafeteria?"

After his long trip by rail, paired with the satisfaction of knowing what sat inside his map case, the oberst decided that he would, indeed, like that very much.

By its appearance, the reception room gave no indication of being situated in the middle of a war-torn city. Rather, it looked to be the very heart of a prosperous empire that provided every good thing—schnapps, brandy, hothouse tomatoes, pickled eels, potato salad, éclairs, and more. Here was everything that could not be found on the streets of this city, nor, one suspected, in any of the homes in this city that were not occupied by the uniformed elite that populated this hall.

This thought, however, did not stop Gunter from loading the fine china plate the steward handed him as he reached the head of the line. He plucked a fork and, as he made to turn and go take a seat, his eyes landed on the schnapps, brandy, and bottles of wine he saw further up the table. Reluctantly, he sighed and turned away. His meeting with Goebbels required all the sobriety he could muster. His body, which between grief and neglect had been pushed to the limits of its endurance, needed fuel.

Goebbels, his lean intensity positively glowing, approached Gunter as he placed a forkful of *spätzle* into his mouth. Gunter quickly swiped his mouth with his napkin and hurriedly stood to salute the Reichsminister, still chewing.

"My dear Gunter," Goebbels said. "I was so sorry about your family, but *Der Fuhrer* was so insistent that this Jew animal, Adelmann, come to justice. I simply could not allow you to leave your duty station. In fact, he is still adamant regarding the capture of this criminal and anyone who is associated with him. Have you *any* ideas how to accomplish this?"

For once, I have what you *need,* thought Gunter, satisfied with his newfound sense of power. Hannah's letter was, as Ermenthaller had suggested, the ticket to holding sway with Hitler. He searched Goebbels' face and saw … what? Desperation. Need. What had this Dr. Adelmann done to draw the ire and full resources of the Third Reich? And what would they be willing to offer him in order to find this man?

"Herr Reichsminister, I have been questioning everyone we have captured for months now in search of that man," Gunter began. "In fact, only yesterday, in an abandoned residence, I found a communication left behind by fleeing Jews. This letter indicated that this *doktor,* the very one you seek, has fled to a country called Suriname, which I believe is in the northern part of South America." The author of the letter, Gunter thought, was of no consequence. That information would remain his alone.

Goebbels brightened visibly. "Excellent! The Führer will be very pleased. How do you suggest we go about retrieving this criminal?"

Gunter swallowed a satisfied smile. It occurred to him that as much pressure as Hitler had applied to him, it had likely been far more torturously applied to Goebbels. Gunter's curiosity about this Adelmann was approaching wonderment.

"If I may, Herr Reichsminister," began Gunter cautiously, gauging Goebbels' willingness to unburden himself by the look of unease in his eyes, "it may aid in my performance of this task to know ... This Adelmann—what exactly is his crime?"

Goebbels' face became more stern as his jaw clenched. For a moment, Gunter worried that he had overstepped his bounds, but as Goebbels looked around the room, presumably to check for prying eyes, Gunter was reassured that he still held the upper hand in this situation. Goebbels needed him. *Perhaps I can manage to convey this trump card into a vacation!* Gunter thought. *Perhaps, even relief from this godforsaken appointment and the dreadful task of herding Juden!*

Goebbels cleared his throat and spoke quietly. "We have reason to suspect that this Adelmann has stolen top secret information, certain pages belonging to the Führer."

Gunter tilted his head in what he thought was a sympathetic look to Goebbels, hoping to extract as much information as possible.

Goebbels scanned the room again, then continued, "This information ... if made public ..." Goebbels appeared to give a visible shudder.

"At the risk of sounding self-important, I have a great deal of recent experience in catching these people," Gunter told him, affecting an appeasing, confident tone that would instill trust in Goebbels. He noted, as he spoke, the reflexive tensing of Goebbel's shoulders, the tilting of the aristocratic head. "Or, should I say, these animals *masquerading* as people." An appreciative nod from Goebbels. "And I have a useful unit of the right size to perform an extraction."

Goebbel's eyes flared. He was interested. Such a task, Gunter knew, could make heroes of them all in Hitler's eyes.

"How many men and what equipment? What supplies?"

"I have twenty-four men under my current command, and twenty-two of them are in my integrated squads. The one remaining SS trooper would be better with a unit of similarly dedicated soldiers now. His training role is done. I will retain the SS feldwebel I have. He is an excellent man. Twenty-two men, two or three trucks, a motorcycle, and two machine guns should allow me to deal with any resistance I might encounter, and allow me transport to penetrate as far inland as necessary to capture Adelmann and any who accompany him. If you could spare me two light mortars, with such fully trained men as I have, I would be able to deliver the strike force of a *company*."

Goebbels cocked his head quizzically. "It sounds as if you intend a revolution, not to simply arrest some *Juden*!" But his smile was warm and approving.

"*Nein*, Herr Reichsminister," Gunter forced a return smile, "but I will be thousands and thousands of kilometers from other German forces, and I honestly have no idea of the political situation in Suriname. If I do encounter force, resistance, I do not wish the honor of the Reich to suffer."

Goebbels slammed his fist into his other palm, a gesture he had slavishly copied from Hitler himself.

"So be it! I will make representation to *Der Fuhrer* tonight." Then he paused a moment, and his face grew serious. "But please understand, Oberst Kramer, that with such vast resources at your command, and with the critical nature of your target, there will be no room for error in your mission. I need not remind you of the consequences the Führer will exact upon you should you fail." He met Gunter's eyes, and his look betrayed not only severity but a trace of fear.

His gaze instantly shifted, like a mask, and grew light once again. "For now, Gunter, enjoy yourself. You are welcome to indulge in as much of our fine food and amenities as you wish. Perhaps tomorrow I will be able to present you to our leader in person." With that, the two men saluted, and Gunter returned to his meal, which was as nectar of the gods for him.

Despite Goebbels' warning, Gunter was quite proud of what he had just accomplished and confident he would prevail in his task. Gunter had met Hitler on several earlier occasions and, frankly, did not care if he ever did so again. Whatever pleased the man was of no interest to Gunter. However, anything that would give him (and his men) respite from the excruciating pursuit of innocents, time to heal, and freedom from Hitler's ruthless, incessant pressure was worth the effort of attending to this mission. *Men are dying in Africa and Poland and on the oceans because of Der Führer's idiocy, and this ass licker refused me a last visit with my girls*, thought Gunter ruefully. *I will take whatever I can get from them.*

Oddly, though, Gunter did not indulge himself that night. He drank a small glass of schnapps, ate two platefuls of the rich food, and trundled off to the distinctly inelegant bed he had been provided in bachelor officer's quarters. There he hung his uniform, patting it in lieu of a press, and slept dreamlessly.

On the following morning, late, Goebbels greeted him effusively, ordered luncheon fetched, and delivered a briefing on the persons and institutions of the Surinamese government. He provided something Gunter had not seen for over a year: real coffee. Gunter found himself nearly swooning. The aroma reminded him of how he and Greta had often taken pastries and the rich coffee of the Austrian pastry shop together while they courted. The realization stiffened and fed his cold determination to extract from this elitist, murderous sycophant all he needed to escape, if only for a few months, the horror that his world had become. But the remainder of his coffee sat in its gold-rimmed cup and became cold through the rest of the interview.

CHAPTER 22

SEPTEMBER 20, 1942
EARLY AFTERNOON

PARAMARIBO, SURINAME

Adelmann's clinic was a sprawl, some parts frame, some adobe buildings, and still more wattle and daub. The doctor had been tacking on bits here and there ever since he'd started the clinic as his business two years ago, and the necessity of housing patients had grown. These days, it was fully stocked with the essentials of preventive care, including quinine and mosquito nets, and, at last, it contained an entirely sterile operating room and delivery room.

Two weeks ago, this had enabled Adelmann—with help from Sarah, who had been working as the doctor's assistant for several weeks now—to deliver the Butlers' third child, a daughter whom they had named Talia, which meant "dew from heaven."

The gorgeous child, who had been born with a full head of chocolate-brown hair and was just as beautiful as her mother, had been remarkably good-natured and easy thus far. Today it was time for her two-week exam with the good doctor. Although George was certainly a proud papa, he had been needed at the store today and would not have come with Lijsbet had this visit not served a dual purpose: He had received a disconcerting communication on the wireless today.

George drove gingerly with his precious cargo, dodging a donkey cart and a man with a wheelbarrow using the middle of the street as he made his way through downtown Paramaribo, which by local standards was a big city. As he parked his Plymouth in front of the clinic, George recognized the doctor's car, a 1938 Buick Special, cream-colored and gleaming. Adelmann truly had a taste for the finer things. George had ridden in that car many a night after imbibing in more than his fair share of Adelmann's fine wines.

"Oh! Talia! My lovely girl! Doctor Adelmann, the Butlers are here!" exclaimed Sarah as she quickly sidled up to Lijsbet to get a glimpse of the newborn. She had looked at no one but the infant. George's face made a half grin. *No one notices the father,* George thought, chuckling to himself, because he knew this was as it should be.

Sarah had never dreamed of working in a clinic, ministering to the sick. Back in Germany, she and Michael had planned a family; she had assumed she would raise children and care for their home while he worked with his father in the newspaper business his family owned. It was this business, Sarah had always suspected, that led the Lipinskis to be among those first targeted by Nazis.

Since he had gone, she had been adrift. Once she and her sister's family had gotten established in their new home, and Jacob had begun earning a respectable living—more than respectable, in truth—she had felt it was time to stop relying on their kindness and have her own home, despite their urgings that she was always at home wherever they were. Remaining with them would keep her tied to the past, and Sarah had never been one for looking back. It was time to find her future.

Within two weeks of having arrived at Paramaribo, Hannah had contracted a terrible flu, and her high temperature and violent coughing had been cause for great concern. Sarah and Rebecca had both ministered to Hannah around the clock, giving her cold compresses and boiling water to fill the basin—along with a few drops of peppermint oil—so that the girl could breathe in the steam and gain a bit of relief.

Rebecca, who would never again feel secure in her children's health after the loss of Ezekiel, had insisted, after one terrible night of endless coughing, that Hannah pay a visit to Dr. Adelmann's clinic. No doubt he would have made a house call, but they also knew how busy his clinic was and how hard it was these days for him to pull himself away. Not to mention that he had done so much for them already. They had no wish to feel even more indebted to him. Not wanting to wait a moment longer than necessary, the sisters had assisted in pulling Hannah out of bed by each offering a shoulder to lean on and wrapping their arms around her back to support her. The poor girl was desperately weak with fever. Sarah had placed a call to George, who had come over in his car to drive them all to the clinic.

When they arrived, they found the clinic in a state of chaos. The lobby was filled to standing-room only; no one occupied the front desk to handle incoming patients, and the desk was covering in assorted piles of papers and files.

Sarah and Rebecca had managed to get Hannah into a folding chair to rest, and while Rebecca sat with her daughter, Sarah went in search of the doctor or any official-looking staff member to determine whether Hannah could be seen and when.

"Oh! Hello, Sarah! What are you doing here, my dear?" had come Adelmann's voice from behind her. She whirled around, relief flooding her.

"Yes, hello, Doctor! Our Hannah is sick, so her mother and I have brought her to see you. Would you have time to examine her? You appear..." she fumbled for the words to express his disheveled appearance and dire administrative conditions that would not insult him, "quite busy."

He sighed heavily. "Yes, my dear, you've noticed." He gave a defeated smile and shrugged. "I apologize. My assistant resigned her post this week, and I find myself rather...shorthanded, indeed. But of course, yes, if Hannah can wait just a few more minutes, I will attend to her as quickly as I can." His arms were full of files and clipboards, and he spun in place, scanning the corridor for a place to set the armload.

Sarah rushed to his side and wordlessly took the burden from him. "Can I help?" she then offered. *Anything to get Hannah into an exam room quickly.* "I'm quite good at organizing. I have helped to care for my niece and nephews for many months now, so perhaps I could provide some relief and attention to patients?"

Adelmann's eyes widened. "Oh! My dear! Could you really?" But even as he asked, he began handing her files that had made up a tall stack on a nearby table. "I would be forever in your debt! Here, please take these files and put them in that room there," he said, handing over the pile and pointing to the room behind her. "We can file them later. How many patients are in the lobby? Can you start making a waiting list?"

Sarah deftly dropped the files in the file room and competently took over the front desk, assembling the haphazard piles into some sort of order and working her way through the crowded room to make a list of patients in order of arrival. Some, she found, had problems that could be addressed without the doctor—cleaning and bandaging cuts, removing splinters, or suggesting home remedies for indigestion. Within forty minutes, Hannah was in Adelmann's exam room; within forty-five, she had medicine to take, and Sarah had a new full-time job as Adelmann's assistant.

The work had enabled her by mid-August to secure a room to rent on her own, but more importantly, it had given her renewed sense of purpose. She had managed to get to know most everyone in this small city—at some point, everyone needed to visit the only local doctor—and had felt she was truly contributing, finding her place. This strange, humid place across the world from where she'd grown up was beginning to feel like home, and she had a real place in it.

Though she had taken no time at all in whipping the clinic's administrative functions into shape—organizing the file room, developing a system of keeping appointments, overseeing all billing—she also had needed to step in and assist the doctor with patients when necessary, and this had proven challenging. Not that she was squeamish, but there was so much to remember! It would be difficult enough to remember many of the names of the various maladies and medications she had encountered, but the language barrier had provided an extra layer of difficulty. Fortunately, Dr. Adelmann had been more than patient with her and spoke to her in German most of the time as she was learning the local languages—she knew a little Dutch, the official language, but English was spoken frequently here, as was the local pidgin, Taki Taki, an odd combination of the two spoken commonly among local merchants and dock workers.

Of course, one of her most memorable, most emotional experiences since working in the clinic had been providing aid during Lijsbet's delivery of little Talia. Hearing the glorious, healthy screams emitted from that tiny body as it breathed its first air, and watching Lijsbet's face as Dr. Adelmann pronounced the child a girl and gently handed her over, had been life-changing for Sarah. Nursing, she now felt, was her calling. Talia had, and would always have, a special place in Sarah's heart.

⧗

"Your little girl is quite healthy!" proclaimed Dr. Adelmann as he gingerly lifted the baby from the exam table and handed her to Lijsbet.

"And a genius, too!" George said proudly, stroking his daughter's forehead. "She naps immediately after Lijsbet puts her down. And look at those eyes! The eyes of a genius. So soulful."

Lijsbet just rolled her eyes and looked over at Sarah, who just shook her head and laughed.

"Well, please bring this genius in to see me in six months," Dr. Adelmann said. "I expect she'll be ready to apprentice in my clinic when I see her next, is that right, George?"

"You see it, too, then?" George said.

Lijsbet, rocking the baby, who had grown a bit fussy, stepped toward the door, with Sarah accompanying her. George stayed behind and called to his wife, "I'll be out in a moment, *Schatze!*"

He turned to Dr. Adelmann and the two stopped walking. "Can we speak for a moment, privately?" George asked, his voice low. "I've received a communication."

Understanding dawned on Adelmann's face. "Of course."

The two men stepped into the clinic's supply room. Adelman found a step ladder, which he and Sarah often used to pull supplies from the uppermost shelves. He gestured for George to take a seat, then leaned against the wall with his arms folded in front of him. "What is troubling you, my friend?"

"Hendrick picked up a signal from a ship in the Atlantic last night. One of his bosom friends, a seaman, who had received a transmission from a ship, the *Klein-Seyditz*. A Nazi ship."

Adelmann looked, puzzled, at George. "I would expect that your night operator frequently hears word of Nazi ships. The Nazis are crawling all over the Atlantic, like a sea of cockroaches."

"Headed for Suriname," George flatly cut him off. "Hendrick's sources are reliable, as you know."

Adelman nodded. Hendrick's sources had provided a vital link to family members abroad when they had been planning to flee Germany. He rubbed his face thoughtfully and sighed. "Why Suriname? Do they know something?"

"It could be anything. Hendrick could not decipher any details about the mission or who is on board. Only that the captain's name is Krager. It left Norway for Belgium yesterday, where it will collect troops and head for Suriname," George explained.

"Do you know when they will arrive?"

"We cannot know for sure, although a trip of that length … perhaps two weeks? Three?"

"We must hold them off."

George furrowed his brow. "How are we to do that?"

Adelmann met his eyes. "Do not forget, I have some very important patients here at my clinic."

George nodded. "Of course. But we cannot hold them off forever. We need intelligence, military assistance … We will need a plan. Our refugees must be told."

"Not just yet," Adelmann said, holding his hand up to silence George. "We don't want to cause a panic. First, we make a plan. Who do we know?"

A moment of silence passed, the two men staring at the floor, thoughtfully rubbing their chins. Then, it was as if someone switched on a light. They looked up and met each other's eyes at the same moment.

A slow grin spread across George's face. "Are you thinking of the same person I am?"

"If you mean Ed Beltran, yes, I am!" Adelmann said, brightening. "Of course! He is just the man to help us! But how can we contact him? We cannot exactly send a telegram into the jungle."

George laughed. "Oh, he can usually be counted upon to purchase supplies at my store a couple of times a month. I would expect to see him in Paramaribo any day now."

CHAPTER 23

SEPTEMBER 20, 1942
6:30 A.M.

SOUTHWEST SURINAMESE RAINFOREST, NEAR KWAMALASAMUTU

Ed Beltran unslung his 1906 Springfield and laid it gently across the buckskin sandbag on the shooting table. Its walnut stock gleamed with hand-rubbed linseed oil, as it had from the day it had been issued to "Private Beltran" at Paris Island in 1918. The flat-brimmed, tan Stetson bearing Marine insignia shaded his hands and the rifle's receiver from the sunlight, cutting the glare.

When he had received his battlefield commission in France as a lieutenant, they had insisted on trading him an officer's .45 Colt for his beloved rifle. The pistol, admittedly, had been invaluable in the trenches, but he had never loved it. He later wound up *buying* the rifle from the Marine Corps so that he'd never need to fear being dispossessed of his loyal friend. It did not leave his side for the rest of WWI, had killed many a German and saved many a Marine.

Just after he had at last achieved the rank of lieutenant colonel, a short mortar round during field maneuvers had sliced up his leg and ended his military career.

Now Ed inserted live .45 rounds as earplugs. Today he was firing full loads and going for the 2,000-yard targets. That meant, he knew, walking about four miles in the freshly fierce sun of Suriname to check them, but that too was part of his daily routine—his way of coping with the damned limp. It was an impediment that he was pleased to see diminishing slightly each year, but nonetheless it was enough to keep him from active service and certainly enough to make trudging through the rainforest extra challenging.

Retired after twenty-two years with the corps, living in a tropical place far from his country and culture, he had found a kind of quiet, if lonely, happiness. A career's savings had been sufficient to buy this big farm in this very small country. It was mostly jungle, but there was enough open grazing ground for him to actually *have* a 2,000-yard rifle range with a good hill for a backstop. All in all, Ed's retirement wasn't at all boring. His gardens, fields, and small herds fed him and the couple he employed, and his military pension was adequate for bullets, booze, and the other necessities of life of a country gentleman.

Although, that pension hadn't shown up for months now, what with the wartime foul-ups in communications. Fortunately, he had enough fuel for months of truck and tractor use, plenty of whiskey, and George, up in Paramaribo, who sent him the occasional convoy guards to train, and bought Ed's coffee crop at fair prices so Ed had a little bit of cash on hand. George saw to it that Ed never lacked necessities, and Ed made sure George's employees could shoot and seek cover.

George and Ed had first met when Ed had driven into Paramaribo, almost in desperation, to find supplies he simply could not obtain in Kwamalasamutu. Conversations with George at his store, and again later at his bank, as well as observation of the bank's rather haphazard security practices had led Ed to offer training for George's people. He had done this intermittently ever since.

That relationship later burgeoned into a job with the mines. Ed eked out pay during his retirement by training security people, not only for his friend George but for the bauxite mines in Suriname. Most able-bodied American men young enough to stand up to the rigors of Suriname were engaged in war preparations elsewhere, and the weaponry skills and discipline necessary to provide mine security simply were not to be found in these backward countries. One of the engineers at the biggest mine had complained about the problem to George, who supplied that mine with food and fuel. George had made a trip into the jungle in person to see whether Ed would take on the job.

Both the Dutch and British had despicably mistreated their slaves in the last century, and the result of people fleeing the cruelty was that several almost-purely West African tribes were now living in the Surinamese interior. There was some intermarriage with the local Indians, but relatively little.

The Dutch referred to them as "Bush Negroes." Those people were terribly poor, universally distrusted white men, and often engaged in violence against travelers and vulnerable businesses in the backcountry.

Ed's answer, in part, had been to take several of those bandits-by-default, captured by Surinamese police after a raid on one of the mines, and put them through his private equivalent of boot camp. At first he had worked them at gunpoint and shackled them at night, as if he were training tigers, but after a few weeks of good food and having being trained in combat skills, map skills, sanitation, and basic English, all but one of his prisoners had become intrigued by the process, just as Ed had hoped, and he had given them a choice: stay and train until he could find them work or go home. Only one had opted for the latter, and Ed had trucked the man to his home village, handed him a sack of food, and waved him off. Ed then stopped shackling his "recruits" at night, began giving them guard responsibilities on his farm, and gave them firearms training at a level they had never imagined. He also fed them at his own table and added table manners and personal hygiene to their training.

When he was done, he had five honed warriors who were in useful awe of him and who had enough basic English to communicate with the managers and engineers at mines like the one they had tried to loot. Those men became the core of the security forces Ed maintained for Suriname's mines, their bush skills allowing them mobility that the coastal dwellers who worked the mines simply did not have.

These days, he only found it necessary to visit the mines every few weeks, to check on routines and make sure his men were being paid and decently treated. Of course, those visits gave him a chance to collect his own contracting fee for their work and his consultation in the development of mine security routines.

If he trained a few more men to officer level, that income would grow to be more than his pension.

Plus, as bonus, he got to eat and drink at his friend George's table and meet fascinating new people.

⧗

The day had become unbearably hot. He stood perspiring on a low hill, looking down at his home, breathing deeply after a couple of brisk miles of walking, stretching away the cramp that always seized him around the thigh when he challenged his damaged leg. Inocente, the young woman he employed to care for the household, would have the copper hip bath in the little gazebo out back half full of hot water by now. In the arrangement Ed had made with Inocente and her husband, Ysidro, when they all had first come here to live, the couple could use the tub while Ed was shooting, and they always had it ready for him when he finished his agonizing walk.

The house was very simple, consisting of two wings of whitewashed wattle and daub walls, along with a thatched roof made of tough reeds from the nearby river. Ed occupied one wing, and Inocente and Ysidro—along with the home's big harvest kitchen—the other. Ed and Ysidro, his cook/workman, were old friends. Ysidro had been one of Ed's sergeants in Nicaragua during the long campaign there. Inocente had been a pretty little girl in one of the villages that the men had been called upon to protect from the Sandinistas' depredations. Ysidro had fallen immediately, deeply in love with her and had plucked her from the village the moment he was able. Ed had maintained a correspondence with Ysidro over the years, partly because he was fond of his old battle comrade and partly to maintain his own fluency in Spanish. Though he had been unable to get leave to attend their wedding, he'd sent a good chunk of cash as a gift.

When he had come to this remote place to retire, he had invited the pair to join him. They had done so happily—the couple providing invaluable service to him, particularly in light of his injury, and he providing additional, needed financial security. Ysidro, though now a master sergeant in the Nicaraguan army, was looking at a tiny pension, not really enough to live on well. It was a good arrangement for all of them.

Ed supposed that when they had children, he would either need to make his house bigger or build another one for them, or perhaps for himself, just out of earshot.

Ed pushed his massive door open, then paused a moment to allow his eyes to adapt to the cool darkness within. He laid the Springfield down on the wicker table by the entryway and sat in the matching chair beside it to unlace the heavy combat boots he always wore to the range and on his hikes. Dropping his socks in the bucket that awaited them, Ed eased his feet into his house shoes and padded across the big red tiles to his bedroom.

Inocente had, of course, already made up his bed and lain a fresh change of clothes out on top of it. Several changes were piled next to the old folding canvas duffle bag. She had included a few dress shirts and some decent slacks, shined leather shoes, and even, against the possibility of dinner at the president's palace, which happened in Paramaribo rather often for George and his guests, added a tie and dress jacket. Ed made these trips often enough that his staff knew the drill as well as he did, and they also knew that he preferred to pack his own bag so he would know where things were.

Beginning to limp a bit as he stiffened in the cool house, Ed shed his sweated-through clothing into another ready bucket, flipped a towel about his middle, and sought the comfort of the tub. Inocente had instituted the bucket program for all dirty clothes. "I never touch them until the boiling water hits them," she'd told both men in her broken English. Considering the usual condition of their clothing after wear in this environment, both men agreed and cooperated.

Reaching his back door entailed passing through his library/living room/workshop. Tools of all descriptions hung or were shelved on one wall and consisted of everything from leatherworking tools to small wrenches, screwdrivers, and the paraphernalia of machining. Along that wall were three massive tables, hardwood-topped and variously burned, pitted, or cut. One held a small milling machine, a drill press, and a medium-sized lathe. An exception to this Catholic assemblage was the meticulously clean stand that held his reloading presses, powder canisters, and brass strategically in front of the best window so that he could see every grain of powder or scratch on a casing while working. There was no room for sloppiness when you were crafting ammunition.

Where tools did not hang, books were racked, their titles mostly in English, but a significant portion were in Spanish and some in French. Ed had accumulated and stored books throughout his career, and one of the biggest expenses of coming to South America for retirement had been the shipment of decades of books he'd hoarded. There were thousands of volumes, from Clausewitz to Jefferson, Machiavelli to Tolstoy, Cervantes to Segovia.

In the gazebo, screened against insects and tightly latticed to chest height for the preservation of the rather casual modesty they practiced, Ed gingerly settled into the steaming tub. He submerged as far under the surface as he could get, then slowly came up again to reach the little table beside the tub that held his mirror, razor, brush, and strop, as well as a massive mug of hot, strong coffee.

The smell of grilling bacon wafted past as he stroked his face with the gleaming blade. At Inocente's insistence, meals were taken at the big table in the kitchen, not, as Ed would otherwise have done, eaten off one's lap while reading or from a plate on a worktable. She did permit reading at the table when Ed was dining alone, as he did at breakfast time, but always managed at least one disapproving look when he did that.

Bathed, shaved, cleanly dressed, packed, and fed, Ed was a very contented man as he carried his bulging clothing bag and rifle to the truck. Inocente and Ysidro awaited him there.

Ed unclipped his web belt, weighted with flap-holstered .45, a Bowie bayonet, and six spare magazines, tossed it to the passenger side of the seat, lay the rifle and bandolier of ammunition across it before he climbed into the pickup, putting the clothing bag on the floor in front of the passenger's side of the wide seat. Despite having trained a handful of the bush folk, and the fact that they and their families liked him, there were far too many of their kinfolk making a living off road banditry to travel unarmed.

Inocente proffered a sizable basket topped with white linen and a thermos that he knew held more of her wonderful coffee. He put them inside the truck, then accepted the bottle of quinine pills she passed him—a prevention measure against malaria. He would, after all, be in the jungle for a couple of days. He took a pill from the bottle and took a quick swig from the thermos to wash the thing down. He made a mental note to stock up on the stuff from George's store when he got to Paramaribo.

He looked beyond his treasured cook to see her husband smirking and could not help but grin back, remembering the hundreds of miles they had ridden and trudged together in the old days. He took the pleasant-smelling bundle and put it carefully on the passenger-side floor, atop the clothing bag. It was heavy enough to feed an elephant, and he would only be gone for two days in Paramaribo, but he wouldn't dare complain to Inocente, whose burgeoning belly was the reason his old friend Ysidro would not be joining him.

"You two take care of the place and each other while I'm gone," Ed said, nodding his thanks to his friends. "I should be back in no more than a week."

The pickup, sturdy old Chevy that it was, started smoothly, and Ed rumbled down the road.

⧗

In no place along this route was it possible to make better than jogging speed. As much as possible, Ed wanted to get through unnoticed. Of course, the engine made noise and in many places the truck left a dust plume, but anyone likely to attack him would be on foot, not mounted or motorized. With any luck, he would be past them before they could set up a stop, but he had to be vigilant. Every time he was about to emerge from a jungle patch or came to a glade's edge, he put the truck in neutral, set the handbrake, and watched the way ahead with the heavy 8-by-50 binoculars whose case was glued to the dashboard. He paid particular attention to places where he knew he would be coming on blind turns.

So went the morning, and after having driven perhaps four hours and topping off the gas tank twice, it was time for a personal exhaust and refill. He went a few feet off road with the shovel, did his business, then stashed the tool and washed his hands and dripping face before finishing off Inocente's food and the last gulp of her coffee.

He had been entering and leaving patches of brush and jungle at lower elevations and sometimes areas of naked rock at the upper elevations. Knowing that over the past couple of hours he could have alerted hostiles far and wide with his truck's exhaust and kicked-up dust, and knowing what ambush-friendly ground lay ahead, Ed took his rifle, bandolier, and binoculars out of the truck and climbed a nearby slope by foot, pausing at the crest behind a tree to scout out the road ahead.

Unfortunately, he had not turned the glass on his own surroundings, and realized his mistake too late when he heard a call that sounded like a war cry and lowered the binoculars just in time to see a man with sinewy muscles charging toward him.

Ed's jaw dropped. As the bandit came at him from around the truck at tremendous speed, he yanked a broad-bladed machete from the sheath that hung along his right leg. He was screaming still, in rage or perhaps fear. He leaped bushes and dodged rocks in a run that was as agile as a cat's.

As the attacker closed in, Ed could see that he faced a boy, not a fully grown man, and relaxed a bit. His own training and weaponry would make this boy an easy opponent. He slid his hand to grasp the bayonet.

As the youngster delivered his first full-armed slice, Ed parried with a reaching glissade that deflected the blade from the boy's high right to lower left, and pushed it toward the boy's still ungrounded left leg, then rapidly twitched his point back from the parry and poked the boy's leanly corded forearm, just an inch in, stopping on bone. It was an almost surgical insertion, precisely directed. The boy's hand spasmed open and the machete clattered onto rock. Ed couldn't help grinning. He stepped back, holding the rifle with his forestock grip, and held up his open right hand in a sign of peace.

It was a mistake. The boy snatched up the machete with his left hand, then, in the blink of an eye, he brought it up in an underhand slice that chopped into the outer edge of Ed's left hand. It was the Springfield's turn to clatter on rock.

Now pissed off beyond all reason, Ed snatched his Colt .45 out of its holster. Tears of pain blurred his vision, and the machete was swinging again, so Ed fired before bringing the pistol fully into line. The slug passed along the youngster's smooth cheek, opening a furrow and taking off the lower third of his right ear. The muzzle blast crisped his skin, and his eyes clamped shut in shock. He staggered back, dropping the big knife, and, clapping his hands over his eyes, fell backwards, his screams now pure pain.

Ed flipped the safety up on the Colt, holstered it, dug out his bandanna, and wrapped his bleeding hand. He then recovered the Springfield, which was just a little scuffed, propped the weapon safely behind him, and leaped upon his wailing foe. The boy wasn't done yet, but a couple of cuffs at his bleeding head and an arm lock had his hands tied securely behind his back in seconds.

Ed peeled back the boy's eyelids to see if his eyes had taken damage and was rewarded by the lad spitting in his face and delivering a fierce curse in a language Ed found incomprehensible. Ed slugged him again in return, then wound the bandanna around the boy's wrists, holding him tightly down to the ground with a firm knee. He grabbed the boy's machete and tucked it into his own belt.

The bound boy attacked, kicking, screaming, and trying to bite. Ed put his rifle butt into the boy's solar plexus, heel-hooked the feet out from under him, added a sharp kidney kick, and left his young opponent retching and gagging on the ground as he headed to the truck for some rope to tie the boy up.

By the time he had the boy back at the truck, Ed's left arm felt like it was going to fall off. He made his way to his foot locker, a good third of the contents of which were medical supplies. Ed first used a clean cloth and water, washed his hands thoroughly, then dug out a bottle of potassium permanganate and, wincing, laid back the clotting flap on his hand to sprinkle the wound full of the painful stuff. He added sulfa powder, put gauze pads and tape on the hand so that he could touch things without flinching, and guzzled a couple of quarts of water.

Then he filled the thermos cup and gave water to the boy, whose eyes widened incredulously but who eagerly sucked that and several more cups down. His eyes followed Ed with an expression of curiosity and apprehension. But he held still while Ed examined his wounds. His clothing was a simple loincloth and kilt of some kind of leather. His only accessory seemed to have been the machete.

The flies had already blown all over the boy's face wound and ear. Ed rinsed the wound with water to prevent infestation by maggots, then poured alcohol and potassium permanganate over the wound as the youngster writhed and jerked about. Ed held him down with one knee, sprinkled on sulfa powder, and as he had done with his own hand, packed the wound with fluffy gauze. Using a long roller bandage, he wrapped the boy's head from crown to jaw to hold the gauze in place, and added tape to secure the roller bandage. Finally, he shook out four big aspirin tablets for each of them, demonstrated that he was taking his, and received no resistance when he administered the same dose to his prisoner. For himself, Ed added a gulp from the whiskey bottle that lived in the footlocker.

He might just try to recruit this little spitfire.

CHAPTER 24

SEPTEMBER 22, 1942
11:00 A.M.

PARAMARIBO, SURINAME

Sarah jumped as the door to Dr. Adelmann's clinic burst open that morning to reveal a startling sight: a large, sweaty man with a rifle slung over his shoulder and a crudely bandaged hand, who was using his other shoulder to support a young, half-naked brown man whose bruised face was encircled by a bloody bandage.

"Doc in?" the large man called abruptly to Sarah, who jumped but took a few seconds to recover from the sight and another to recognize the American accent and his casual way of speaking before responding.

"Oh! Yes!" Sarah finally answered, remembering herself. The realization dawned on her that she probably should get up and help him, so she jumped up from the desk, where she had been organizing files from the morning's patient visits. She scrambled around the desk and went to the young man's other side. "Right this way," she said, helping to lead the two men directly back to an exam room.

Upon finding the good doctor at the hallway prep sinks, scrubbing his hands and splashing his face, Sarah called out to him. "Doctor Adelmann, please help us!"

Adelmann turned with an instantly serious expression on his face. But then Sarah saw the most extraordinary thing: The serious face changed as a broad smile spread across his face, and he stood watching as Sarah helped the larger man maneuver the injured boy into a chair in the hallway.

"Ed Beltran!" the doctor said in a mocking tone. "As I live and breathe. George and I were just speaking of you the other day. I presume you're in town for a supply run?"

"Hey there, Doc," Ed said, standing up and answering with a guilty grin. "That's right. But, uh…I've brought you something."

"I see that. What have we here?" Adelmann asked, gingerly approaching the boy and peering down to get a closer look. Sarah looked on in wonderment. Dr. Adelmann knew this man?

"Happened a couple of days ago, deep in the jungle. It's been a rough couple of days, Doc, let me tell you."

"Yes, I'm sure," the doctor said, peering at the boy's bandaged ear.

"Gunshot wound, shallow, half the ear gone," Ed answered the doctor's unasked questions, sketching the direction of the wound with a finger held above the bulging bandage. "Didn't break through into the mouth, but it did get flyblown before I could clean it out with water and alcohol and then put in potassium permanganate and some sulfa powder."

Adelmann looked at Ed, startled. "You were there?"

Ed grinned sourly. "Well… see… *I* shot him."

A gasp escaped from Sarah before she could stop it. It was enough to stop Ed, who, now that his load had been lightened, seemed to just remember that she was there.

"It seemed like a good idea at the time," he told her by way of an excuse, shrugging and giving her a grin. *A criminal in our office!* Sarah thought, panicked.

She directed her own gaze to Adelmann, whose eyebrows raised. "Is that right?" Then, noticing Sarah's expression of fear, smiled. "Ed, my assistant and nurse, Sarah Lipinski. Sarah, my dear, this is our old friend Ed Beltran. You need not be afraid, I assure you, he does not make a habit of shooting people." Then, turning to Ed, he added, "Unless you've changed since last I saw you? I know that life in the jungle can be harsh."

"Nah," he answered, brushing off the question. "Self-defense. This one jumped me in the bush. Got me pretty good, too," he chuckled, holding up his bandaged hand. "Machete. I was impressed. He may just be my newest recruit." His chest seemed to puff up as he said this last proudly.

"Recruit?" Sarah repeated. Although she had come very far with her English and could now carry on daily exchanges in the language, this was a word she had never encountered. Ed eyed her quizzically.

"My dear," Adelmann began, turning his attention to Sarah and switching to German for clarity, "Ed is a former Marine from America, and he trains young men for combat, for security purposes. A 'recruit' is a new trainee. I assure you, he is quite safe."

Ed looked on at the exchange, taken aback at hearing German—an unfriendly tongue these days, Sarah knew. She tried not to use it as much as possible.

Adelmann then switched to English upon seeing that he had unintentionally unnerved Ed. "Sarah, I am sure that Colonel Beltran will tell you the entire story, but first, I must ask you to scrub again and prepare to assist me with our patients."

⧗

Between the three of them, moving the injured boy, whose name turned out to be Azi, had been fairly easy. He was lain on the exam table. Adelmann immediately began calling out orders to Sarah in rapid-fire German. "I will need a scalpel, a flushing syringe, hydrogen peroxide, a liter of the sterile saline solution, and…one of those quart ball jars. Two large suture kits and one small one, gauze, bandages, including a roller bandage… Is there water boiling still? We will need to bathe the affected areas."

Sarah looked terrified but scampered to respond. Despite her weeks of service to the doctor, the majority of her assistance had been with minor cuts and scrapes, fevers, and very occasionally a bone break. She was in new territory here.

"You didn't have a nurse the last time I was here, just those ham-handed assistants who used to call themselves doctors," Ed said to the doctor as Sarah walked away. Ed's eyes followed her retreating figure, a gesture that Adelmann noticed with amusement.

"Sarah is a widowed lady of my faith who arrived with a group of refugees quite recently," Adelmann explained. "She will be a good field doctor in another year. She is already an excellent midwife and a fine operating room nurse." He drew a steaming bucket of water from the reservoir on the large wood stove that stood against the brick sidewall of the lobby then poured in another from a line of buckets against the same wall. Opening a cupboard, he extracted a stack of towels and washing cloths, dropped them into the water, seized upon a jug of liquid soap, and added, still quietly as he strode toward the operating room, "In all justice, she is progressing faster than my local doctor trainees, not only because she is smarter, but because she can read German, and all of my textbooks and references are in German."

Ed was dumbfounded. "A woman *doctor*?" He had never heard of such a thing.

Adelmann was amused. "Think about it. Women have to make hard choices all the time. They are caring, have good hands, and are often clever with them. In caring for themselves and children, they are trained in dealing with unpleasantness. In fact, there are a few women with medical degrees in Germany already."

It was a messy business, working on Azi's wounds, because the only thing available for pain short of full anesthesia was opium pills, which didn't dull facial sensation too well. Still, the boy cooperated, and Sarah was truly deft, debriding the cheek wound, suturing it where that was feasible, trimming and stitching a new lower edge for the ear, then flushing the bayonet wound in Azi's forearm, spreading the lips of the thing and probing. Everyone flinched when her probing brought forth a small geyser of pus (though Sarah did fairly well at concealing her disgust), but Dr. Adelmann gave a sigh of relief at the sight.

"Get in there and flush as forcefully as you can, Sarah." She gritted her teeth and nodded assent, holding her breath to avoid the odor that was wafting up from the wound.

The doctor began to wash down the smeared arm and blot up the puddles on the operating table. "And Ed, if I may solicit your help, I need another bucket of very hot water and about half as many towels as I put in this one."

Ed nodded, seeming to appreciate being given a direct order. *Military men are all alike, no matter where they are,* Sarah thought with some condemnation. She had had her fill of military men. Unaccountably, she bristled at him as she watched him leave to find a bucket.

Adelmann looked at Sarah and Ed, noting the tension between them. Suppressing a grin, he spoke English.

"Sarah, we will put this young fellow in the first sleeping hut and start compressing the arm immediately. Get another bucket and more towels and put them in the hut. Ed and I will get the boy in there and get the oil cloth under his arm. And I want the compresses to be renewed at ten-minute intervals for at least two hours." Sarah looked stricken. She couldn't help it. She would be forced to spend hours at this roadside bandit's bedside?

"I will begin the compresses, and I want you to scrub this table, get fresh instruments after you rescrub and reglove, then please treat Colonel Beltran's hand in here, and determine whether it requires hot compressing as well. When you have made that determination, let me know, and one of us can go fetch one of the housekeepers to keep the compresses going for one or both."

Sarah sighed and nodded again. She could feel Ed's eyes upon her, but she refused to look at him. "Yes, Doctor."

As Adelmann made his way out the door with the bucket of dirty towels, he stopped and looked toward Ed. "And Colonel, will I be seeing you at the Butlers' home this evening? George and I have a certain matter to discuss with you."

"That's right," Ed nodded, tearing his eyes away from Sarah. "I'm looking forward to some of that twenty-year scotch of his."

"Very good," Adelmann nodded, satisfied, and smiled quietly as he left the two alone, shyly glancing at each other.

Azi was already sleepy from the opium, and within a minute or two of being compressed, he went abruptly to full sleep.

Sarah used a sopping hot towel to soak the crusty wrapping of Ed's hand. He sighed heavily. The thing must have been a painful nuisance, Sarah realized, noticing that he seemed to release tightened muscles in his shoulder and neck as soon as the warm towel was applied.

"Thank you."

She smiled softly. This was what she enjoyed most about her work. She obtained enormous satisfaction from providing relief to patients. Even patients like Ed Beltran. "This wound is…healing. But I am going to have to debride the edges where there is dead or dying skin. It will hurt. Do you want some opium?"

"No, I have to get to the Butlers' house tonight. Sounds like they need my attention. Can't do that if I'm nodding off every few minutes. I owe them that much."

She nodded, going about her work. After a few silent moments, her curiosity overcame her. She inquired, "What are you doing here in Suriname, driving alone along roads with bandits?"

"An artillery accident. I have to heal up before they'll let me out of retirement."

"And you live…?"

"I have a *finca*, a ranch, in the jungle down south," he answered, wincing as she attended to his wound. "I live with my housekeeper and her husband, one of my old noncommissioned officers from Nicaragua."

"Nicaragua?"

"There were trail and road bandits there, like our young friend, but more organized and better armed. Called themselves *Sandinistas*. It was back in the '20s, when I was still young. I'd been fighting *your* folks in the first big war," he motioned to her, "but America cut her forces way back after that war, and those of us who were military officers had to find other work for a while."

At his words, her face registered revulsion. How could he associate her with the war-mongering Germans?

"They are not my *volk*!" she insisted, anger and sadness welling up inside her. "They are *Germans*, and I am a *Jew*, and they are *killing* us! And they killed my husband, too!" Tears escaped from her eyes, and she turned quickly to the cabinet to retrieve a towel, silently berating herself for her emotional display and attempting to pull herself together. It had been months since she had been overcome by emotion about the war and Michael, but for some reason, Ed Beltran was pushing uncomfortable buttons.

"Whoa, now," Ed replied, both hands up in a gesture of surrender. "Look, I didn't mean anything…" The sincerity on his face told her that he meant it. Her stony expression softened and a smile crept up one corner of her mouth.

"Now, Colonel Beltran," she said, regaining control of her emotions, "you must hold still, because I need to suture your hand, and it is difficult work."

He nodded his consent, and the two remained silent as Sarah worked and Ed watched her face. She could feel his eyes on her, and her face burned under his attention.

It was evening, after dinner. Lijsbet, on her feet in the kitchen and hold-ing Talia with one arm, used her other hand to pour cups of coffee for her husband, Ed Beltran, and Ben Adelmann with the other. She chuckled at the sight of them, all three leaning back in their chairs and patting their bellies, which had all been properly stuffed by Carmina's delicious cooking. This evening's feast had been traditional Surinamese fare—with curried chicken and potatoes, green beans, and fried plantains. The Butlers' efficient, beloved housekeeper had disappeared shortly after serving dinner and putting four-year-old Skye and two-year-old John to bed—too quickly even to enjoy the moans of delight when the group had taken their first bites.

"I tell you, George, that Carmina's a keeper," Ed said, knocking back his last gulp of scotch and taking Lisjbet's cup of coffee with a nod of thanks.

"This I know, my friend," George said, smugly. Then, catching himself, he added, "Of course, Lisjbet here is a wonderful cook as well…"

"Carmina is a godsend," Lisjbet mused as she looked adoringly down at the sleeping bundle in her arms, then reaching over to pat George's shoulder. "You have not wounded me, *Schatze*, do not worry. Thank goodness for her help around the house, and with Skye and little John, and for Sarah, who attends so wonderfully to little Talia here, so that I may sleep. You owe them a debt of gratitude, those two, for keeping your wife in happy spirits."

Ed's eyes flashed interest at Sarah's name. It was only for a second, unno-ticed by all but Dr. Adelmann.

"She is in my prayers every night, my dear, I assure you," George replied, giving his daughter a soft kiss on her head and another to Lisjbet's cheek as she bent to say good night.

"Good night, *Schatze*. Gentlemen," she said, bobbing her head and head-ing to bed. She stopped and turned. "Ed, the spare room is ready for you."

"That's my girl!" he replied, winking at her. "Thank you, Lisjbet. You are ever the gracious hostess."

Once Lisjbet had left the room, Ed cleared his throat. "So, this Sarah of yours," he began, looking over at the doctor a little too casually, "does she … is she … how did you …?"

An eruption of laughter burst from both George and Adelmann. The gruff, brawny Marine colonel had a school-boy crush!

"Did I miss something?" Ed asked, blushing. "What's so funny?"

"I believe Colonel Beltran is besotted!" George chuckled, sipping his coffee. "But I suppose it must get lonely in the jungle."

"What?" Ed retorted, offended. "You two are nuts. I was only asking a polite question."

"It wasn't your *words* we noticed," Adelmann said, grinning. "Your eyes, and the way you stand at attention at the sound of her name…they told us all we needed to know."

Ed could do nothing but shake his head, embarrassed and disgusted.

"Don't worry. You could do far worse than Sarah Lipinski," Adelmann responded. "She and her family are marvelous people."

"Refugees? Latest batch?" Ed asked, still looking at his coffee cup.

"Yes. In fact, that is what George and I wanted to speak to you about tonight," the doctor said, exchanging glances with George.

"Is that right?" Ed asked, looking up with a raised brow. "Something I can do for you fellows to return your hospitality?"

George cut in, his tone turning serious. "Actually, Colonel Beltran, yes there is. It seems we could use your special training for a situation that has arisen."

"Oh yeah? What kind of situation?" Ed asked, reaching across the table for the nearly empty bottle of scotch and refilling his tumbler.

"It seems a Nazi ship is making its way to us," Adelmann said, looking Ed square in the eyes.

"Nazis? Here? To Suriname?" Ed asked, startled. "What do they want with this place?" Then, instant recognition dawned in his eyes. "Wait a minute… Your refugees, right?"

"Perhaps," Adelmann admitted.

"Herr Adelmann, the good doctor's uncle, was among them," George added.

"But," Adelmann interjected, "there may be more to it. I have a little intelligence of my own. You see, Hitler's plan, his 'Final Solution,' as it is being called—I have reason to believe that it has been stolen."

"Plans? What kind of plans?" Ed asked, noting that even George seemed surprised by this revelation of the doctor's.

"Plans for exterminating Jews," Adelmann said bluntly. "Written proof of Hitler's plans to eliminate Jews. The officers on this ship are hunting for it."

George and Ed sat, blinking at Adelmann. Finally, Ed, the former intelligence Marine, put the pieces together. "If that wound up in the Americans' hands, they'd join the war. It would *end them*."

Ed's words hung in the air as the three men sat in silence.

"Well, I wouldn't mind fighting some dirty ol' Germans again, for old times' sake," Ed said, slapping both hands on the table. "I'm in. When can we expect them?"

"The ship left for Belgium a few days ago. They will gather men there. We estimate … a couple of weeks," George said, looking to Adelmann for confirmation.

"Can we get the president to work with us? You know the guy, Doc, right?" Ed asked.

"Yes, he is a patient, and I believe he will do what he can to support us," Adelmann said. "But we must protect our sources. Until the president himself picks up intelligence of the ship, we say nothing. Agreed?"

The other two nodded solemnly.

"Now," Adelmann said, "to our plan."

"Wait a sec, Doc," Ed cut in, swiping the air with his hands. "What does all this about the Nazi plan have to do with your refugees?"

A slow smile spread across Adelmann's face as Ed and George watched. His eyes went from one to the other, wordlessly. Then, he placed both hands on the table and stood up.

"Gentlemen, let's get to work!"

CHAPTER 25

OCTOBER 8, 1942
7:00 A.M.

SCHEPEN SIFFERDOK, PORT OF GHENT, OCCUPIED BELGIUM

Ermenthaller had them well in hand. Of course, he always did.

Behind the men, who stood in ranks at attention, sat Gunter's favorite half-armored Mercedes, two other trucks with small cargo trailers, and Kucher's sidecar motorcycle. Each truck's cab roof bore a mount that could accept one of the three bipod-equipped MG42 machine guns, now slung from trooper shoulders. Tripods for those were bagged for long-range needs off roads. Crated and stowed in the trucks and trailers were two 8-cm Granatwerfer 34 mortars, two hundred of the finned rounds for them, twenty-thousand rounds for the machine guns, five thousand rounds for the Mausers, field rations for two months, water cans, aid supplies, tires, gasoline cans, and even a couple of cases of schnapps.

Gunter was astounded to realize that the company would be equipped with far more weaponry than he'd requested. And he had never, even in peacetime, been able to assemble weapons and supplies so easily and quickly—even, he noted, with shiny new boots for everyone, despite the recent difficulties in collecting even the barest essentials for his men. Gunter was smug in the knowledge of how desperately Goebbels wanted Adelmann's capture and felt pleased to, finally, be in control.

Three men to each mortar, two to each machine gun if they were on tripods, one to drive each of the trucks, and two men with the motorcycle. That left five riflemen to carry extra ammunition. With each man having a rifle or pistol or Schmeisser submachine gun, he could operate them as one unit or two, with or without the heavy weapons. The medic would not be burdened with anything other than his Luger and kit.

Despite his continuing distaste for their task, even this long-distance and less-intense version of it, Gunter felt pride at his creation. This was a strong, agile unit and could project great force.

Their formation was beside the cobbled road leading to the Schepen Sifferdok. And at that dock was moored the merchant vessel *Klein-Seyditz*, a freighter of 6,000-tonne capacity owned by Kreigs Marine. It was very nearly the largest vessel that could possibly navigate this inland port.

Gunter noted that the handful of sailors on board were lining the rail, staring out with what he believed was some distress. Goebbels had explained that putting soldiers on board a merchant vessel entailed some negotiation, even with the control the Reich exerted over German businesses.

"Oberst Kramer!" Goebbels barked, interrupting Gunter's thoughts. The men exchanged salutes. "They will be able to feed your men while you are on board and to offer shelter in the hold. But you are five times the number of men normally carried aboard. You will have to take some pains to reduce your impact on the crew and their jobs."

"*Jawohl*, Herr Reichsminister," Gunter replied. "I will be drilling my unit and performing vehicle maintenance some portion of each day, and we will offer assistance to the crew in tasks we can help them with."

"You are soldiers of the Reich and are due your dignity," Goebbels nodded, signaling approval. "However, when you return, you may well have two or three dozen prisoners. It is essential that you make friends of the crew on the outbound trip."

He fidgeted for a moment, twirling a letter opener shaped like a miniature saber. *The pressure he is under!* thought Gunter with some relish.

"The Jew, Adelmann, and his immediate family are your primary target. Any other prisoners who interfere with your movements may, and should, be eliminated at your convenience. The Surinamese government is a reluctant cooperator in this effort, so you will need to exercise some discretion at that."

He had just been given blanket permission to murder civilians. Gunter had suspected as much. He just had not been brave enough to think too hard about it.

"I understand, Herr Reichsminister."

Meanwhile, what had occupied Gunter's mind ever since receiving notification of this mission was the length of time it would take: two weeks outbound voyaging after two weeks of staging, then time ashore necessary to make this capture, perhaps a few days after that ashore, and two weeks to return. *Two months at least away from this filthy duty.* And a good portion of it in a warm, tropical place. This would be an independent command, a unit he had put together by himself, and enough arms that they could face two companies of regular troops. He could not have done better for himself, or his men. Nonetheless, Gunter did his best to remain grave-faced and earnest.

Goebbels looked at him intensely and stated, equally intensely, "The Führer is counting on you, Kramer. You are young, but young as you are, this could mean another promotion. I wish you the best of luck." He locked into a position of attention, making it look elegant with his lean, broad-shouldered build, and snapped out his arm in the Nazi salute. "*Heil Hitler!*" His arm quivered with the force of his delivery.

Gunter responded in kind, feeling like a stick figure on a *Punch and Judy* stage.

Now they were ready to embark. The machines would have to be lashed on deck.

Gunter had wanted to leave everything, tarped, on the trucks and trailers, but Ermenthaller had warned him against that, having experienced sea transport of equipment on a deployment to the Sudetenland many years before.

"Herr Oberst, the force of wind out at sea is unbelievable sometimes. I have seen tarps and truck canopies shredded like tissue paper."

Gunter had the greatest of respect for his noncommissioned officer and followed his advice without a second thought. Everything must go into a hold.

When they were done stowing their gear and supplies, Gunter realized how much of their tiny corner of hold space was taken up by them, so he had the men arrange crates and bags as furniture and flooring and left them to make the best of it. Gunter himself had been given the First Mate's cabin out of respect for his rank. He had offered to share it with Ermenthaller, but the sergeant had declined with thanks.

"Herr Oberst, it is not good for young men to be bored with so many weapons close at hand. They need someone older and with authority to keep them behaving safely." Gunter conceded the point, shuddering at the thought of a carelessly fired round ricocheting around the hold.

All of his transport was both chained and rope-lashed to the upper deck, as were the segments of the ramp that had been employed to let them drive on board. Gunter was taking no chances on not being able to offload his machines. The idea of extended marching in a tropical country was not appealing.

There also was an unpleasant surprise. The *Klein-Seyditz*'s captain had no intention of setting sail until the following night.

"And why is that?" Gunter probed. He had thought all the arrangements had been made for this trip. Herr Goebbels, Gunter knew, would not be at all happy when he heard of a delay. They had already been in Belgium for nearly two weeks.

"Because I do not wish to commit suicide or have my ship sunk, Herr Oberst!" the captain said. He was a squatty, bald little man, whose natural stance was bowlegged and balanced. His wry smile was not at all humorous.

Gunter cocked his head inquisitively.

"Tomorrow night will be cloudy. No moon. We have embarked you here, away from the coast, so there is less chance of one of the *verdammt* British seeing you come aboard, but my *Klein-Seyditz* would be a prime target from the air in the *kanal* or the river, and certainly at sea, where there are British vessels. And loyal as we are to the Reich, we are not a military vessel. We have one rifle—for sharks."

Gunter was forced to concede the necessary time. He and Ermenthaller made the best of it. It was a chance to take the men ashore and exercise them, to find thin mattress pads at a local supply depot to make the hold more bearable, and to provide a night of liberty so the men could find women and beer. Even in an occupied country, wherever there were sailors those commodities were available.

On the following night, they slid out to sea—not silently, because the diesel throb echoed, but at least they were not a target luminous with moonlight. There were no running lights, no matches or cigarettes on deck, no flashlights, and no lights in compartments with outside portholes.

By dawn, they were many leagues out to sea, and Captain Krager set a course to put them in fog banks as much as possible all day.

When, on the third day out, cloud cover became a tremendous storm, and the world around them was all immense crashing seas, spume, and spray, he beamed ecstatically. Gunter, on the other hand, was doing all he could just to grip the edge of the chart table and hold on for dear life as he fought back enormous waves of another kind: nausea.

When he had to dash out of the bridge and to the rail, clinging there and heaving, he discovered at least half of his unit already there, with Ermenthaller watching from a hatch and roaring with merciless laughter.

The feldwebel kindly muted his laughter at the sight of his Oberst but was still chuckling helplessly when Gunter staggered over to him and glared. But he soon cracked a smile, though he was wiping dribble away to do so.

"Feldwebel, the least you could do is to get a rope through everyone's belt. We are going to lose men to one of those waves any minute."

Sobered, Ermenthaller whirled to comply, and Gunter lurched again to the rail.

Two days of safety from observation and interception led to Gunter becoming several pounds lighter and very much disenchanted with sea voyaging.

Entering the hold became an olfactory challenge. Not everyone could make it out and to the rail, and for some, the stress of nausea had induced diarrhea.

As soon as it was possible to be on deck without being tethered, Gunter had Ermenthaller bring everyone there for a unit wash down with buckets of sea water. There was a great deal of whooping and gasping. But there was a great deal of laughter, too. It struck Gunter that he had never seen them with such fine morale. It was good to have a break from their terrible duty.

One of the sailors showed them a trick involving ropes and the foaming wake of the *Klein-Seyditz*. Some of the mattress pads had to come above decks and be scrubbed down as well.

Dismayingly, just as they had cleaned up and gobbled down the hot meal the ship's cook produced, another storm, an even more violent one, overtook them.

Of course, the captain was delighted. Gunter retreated to his dark cabin.

Perhaps because he had not eaten, waiting for his men's empty bellies to be filled, he did not become seasick this time.

His own illness was deeper and more threatening and had been growing in severity over a period of months. *Gerta. Emma.*

The depth of wretchedness over their loss came over him occasionally and was as physically powerful as the waves tossing the ship. There was nothing left for him. He no longer had pride in his profession. He had no wife, no child. There was only his duty to those young men in the hold to stand between him and his little pistol.

He had a bottle of schnapps in his kit bag. The thought of drinking from it clenched his stomach. During two weeks of intense refitting and supplying, moving his troops, and then the anticipation of setting sail with the new moon, he had never *thought* of taking a drink. And now, when his mind needed to crawl under the rock of alcohol, he *could* not. It was horribly unfair.

And how many people had he sent to this same misery or worse?

Alone, sober, empty, exhausted, and utterly sick to his soul, Gunter cried in the dark.

CHAPTER 26

OCTOBER 18, 1942
6:30 P.M.

PARAMARIBO, SURINAME

Hannah was entranced; Sarah was humming, almost singing, when she came home from the clinic, helped mother a bit with dinner, and took buckets of hot water out back to their little bathhouse for a bath. She took far longer than usual at that and came to the table a tad late with a towel wrapped around her wet hair, face glowing with scrubbing.

Sarah had been like this frequently in the weeks following the American colonel's arrival into Paramaribo. Though she would never admit it and was shy to talk about it, it was clear to all who knew both of them that there was a strong mutual attraction. While Sarah had been a rock, sure and steady, for Hannah and Amos, and certainly for Rebecca over the last several months, her liveliness, the bloom in her cheeks, and the glint in her eye had been lost the day Michael had been taken from her. Lately, however, all had noticed that they seemed to have returned.

Sarah missed her late husband every day and still wore his ring on a chain, hanging close to her heart. But lately, the feeling wasn't the bone-deep ache, an almost physical punch at the memory of him; now, it was melancholy, sweeter, and now, more than simply the pain, she could feel joy at having known and loved him at all. More than that, she could envision a future that might, someday, involve that kind of love again.

Ed was teased frequently and mercilessly by Dr. Adelmann and George, who noticed that this big, strapping American Marine would go sloppy and doe-eyed whenever Sarah's name was mentioned or when she happened to enter the room (which she did a lot, because he managed to find reasons nearly every day to appear at Adelmann's clinic during her work hours). Though he kept an eye on her always, he rarely interrupted her work, which she appreciated, admiring him all the more for it.

Hannah, being a teenager and thus attuned to such things, took little time to comprehend the look of serenity on Sarah's face and register the blossoming attraction between them. Rebecca and Jacob, however, still had not. She knew that were her parents to be observant enough to notice, they would immediately worry about the fact that Ed Beltran was not a Jew. Hannah, who considered herself a modern young woman, didn't believe such a thing to be an insurmountable obstacle, but she knew that her traditional parents did.

Her traditional parents had also resisted when she'd first proposed working the bakery counter at George Butler's general store. It was Jacob's sense of indebtedness to George that had enabled him to allow his young daughter to take a job. That and his vivid memories of the delicious *apfelstrudel* she and her mother had prepared for Captain Cervantes and the crew of the *Bon Chance*.

Hannah had arrived in the middle of the workday to give the two men a traditional German *kaffee und kuchen*. She had brought a carafe of warm coffee and a basket of *butterkuchen*. "The girl has a gift," George had told Jacob, brushing crumbs from his third piece of pastry off his shirt. The girl had turned this simple treat of yeast dough, butter, almonds, and crumb topping into something utterly magical. "Our patrons would pay good money for her baking talents. Perhaps Hannah could take over our bakery counter, Jacob? After all, our current meager selection of baked goods isn't exactly packing them in. But this..." he said as he reached his hand into the basket for his fourth *butterkuchen*, "for this, they would forge a path through the jungle."

"Oh please, Papa!" Hannah pleaded with Jacob. "Please say yes! You must!"

The truth was that she had been baking for hours on end out of sheer boredom. The prospect of being useful, a contributing adult in the household, pleased her enormously. Amos and Dr. Adelmann's cousin, Levi, had secured dockworker positions shortly after arriving in Suriname. With Amos, Sarah, and Jacob gone all day, it had fallen to Hannah to absorb all of her mother's attentions, and also her grief and worries. The times when mother and daughter baked together felt to Hannah like the only times when things felt happy, normal. She worried that her mother might never be herself again now that Ezekiel was gone, no matter how much time passed. And although she worried what might happen to Rebecca once left alone all day, Hannah could think only of getting out and experiencing some long overdue independence.

Once Hannah took over the bakery counter, the pleasing aromas of butter, cinnamon, cardamom, molasses, and chocolate seemed to hover over Paramaribo. Patrons, having caught a waft of sugary goodness on the wind, would follow their noses to George's store, and not only had the bakery counter become a huge success in a short period of time, but it took no longer than a few days for his entire store to benefit from the additional traffic. Even better, Hannah thought, was that Rebecca had taken to joining her daughter in the morning baking and frequently offered George useful advice about merchandising his shelves to better appeal to wives and mothers—the people who most often did the household shopping. Hannah got great pleasure out of seeing her mother busy and purposeful. The arrangement was working out for all concerned.

For his part, Jacob had proven himself time and again to be invaluable to George and kept things running like an expensive Swiss watch. When he had first arrived and seen George's scattered method of bookkeeping—not really a method so much as a series of piles—he had been secretly pleased to know that he could immediately be of help here. He would never stop feeling indebted to Dr. Adelmann and George for giving him and his family a new life, despite George's urging that it was they who repeatedly benefited from the Roseweigs' arrival.

At dinner on this particular night, the family sat astonished, watching Amos silently shovel the dinner of sausages and boiled potatoes into his mouth in a concentrated stoking. It seemed the boy might never stop growing. He was already bigger than Jacob; his mother often reasoned that Amos just "needed material for construction."

When Amos finally came up for air, he swabbed his mouth with one of Rebecca's new napkins and turned to his aunt. "Could I come with you to the clinic tomorrow? I'd like to talk to the colonel."

Around the table, all grew silent, forked poised mid-air in anticipation of what Amos would say next. Amos was many things—stalwart, kind, endlessly useful to his father and protective of his family—but caretaker of the sick and injured, he was not.

"What on earth for, Amos?" Jacob asked.

"Of course you may," Sarah interjected quickly, stealing a reproving glance at Jacob. "Is there something in particular you'd like to talk to him about, Amos?"

Amos looked anxiously around the table at the faces watching him, then down at his plate, shrugged, and stabbed another bite of food without looking up. "I just want his opinion about something."

"Oh?" Jacob asked. "About what?"

"Just something I heard at the docks yesterday. I thought …" He looked around the table at the faces staring at him. His expression was unreadable. Guilt? Sadness? Fear? After a moment, he sighed and said, "I heard he trains people in the jungle how to fight and to shoot guns. I want to ask if he'll train me."

What does he know? Sarah wondered. She had noticed Ed, Dr. Adelmann, and George exchanging looks and private whispers when they were together at the clinic—and now Amos. Something was happening, and it wasn't good.

Jacob shook his head ruefully. "No, boy, if you have a day off, we need to repair that leaning fence behind the jakes. And we need ground dug for a garden." He looked thoughtful. "Though learning to shoot is a good idea for everyone. It is time we Jews learned to protect ourselves if need be. Sarah, perhaps you could ask the colonel about this?

"*Yakob*, why are we not hiring someone to do that work?" Rebecca asked, sounding a bit scandalized. "You are a business person. Surely we have the money for this." Hannah realized that her mother's ideas about dignity were reemerging now she was again a respectable *hausfrau*. She had taken to readjusting Hannah's blouse in the mornings, sometimes stitching top openings tighter, and Papa's shirts always gleamed and were perfectly ironed since she had acquired tub, washboard, and irons.

Papa smiled and winked. "Not so much as you might think. I am putting twenty percent of my pay toward this house."

Rebecca looked sick. "But Herr Butler said the house came with the job! He is charging us *rent*? Some days you work twelve hours!"

"Rebecca, it is not rent. It is payment. We are now *buying* this house. Clear title in four years! We are living here rent-free as was promised, but it will be better to own it. And this way, when we make improvements, we can count on keeping them. It is always better to own. And to be honest, most days we have a nap after lunch at the store, or sometimes George locks it and takes us to lunch."

Then, turning to Amos, he said, "There are good vegetables in the market, and they are cheap, but if we have our own garden, your mother can simply pick what she wants to cook. Also, next week, you and I are going to build a chicken pen. You may have noticed that almost everyone here in Paramaribo has a garden, fruit trees, chickens. It is just part of living here."

⌛

The next morning, Sarah and Hannah strolled off to town for work at their usual time, but today Sarah carried not just a little parcel of her own lunch but a sizable basket full of gingersnaps baked by Hannah. Sarah hoped that plying the colonel with sweets would help encourage him to take the Roseweigs on as "trainees" and teach them—even her and Hannah—how to fire a gun.

As they turned onto the main street through town, the two were halted abruptly when a tall, handsome man stepped in front of them.

"*Guten morgen*, Frau Lipinski. George told me of your usual route to work, and I thought I would walk with you and help you open the clinic." Ed seemed elaborately formal today. Sarah smiled at his attempt to speak German.

Sarah smiled politely. "Very well, Colonel. But we often have a line waiting at the clinic when we open. You may have to wait a little bit for Dr. Adelmann's attention." She couldn't help the blush that crept up her neck to her cheeks but silently cursed it all the same.

"May I carry that for you?" He reached automatically for Sarah's basket. He brushed that hand, and Sarah's blush, unbelievably, deepened. He held the basket up and sniffed appreciatively. "Work supplies?"

"Actually, gingersnaps. Hannah and I ... Colonel Beltran, this is Hannah Roseweig, my niece."

The man put the basket down carefully and extended his hand; Hannah's met it in automatic courtesy. Hannah noted the strength in his handshake.

"Oh yes, Ms. Roseweig! So *you* are the baker at George Butler's store that I've heard so much about! I think Lisjbet has been forced to let out the waist of George's pants thanks to your delicious treats."

Now it was Hannah's turn to blush. She nodded her head and quietly said, "Thank you."

"Colonel, I'll be honest. These gingersnaps are for you, as a sort of payment. You see," Sarah said, looking down shyly, "my family and I were talking last night and, well, we hoped you would be willing to share your military experience with us? We feel it's time we learned to fight. To shoot guns."

Ed stopped in his tracks. "We?"

"Yes, my nephew, Amos, first brought it up, but we all feel it's a good idea. I, for one, would like to know how to defend myself should our party face further danger."

Before he had a moment to formulate a response to this odd and totally unexpected request, he saw that they had arrived at the clinic. There *was* a line: five people, three of whom were worried parents with a baby.

"Colonel, would you put that basket down on the other side of the stove? Hannah, please stoke the fire." To the plump Dutch housekeeper who bustled in from the door that led to the patient rooms, Sarah said, "Maartje, put the pressure cooker directly over the firebox." Then, in their shared pidgin language, Maartje, plainly ready for the end of her shift, shared the updates from overnight, hung her apron inside the door of the utility room off the lobby, waved tiredly, and left.

"Well, Colonel…" Sarah began, realizing that her request would have to wait.

"Please call me Ed, Ma'am."

Sarah looked startled and pleased. Perhaps a little timid. "Ed, then, there will be a short delay before we can finish our conversation, unfortunately. This little boy has malaria, almost certainly. He has not been nursing well, is fussing a lot, and had a very high fever this morning followed by sweating. And his diaper is dry. I have to start him on quinine injections, and I have to take care of anyone who is bleeding as fast as I can."

She sounded as though the recitation of symptoms was as much for her own benefit as his.

"Understood. Can I help?"

Sarah's smile was distracted. "If you would go outside with some of those buckets and fill them from the well, I would appreciate it. Maartje used all the water for compresses overnight."

By the time the man who had put a chisel through his palm had been cleaned, stitched, and bandaged; the baby injected with quinine-infused solution as both medication and hydration; and the remaining patient, another carpenter, who had been carrying a rough timber, had had a one-inch splinter removed from his shoulder, it was midmorning.

Dr. Adelmann had arrived, his car seat full of supplies from George's store. When he entered the clinic, Sarah reported her updates and received compliments for her decisions.

Adelmann queried Ed, "Have you been added to my clinic staff? We're seeing a lot of you these days."

"I *think* I volunteered. I came early to, uh, to have you take a look at my hand again."

Adelmann had to laugh out loud. "Is that right?" he asked with a mischievous grin. "Have you had Sarah take a look at it? I'm sure she has the cure for what ails it."

Colonel Beltran looked more than a little startled that the doctor had so overtly called him on his trick. Sarah bowed her head and pretended to busy herself with the bags of supplies, but it was only to hide the grin of pleasure on her face.

"Sarah and I will put away all the things I brought from the store, but then we must talk," Adelmann said. His voice took on a serious edge, and the room grew still and somber. "Then, I am afraid that we must gather the fathers of all the families immediately, including my uncle. We have received information from American intelligence that the Germans are sending an expedition to capture your group."

He looked sick. Sarah's face went slack. Ed's tightened, and his eyes glared.

"We have known about this for some time, and we are working on a plan, which includes the colonel, here," Adelmann said, and Ed bobbed his head.

The fear seizing her heart moved down into Hannah's gut, and she had to go outside and retch.

After a moment of silence, Sarah spoke up. "So, Colonel Beltran, can we speak now about those shooting lessons?"

CHAPTER 27

OCTOBER 20, 1942
11:00 A.M.
GOUVERNEMENTSGEBOUW

PARAMARIBO, SURINAME

Jacob Roseweig, Ben Adelmann, his uncle Herr Adelmann, George, Ed Beltran, Eli Rabin, and Albert Levin, all of whom had established new, comfortable lives in Paramaribo by now, gathered in the small conference room in the back of the presidential palace. Despite their present lives of relative comfort, they were now, for the first time in many weeks, made uncomfortable again.

Every detail of this room bespoke elegance. Dark wood wainscoting was interrupted at the leaded windows by tall, red velvet drapes. A map of Suriname was framed in gilt between those outside windows. All the lettering on the map was in Dutch, and the map had been hand-drawn in oils.

George, who had seen Buckingham Palace years ago, had never thought this palace to be all that grand, but he was thankful that it was at least large enough to accommodate all of these men with quiet, private quarters.

The president was a small man for a politician. He spoke as if he were alone, seeming to muse in speculation. He had his fingers interlaced over his vested paunch, and his balding blond head was bowed a bit.

"The situation is a delicate one. We are supposed to be in a neutral stance *vis-a-vis* both America and Germany. Of course, we are of far greater importance to the Americans because of our bauxite, which they need desperately for their war effort. However, any diplomatic or intelligence help we receive from the Americans has to be clandestine. They are not involved in the war in Europe, or the Japanese activity in Asia, and, for the most part, they do not want to be. While President Roosevelt, as you know, Colonel, favors entering the European war on the side of Britain, so far he has not had the political strength to do so."

He had been gazing out the window but turned to look sympathetically at Dr. Adelmann. "Not only are we reluctant to give any more help than we must to these creatures who have invaded and looted what was homeland for many of us, but *you* have become a friend to all of us, and we all owe a huge debt to you for the countless lives you've saved and improved."

Adelmann nodded his head modestly and appreciatively.

"Of course, other than the fact that it was communicated by an American from the embassy, the source of this information is anonymous to us," the president continued. "However, we know that the freighter *Klein-Seyditz* set sail from Belgium some time during the night of October ninth. We know that it carried a force of German troopers, with some motorized vehicles, under the command of an Oberst Gunter Kramer."

Ed jerked erect. Today he wore slacks, a dress shirt, and tie, but had of necessity laid aside his blazer. Both the president and Dr. Adelmann swiveled to gaze at him.

"You said *Gunter Kramer?*" Ed confirmed.

"Colonel? You know this man?" the president asked.

"Luftwaffe intelligence. I met him in Britain about seven years ago, when we were working in our respective embassies. The man has a whacking great scar across his face from one of those ritual duels at Heidelberg. Of course, he had a diplomatic title, 'aide de' something, but he was Intelligence. At that time, I was in command of the London Embassy's guard. If he's an oberst now, he's impressed somebody enough to get up through the ranks fast. He was a brand-new captain then."

"What's your personal estimate of him?"

Ed considered. "Smart. Very controlled, a courteous and careful man. Not good news, I'm afraid. I judged that he could be a very hard man if he had to be. I met German officers like him during the first Big One, and they were never easy opponents."

The president swiveled again to gaze pensively out his window. "I can delay, but I cannot prevent their landing. I can resist their bringing weapons ashore, but if they insist, I cannot present armed resistance. While I have an 'army,' it is really nothing more than one barracks of soldiers who are most useful as palace guards and sometimes against organized banditry." He nodded respectfully at Ed. "Less useful than the little pursuit group you have formed, Colonel. The Germans will outnumber the police I have available in the city. Perhaps," he swiveled back again, to face Dr. Adelmann, his face sad, "you should consider going with the colonel to the southern part of the country, or maybe Guyana, while they are here. And taking your friends with you."

Ed shook his head while George snorted. The doctor looked around at them, nodding, and replied, "That is totally impracticable, sir. There are women with infants, there are numerous small children, and there are very few routes, if any, into that area that do not cross through bandit territory. None of these people are trained in how to care for themselves in primitive situations in the tropics. With time they could learn, but I am sure we would have deaths as a result of such a flight, from disease or injury, if not from bandits. Also, we have no place to go. There are far too many of us…"

Ed stirred uncomfortably in the high-backed, leather-cushioned chair. "Yeah, Mr. President, I have to concur. I could take no more than a few to my finca, but it would be dangerous, especially for the children. Trucks could not carry both enough gasoline and people to reach all the way to the coastal settlements in Guyana, the monsoon is only weeks away, and we have no assurance the Germans will not come inland…"

Adelmann held up his hand as if to say, "Don't worry, I'll handle this."

"Of course, Colonel Beltran, we would never expect you to put up our entire large party. But Mr. President, I feel strongly that the colonel's military training would be of great value to these people, right here in Paramaribo."

Ed nodded in agreement. "Absolutely, I do this for a living. Leave that to me. But I feel, Mr. President, that beyond that, if you pooled your army and police, and I pulled my trained officers from the mines, we could probably crush them, even without these people's help."

For just a moment, the president looked thoughtful. But he shook his head and rose from his chair, as did they all, in courtesy.

"Gentlemen, all I can offer is something like your Admiral Nelson's blind eye," he smiled at George. "Neither the Army nor the police will interfere with your movements. But I cannot take overt action against German forces without endangering both this country and our parent one."

⧗

The contingent of men exited the president's compound through a rear door and gloomily and silently walked the short distance to where George's and Dr. Adelmann's cars were parked. Only when they had reached them did the doctor speak. His voice sounded starkly flat.

"I think we should go to my clinic. My lobby is the only place with enough chairs, and it is where wives will not be frightened to death."

"Okay, Doc, we need to get this hashed out, so I can start putting together men and weapons," Ed said.

Rabin and Levin, who were unfamiliar with this American's brash ways, looked at him apprehensively.

Sarah and the other assistants had dealt with all of the patients for this morning. The doctor closed and locked the doors. He pulled forward the big percolator that always occupied the back of the stove and indicated a hanging line of mugs. Ed and George immediately poured themselves dark coffee; the other men sat nervously.

Albert Levin said quietly but firmly, "I want us to examine all solutions that avoid killing first."

Ed grimaced. "If I pulled my trained men off the mines, and managed to borrow a few troopers from the American 'embassy,' we would still be outnumbered two to one. I agree, we need to look for solutions that avoid killing." What he seemed to be thinking and not saying was, *because we'd likely be the ones getting killed.*

Jacob, worry a mask on his face, asked, "George, Colonel, is there *anywhere* in this country we could hide our people?"

George and Ed exchanged a resigned look, and George replied, "There are the mine sites, plus a few ranches and estates. At most, we would have the same shelter problem, and all of them are on major roads. Questioning people as to the passage of a number of vehicles would give the Germans our route within hours. That number of German troopers would destroy the guard force of any single one of the mines very quickly. None of them are set up to defend against a major assault—only to protect supplies and mine operations."

Jacob looked even sicker but persisted. "Colonel, did you mean what you said about your home in the jungle? There really is no place for us there? You don't feel it would be worth trying?"

"It's a question of shelter. I could put up eight or ten people in my house with everyone being very uncomfortable and crowded, but there is a serious problem with wildlife, and the monsoon will be here within weeks. Europeans could not possibly endure our monsoon without solid shelter. Additionally, my place is almost three hundred miles away through some awfully danger-ous jungle. Not really an option for more than a few people, if you all could even make it through the trip. And a few would require armed escort to get there safely. Also, I don't think there are enough trucks in Paramaribo to carry all of you."

"Coastal Guyana?"

"We thought of that already. Same argument about not enough transport, and many more hundreds of miles, equally dangerous. On top of that, I have no idea at all if the roads are passable. I've never tried to go from Suriname to Guyana's coast. I've always traveled by truck and ferry and have stayed *within* Guyana. In any case, even if we had enough trucks, we couldn't carry enough fuel, and there is no place to refuel short of the coast. Even worse, there is literally no spare housing at Guyana's coast."

Jacob's face grew resolved. "Then we have no recourse but to fight and die or wait for the Germans to run us down like rabbits?" He sounded angry.

There was a flurry of speech, men talking over each other, and Sarah, who had been hovering in the back of the room and seemed to have been forgotten by the preoccupied men, overrode them abruptly.

"Enough!" The men were startled into silence. Sarah remembered a day not so long ago—although it seemed another lifetime—when she had done this before. Nothing could cut through the din of men arguing like the sure, clear tones of a woman's voice. "Colonel, what chance would we have in a fight? Could we disperse people, a few here and a few there?"

Jacob shook his head. "That would put us in the same horrible situation as in Amsterdam. If the Germans choose to ignore the local authorities and begin the kind of sweeps they did in Haarlemmermeer and Hoorn and Amsterdam, we would be just as powerless to resist them as we were there."

Ed closed his eyes, going through the kind of checklist he had gone through before so many battles, and decided to speak to Sarah's first question, figuring Jacob had pretty well answered her second.

"I do have a few trained men I can bring here within a day. They're already armed, and I can get dynamite, TNT, and detonating caps and fuses from the mines just for asking. George has a storage shed of that stuff as well. If we attacked with complete surprise, using a lot of explosives, and got dead lucky, we *could* destroy or cripple the German force. Problem is, we do that and your president will have the kind of international incident he needs to avoid."

Dr. Adelmann stood, shaking his head sorrowfully. "Let's think about this overnight. Jacob, Albert, Eli, I think just now the women should not be told. We have a bit more time. Let them have a day or two more of calm." He transfixed Sarah with his gaze. "I hope you agree with that?"

"Yes, Doctor. I don't want to ever have to tell them." Tears glistened down her cheeks. She and Hannah could not bear the thought of telling Rebecca and had decided together the previous day that they would not until it was absolutely necessary. They weren't sure she could handle it, after all she had been through. And she was only starting to come back to life.

"Then we will meet here tomorrow morning at eleven o'clock. That will give us time to deal with the morning patients."

Ed made a beeline for Sarah as the meeting dissolved. He took her hand and tugged her down the hall. He noted Adelmann's and Jacob's startled glances but ignored them. "Are you serious about learning to shoot?"

"Of course," she said quickly, unblinking. "So is my nephew, Amos. And Jacob. We all want to learn to protect ourselves. Will you show us?"

"You bet," he said. "Get your nephew and Jacob, and the three of you meet me at George's store in an hour."

Shirts, trousers, boots, socks, a broad hat, a belt, and a knife to go on it, a mosquito net, a blanket, and, last but not least, a Smith and Wesson police special .38 revolver, flapped holster, and two boxes of ammunition all were laid out on the ground before them. Ed had guided Sarah, Jacob, and Amos in their purchase of field kits, believing that if he was going to train them in military-style fighting, he would need to do it right.

With their kits ready, Ed had borrowed one of the trucks from George's small fleet, each of which was the size of an American six-by-six military jeep, and driven them outside town to a rural area where a dilapidated fence stood in sections at the end of a large, filthy field. Ed had unpacked the truck and laid their new equipment out on the ground before them, intending to school them all on the uses of each item.

"We don't know how to use any of this," Sarah said. She was fascinated by the gleaming blue pistol and squatted down, reaching out a finger to stroke the fluted chamber like someone greeting a strange cat.

"You will before you leave. That's just a revolver. Double action, no safety, just point and pull. Not complicated, and you can learn enough for short range with one box of ammo."

Ed proved to be a patient, helpful teacher. He expertly guided them all through the safety procedures, ensuring that they understood how to safely handle a gun before even allowing them to load the ammo.

He showed them the "power stance," like a boxer in the ring, with both legs slightly bent, the body leaning a bit forward, and one leg stepped just in front, which he told them offered stability. He showed them how to place their hands high on the grip for greater control.

"And don't let it wiggle around in your hand," he instructed, grabbing the revolver in Jacob's hand and jerking it in his grasp to illustrate the older man's unstable hold on the weapon. "This is a weapon of destruction. Hold it like one." He pushed it more deeply into Jacob's hand and encouraged him to tighten his grip. "That way, the recoil when you fire won't cause the bullets to fly into the air, and it won't knock you on your *tuches,* as they say, right?"

Jacob, Sarah, and Amos gave a chuckle at the colonel's attempt at humor in their language.

He continued to show them how to use their front sights and how to smoothly pull the trigger rather than rapidly jerk it back so that they maintained their targets—cans pocketed from the general store—in their sights. He had them practice clicking the trigger without any ammo in the guns first, to acclimate to the feeling. Then, once loaded, he stood behind each of them, held his hand over theirs, and operated their guns for them as they simply held them, learning the feeling of a firing gun in their hands and a smoothly pulled trigger.

Amos was a natural and needed very little coaching. Jacob, shaky at first, was a fast learner, and Ed admired his determination to learn this skill, which clearly was uncomfortable for him.

When it was Sarah's turn, Ed did what he could not to be distracted by the clean scent of her long, dark hair, and the musky fragrance of her skin, and the fact that their bodies were so near each other. Sarah, too, was highly aware of every part of their bodies that were touching or even close, and it put every nerve ending on edge, which actually seemed to help her firing accuracy.

They managed an hour of slow-fire practice, and although Ed occasionally had to step in to correct their posture or slow down itchy trigger fingers, in all he was pleased by the training session, which it seemed had made capable gun handlers of them all. It still did not make them experts; if brought face to face with Kramer and his fellow German soldiers, they likely would not stand a chance. But they would be able to defend themselves, and right now, that was all Ed was concerned with.

When target practice was finished, Ed returned his cadre to George's store, along with the truck, and made his way back to his lodging at the Butlers' home, where Carmina had prepared a delicious meal of lentil stew. Once he was heartily full, Ed went to his room to write an important letter.

Ysidro:

Old Friend, I am sure you must be concerned about the large convoy that has just arrived on our doorstep. I am writing to keep you apprised of events here in Paramaribo and to explain why you must do as they say. It seems our old enemies, the Krauts, are on their way here in pursuit of Dr. Adelmann and some of his friends who have fled here. I need you now, friend. Please do not delay. I have sent a convoy of three trucks from George's store and five guards, all of whom you know because we trained them. One truck is equipped with padding in the back and a tarp roof and mosquito net so that Inocente can be brought here to Paramaribo. I am also sending the enclosed money for anything else you may need for the journey.

The two youngest guards are to stay there and take care of the finca while we are gone. They already know everything about our stores and routines from living with us, but be sure to point out the breeding stock we want to keep. You know how they are when they get meat-hungry.

Come with all three trucks, three guards, and Inocente to meet me here in Paramaribo. Make all possible speed.

Bring with you:

Both Thompsons, all six magazines, all my spare .45 ammunition, both cases of grenades, and both of our pump shotguns, and all of the ammunition for them. Also, of course, your own llama and Springfield.

Bring my lockbox as well. Whatever happens, we will have to live here through the monsoon.

We have an action to fight. I need your experience.

Take care of the mother to be.

Your friend,

Edward Beltran,

Col., U.S.M.C., (Ret.)

CHAPTER 28

OCTOBER 22, 1942
5:30 A.M.

IN THE DEEP ATLANTIC, ABOARD THE FREIGHTER *KLEIN-SEYDITZ*

Gunter roused from his dismal hibernation. The *Klein-Seyditz* was in calm seas, and he now had to go on deck and interact with his men.

First, he went to the captain on the bridge, and, once informed that they were not likely to encounter more storms before coasting, he went to his unit and began preparations for disembarking.

"Ermenthaller. Turn out all the men, all stores up on deck, into the trucks and trailers, mortars and machine guns on top. Then, everyone prepare a fresh uniform, with dubbined boots, and oil the weapons."

"*Jawohl*, Herr Oberst. Are we nearing shore?"

"That is the case, Oberfeldwebel Ermenthaller. Roughly the day after tomorrow." Gunter kept his face immobile as he held out a handful of insignia.

Ermenthaller looked absolutely flabbergasted, staring at the little bundle that represented promotion. It was time for Ermenthaller to be an oberfeldwebel. This had been Gunter's Wehrmacht rank and insignia, and not SS, but it would have to do—it was all he'd put in his kit before embarking.

Gunter pivoted and strode back to his cabin.

He would need to go ashore and talk to the German embassy and the local government, before bringing his men ashore. Goebbels had told him that there was no foundation of precedent for the Reich to bring its forces ashore, except the fact that it was probably the superior force in that theater. The embassy would know how he should proceed.

I need to talk to Captain Krager, borrow an iron and a brazier to prepare my uniform, and I should ask Ermenthaller if he has a dress uniform in his kit, Gunter thought, making mental notes of the work ahead of him upon arrival. *I am the only officer, will have to attend any invitations, should respond with a minimum cadre. A senior N.C.O. is perfectly acceptable at an embassy party … If they try to keep us on board …*

All this worry was futile, he knew. He could have no idea how to react until he was ashore and could established diplomatic contact with the Surinamese government.

But with the activity of the morning, and his purposeful planning, Gunter had not even noticed his depression ebbing away on the sea.

CHAPTER 29

OCTOBER 22, 1942
7:00 A.M.

AMERICAN EMBASSY, PARAMARIBO, SURINAME

"A t-ten-HUT!"

The Marine sergeant at the desk barked out the command, coming to his own feet and bracing to attention, as did the rifle-armed private who had been standing at parade rest beside the door. Both wore huge grins, in violation of normal Marine military behavior.

"Colonel Beltran! Good to see you, Sir." The sergeant saluted with the crisp precision the Corps had ingrained in all of its personnel.

Ed nodded deeply. He was in slacks and shirt, not in uniform, and so did not return the salute but acknowledged it courteously, as was proper.

"You too, Sarge. At ease."

He glanced around the distinctly inelegant lobby of the equally inelegant American Embassy.

"Captain Hodgins in?" Ed asked, looking for the man who commanded this tiny unit of Marines.

"Yes, Sir. He's off duty, but only as of a few minutes ago. He's probably still in the guard room." The sergeant gave the open-palmed directional wave of a Marine guard, and Ed made his way to the guard room. As he did, he grinned, thinking to himself how odd it was that this Marine salute-to-wave gestures were never part of any Corps training, though it was deeply ingrained in that military culture and was displayed at every Marine post he'd ever seen.

Hodgins was a very junior captain, in a not-very-junior post. He wore the requisite dress blue uniform and white web gear, his .45 in a white holster, and his hair cut in a strictly regulation flat top, with the hair at the temples and the back of his neck in the very short trim called "white walls." Hodgins' posture always bespoke the utmost seriousness, displaying respect for this post that Ed knew he felt lucky to get. That's why it struck him as humorous to enter the room and find Hodgins' broad white-billed cap lying casually on a table and the captain himself slumped tiredly against the wall as he slurped coffee from an immense white mug.

"Got some of that to share?"

Hodgins almost spilled on himself, coming to attention. But he managed to avoid that, stabilizing the mug just in time, and his freckled face broke into a grin as broad as the sergeant's. Ed was a popular visitor.

"Well, okay, Colonel, if you want to take the risk on this stuff. Pot's been going all night, and it's fit to use as paint remover." Knowing what Ed's reaction would be—coffee was his nectar—Hodgins was already pouring into another huge mug.

"Fred, I need to talk about something I'm not supposed to know. You okay with that?" Ed asked as he nodded thanks for the coffee.

Hodgins' return gaze was intelligent and amused. Both men seated themselves at the table in plain wooden chairs and hunkered forward, their forearms bracketing their mugs.

"George Butler owns the only big store in Paramaribo. He supplies the doctor who takes care of the president, supplies the president's palace, and this embassy, and the other two embassies, and the mines. You stay at Mr. Butler's home when you're in town," Ed looked at his old friend, who was nodding. "So you *know* the Germans are sending a platoon or so."

Hodgins, who had been nodding agreement, froze as Ed said this. His eyes never left Ed's as he slowly drew the coffee to his mouth and sipped.

Ed interpreted the gesture as one of silent agreement and leaned back, grinning. "This is your first embassy post, and you already have a good grasp of how hard it is to shelter intelligence. It's no different in the big capitals of Europe. All diplomatic circles are actually small towns like Paramaribo."

"So?"

"So the people the Krauts are coming to take away are just living their lives here, doing no one any harm, and it's not right."

"Yes, Sir, I agree. But America is still neutral. So we can't do anything about it, unless … You were thinking of putting them here for sanctuary?"

Ed was totally flummoxed. The thought hadn't occurred to him, but it wasn't a bad one. He also knew that the Americans wouldn't remain neutral for long if they knew what was in those papers that were missing—the ones he felt sure Adelmann had. But this wasn't information he had plans to reveal.

But before Ed could reply, Hodgins interjected. "Thing is, Sir, I have just seven men, including one sergeant and one corporal, which is barely enough to have two men in the lobby and a standby for latrine relief and grounds patrol around the clock. If I want to give someone liberty, I have to stand watch myself."

"I honestly hadn't thought of sanctuary here, but, of course, if you give someone sanctuary, it's not a question of being able to fight off an intrusion, but whether someone is willing to violate American sovereign territory."

"I know that, Sir. I was thinking more in terms of room. I live in a house near here, a couple of the ambassador's staff share that house, and my enlisted people live in a very small bunkhouse behind this building. We don't *have* any accommodations."

Ed slumped a bit. For a moment there, it had sounded like a way out, but Hodgins had nailed that coffin shut.

"On top of that, Colonel, this is not an official embassy. Suriname is not 'officially' a country; it's a possession of Holland, which is occupied. Our 'Ambassador' is legally a 'Representative.' We *rent* this joint from the Surinamese government. It's not sovereign ground—not ours, anyway."

Ed sagged a bit.

"What I wanted to do was to borrow a few of your fellows, in mufti, to join me in a *maybe* fight."

Hodgins braced up in his chair. *It's nice to deal with Marines,* thought Ed. *We're so predictable; we all just love a good fight.* "The Ambassador has instructed us to stay on embassy grounds to avoid any contact in town with the Germans and to avoid any provocation," Hodgins said.

Ed's nod was resigned.

Hodgins continued, straight faced. "I must have three men on duty at any given time. The other four, and I, can be anywhere you want us, in plain clothes and armed, with an hour's notice. An hour because we have to sneak out."

Ed smiled.

"If I may ask, Sir, why is this your fight?" Hodgins asked.

"Well, aside from the fact that I owe—we *all* owe—Ben Adelmann an eternal debt of gratitude, it's the right thing to do, Hodgins. These Krauts, they can't get away with this. These are good people. One, in particular…" Ed's voice trailed off, and when he realized Hodgins had caught him in dreamland, he straightened up. "Anyway, she's Adelmann's assistant, and she and her family are good people. My country won't let me fight on their behalf, so I'm helping in my way."

It was Hodgins' turn to grin. He and Ed had gotten drunk together a few times, and Ed sometimes took a couple of the guardsmen out of town for high-end rifle and bayonet instruction followed by beer. He was entitled to a little teasing.

"A woman, Beltran? A leg trap baited with petticoats. As good a reason for a fight as any," Hodgins said, shaking his head and repressing a chuckle.

"Hmmph," Ed said grumpily. "This fellow they're looking for specifically is the same man who treated *you* for malaria a few months ago, as I recall."

"Wondered at the name."

"I've talked to him and his people," Ed continued. "Seems the Krauts are not just putting Jews and gypsies and queers and everyone else they dislike in camps, but they're carrying out systematic executions. Without trial, of course. Personally, I think the Germans are shit-scared that intelligence about that will get to Roosevelt."

"Intelligence? Do you have proof? Plus, Mr. Roosevelt is Episcopalian."

"I know that," Ed said, disregarding his question. "We used to go to the same church in D.C. But in '37, he addressed freedom of religion, not only in our country but in the whole world. You think he wants to fight the Krauts now? Wait until he hears about this."

Hodgins grinned. Ed got down to the brass tacks. "I have three trained guards, and two mining engineers, Evans and Williams, you know them, they want in." Hodgins nodded as Ed continued. "My old sergeant from Nicaragua is coming, and four of your troops, plus you and me make twelve. That's still almost two-to-one odds, and I don't like that against regular German troops. Adelmann's people can defend themselves, and they're prepared to, but I don't see them doing any real fighting. What do you have for heavy arms?"

"Not much, I'm afraid. This is just a ceremonial posting. I have my sidearm, all the troops have Springfields, and Sergeant Lone and Corporal Sutter have both .45s and rifles, so they can sit at the desk. I don't even have any grenades."

"My guards have Springfield rifles like yours, I have a couple of 12-GA pumps coming, and some slug and buckshot ammunition I can let the engineers use, no time to sight them in on anything else. Also, I have a couple of Thompsons coming, with three drum magazines apiece. Those would be best off in Marine hands. My sergeant is trained, but both he and I are really riflemen. On top of that, I have a couple of dozen grenades, and I will have a bushel or two of dynamite and TNT available."

"Damn, Colonel, you're better equipped than the whole Corps in Suriname!"

"You have to remember, I gotta go through bandit country to get to the corner store. And I live in the back of beyond."

"Good thing. The Germans usually have MG 42s even down at the squad level."

"Been paying attention, have you?" Ed gave the young captain a sly look.

"Mr. Roosevelt wants us in that war, and he's been getting his way for quite a while. I figure it's just a matter of time."

"I figure you're right. I just hope I can get off the disabled list in time for it."

"I don't know, Colonel, doesn't the Corps have a mandatory retirement age?" Grinning widely, he gestured with his fingers. "You start fossilizing around the edges once you're over the hill."

"Captain, there is only so much nonsense I will take from junior officers with wet ears. I'm not even forty yet." *At least for another three weeks,* Ed thought.

Hodgins was looking energized at the prospect of action. Ed kept his advice short.

"You know your own men best, but I would advise picking anyone who has already seen any combat, and after that, looking at their shooting ability."

"Already know who to bring to the party," Hodgins said readily. "Corporal Sutter is smart as a whip, but he wears glasses like pop bottles and barely makes marksman. He'll be in charge of the embassy, with Private Murkowski, who I *suspect* is under eighteen, and someone else who pisses me off between now and then."

"Good enough, Hodgins. I figured you'd come through. If it comes to a fight, I'll try to use you and your boys at enough range so that any Krauts who live through it won't be able to identify you."

"Can't ask more than that. It would be nice not to be assigned embassy duty in Iceland … as a private."

Ed waved airily. "Actually, I understand the Icelanders are nice folks, and their girls are friendly."

"How are we going to deal with the local cops?"

"The president has sort-of promised a 'see-no-evil' attitude on the part of his cops and that little excuse for an army he keeps," Ed said. "But if we do have to shoot, I want it fast and mean. If it goes on too long, he'll be up against it with the German embassy people. They push him pretty hard anyway."

"Friendly girls in Iceland, eh?"

"Yep. When I had the embassy in London, they used to fly the boys from the Iceland embassy in every few months to defrost."

Hodgins widened his eyes a bit. "Defrost?"

"Oh, no big deal. We'd just run them through a crematorium in a funeral home that operated off Hyde Park, and they'd be limbered up in no time."

Hodgins dropped his head into his hands and moaned eloquently.

Ed rinsed his cup at the sink and put it back on the shelf.

"Thanks for the java."

As he exited, Ed grinned. That would teach Hodgins to call him old!

CHAPTER 30

OCTOBER 22, 1942
2:30 P.M.
GOUVERNEMENTSGEBOUW
PARAMARIBO, SURINAME

There were only four men in the conference room this time. The president sat in one of the deep armchairs along the wall. George and Dr. Adelmann occupied identical chairs on either side of him, and Ed sat in one of the high-backed straight chairs facing the semi-circle made by the others.

The president spoke softly, and, in this room of dark woods and heavy velvet and leather, his voice sounded even lower.

"Gentlemen, have you come up with any solutions?"

Adelmann spoke at equally low tones. "We have examined the logistics of taking *all* of our recently arrived coreligionists somewhere else while the Germans are occupying the area. Logistically, that is simply impossible. Questions of transport, fuel, and actual shelter preclude doing it. Even with taking only those people who last arrived here and who may be at greatest risk of being seized by the Germans, evacuation is simply not feasible. The idea of taking sanctuary in the American embassy also has been ruled out by Captain Hodgins, commander of that post. We have examined the idea of dispersing the threatened people to smaller settlements and towns. But because search forces of similar size effectively destroyed refuge for our folk towns throughout Holland, we have come to the conclusion that that is an unacceptable solution."

The president sighed heavily. "Have you *any* idea of how to cope with this situation?" His eyes moved instinctively to Ed.

Ed sat as erect as he could. He tried to keep the intensity of his voice under control.

"First, it would be extremely helpful if we could know precisely when they are going to make landfall, and where. Secondly, if you could make some excuse to hold them offshore at anchor rather than allowing them to dock where they can debark their vehicles, we would retain the upper hand. And thirdly, and the most important, is to forbid them to come ashore armed."

The president looked alarmed.

"You are not considering murdering all of them, are you?"

"Sir, I cannot deny, the thought has occurred to me. But no, while I am not sure precisely what to do, *yet*, it will not involve *killing* unarmed men. You have my word as an officer."

The steel in his voice rang true, and the president visibly relaxed into his chair. Ed continued.

"Any delay you can provide will be useful and will reduce the possibility of violence. Ideally, if you could separate the soldiers from their weapons and house them ashore, it would give us the greatest scope of possible operation with the least effect on the international situation."

George spoke up for the first time.

"Sir, you have that new wing on the army barracks. You could put twenty or so men in there and provide them mess facilities and sanitation." He smiled, evilly. "At the expense of the German Embassy, of course."

The president began to look engaged. He smiled a very small smile and tented his pudgy fingers.

"As tiny as this country is, I am afflicted with a full-grown bureaucracy. The least I can do is to share it with guests."

Ed grinned happily at this show of bureaucracy engaged in deliberate obstruction—for once, to his benefit. "Mr. President," he continued, "I will endeavor, if we *must* do something noisy, to do it as quickly as possible so as to give the Germans the least excuse to blame *you*. If police arrive no sooner than one half of an hour after an ... occurrence, it would be best."

The little man in the big chair nodded amiably. "Giving me the grace of knowing when police would best be occupied, say, on the outskirts of the town, would help as well. However, this should be our last group meeting. In anticipation of their forces' arrival, the German diplomatic staff have been omnipresent in this compound." He looked sincerely irritated by that. "In future, my aide, Andreeson, is a good channel, and speaking to him precludes your having to request a formal interview or to sign the guest book. Also, Police Captain Voon is already apprised of our arrangement. A very quiet man, Voon." He cocked his head at George. "Has he become oppressive?"

George smiled. "I usually send him a sample of nice things I get in, a few bottles of wine now and then, and I remember his birthday. Nothing oppressive at all."

The president nodded and made his way out, pausing only to shake each of their hands. When he had gone, Ed shook his head. He knew George had to keep the president and the head cop happy, but what they seemed to take for everyday business, they'd call serious crime anywhere in the states, outside Chicago.

Before adjourning themselves, George needed to address their early warning system.

"I have part shares in a few fishing boats and do a lot of business with the radio telegraphy office. I can have boats out, offshore, with visual contact with each other, covering an arc that's likely to intercept the German freighter's course," he said, impressing Ed tremendously. "I can keep them out there for four days, and after that I'll have to rotate them in. They have rather primitive crew accommodations. We can get maybe a full day of notice. All my share boats have radios."

Ed was not so happy about his own communications. He would have one of George's trucks at the outlying mine, where one of his first "trainees," his old friend Bolagi, commanded the force. Once he got a message out there, Bolagi and George's driver, Otto Rabin, who also happened to be one of Adelmann's refugees (and therefore extremely motivated), could come in toward Paramaribo, gathering the force as it came. Weapons and explosives would, if Ysidro successfully executed Ed's plan, already be staged in town.

He resolved to see if the radios at the American embassy or the radio telegraphy office could reach the mine's radio. Considering the iron-bearing clay soils here, he wasn't altogether hopeful about that. Seaward communication was a lot easier, but the hills here tended to swallow radio waves. Ed thought ruefully that he might wind up doing Revere's ride himself, with the Chevy.

CHAPTER 31

OCTOBER 24, 1942
4:50 P.M.
GEORGE BUTLER'S STORE
PARAMARIBO, SURINAME

"Baas." Bolagi looked as stolid as ever, standing in the doorway of the store, the sunlight outside creating a luminous silhouette around his bulky, dark body. Road dust coated his uniform. Ed noted approvingly that the rifle Bolagi carried had recently been wiped down and gleamed with oil, and a Merry Widow had been placed around the muzzle. Suriname was home to wasps small enough to build mud nests in the bore of a 30-06, so it was always better not to take chances. He was also impressed at the speed with which the convoy had arrived. The drivers must have held their bladders and maintained leaden feet for the entire trek through the jungle. Ed had certainly trained his mine guardsmen well.

"All weapons in truck."

"How is our mother to be?"

"She good. Still big." He grinned, expansively miming just how big Inocente was with his hands.

Looming behind the black man was a beloved face. Ysidro slapped a hand on Bolagi's shoulder, amiably shifting him aside.

"*Hola, Coronel.*"

"*Hola, Sargente. Bolagi dice que no estas un padre aún?*" Ed said, using the familiar form of the verb to remark upon Ysidro's still-childless status—Ysidro and Inocente were family, after all.

"No, *Coronel*, but every bump on the road I thought I would be," Ysidro said, visibly relieved to have completed the trip. He and Ed exchanged brotherly hugs.

"Inocente in the truck bed?"

"*Si*," Ysidro nodded. "She is resting. With the mosquitos, the bumping, the heat ... I do not want to wake her. We have sweated enough to fill buckets."

"Speaking of which ... Bolagi!" Ed called over Ysidro's shoulder to the retreating figure in the doorway. "Would you please bring Inocente some cool compresses for her mosquito bites and a tall glass of water? Make sure she's got plenty of fresh air and shade back there." He pointed Bolagi to the small kitchen sink in the stockroom, where padding and blankets had been set out for the guardsmen to sleep on that night.

Bolagi nodded soberly and did as he was instructed. Ed pulled up a couple of chairs and motioned for Ysidro to take a load off.

"I'll take you both with me to the Butlers' home, where you'll be staying tonight, in a bit. But for now, come sit down, have some coffee, and I'll tell you about the situation we have here."

⧗

The next morning was slow at the clinic, to Sarah's great relief. It had seemed lately as if the whole of Paramaribo had taken ill this week, and she'd hardly had a moment of peace to herself in which to just *think*. She felt that the oppressive weight of what was to come required that she give it her undivided attention.

Since discovering the truth of the approaching Nazi ship, Sarah had been plunged again into the darkness that she had grown accustomed to a lifetime ago. It was as if no time had passed. Just when she had thought that freedom was theirs, and that the Nazis could be left behind like a bad nightmare, she saw now that this could never be the case. Their persecution was an incurable disease, a cancer, rotting away her insides and leaving her with a cold, crawling fear that was like a knife hollowing out her insides. All that she and her sister's family had built here, all the friends they had made, all their hopes for a happy future, all could be swept away. As if the loss of her dear husband could be made worse ... these potential losses could not be borne. She'd rather die. And she would fight to the death to prevent it. She would never go quietly.

It was her biggest regret—it had plagued her in the months after Michael had been taken—that she had not fought hard enough, not kicked and scratched and bitten, clawed those filthy Nazis' eyes out to keep her husband with her. Out of fear, she had cowered. No more of that. This new life, and the lives of her family and loved ones, would not slip away from her. She would fight the dirtiest of fights.

Thanks to Colonel Beltran's field training, she might just stand a chance. She warmed at the thought of him, his voice in her ear as he had coached her that day, the heat emanating from his chest as he stood behind her…

It was as if she had summoned him with her mind. The bell on the clinic door jingled and in stepped Ed Beltran himself, with a look in his eyes that told her it was likely that, at that moment, he had been having similar thoughts about her. Relief coursed through her veins at the sight of him.

"Colonel!" Sarah said, jumpy at having been startled out of her reverie. "Good morning! May I help you? The doctor is out, I'm afraid."

"It's okay," Ed said, sounding more serious and quiet than she had known him to be. *It must be even worse than I'd thought,* she realized. "I just wanted to, uh, keep you apprised of what's happening and check on you." His face looked abashed, and he looked at her to be sure he hadn't overstepped his bounds in admitting his errand.

"I am well, Colonel, thank you," Sarah said, bowing her head slightly to hide the blush rising in her cheeks. "But what news? What is happening?"

"It's a busy day. The Germans could arrive at any time now," he said gravely.

All the color drained from Sarah's face. "So soon?"

He nodded. "Yeah. George must put all his boats out to sea today to keep lookout. I have to fuel the Chevy, check the oil, and George has to send the driver and a truck back to the mine with Bolagi. Bolagi will need to set up radio watches, at all of the mines where I have people, on his way out."

"Have my family been told?" she asked.

"Not yet," he admitted. "I … came to see you first. But I'm headed there next. I want you all armed and ready. I want us all as ready as we can get. But if the president plays the delay game, we may not have to fight for days, if it all."

"You say you have men who will help us?"

"Yep, I have my old Marine buddy who just drove in from the jungle and several of the mine security guards that I've trained. I'm calling in all my favors. But the mines have a real problem with security, which is why they employ my men in their guard forces. I need to keep those fellows riding herd on their mines as long as I can. So we're already thin on the ground, with two of those guards holding down the fort at my ranch down south. I also have two engineers who are going to help; both work for Alcoa, and they need to be available to go to any of the mines on a day's notice. I can't call on the Marines at the embassy until the last minute, because they're helping on a totally quiet basis. Anyway, the timing's tricky here, but I think it'll work."

As he explained, his eyes were fixed on the desk between them, but he slowly approached her as he spoke. When he finished, he lifted his head and looked at her fully, letting his eyes meet hers. What he found there was defiance. He was impressed. She was readying herself for a fight. This was no shrinking violet that stood before him.

"If my arrangements work, I can put together a fighting force in less than six hours. I'll need Doc and George to help me with preparations today, so you'll be needed more than ever here."

"But I want to fight," she protested. "I am ready. This is my freedom, and that of my family's, and I want to protect it."

"I know, but you have skills the rest of us don't, and we need them," he assured her. "Now, I'll need to know whether there is a good supply of sterilized bandages on your shelves. I realize that neither you nor Dr. Adelmann has had much experience with gunshot wounds, except for that of our mutual friend," he paused, and they both chuckled as they remembered how they'd met over Azi's wounded body, "but he tells me he has to deal with blasting accidents at the mine sometimes, and that's close enough."

Her dark eyes grew even bigger. "You expect much wounding?"

"Hopefully not. If we have to fight, and I do it right, I'm hoping all the wounding will be on *their* side. But no battle plan lasts beyond the first shot. They always have to be changed to accommodate what actually happens and how the enemy actually responds."

She nodded in understanding. "I'll do anything I can to help. Our supply shelves are full. We are ready."

"Good," he said, with a small smile. And he saw in her face that she did indeed mean *anything*. "I must be on my way. But, um…" he began, stammering and shifting from foot to foot, "I would, at some point… Well, you see…"

"Yes?" she prompted, hoping she knew what the Colonel was getting at.

"Well, it's just, I wanted… Could we… you know… when this is all over, could we, well, get to know each other a bit?"

Sarah couldn't help but smile broadly at the big Marine's vulnerability. It gave her hope that this nightmare really *would* be over, and her spirits buoyed immediately. "Yes, I would like that very much," she said warmly. "Goodbye, Colonel, and good luck." He smiled, nodded, and turned to leave. Before he reached the door, she called, "Oh, and thank you, Colonel!"

"Ed. Please call me Ed." And with that he left, pulling the door gently closed behind him.

CHAPTER 32

ABOARD THE *KLEIN-SEYDITZ*, APPROXIMATELY 100 LEAGUES FROM THE COAST OF SURINAME

Captain Krager was livid. He put the microphone down with a crash, tore off the earphones, and slammed those down as well.

"*Gottverdammt* Surinamese want us anchored offshore, in international waters. I am not even sure I can find bottom with my anchor that far out, and that leaves us exposed to any passing ship!"

Gunter asked, carefully, because Krager was obviously in a rage, "What reason do they give?"

"They say that they are a neutral country, of course, and bringing troops to their shore is a violation of international law. They say they know we have troops on board." He looked accusingly at Gunter, who braced himself.

So much for sneaking out of port during darkness, Gunter thought, fuming as he remembered the enforced wait and the liberties his men had been given, which had undoubtedly allowed this intelligence to reach the enemy. And they would share it. Anything to put a thumb in Germany's eye.

"So we are not approaching unexpectedly," Gunter said, trying hard to appear unruffled. "Of course they say this, but, as you know, the position of the Reich is that because we have conquered Holland, and Suriname is a possession of Holland, *we* are sovereign here. They are not an independent country. Also, of course, this argument has been going on ever since we occupied Holland." He pondered and asked, "What is to keep you from just going ashore in any case?"

Krager looked at him as though he were an idiot. "*Only* a couple of little gunboats, really American PT boats, bought from them, complete with machine guns, side-slung *torpedoes*, and room on board each for a dozen soldiers. They could put us on the bottom in a matter of minutes."

"If we do not stop, how soon could we reach port?"

"Late tonight. But, Oberst Kramer, I would not approach that coast during darkness any more than I would pet a shark. So, tomorrow after sunrise it shall be."

"If you please, Captain, try and raise the German Embassy in Paramaribo." Gunter reached into his pocket and produced a slip of paper. "Here is the frequency Herr Goebbels provided. Perhaps the diplomats can bring us in. What is our fuel situation?"

If it were possible, Krager looked even angrier now. "Insufficient to return to any port in Europe! We would have to divert into the Caribbean, where fuel supplies are very irregular, or down the coast to one of Brazil's larger ports. And my *verdammt* cargoes are all bound for Suriname, which is why we were asked to carry *you*!" His face was alternately red and patchy white with rage.

"I will wait in my cabin, Herr Captain. Please call for me if you make contact with the embassy. *Danke*."

Gunter felt the skin on the back of his neck tense as he exited the hatchway from the bridge.

The voice through the earphones was polished despite the static that distorted it. "We will make a presentation to the government of Suriname that you be allowed to come ashore and negotiate cooperative police efforts to recover these *Juden* criminals. In the meantime, please stand by outside Surinamese territorial water. That is generally accepted to be three miles, three British nautical miles, offshore. Do you understand, Oberst?"

"*Jawohl*, Herr Ambassador," Gunter said. "Can you tell us approximately how long this process will take? The captain and Krieger Marine are incurring considerable expense at this delay." The captain stood, a clenched knot of anger uncoiling itself, listening as best he could to the incoming voice spilling from the earphones. Gunter's reference did nothing to alleviate his tension.

"Today has been declared a governmental holiday, because the government offices suddenly required fumigation," replied the voice. "Therefore, it will be 24 hours before we can make your presentation to them."

The polished voice over the radio managed to be both dryly amused and precise. Gunter squeezed his eyes shut. There was nothing to be done; he must request of the captain that they remain out here and expend his diminishing fuel for at least another day, with no certainty that there would be a resolution to the situation.

When the call had ended, his ears still ringing and his cheeks flushed from as categorical a dressing down as he had ever received, Gunter paced the deck, pausing to examine the lashings on his truck and motorcycle pool. Kucher was there, gently tuning his pet motorcycle.

"Good to see you, youngster. Can this thing fit in the big lifeboat slung behind the bridge?"

"I… I don't know, Herr Oberst."

"Do some measuring and find out. It may be necessary for me to go ashore and do some talking before we can debark, and I do not want to be on foot."

"Would *you* take the cycle, Herr Oberst?" He looked apprehensive at the thought of his lovingly cared-for device in anyone's hands but his own.

Gunter snorted. "I would wind up on the back of my head. I have never had a chance to play with one of these." He tried fitting himself into the sidecar, discovering that with his height, his knees would end up around his ears—not the most dignified of postures for an officer making presentations in a moderately hostile country.

He caught Kucher smothering a grin in the greasy sleeve of his coveralls. He grinned back. "It might be more dignified if I simply walk and die of sweating in this humidity."

"Sometimes, Herr Oberst, when we are moving slowly, the passenger can sit up on the back rim of the sidecar, and that would put you up higher and look much more dignified. If there are no big bumps."

Gunter tried that posture and it was certainly a more dignified one. "I must trust you to avoid the big bumps and not drop me in a mud puddle on a diplomatic trip."

He left the young messenger chuckling and returned to his cabin, not daring to go to the bridge and perhaps receive even more of a lashing from the infuriated captain.

This whole mission was turning out to be what he'd once heard an American soldier call, "a cluster-fuck." He chuckled and shook his head, trying to determine whether or not he even cared.

⧗

Their next communication from the shore, late on the following day, was from the German Embassy, informing Gunter that a presentation had been submitted to the Surinamese government regarding "a representative having a joint police meeting."

They were barely making headway on a frequently reversed course, at right angles to their former route. While the seas were calm, the swells were large enough that they had to maintain headway to avoid being turned sideways and potentially broached. The captain constantly emanated rage. Still, there was hot food and coffee, and it was possible to exercise on deck.

The men's morale remained high. And while the captain was livid, the crew, not privy to fueling costs and potentially blocked cargoes, maintained an attitude of friendly cooperation.

Two days later, another call was placed to shore: "Herr Ambassador, the fuel situation with this ship is approaching critical. It is absolutely necessary that the *Klein-Seydity* be allowed to at least anchor close to shore. If an extended storm catches us out here, we could be in peril of losing power as we seek a place to refuel or even to weather the storm. If, after we anchor, the Surinamese government would permit me to present my papers and our government's position regarding these *Juden* criminals, I could make a landing with a small boat and come alone for discussion."

The returning voice, though still suave and polite, held a hint of irritation. "Herr Oberst, it is the task of the *diplomatic corps* to explain our government's position. However, we will request that, for humanitarian reasons, your vessel be allowed to anchor inshore and that you yourself be permitted to come ashore for discussion."

Gunter was finding it hard to conceal his own irritation. Despite fervently wishing, a few short weeks ago, to extend this trip as long as possible, he could now think of nothing but stepping foot off this damned ship. "Herr Ambassador, that would be greatly appreciated. Reichsminister Goebbels is very concerned with this mission." Gunter was sure that the mention of Goebbels might provoke fear and stir the embassy on his behalf.

"Herr Oberst, we will move as fast as we can and get back to you immediately when we have an answer."

"*Danke.* Out." The captain did not even bother to turn around from the window, and Gunter exited quietly.

⧗

Another two days passed, and it was November when Gunter finally received a call from the embassy. "We have achieved permission for you to anchor inside Paramaribo Harbor, where one of the Surinamese naval vessels will indicate your moorage place. Do you have a landing vessel?"

"There is a large lifeboat with apparatus for lowering it," Gunter replied, his spirits lifting. He was no sick of the sight of the *Klein-Seyditz.* "It has both oars and an outboard motor. I must ask the captain's permission to employ it." Across the bridge, the captain locked eyes with Gunter, nodded emphatically, his lips tight, and then looked back intently at the fuel gauge on his console. It was indeed a miracle—and a true demonstration of the captain's genius at fuel management—that the ship had held on this long without refueling.

"He has granted that permission, Herr Ambassador. Can you send a car to the dock to fetch me and carry me to the embassy? I can bring ashore a motorcycle and driver to provide my own transportation if that is impossible."

"At this time we have only permission for one person to come ashore. The government here is, at this time, very resentful of an armed party being sent without its express permission. Of course, we hold legal sovereignty over them, but that situation has not yet penetrated their thinking, and we are reluctant to precipitate a conflict."

"*Jawohl!* I am eagerly looking forward to making your acquaintance in person, Herr Ambassador. Kramer out."

Without speaking, the captain strode to the wheel, moved the seaman there out of the way with one hand, and spun it to change course for the harbor of Paramaribo.

"Kucher!" Gunter called to the young man who stood nearby, "the embassy is sending a car to pick me up, so we won't be able to practice that bit of mechanical acrobatics after all." The boy looked vaguely disappointed. He felt for the young man who, along with many of the young seamen on board, had never been anywhere outside Western Europe and were eager to see the tropics.

"Men, I will attempt to get us all ashore as soon as possible," Gunter called to those nearby. "The government here does not realize as yet that they are under German legal control. Our task is not to teach them that reality but to capture one specific criminal. And, of course, any who accompany him and who may have been accomplices in his crimes against the Reich."

Later that afternoon, Gunter was leaning against the outside bulkhead of the bridge, exulting in the benevolent radiation of the sun and in being out of range of the malevolent radiation of Krager, when he heard Kucher and one of the troopers from his unit talking. The boys were huddled against a tarp that shielded a deck-lashed pile of cargo, and Gunter realized that they had no idea that their conversation echoed up to the deck. He'd noticed that everyone still seemed to be shouting, although now the engines were silent, and the sea no longer pulsed along the hull.

"Wish we could just go ashore, find jobs, and forget this *verdammt Juden* chasing."

"*Jawohl*, it is like being recruited by the devil to pitchfork souls into hell."

"Do you think the oberst *believes* that the Reich owns this country, this Suriname?"

"He is a good officer, and he takes care of us, but who can know what an officer believes?"

"This is true; they say what the Reich tells them to say. But Oberst Kramer is better than most."

"Even so, he says what the Reich tells him to say. I carried the message that told him his wife and daughter were sick. I found out later from the feldwebel at the radio telegraphy office in Amsterdam that command denied him permission to visit them before they died. What do you think he really thinks of the Reich?"

"Who can know?"

Gunter ducked into his cabin, avoiding any possibility of acknowledging that he had heard the conversation. And, in any case, the tears flooding his face precluded his ability to chew out his troops for unnecessary and inappropriate conversation. He wasn't all that angry, anyway. In fact, it was of some comfort that someone else knew.

Gunter's tears seemed to be drawn from a well of infinite depth. The pain and loss were unending. And now faces from railway sidings and brutally filthy railcars were superimposed over the beloved visages of his wife and daughter. He remembered the frilly pink letter and envelope in his message pouch.

When he had finally composed himself, he placed the call. "Herr Ambassador, I will be at the dock in one half hour."

"*Jawohl*, our limousine will be there to pick you up. Be aware that there will be representatives of the Paramaribo police force and the Surinamese army there to greet you."

Could it be that he himself posed the threat of an entire army to this tiny country?

Fully twenty of the army were there, with medals, trumpets, bannered staffs, and white-gloved officers saluting. The police were less flamboyant, but at least a dozen of them stood ready to deal with any unlawfulness, arrayed in front of their U.S.-built jeeps.

Gunter stumbled only slightly as he topped the dock ladder and returned the salutes, with the Wehrmacht salute, not the one preferred by the Führer. He felt like an absolute ass, centered in this mass of attention.

"Herr Oberst, the Ambassador has sent me to see you to the embassy." Gunter turned to the voice and saw, wearing the plainest of Wehrmacht uniforms, a fresh-faced youngster standing by a weathered Mercedes, holding the rear door open.

"*Danke*. How far is it?"

"Just about one half of a kilometer, Herr Oberst." He shut the door percussively on Gunter, then circled the vehicle to get behind the wheel.

There was an authoritative knock on the roof. The driver rolled down the window for the police offer standing there who, ridiculously, bore three stars on his collar. His stolid Dutch face was unbending in its sincerity.

"German officer, we see you are bearing arms on our soil. Is this deliberate provocation of our sovereignty?"

"My sidearm is part of my uniform. Note that our embassy guards are armed." His response was off the cuff. Never had he expected a challenge to an officer's sidearm.

"Nonetheless, their arms are on German sovereign territory, your embassy. Please surrender your sidearm until you are on German sovereign territory." He held out his hand, obviously expecting surrender of Gunter's pistol.

Gunter snapped to the driver, "Drive to the embassy, now!"

The Mercedes managed only an abortive move forward, when one of the Jeeps of the police contingent drove across its path. There was an ominous lowering of shoulder weapons about them.

The police officer returned to the window of the Mercedes. "Mijnheer, your pistol. Now."

Gunter extracted his pistol slowly and put it in the officer's hand, like dropping a turd into a cesspool, his face frozen with affront.

There was a police jeep in front of them the entire way to the embassy, and the speed was kept very low. This was adults chastening children.

Gunter emerged, unfolding his length from the depths of the leather-clad interior of the limousine, only to find the same officer in front of him, holding out his pistol, face unperturbed. "Here, Mijnheer, is your sidearm. Be careful not to carry it onto Surinamese soil again." He did not allow Gunter response time but pivoted on his heel and returned to the Jeep that had borne him.

Gunter felt his neck and ears flame. This was beyond endurance. But, surrounded by overwhelming force and alone, he could at best maintain dignity and retreat within the German embassy. The Swastika banner across its front was reassurance of normalcy, until he noticed the stains of thrown tomatoes and dung across its surface.

He checked his pistol for load and completeness before he holstered it. After all, he might want to shoot someone here.

CHAPTER 33

NOVEMBER 1, 1942
5:20 P.M.

PARAMARIBO, SURINAME

Ed peered through his binoculars at the dock. *Yep, there he is,* Ed thought, recognizing Kramer immediately. It was the scar that gave the oberst away. Kramer's face looked gaunt, his form was lean to the point of boniness, and his movements were deliberate, as if they cost effort. Still, his stride had the same power Ed remembered from years ago.

As the encounter on the dock proceeded, Ed chuckled. They were doing the whole nine yards on the German, showing up with more people than the Nazis had on board to greet just one man. They were armed to the teeth, and unless the Kraut could get his troops and any heavy weapons onto land, they had him pinned like a butterfly.

That was emphasized by the PT gunboats that bracketed the German freighter, aimed inward toward it. While anchored themselves, their mooring ropes held buoys, indicating that they could drop their anchor rigs and power up immediately without losing their ground tackle. These Nazis were stuck between a rock and a hard place. Ed felt it might even be overkill. The very pointed naval standoff was startling. He had not expected such a direct threat from the president; he had expected the action to primarily consist of note passing and obfuscation. *The little man has bigger balls than I thought,* Ed thought, and couldn't help but smile.

Ed lay in the loft of a warehouse just fifty yards off the dock road. From the shadows here, his lenses would not glint and warn the Germans of the observation. Earlier, from a spot nearer their mooring, he had used the spotting scope he kept at George's for those times he trained shooters here. Even five hundred yards away, he had been able to distinguish figures and weapons clearly with the tripod-mounted scope. So now he had a count of German troops, though still no idea of their equipment, except that he had made out two slung MG 42s in the formation that had seen their commander off on his trip to the dock. Wanting to get to this observation point before the German officer did had precluded any more detailed analysis of the unit. He figured the ship to hold twenty-one or twenty-two men, with a senior sergeant of some kind, and, with the exception of the noncom, they all wore standard Wermacht gear.

Ed was puffing a bit from the quick drive up and through town to this location and the scramble to get into the loft. Sweat prickled under his shirt. Since arriving in town a little less than a month ago, his exercise regimen had taken a backseat to strategic planning, and he was feeling a little soft around the middle.

Not that he had been taking it easy. There was plenty of work to be done. In the weeks since learning of the Nazis' approach, Ed had guided Sarah, Jacob, and Amos in target practice nearly every afternoon. He had come to feel confident in their ability to stand their ground and even, potentially, give a German soldier pause in an attack, which was all that mattered.

He had briefed Jacob, Ysidro, and Bolagi, as well as Captain Hodgins, on everything he knew about Oberst Kramer—his ambition, his cold and calculating manner that Ed had observed in him during the war. Working under advisement from George Butler and Dr. Adelmann, Ed devised a strategic plan for communications with each member of his Surinamese "force," and this small but mighty team had run through it repeatedly in recent days, perfecting their signals and codes and ensuring that all radios were in top working order. No one would move in the coming days without these few men knowing about it.

As the days wore on, heightening the anticipation and stress for the Roseweigs—he had learned from Sarah that Rebecca was actually suffering panic attacks—Ed grew more appreciative of the president. The man had made good on his promise to hold off the Nazis for far longer than had been expected. Though the tension could have been cut with a knife, Ed for one was glad for the extra time, and, with each day, he felt more confident about the possibility that, if everyone executed their parts in the plan as assigned, this would all soon be just a memory—one that might even induce laughter at some point in the near future.

The only source of real stress for Ed as time wore on was Ysidro, particularly with regard to Inocente's burgeoning belly, which threatened to pop open at any moment. At least her unusually large size was no longer a mystery. Dr. Adelmann had come out of the examination room the afternoon after they had arrived, grinning and slinging his stethoscope around his neck as he explained that he had heard not one but *two* heartbeats in there. Inocente, who had a new bed in a newly rented house, had been given strict instructions for bed rest until she delivered her twins, and Ysidro feared that his leaving might provoke early labor. If her husband had tended to hover before, his hovering only doubled when he learned there would be two babies. He was driving her crazy, so she often sent him on errands to split firewood or to retrieve foods or spices from George's store. She insisted, and Adelmann had seconded it, that it was merely a short walk to the clinic when it was time to deliver, and her good health had assured the doctor that this would be safe. In fact, she seemed fearless in contrast to her husband, who was just a bundle of nerves.

Thankfully, Sarah had been at the clinic on the day they had learned of the news and had become fast friends with Inocente during the exam. Anxious to be of use, she had suggested a plan that Ed had thought genius: The three Roseweig women would rotate shifts at Inocente's bedside while Ysidro was gone during the day, training with Ed. They attended to her needs, brought her delicious foods, and, in return, Inocente even taught them a little bit of Spanish. It also seemed that the distraction of these visits helped to ease Rebecca's anxiety a bit, had given her purpose, and, as she shared her mothering wisdom with Inocente, even provided a bit of needed therapy. All three had begun to think of Inocente as a dear friend, and Hannah had made sure to tell the mother to be that she would volunteer her babysitting services happily.

As Ed lay quietly, observing the welcome being given to the Nazis, he grinned smugly, deeply satisfied with how well everything was working out.

CHAPTER 34

PARAMARIBO, SURINAME

Hannah felt shaky but braced herself against the counter with her hands and summoned a smile to mask her fear. The young man who swung aside the screen door to enter the general store was not threatening. His gray trousers and white shirt were clean and pressed, his smile automatic and friendly. The other less-handsome but equally neat young man who entered behind him smiled at her as well.

Amos had raced ahead minutes earlier to warn her, Papa, and George of the two Germans' approach and then just as quickly ducked out the back door through the office to run home to his mother.

Only the knowledge that they needed every bit of information they could gather was what kept Hannah from fleeing. Amos had proven an excellent, even somewhat ghost-like spy, watching the docks for hours during the day and then darting, absolutely unseen, to share his intelligence with Ed, Ysidro, Dr. Adelmann, and George. Also, knowing both Papa and George Butler were standing in the back, in the bakery's kitchen and with axe handles in hand, lent a certain reduction of fear. Remembering dear, brave Alexandra and how she had dealt with the military police that terrifying night at the dock in Amsterdam gave her guidance and inspiration now.

She wiggled her shoulders, letting the wide top of her blouse down another bit, and tried to pretend this was just a handsome young man and not a Nazi. *Mutter would be very angry to know I took out her stitching*, she thought. She cringed to think that her father might see this display, forgetting herself and the situation at hand momentarily as she made room for this teenage dilemma. But hearing the officers speaking in German immediately brought her back to the present.

She was *not* to let them know she spoke German. It was the native Taki Taki or her small stock of Dutch, but absolutely no German. The idea was to gather information on the Germans, never letting on that she understood a word, never giving these wolves the slightest inkling that here, right in front of them, was their prey!

"Mijnheeren?" Hannah prompted, batting her eyelashes.

The men (boys, really, she thought, as she now saw up close that neither could be as old as twenty) were transfixed by the smells of the place. They grinned, chins up and smiling as they inhaled ecstatically.

"*Guten morgen, Fraulein.* How much is the… do I smell *apfelstrudel?*" The handsome man's eyes flicked over her blouse, with a different kind of hunger—better suppressed but almost equally obvious.

In Dutch, cocking her head as if she did not fully understand him, she asked, "You want *apfelstrudel?*" and gestured to the large pan in the glass display case.

"*Jawohl!*" came the duet, along with enthusiastic nods. Both boys licked lips, obviously on the point of drooling.

Hannah dished two generous servings on to small white plates, drizzled vanilla sauce over the tops, placed a small fork on each plate, and came around the end of the counter to place them on one of the small tables next the front window. The lead boy had bills in his hand, obviously expecting to pay up front for his treat, and Hannah gestured to the carafe that sat on the counter. "*Kaf?*"

"*Danke,*" they again chorused, with nods. Hannah filled mugs of the same heavy white china, then placed those on a tray with a little pitcher of cream, a covered sugar bowl with its own spoon, and two additional spoons, and carried it to the table. She smiled and curtsied slightly. The boy proffered money again.

Hannah made her smile friendly, though the Germans' closeness was causing her throat to close. Behind them, in the kitchen door, she saw George's face for a moment, offering her an encouraging smile. She shook her head slightly, and, still in Dutch, replied, "Mijnheeren, pay when you have finished. Now, eat, drink, and enjoy."

They were concentrating to catch the Dutch but sat, grinning and watching this pretty young woman, and then seized their forks.

Hannah busied herself cleaning counters, buffing glass, restocking the displays. This was early afternoon, and she noted as she cleaned that the rush of lunch customers had seriously depleted the offerings.

Need to put out the breads for the men going home after work and the morning pastries for their homes... Hannah thought automatically. For a moment, there, she had forgotten she was just then sharing the room with two of the terrible Nazis who had chased her little brother and Sarah's husband, and who knew how many others, to their deaths. She set her face in a smile and hustled out with the carafe to offer refills, wishing fervently that she could pour poison into their cups.

With their appetites dealt with (already both plates were empty), both youngsters leaned back, sipping and chatting, looking appreciatively at their waitress. They were very like many other men who came here, she realized. But these men did not make Hannah appreciate her growing attractiveness—only to realize that it was a useful weapon.

In German, the better-looking boy, whom she'd gathered was called Kucher, offered a compliment quietly to his companion, and Hannah fought the instinct to raise her head at her native tongue. "This is as good as any apple strudel I have ever had at home. *Gut!*"

It had better be, Hannah thought as she listened. *My mother is as good as any cook in Germany, if not better.* It felt a sort of betrayal to share her mother's talents with these men. *All for the greater good,* she reminded herself.

She had stopped moving for a moment and realized that she might appear suspect if she didn't continue her charade. She approached the table and asked, "May I interest you in some sweets for the upcoming Diwali celebration?" She opted to use pidgin now, feeling sure that it was least likely to be noted as false by these men. Both Germans stared at her, dumbfounded, clearly not having heard the language before. It had been the right choice.

"*Wie bitte?*" the formerly quiet man asked, begging her pardon.

Bringing a bowl from behind the counter, she mimed putting named items in it. "Dutch. English. Hindi. Urdu." Then, using the spoon from their sugar bowl, she stirred, and then, pointing at the imaginary mix. "Taki Taki."

They grinned ecstatically, enjoying both her and her illustration.

For several minutes, the three made a hilarious language lesson, interspersed with slurps of coffee and spoons of the sweet fruit cobbler and crisp strips of crust—they had asked for seconds, passing on the offer of traditional sweets for the approaching Hindu holiday. The Germans kept her talking, flirting with her by asking strategically for translations of such words as blouse, skin, hair, or skirt, and obviously appreciating the lesson. The flirting was just male reflex, she knew, but she felt violated all the same, despite the bright smile on her face.

George had been open about that. He'd spoken to all of the Roseweigs before he'd recommended the bakery to the German officer. In the kitchen of the new home Rebecca was furbishing with such pride, he had sat on a reversed kitchen chair, big hands folded over each other. Colonel Beltran had leaned against the wall, having declined Amos' offer of his chair. The Roseweig house was not yet fully furnished. None of the chairs matched, and the table bore oilcloth, not the linen Hannah knew her mother would have spread upon it in Germany.

"The American protests have enabled the local government to stave off the Germans, keeping them unable to get their vehicles and weapons ashore with their men. But the Germans can make trouble in Holland for Suriname, which we cannot afford. The president can be stubborn, but sooner or later, if the Germans persist, they will be ashore, armed, and doing the evil they were sent to do."

He bowed his head to his hands for a moment.

"Ed, er, Colonel Beltran," George corrected himself, "has some ideas for what he calls 'intelligence gathering,' and which I call eavesdropping and sneakiness." He grinned at his friend.

The colonel grinned his own tight grin and put it simply. "All of you understand German. We have the German troopers ashore, and they will want food, coffee, drinks, things from the store, when they have liberty." He looked carefully into Jacob's eyes, and, when met with an understanding though reluctant nod, his eyes moved to Hannah's. "If one of you is in place to hear them talk with each other, we can learn some important things. Hannah, I believe your delicious German pastries would make irresistible bait." She, too, nodded in understanding.

Rebecca, who was still a bit stiff with the American colonel who seemed to keep bringing trouble wherever he went, spoke up. "And what is important enough to risk exposing our people, our *family,* to these horrid creatures?"

"We know how many Germans there are. We know their ranks and names from their disembarking records. We *need* to know which ones are drivers, which ones are machine gunners, and if any of them have any combat experience. Also, we need to know what extra weapons, what heavy weapons, and how much ammunition they have."

The expression on Rebecca's face was scathing. "That kind of question could cost me another child! No. We will do no such thing."

Jacob raised a placatory hand. "Hear him out, Rebecca, my love. I'm sure the colonel is not asking any of us to take big risks."

Sarah too, smiling, put a hand on her sister's arm, soothingly. She looked up to Ed admiringly, and the glance between them was, at least to Hannah, obviously sweet and affectionate.

Ed, catching himself, rearranged his face into solemnity and nodded. Ed proceeded cautiously, knowing the best way to win Sarah's respect was to earn that of her family. "All due respect, Ma'am, I don't think you're following me. I don't want *anyone* to ask *any* questions. The plan won't work that way. I don't even want anyone to *talk* to these men in their own language. I just want people in place who can understand them, to listen."

George spoke up again. "Apparently, most of the Germans have taken opportunities to visit the houses where women act as ..." he glanced around the room, "temporary wives for money."

He then flushed, looking aside at Rebecca's somewhat indignant glare at bringing this subject up in front of her children. Hannah fought to conceal a giggle and looked at her brother, whose eyes were on his shoes. As Jacob had become aware of these places, he had sternly pointed them out to his children with caution, instructing them not to go near them. But Hannah not only knew exactly what went on in these houses, she'd lately seen her brother trying to peer into their windows.

George nodded apologetically. "Just want to make the point that girls and women are probably not at risk around these men in the course of one of their liberty periods. They have . . . relief for their impulses. "

"Even so, Herr Butler, I do not want my Hannah alone with those terrible men."

And, so, as Hannah played host to two Nazi soldiers, Jacob and George stood in the kitchen with axe handles.

There was astonishment as Hannah remembered how much she, too, had wanted the security of armed guards. She was feeling quite smug now as she bantered pleasantly with them, and felt sure she could toy with them for hours if she liked. She had even sold them more pastries for the road, which they would bring back to their oberst, whom, they explained, was currently unable to roam the town but, they insisted, was a "good officer." In any case, it seemed clear that Kucher, a motorcycle messenger, liked him and thought it was a shame he couldn't relax a bit, since having lost his family so recently.

Indeed, their bill was a nice one, and the handsome Kucher pressed a tip into her hand, gently, as they left. As the door shut behind them, she smiled to herself. She was a spy, and a successful one at that!

She darted into the kitchen, excited, to find George Butler and her father up on stools, axe handles laid aside, munching pilfered jelly rolls.

Hannah put her fists on her hips in pretend outrage. "And how long have my *guards* been loafing?"

George coughed as crumbs went down the wrong pipe from his chuckling. Papa swallowed carefully before he waved a hand in the air. "Since my *innocent* little girl reeled those boys in, netted them, and laid them out in the market!" He looked at his growing daughter speculatively as a blush began creeping into her cheeks. "How many *other* boys are spending too much on pastry since you started working here?"

Hannah's blush became full when George, still coughing a bit, said appreciatively, "Recall, Jacob, that sales for this establishment have risen thirty percent in the last month."

Hannah stared at her father, noting that the look on his face didn't exactly appear disapproving.

Jacob snorted. "I had not realized that the increase was due to my *daughter.*"

"Her pay will reflect that after this next month, Jacob," George said, arms spread in a gesture of openness. "Fair pay for good work." George rose, dusting his hands, and said to Hannah, "Lock up for an hour and come over to the clinic with us. Colonel Beltran said he wants to personally 'debrief' everyone who has overheard anything from the Germans."

Oh, yes, the colonel. The most experienced fighter among us was curiously absent, Hannah thought. "Why wasn't *he* here?" she asked aloud.

George looked solemn for a moment. "He was. In a vacant house a hundred yards from here. With his rifle. He was poised and ready to kill those Germans on the spot if they realized who you were and seized you."

"Oh," Hannah replied, contrite. "Papa, did you know that?"

"Sarah told me. Apparently, she had offered to stand out there herself with a rifle, but Ed had assured her that it would not be necessary." Papa smiled.

⧗

Jacob's heart felt as though it were in his mouth. The immense noncom stood just one counter away in the store, browsing through boxes of cigars and seeming to be in no hurry to finish, sniffing with the occasional hum of appreciation. The man was built like a big icebox, all one width from his wide shoulders through his hips. Now he knew how Hannah must have felt every time the German beasts stepped into the store.

Jacob bent to stock the shelves of towels and washcloths, keeping his face averted from the oberfeldwebel and waiting until the man approached one of the other soldiers in the store before selecting his next task, in order to position himself closely enough to listen to any conversation they might have.

They were buying polish for their boots, soap, Cuban cigars, and pre-rolled cigarettes, showing a preference for the American brands Lucky Strike and Camels.

"Oberfeldwebel, should we buy some oil for the weapons? All they have on board is engine lubrication, and I see some American three-in-one here."

"Buy three of those larger cans, but go on using the engine oil. In fact, swab some grease through the bores of everything while they're still on board. That sea air would destroy any barrel ever drilled. Note the price, Kleinhoffer. The oberst will make it up from petty cash."

"Any idea when we can get them ashore, Oberfeldwebel?"

"They are going to bring the *Klein-Seyditz* to dock for unloading in a day or two, and we will be putting guards on board so the dock workers don't walk off with all of our ammunition and grenades."

"And the guards will be the drivers?" the man asked, in a sly, lowered voice.

"You figure it out, Kleinhoffer. You're the clever one." In point of fact, the noncom sounded approving of the trooper's perception.

"But when we do get them ashore, we need to clean all the weapons immediately, first with diesel fuel to cut the grease, and then with good gun cleaner, before we oil them. Buy three big cans of that Hoppe's number nine over there, too."

Jacob knew that what he'd overheard was terribly important and became desperate to share the information with George and Ed. He hoped they would be able to talk to the police to block this. None of them knew yet which ones were the drivers, with the exception of the motorcycle boy, Kucher, who seemed to spend all of his money at the bakery, chatting up Hannah.

While they had been conducting this eavesdropping surveillance of the Germans over the past couple of days, others had come up with bits and pieces of information. This very tactic, of putting drivers on board as guards and seizing some opportune moment to speed the military vehicles and their cargoes onto shore to arm the German troops already there, had been anticipated by Ed and Ysidro and discussed by all. Jacob was pleased and surprised to find that so much had been accurately anticipated.

Jacob shouldered a pile of towels, and, keeping his burden between his face and the Germans' (eerily recalling his trek through the slushy streets of Amsterdam), made his way to the back room. Though he silently credited the colonel for suggesting that Jacob employ these subversive methods, he also wished that he would never need them.

There were two clerks working in the store, one in the front, behind the counter, and another just reentering the back room from a visit to the jakes. He approached the latter clerk as he walked past.

"I am going to George's house to talk to him. It might be better if both you and the other clerk stayed in the front room while the Germans are here. No Dutch. Just Taki Taki."

"All right, we will. When they buy things for their friends in the barracks, or for their unit, they always want receipts to show cost. That takes a little longer."

George employed no one that he did not trust completely. And, most often, transactions in the store were unrecorded. As far as Jacob had been able to tell, clerk theft was nonexistent. On a few occasions, some of the poorer public had apparently shoplifted items, but that was much more a rarity—as Jacob had learned from his friends who had operated shops in Germany—than it had been in Europe.

Jacob stepped quietly and quickly out the back door of the store and began running at top speed toward the Butlers' house. *I am no athlete,* Jacob thought wryly, *so why is it I keep finding myself clinging to cargo nets, staggering across tossing decks, and running in jungle heat?*

George was not at home. Jacob leaned in the doorway, gasping, his sodden shirt clinging to his pale skin, and Lijsbet insisted he drink some iced water before he made his way to the café, where George was meeting his truckers.

By the time he reached the café, Jacob had done the better part of an English mile and his knees were wobbling, he was seeing spots in his vision, and his breath came in great gasps that seemed to give him no strength. George saw him coming through the window by his usual table, and was outside instantly, a big glass of wine extended helpfully. Though it wasn't exactly refreshing to his thirst, Jacob gulped the rich stuff anyway, surprisingly feeling the alcohol he rarely drank lend him instant energy.

"They are going to use the trick of putting drivers on board as guards, just the way we thought they might!" Jacob said between heaves and pants. "And we don't know any of the drivers' names."

George was grimly disgusted. "Jacob, sit in the shade here, and then I will drive you to the clinic, where Ed and Sarah and the doctor are this afternoon."

George ducked back into the café, reemerging immediately with a huge beer mug of water, which he placed beside Jacob on the bench before returning to his meeting. As Jacob gulped the mug of water in just a few swallows, he felt grateful, yet again, that he worked for such a thoughtful, kind man. George had been helping the family, without keeping account, for weeks. But Jacob, by instinct, had kept count—of every expenditure, every gallon of fuel, and all the other ways great and small in which he and his lovely wife had helped his family. He would see to it that George was repaid, once this infestation of vultures had finally passed.

The meeting at the clinic went very much as Jacob had expected. No one had any more intelligence about the identity of the German drivers. Unexpectedly, Ben Adelmann and Sarah looked at each other and began smiling broadly. She had been clued in on this plan the day before and was positively brimming with enthusiasm, not only with the plan itself but also with having been included in it.

George, Ed, and Jacob looked at them, bewildered.

Dr. Adelmann hooked his thumb over his shoulder in an American gesture he had recently adopted from the colonel. "It seems that our German visitors sometimes forget their quinine. I have two of them, delivered this morning by Surinamese Army Jeep, with fevers, terrible headaches, and all of the other symptoms of severe malaria. I am administering quinine, of course, but one of them is delirious, and, with a little bit of ethanol added to their next injections, both of them can be. And we have," he gestured at himself and Sarah and Jacob, "three fluent speakers of their native language to question them as long as we have to. "

Colonel Beltran actually applauded; Jacob, if he had not been on the edge of exhaustion, would have done so, too.

"Bet they'll have worse headaches when they wake up!" The colonel looked not at all sympathetic.

"No, they won't, because I will over-hydrate them a bit afterwards. I have sworn an oath and cannot harm someone under my care." Adelmann's face was set adamantly into stone. "But," he brightened a bit, I have some medicine called sodium pentothal. I had planned to try it on the Villers' daughter the next time she has an episode of mania. Some practitioners have been reporting successes."

The doctor was met by confused expressions. "I can use a bit of it on one of the Germans. It is called 'the tongue-loosening medicine.'"

Sarah went with him, bearing a tray of apparatus. On the way, Adelmann paused at the big icebox and took from it a tiny vial. He looked grim.

Sarah knew that perhaps this came close to the very edges of the doctor's oath. But if it worked, it would save many lives—lives that were far more deserving of continuing than those of the Nazi butchers.

At that moment, she looked to Jacob and was astonished to find him sound asleep.

"Turn this. Look through here. Do *not* touch the glass." Ed blew breath on the lens of the tripod-mounted telescope and used a clean, years-softened handkerchief to gently wipe it. Azi watched, entranced. It took fifteen minutes with Ed's reluctantly expanding Taki Taki vocabulary, Azi's minuscule English, some wild gestures, and drawing in the sand to give Azi his assignment: to watch the *Klein-Seyditz*, and if he spied Gunter Kramer coming ashore, make haste to the store and let Ed or George know. Decent treatment of the currently irreplaceable scope was of critical importance.

Ed left the boy in a clump of tall grasses, deep in shade, and left a water bottle, a loaf of bread, and a big sausage for him as well. Since recovering from his infection and being introduced to regular meals, it seemed Azi was eating nonstop. Obviously in a growth spurt that might never have happened on the protein-poor diet he had grown up on so far, he'd gained almost an inch in height and at least ten pounds in the past month. Ed, Dr. Adelmann, and Sarah had taken to just putting food in front of him and watching in amazement, as if he were some sort of caged animal. Sarah had been teaching him table manners and the myriad courtesies and behaviors the boy was lacking, as he recovered, first in the clinic bed and then as he returned daily to be put through the rigors of Ed's security training. Ed had no idea where the boy had been staying—he suspected the boy was sleeping outdoors someplace—but each day he arrived at the clinic, first thing in the morning, for training.

Using table tools barely slowed the kid. Even though some of his natively acquired courtesies, such as not making eye contact with elders, had to be trained away, he was a willing and eager learner. His world had become bigger and richer.

"My officers can't do their jobs if the other guards can't trust them," he had explained to Sarah when she had asked why Ed's training had included such things. "If they are *too* different, they won't be trusted. So to some extent, I have to train up officers and gentlemen."

A smile had grown on Sarah's face. "To be marrying men?"

Ed collapsed into laughter, remembering how he had been startled when he'd discovered that Bolagi had acquired *three* wives since beginning his unheard-of *paid* job at the mines.

"Why is that so funny?" she had asked in an endearingly earnest way, fixing her gaze on him as he explained what had made him laugh. Then she had crinkled her nose and thoughtfully asked, "That is *legal* here?"

"Well, the bush folk have their own law."

Now, striding through the tall grass back to his jeep, Ed couldn't help but smile warmly at the memory of that exchange with Sarah. No matter the ugly task before them all, he still felt like a school boy, excited for this opportunity to get to know her, even under these conditions.

CHAPTER 35

NOVEMBER 5, 1942
ABOARD THE *KLEIN-SEYDITZ,*

IN THE HARBOR OF PARAMARIBO, SURINAME

First it had been the note to the Surinamese government requesting a joint conference between "the visiting German Police Representative" and the equivalent Surinamese police officials.

Then came the back-and-forth negotiations as Gunter's role as "Police Representative" was defended, despite his German military uniform.

Following that was the request, channeled through Gunter to the German embassy and then to the Surinamese, that the *Klein-Seyditz* be allowed to offload her cargo. That had met *three days* of silence, until a response came that while the German military and their transport were poised on board to debark, the unloading of the *Klein-Seyditz* simply was not feasible.

Each of these transactions had required Gunter to boat over to the dock, surrender his pistol to the policeman awaiting him, and be driven to the German embassy in a Mercedes sandwiched between two police jeeps. The courtesy of the Surinamese, though absolutely impeccable, was totally inflexible. The contingent awaiting him eventually dropped to a few men and two jeeps, but they were there every time.

Astonishingly, on Gunter's second trip ashore, the police commander had presented him with four boxes of cigars and a case of the local rum upon his return to the *Klein-Seyditz*.

"You understand, Mijnheer, this is governmental policy. We do not want you to think us devoid of hospitality."

Gunter had blinked in astonishment for a moment, before bowing and thanking the man.

His troops and Krager's crew were delighted with this taste of the shore they were denied.

On the third trip ashore, Gunter was tendered a letter from the president's office, in Dutch. It was businesslike, but still astonishing:

> To: Oberst Gunter Kramer, resident on board the freighter Klein-Seyditz, Paramaribo Harbor.
>
> From: Office of the President of Suriname.
>
> Subject: Permission for shore access for crew of the Klein-Seyditz and enlisted members of the German military on board the Klein-Seyditz.
>
> Access shall be during the hours of daylight only.
>
> Access is for recreational and commercial purposes only.
>
> All personnel are to be unarmed, and without insignia.
>
> This is solely a consideration of the extended time on board your personnel have spent and not to be construed as permission to land as a military party. The sovereignty of Suriname is not to be imperiled, and any action taken to do so will result in immediate revocation of this permit.
>
> Signed,
>
> Nicolas Anders,
>
> Aide to the President of Suriname

Krager and Gunter consulted with each other, stiffly, and decided that half the crew and half the troopers at one time could take advantage of the offer. All the men were indeed becoming restive, as the smells of shore and distant sightings of swaying women tempted.

The *Klein-Seyditz* was still forbidden to dock; Krager was, despite taking a night or two ashore himself, still fuming; and, of course, the troopers who came ashore were watched openly by the police, a polite surveillance. The troopers actually reported that some of their watchers had bought them drinks and told them where the best bordellos were. It was a very civilized captivity.

Now, after three weeks on this ship, and without any answer for his increasingly restive troops, Gunter had to make some concessions.

"Captain Krager, they offer onshore accommodations for my troops, as long as they do not debark your ship at the dock. I am inclined to accept; they are offering barracks accommodations for my men, and, after you are offloaded, refueling and galley restocking for you. They insist, however, that my transport and weapons remain on board and that you return to anchorage after offloading."

Krager's rage had subsided, just a bit. "Anything that lets me offload my cargo and refuel is enthusiastically endorsed, Herr Oberst."

"Yes, well, it means offloading my people via your lifeboat, as they have been insisting I do during *my* onshore excursions. Only *after* that are you to dock and offload and refuel."

"Herr Oberst, your operations on my ship have been *in ordnung*. I have no complaints of your courtesy. However, Krieger Marine is out a great deal of money for the extended delay in making landfall and offloading that has occurred because of your unnecessarily publicized presence on board my ship."

"*Jawohl*, Herr Captain. And I am sure the Reich will compensate your owners suitably."

"I certainly hope so, Herr Oberst."

Despite that civil exchange, whenever Gunter's back was to Krager for the next few days, the hair on his neck rose.

Then came another tedious trip to and from the German embassy. A couriered communication from the American representative was a copy of the text of one that had been sent officially to the Reichstag in Berlin, and was signed by a state department functionary in Washington, D.C.:

> *The government of the United States of America herein for-*
> *mally protests the attempted armed invasion of a neutral territory*
> *with friendly and commercial ties to the United States of America.*
> *We call upon the Government of Germany to immediately cease*
> *such provocative actions in the American sphere of influence, a*

hemisphere removed from any possible legitimate interests of the
German Government.

The German Ambassador sounded resigned. "We have war still with Britain, where the fools have not surrendered despite the punishment we have meted out to them from the air, the campaign in North Africa, particularly, and irregular resistance in Holland, France, a bit in Belgium, and some, though ineffective, in Poland ... Just *franc-tireurs*, snipers, and some sabotage, but requiring troop presence. Also, for some reason, our resupply for Rommel's work is suffering badly. We do not need another enemy just now. The Reich will rule for a thousand years, but we must time our conquests wisely. This must be responded to, and our position *vis-a-vis* the criminal fugitives made clear."

"So when may my men come ashore? As unarmed guests, I mean."

"In perhaps another three days. The barracks the Surinamese are offering are being completed as we speak. Paint is still drying, for example. Purely a *practical* delay this time, Herr Oberst."

This diplomat was a Hitler fanatic, much as the detested and long-gone Eberhardt had been, only a diplomatic version. He was, despite that, a likeable man. Gunter found himself returning his wry grin reflexively.

It took four days. And the contingent of police and army was again at full strength to meet them as the lifeboat brought its first load to dock.

The offloading of the unit was attended with another bit of humiliation. At the dock, as each lifeboat's load arrived, the Surinamese insisted on open luggage and packs. No weapons were allowed on Surinamese soil; Gunter's word that no weapons were carried was simply and humiliatingly disregarded.

"This is an absolute insult to the Reich!"

The young diplomatic aide stood stiffly in front of the police commander. His face quivered with affront that Gunter believed for once was sincere.

"The oberst has stated that his men are unarmed and that their luggage does not contain arms," he argued, clearly feeling the pressure of Gunter's eyes on him. "The word of a German officer should not be challenged in this way."

"The oberst himself has attempted to violate our sovereignty," responded the commander, unfazed by the plea.

Gunter recalled the incident with his pistol. Perhaps it was a slight exaggeration, but nonetheless it was true.

After their initially firm resistance and the courtesies that had been extended after that, Gunter found himself reluctantly growing some small admiration for these tropical popinjays with their silly ranks. As if they were playing a chess game, one might say they had forced a stalemate.

The blocking tactics continued, the American representative insisting that a *hard copy* answer from the Reichstag must be relayed to him through the American state department.

"Of course he has no means to enforce that, and no real standing here, but because the Americans do so much trade here, this colonial excuse for a government is not going to shift position without American acquiescence," said the Ambassador, again being wryly practical. "Of course, it is always easier to seek forgiveness than permission, and Reichsminister Goebbels has sent a coded communiqué to encourage you to seek a solution which will allow you to seek forgiveness."

The message was loud and clear: Get the unit ashore and out from under Surinamese Coast Guard control. There were no suggestions how, but he was expected to take some initiative. It was a chilling reminder that the Reich was everywhere.

Gunter had three months' pay for his men stored in a lockbox. It was in Reichsmarks, of course, but while ashore, he had discovered that the local bank would convert them to the local currency at a small charge, which Gunter found to be quite restrained. The proprietor was a charming Englishman named Butler, which Gunter found astonishing; he would have expected hostility (after all, the Germans had been bombing the English homeland until just last month), but he received only politeness and a referral to the proprietor's store, which apparently contained a good bakery.

"Unfortunately, I must clear all of *my* movements through my embassy and yours at this point," Gunter replied to him upon receiving the recommendation. "I will, however, pass your recommendations along to my oberfeldwebel and men. *Danke*."

Ermenthaller had been leading exercises on a daily basis for all the men, allowing just half the force their liberty every other night, and on several occasions the oberfeldwebel had marched a work party to the dock to flag the *Klein-Seyditz* and come aboard to perform maintenance on machines and weapons. Of course, when they reappeared at the dock, they were inspected. All of them were watched.

So the force was well in hand and the men content, well fed, sheltered, and exercised. Gunter could pull them into fighting shape in just hours. If only he could unite them with their weapons.

And so the stalemate continued. As long as his transport and weapons were not ashore, he was helpless there. As long as they remained at sea, the locals had overwhelming force available to sink the *Klein-Seyditz* and all his resources with her if they found it necessary.

It had become too oppressive for him to remain long hours in his cabin and on the freighter between interminable visits to the embassy.

Krager, while no longer radiating hostility, was resigned to billing the Reich for his ship's and crew's idle time and was less-than-stimulating company. All the man had done since the previous war, apparently, was to captain this ship and some others in remarkably routine voyages. He knew invoices, billing, and diesels, and he knew his coasts and courses. Apparently, though, he did not read books, have any hobbies, nor have any family.

There was a miniscule library at the German embassy. Gunter had exhausted that within the first few days here. He even tried fishing off the side of the deck away from shore. It was too banal an occupation for the leader of a German force, and Gunter was sure, though he had seen none, that the *Klein-Seyditz* was under observation at all times. The occasional large perch made for small triumphs.

Krager even smiled at one such repast. There was nothing better than fresh seafood.

The German ambassador had held a small reception for Gunter after four days of stasis. The commander of the American Marine contingent, Captain Hodgins, had attended, with the American ambassador. The British ambassador had pointedly not attended, and the ambassador for the "free" French had attended, as had, of course, that of the Vichy government. Gunter suspected that they had all come from complete boredom and for the schnapps. Conversation had been polite, if frosty to the point of homicidal between the rival French contingents.

Captain Hodgins had worn the ornate blue and gold uniform of his corps, an ivory-gripped, mameluke-hilted saber at his side and his Colt automatic in a spotless white holster. He and Gunter had gravitated to each other after the reception formalities.

Hodgins saluted first, of course, as a simple courtesy. Gunter returned the similar Wehrmacht gesture (not the Hitler telegraphy pole one).

"Saber?" Hodgins gestured at Gunter's scarred face.

Gunter smiled. "When I was a foolish and immortal student, yes. Have you ever employed that one?"

Marine officers' swords, he knew, were made and measured to each officer as they took their commissions. They were magnificently real blades, not the showy, often pot-metal things of other forces.

"Saluting, gesturing, and polishing, yes. Fighting, no." Hodgins grinned a youthful grin. "But I used to do Olympic saber in college myself. We, however, wore masks and used those toy blades."

Gunter brightened. "The ambassador's son has a set of those, with the straight hilts, and masks and plastrons. Would you care for a match or two sometime?"

Hodgins was momentarily taken aback. Then his face firmed and he smiled a smile that greeted and challenged at once. "Of course. Here, or at my embassy?"

"Either. Are there any other fencers in Paramaribo?"

"A couple of the Frenchies in each embassy, as you'd expect," Hodgins said. "I don't know anyone else."

"The ambassador's son, young Yost, will be disappointed if he is not included. Especially if we are using his weapons."

"He's what, fourteen? With the masks and plastrons? Why not?"

And so it had developed that on several afternoons, after his seemingly inevitable conference at the German embassy, Gunter would be driven to the American embassy, a much humbler building, and the two officers, as well as the boy and sometimes one or another of the French diplomats (though never from competing embassies at the same time, because they were "too damned likely to whip out real blades," Hodgins had said, straight faced) would gather at an impromptu *piste* made by putting the enlisted men's bunk beds and lockers against the walls of their bunkhouse. Two of the French, it turned out, had full sets of blades and protection, including fine gloves. It was possible to have two engagements at once.

The very first time Gunter and Hodgins had faced off, Gunter had expected aggression, and he had received it, but Hodgins had played a drawing game, retreating only to exploit overextension or imbalance. They were evenly matched, though Gunter had a far stronger wrist and he suspected the American of not revealing everything he had. He found he enjoyed the action that did not require thought, only pure, trained instincts and an opportunity to sweat deliberately for once.

Off-duty Marines were an enthusiastic audience. The sergeant, Lone, had even managed to get both his own captain and Gunter to teach him some blade work. He had become unexpectedly good very quickly.

"Sergeant, you have no previous blade experience?" Gunter had been gasping after barely averting the sergeant's determined and merciless attack. His English had fully returned by then.

Sergeant Lone had smirked. "Just a few hundred hours of bayonet training, Sir. I used to teach it, and Colonel—" He had glanced over at his own officer, and Gunter had caught a cautionary look from Hodgins to Lone. Abruptly, Lone had shut up. Even though the men had become jovial together, it had appeared that some training still was not up for discussion. Gunter had been determined not to pry, only to listen.

"Where was it you performed such long instruction?" Gunter had inquired.

"Paris Island, Sir. And, after that, with the Fleet Marine Force." This had been said with obvious pride.

"So, Captain Hodgins, you have put a … 'ringer' in against me," Gunter had said with a mock glare at the American captain and a bit of exaggeration of his breathlessness.

Everyone had laughed. But Lone was very good and stretched everyone, more so every time he picked up a saber.

After that first session, the police escort had taken to watching as well, perched cheerfully on footlockers with the Marines, as did the Wehrmacht driver from the embassy.

By now, just days into this routine, Gunter was already feeling the benefits of regular exercise. He was becoming aware of his body again, after so many months of just being a passenger in it. He was also becoming aware of the female half of the local population—a truly odd sensation. He had not thought that reaction could ever occur again, after losing his family.

Gunter chose to ignore it. He had no private time in town, in any case, and therefore no opportunities.

CHAPTER 36

NOVEMBER 7, 1942
THE EVE OF DIWALI
4:45 P.M.

PARAMARIBO, SURINAME

Despite Suriname's large contingent of European natives—particularly Dutch—nearly one quarter were Hindu, having been indentured servants sent here through partnership with Dutch Guiana. This explained why Hindu celebrations such as Diwali were so widely observed, and Gunter could understand why the joyful traditions of decorating homes, hanging lanterns, exchanging sweets, playing music and drumming at all hours, and dressing in the colorful costumes of the Hindu gods and goddesses involved in this five-day celebration would be appealing. Tonight, on the eve of Diwali, it was traditional for people to come together for parties, to celebrate in costume, to dance, and to gamble, which was considered an auspicious activity that honored Lord Shiva and the goddess Parvati, who were said to have engaged in a cosmic game of winning and losing.

The embassy would be hosting a gathering that evening, and Gunter could not resist attendance, though he wanted to. He tried to include Ermenthaller, as a matter of policy, as well as a means to have someone present he could talk to. The embassy staff were too likely to be exercising their linguistic skills.

He had to admit to himself, though, that he was drawn by the glowing lights of the oil lamps, or *diyas,* that had been increasingly casting a collective glow upon the streets and waterfront, as well as the smells emanating from bakeries and sweet shops in town that were now operating around the clock, and he hoped to absorb some of the celebratory spirit and perhaps experience a lightening of his mood. Diwali was, after all, a celebration of the triumph of light over darkness. He hoped that the darkness in his soul might someday give way to light, though he had no idea how that might be possible.

Hodgins, as he learned, was Catholic and avoided such Hindu traditions. The two men stood sweating as a variety of Frenchmen and the American sergeant, Lone, contended in the *piste* spaces. "Back in our half of the world, there's a chill in the air, but here in Suriname, it's November, and we are sweating like pigs, even when we are not dueling," Hodgins said irritably. "This evening we will be sticking to our dress uniforms."

"Well, they will have to be content with my one surviving uniform and its attendant mildew," Gunter replied.

Hodgins gave the German a sidelong look and a half grin. "Too bad you didn't come prepared for the diplomatic life, Oberst." He gestured grandly. "I, on the other hand, came with no less than five varieties. I never will understand why the military spends so much time dressing up professional killers."

Gunter gave him an assessing look, knowing the captain well enough by now to know when he was being teased. Nonetheless, he gave a serious answer, rather than the indignant one the younger man was pushing for.

"Dress uniforms remind soldiers that they are part of society and are an attempt to give soldiers a feeling of being valued and respected." Why the sudden defense of the Reich's policies on dress? A long-honed instinct, he supposed.

"Textbook answer, Oberst. But why so damned *many*?" He sounded genuinely aggrieved.

Wishing to lighten the tenor between them, Gunter's face reflected amusement. "Because, as I am sure you have already realized, soldiers are display racks for politicians, who treat them as pets."

They both snorted, resuming masks for their final matches of the day. Today, Lone scored two slashes and a thrust on Gunter, receiving only a bare touch to his own mask that would not actually have kissed skin.

Gunter saluted, chest heaving, shirt soaked, feeling his heart working to circulate the oxygen his exhausted cells demanded. Lone returned the salute, looking annoyingly fresh.

"Sergeant, you have become one of the most seriously dangerous saber fighters I have ever met. You should consider acquiring a practice blade of full weight and working with it. The only times I am a serious threat to you now are when I am in close, we are locked, and I succeed by pure weight and height, or when my stronger wrist drops your *glissade* block."

Lone nodded respectfully and gratefully. "Thank you, Oberst Kramer. It's been an education."

Gunter glanced down, nose wrinkling, "And a sweaty one."

"Well, that too, Sir. Good afternoon."

Gunter smiled to himself, feeling confident in his approaching mission. He was winning, if not friends, at least a bit of trust and warm feeling from the Americans stationed here. It would all be gone tomorrow, after he and his unit took advantage of the distractions of the Diwali festival—its parade and ensuing fireworks—as well as the darkness of the new moon to perform the duties he had been sent for.

He began making a mental list of what must be done. He would have to turn over the engines on the trucks himself before cleaning up, not knowing how long it would take to fire them up if they were not recently warmed. Tonight, the offload would begin. He would put his "guards" aboard, and then, the following night, with the gangway still in place and leaving just the one fireguard on board during the city's festivities, the men would take their vehicles and weapons from the dock and stage somewhere out of town while he and the fireguard uncrated mortar and ammunition. Gunners would stage a few streets away, looking as if they were simply enjoying the celebration, and would be unstoppable as they proceeded to the barracks to gather the rest of the men.

His satisfied smile about the prospect of finally bringing an end to this mission drew no attention now, here in this makeshift fencing arena. After all, the police detail that was with him was jocular, again having enjoyed watching the increasingly exciting saber play for the last couple of hours.

In the slow Dutch he had acquired while working in Holland, Gunter asked one of the police officers, "Do you have duty during the festival tomorrow?" Sodden shirt at his feet, he swabbed his torso with one of the wet towels the Marines had provided and then shrugged into the fresh shirt he always carried along. In the heat, of course, it too would be soaked by the time he regained the *Klein-Seyditz*, but he sought to minimize the odor as much as possible

"Oh, no, Mijnheer Oberst. No one works on Diwali, unless you count the townspeople hanging the lights and the fishermen catching their last for the late-night feasts."

Gunter was surprised by this local officer's casual reply, revealing such a significant weakness. While the local government clearly saw him and his men as a threat, these impromptu fencing sessions and light banter with the police had clearly gone a long way toward establishing trust—trust that was unearned, he thought with a moment's guilt before dismissing it. *Dummkopf.*

"So, many people on the docks?" Gunter probed, trying to maintain a tone of disinterest as much as possible.

"Oh, yes," the policeman said, realizing too late the need to assure this oberst of a local presence. "Half the town will be there in the late afternoon, then there is drinking and dancing in the streets, little celebrations all over the city, for most of the night. The fireworks are tremendous, done on the North Beach, and everyone in town will be up on their roofs to watch. Many eyes will be on the docks, Mijnheer."

"I will need to double the guard I put on the *Klein-Seyditz* while she is at dock, then. Some of our cargo could be of great trouble to you police if it fell into the hands of criminals."

"Yes, that's true. How many?"

"I think four is a good number; that way they can take turns sleeping."

"No problem, Mijnheer. But please remember, they are not to be on the dock with weapons at any time."

"Understood." Gunter was more than satisfied. The four men would be the drivers and Kucher, ready at a moment's notice to launch their attack at Gunter's word. The many eyes will be directed at the wrong place.

Gunter had an afterthought as he sat in his lifeboat, on his return trip to the *Klein-Seyditz*. He hoped they would not have to hurt any of the young men on police detail. They may be *dummkopf* officers, but they had done everything *in ordnung* and politely. Not to mention the rum and cigars.

⧗

Ed sat in the clinic, sketchpad on his lap, and surrounding him sat or stood what had become the planning council. Outside the windows was a dark, almost entirely moonless night, with only a few remaining *diyas* lit in the doorways of a few homes and businesses. In the distance was the soft, almost imperceptible sound of a drumbeat—the first of many that they would hear over the next twenty-four hours. In the room were George; Herr Adelmann,

Levi, and the doctor; Jacob; Amos; Hannah; Sarah; Rabbi Levin and a member of his congregation, a small, middle-aged man the rabbi called only David and insisted was trustworthy; Eli Rabin; Captain Hodgins; Ysidro, who looked haunted because Inocente, astonishingly, had continued to swell; and three of George's drivers, two of whom were neither Jewish nor had Jewish relatives and one of whom, Otto, was Eli Rabin's son. All three sat close to George, who had brought them tonight for the first time.

Ed stood amid the quiet chatting, the better to cast his voice throughout the room.

"Tonight is our last meeting. Late today, the German freighter began offloading at the dock. That will continue throughout the night. We're estimating that will take about ten working hours, and, since nobody works during Diwali, the vessel will remain at dock for two nights."

"Captain Hodgins," Ed nodded to his old friend, "heard code on the Germans' embassy frequency. That's not unusual before one of the pursuit group officer's excursions ashore, but it *is* unusual in late afternoons. The troopers who showed up to guard tonight were identified, as usual, by the police. Those troopers also gave the police a list of names and ranks for the troopers who will come to relieve them tomorrow morning, and all the names were given to the good doctor here, when he was called to the palace for an 'emergency attendance.' Tomorrow's replacements are the drivers and the motorcycle courier."

Hannah flinched slightly. Kucher had spent many innocent and obviously friendly hours at the bakery. Despite the evil he represented, and against all her sense of reason and propriety, he had become someone she knew and, against her better judgment, actually liked. Nonetheless, she had no intention of backing out on this mission. In fact, this friendship was why she had been invited to this meeting.

"That means the Germans are planning a break with their vehicles and weapons from the dock," Ed went on. "Probably tomorrow night, during the festivities. If they unlashed the trucks during daylight, it would be visible from shore, let alone from the dock. Captain, I want you and your team with me tomorrow afternoon."

Hodgins nodded in satisfaction. "I can be there when you want; I got liberty for my troops for the festival. Just two have to stay at the embassy, which is closing for the holiday."

"I radioed out to the mines earlier, and Bolagi and my other two officers and the engineers are *en route* or being picked up as we speak. They will come here, to the clinic, and should arrive late tonight or early tomorrow morning." Ed tried not to sound worried at having his force moving over primitive roads through darkness. The loss of even one vehicle could mean failure.

Rabbi Levin spoke up. "Colonel, we discussed the explosives you have stored. Are those ready?"

Ed winced. "No, and I have to put in caps and fuses before I sleep tonight."

"David here is the blasting technician for the nearby mine. He has decades of experience, and if you take him to your stored material and tell him what you want done, it will be done professionally." The solid-looking but short man who, Ed noted, had singularly blackened hands, just nodded.

"Also, there is a local chandlery operated by a member of my congregation. The owners' truck is on the docks almost every day, a regular sight. We can arrange to put the prepared explosives under lock and key in a dock shed that they own, close to the mooring spot of the *Klein-Seyditz*, during the working day tomorrow. Since they have to make several trips tomorrow because all the ships are party places during the fireworks show, we can put you and your boarding party and the drivers in that same shed toward nightfall."

Ed was amazed. This level of thoughtful logistical support made several of the uncertainties that had been keeping him awake nights go away. He nodded respectfully at the little man whom he'd always believed to be rather ineffectual. "Thank you, Rabbi. I think *you* would have made a good officer."

Rabbi Levin nodded calmly and smiled his appreciation.

Ed turned his attention to Hodgins. "I want you and your boys, with boots, weapons, and ammo all bundled up for carrying—sea bags are good—to stage at my truck, a street over from the embassy, by that big fig tree, at fourteen hundred hours tomorrow. It looks like we'll be moving into attack position with the help of the rabbi's chandler friends, and we should probably be in our civvies for getting there."

"Aye, aye, Sir!" Hodgins replied enthusiastically.

"I will keep Bolagi and my other guards with me," Ed said. "They know me best. Captain, form yourself and your men as two fire teams. I may need to split you. You in charge of one, Lone of the other, if you please." This was phrased as a request because Lone was under Hodgins' command; nonetheless, it was an order, and both of them knew it.

"Aye, aye, Sir!" Hodgins repeated, exercising considerable volume.

Hannah and Sarah exchanged glances and fought back giggles over his bravado. Ed, somewhat charmed but trying to maintain authority, mock-glared at them and continued, returning his attention to Hodgins.

"I'm going to have the engineers with the shotguns stay with me. Both were army officers when they were younger, and if I put them with your teams, they may automatically start trying to give orders."

Hodgins nodded understanding. Clarity of the chain of command and instant obedience were at the very core of the Marines' combat effectiveness.

"I'm going to form three of my own two-man fire teams as well—Bolagi running one, Sergeant Ysidro the other, using the engineers for the third (probably to stand guard for the drivers), and Ysidro will keep one of the Thompsons. I'll lend you one for each of your teams."

Sarah and Hannah were waiting for the captain to bark again, but this time no order had been issued. Hodgins just nodded, and both ladies looked disappointed. Despite the seriousness of what was about to happen, it was so nice to find small reasons to laugh.

"Doctor, you and Sarah are to be here, with the operating room prepped for work. If anyone gets hit, fast treatment may mean saving lives, as you know. If we succeed in requisitioning the Krauts' gear, we'll stage here in any case on the way out of town."

He then turned his attention to George and his drivers. "Make that clear to them, please, George. Also, that they are to *stay in that shed* until one of us comes back to fetch them." George turned to his men and began a low conversation in Dutch.

"Colonel?" It was David, the blaster. His English was accented with Dutch but easy enough to understand.

"Yes?"

"I think I should be there, too, to plant the charges and lay the fuses and detonation cord."

Ed was genuinely startled. He glanced at George, who had finished relaying instruction to the drivers, and raised a querying eyebrow, as if to ask whether this man could be trusted.

"David is a solid man, Colonel," George replied, looking him straight in the eye. "I have known him for years. He is absolutely trustworthy, and everyone knows he *cannot* be panicked. I believe that's a quality we must have in an explosives man, is it not?" George's mouth turned up in a slight smile on one side.

Ed nodded quickly. George's word was as good as gold. "David, that would be very much appreciated. I haven't done blasting for years. But you stay safe until one of us brings you aboard. Got that?"

"Yes, Colonel."

"Why are you in this?" Ed couldn't help but ask. After all, the man had been here for years; he may be a Jew, but he didn't have skin in this fight.

David looked puzzled for a moment. "They are my *people*. Caleb and Deborah Zeitweg, who came to live here last year, and Dr. Adelmann … they are now my family. And…" at this he grinned, "my oldest son very much likes Yael Zeitweg."

Hannah clapped a hand to her mouth, radiating delight. Jacob and Eli Rabin gave a slight chuckle as well.

"Very good. But remember, we have to get the *Klein-Seyditz* away from the dock and out of the way before we sink her, or she'll make trouble for years. Can you swim?"

David looked startled. "No . . ."

"Well, then, you'll need to set up radiating det cord from one or duplicate fuses and get yourself off her while she's still at dock. Someone else will have to light her off."

David nodded.

Jacob gently raised his hand.

"Jacob?" Ed had little in mind for Jacob except to assist Hannah in her role, but he was committed to assisting and had proven a pretty good shot in Ed's training sessions. The older man seemed keen to participate.

"The *Klein Seyditz*, it turns out, is a slightly younger version of the *Bon Chance*. It has the same configuration. On the *Bon Chance,* I did inventory for weeks as part of getting Captain Cervantes' affairs in order. I can take you and David to the seacocks, the engine room, and the fuel tanks in minutes, where you might need to search for far longer." Jacob looked full of resolution, but Ed saw his Adam's apple bob as he gulped back what was obviously real trepidation.

"Can you fight?"

"Shamefully, I have no skills in that direction, Colonel. But, with your training, I can shoot a gun." Jacob turned to Amos, reaching out his arm to pull the boy up and draw attention to him. Amos, gangly and unused to attention, looked at his feet. "And my son, Amos, he shoots ably, thanks to your instruction. But more important, he is a natural spy. He and Nathaniel," at this Jacob turned to his son's friend, and Nathaniel looked up, nodding slightly, "they have been working on the docks, making frequent reports to George. They are as sly as ghosts."

Ed nodded. "I agree. Okay, boys, you're in. But Jacob, may I respectfully ask, Sir…" he stole a quick glance at Sarah, seeking her approval, "do you have the stomach for this?"

"Surely you do not think I would miss acting to protect my family?" Jacob stood proudly, his arm still around his son's shoulders.

Hannah's eyes were wide and concerned. She stood and hugged her brother and father, proud of their strength and cleverness.

This evening had taken many different directions, and Ed was realizing that he didn't have the control he had thought he had. He felt ashamed to realize that he had been thinking of these people as helpless. Helpless they definitely were not. Even the Roseweigs' young daughter was prepared to place herself in harm's way. He directed his attention to her.

"Hannah. We want you to make a delivery during the festival, to the motorcycle courier on guard duty. Are you willing?"

Jacob tensed. He had suspected that Hannah would be asked to continue relying on her feminine wiles, but he had hoped she was done with all that.

Hannah's bright, determined eyes remained fixed on Ed, her steady gaze giving her consent and encouraging him to continue.

"Dr. Ben will make some 'modifications' to some really nice pastries from your bakery, and they will make getting on board and dealing with the Germans much easier."

"Will these 'modifications' kill?"

It was a very adult question, and Ed answered her as he would an adult.

"No, they are just to make resistance, and killing, less likely. Let's call them a safety precaution. The delivery will be in broad daylight or, at worst, at sunset; you will never actually go on the ship, and we will be watching to protect you if the Germans become suspicious and try to grab you."

"Yes, I will do it," she replied without a hint of fear or hesitation.

"Good."

Rabbi Levin looked embarrassed. "Colonel, I have to ask, even though I myself have argued for no killing, what are we going to do about the Germans after they lose their transportation and weapons? And *why* are you stealing those instead of just sinking them?" He made a dismissive downward gesture.

"Good questions. First, to the second one. If the *Klein-Seyditz* goes down in shallow water, and Paramaribo is a *very* shallow harbor, the weaponry could possibly be recovered. We don't want that. Second, *I want* the weapons and trucks and so on, so I can offer the Krauts employment."

Hodgins looked at the Colonel sourly. "Colonel, I can tell you that the ambassador does *not* want these assholes…" He blushed, violently, and half bowed to the women, who once again found themselves suppressing giggles. "Sorry, pardon my language." He turned resolutely back to the Colonel and continued. "He does not want them anywhere *near* the bauxite mines. America needs the aluminum. And as we talked about, we are probably going to be fighting the Reich sooner rather than later." He was deferential to his superior officer but making a point decisively.

Ed nodded amiably. "I've thought about that. But there's a need for transport into Guyana and Brazil. The roads are really dangerous with bandits and even some local cops, who are only little better than the thieves. The Krauts would make good road guards; it would get them off the coast, away from the mines, let them have time to learn the language. And I, incidentally, could get rich selling their services."

The rabbi, Eli, Jacob, Sarah, and both Adelmanns stared, mouths hanging open. George smiled.

"If they have their weapons, they're more valuable. Of course, I'm not talking about re-arming them while there's any chance of them turning on us. And I wouldn't put them out as a unit big enough to come back here and make trouble.

"But they can build themselves a barracks on my place, and I can feed them, with some buildup of my plowed ground. They'd be away from here, making themselves useful. And even when their home country and ours go to war, which, as the captain says, is likely sooner rather than later, they'd be deep in the jungle, safe from both sides."

There was silence about the room as everyone thought over the idea of *profiting* from the Nazi pursuers. Ed's retirement had made him impressively enterprising.

Hodgins began to smile. Then the rabbi chuckled, and George literally bellowed his delight.

There was little left for the group to discuss, and the mood in the room was surprisingly jovial. Giving the drivers and David instructions for rendezvous, and then instructing Hannah about what to bring to the clinic for 'modification' and when, took another twenty minutes.

Before the group disbanded, Sarah stood with fire in her eyes. "Thank you, Colonel. We trust you. *I* trust you."

Ed smiled appreciatively, warmed thoroughly by her words.

Then, the lighthearted tenor of the room changed. All eyes were riveted to the young woman who sought now to take control of the room. She turned her attention to Amos, Hannah, and Jacob. "We cannot fail. I know that you will do your best. But too much is at stake! This mission cannot fail! You will be my eyes. My spirit, the spirit of Michael… We are with all of you."

A minute of silent solemnity fell over the room, and in that minute the Roseweigs were alone there, as they had been another lifetime ago in Amsterdam. They exchanged affectionate gazes and hugs, wiping tears from their eyes.

Ed stood from his corner and watched, utterly respectful of Sarah and her family, barely able to comprehend all that they had been through to get here. *That is my bride,* Ed thought. *That is my family.*

Finally, the group disbanded with their marching orders. Ed gathered his notes and looked up in time to see Sarah following Dr. Adelmann into the clinic waiting room. She turned to glance at him and their eyes met. She lowered hers, bowed her head, and smiled a silent "thank you" to him. Blossoming love swelled in his chest. He would have done all this for her alone.

CHAPTER 37

NOVEMBER 8, 1942
DIWALI
7:00 A.M.

PARAMARIBO, SURINAME

Ed woke to a brilliant, beautiful day, and rather than thinking first of the battle to come that night, his first thoughts were of Sarah.

He rose quickly, enjoyed a delicious breakfast of honey ham, sticky buns, and sliced mangoes prepared by Carmina and left George's house with all the demeanor of a man about to enjoy a day at the market and not one about to embark on the fight of his life.

Outside, the early morning light made the mynah birds, which were hopping hopefully along the street, almost glow, and the parrots flying overhead were like airborne brushstrokes of vibrancy. He shook his head, catching himself waxing rhapsodic about birds—what had Sarah done to him?

He inhaled deeply, taking in the humid, fresh morning air. It was a good day for a fight.

He made his way to Ysidro and Inocente's little nest. Inocente was up and cooking already, her usual happy bustle reduced to a serene waddle, but she was intent on her kitchen, her domain. Ysidro sat at the table, watching her with loving wonder. Coffee steamed from mugs, and the smells of corned beef hash and frying eggs filled the air intoxicatingly. Ed was full from his own meal, and still his mouth watered.

Within moments of having sat down at the table for a cup of coffee with this old friend, Ed looked up to see Azi was at the door, not panting but breathing deeply, a sheen of sweat coating his coal-dark skin. He had run here, obviously, and even before a word was said, Ed knew that meant German movement.

It took several minutes, between shortness of breath and language gaps, to get Azi's report. The guard exchange had taken place at daybreak, as expected. Also as expected, the police had required one group of guards to leave the dock before their replacements were allowed onto it. No weapons had left the ship.

Kramer was still on the ship. But the limousine from the German embassy was waiting at the shore end of the dock and had been for some time. Azi was still a stranger to clocks and the counting of time, but Kramer was probably going to the embassy soon. Ed was confused by the unexpected move. He had expected Kramer to be off the freighter when the troopers pulled their bugout, and he knew Kramer had been invited to the embassy celebration that evening, but why come ashore this early?

Inocente was putting out a plate of food and a mug of coffee for the boy, who smiled thankfully and tucked in gleefully, as always.

"Dammit. What's he up to?" Ed squinted, then turned to his old friend across the table from him. "Sergeant, I need to keep that Kraut bastard under observation all day." Ysidro stood at attention immediately to gather his things. "Drive up to George's place and tell him that, please, and that I want him to relay any movements to me here. Then come back."

George had what he referred to as his "Baker Street Irregulars"—local boys and girls who let him know what was happening with ship arrivals and departures, incoming trucks, and so on. He paid in coins and candy, small expenditures to keep abreast of his business environment. In Ed's mind, it was a scouting force to be called on. He would do it himself, having an unnatural desire to observe Kramer himself, but felt it best to remain here at "headquarters" should any more updates come in.

"*Si*, Coronel." Ysidro gulped the last of his coffee, carefully hugged Inocente's head, planted a gentle kiss on her cheek, and strode out.

Azi was mopping his plate with bread, and Inocente automatically reheaped that plate. The boy's appetite was a force of nature. She refilled her own as well. Inocente was eating for three, after all. Ed sat drinking coffee and thinking, waiting for more news, anxious to do something but afraid to leave his post, being the center of this plan. He'd have plenty to do soon enough. For now, he could only wait.

Before him on the table were blueprints, plans of a ship resembling *Klein-Seyditz* that George had secured for him. Though it was likely the Nazi ship differed slightly, it gave him a sense of an approach. As he waited, he unrolled the plans and, again, studied them anxiously.

Within the hour, Ysidro returned, sending Azi back to his observation post with a big egg sandwich wrapped in linen to help him survive until the next meal. And they all waited.

Late that morning, Amos appeared at the door, perspiring more than had Azi that morning. His German skin was still not used to tropical heat, though he certainly was not out of breath. The gangly boy was an experienced messenger.

"*Guten Morgen*, Colonel."

"Amos! Is there news?" Ed stood, and Inocente pulled out a chair for him. Amos's eyes widened at her horizontal breadth, then he smiled politely at her and took a seat.

"The children say the big German officer is in their embassy still. And even though the embassies are all closed for business today, for Diwali, every German diplomat and worker is there, too."

"How can the kids know *that*?"

"They talk with the maids and gardeners, it seems. At least a couple of George's informants have parents who work there." Amos' tone implied admiration.

Ed shook his head in wonderment, making a mental note to never try keeping a secret from George in Paramaribo.

"Now, I wonder what in hell has them all worked up?"

The answer arrived almost immediately in the person of Sergeant Lone. He drove the embassy sedan with exquisite care, obviously either not very experienced at the task or terrified of denting the glossy vehicle. When he emerged from the vehicle, Ed saw he was wearing the loose shirt, trousers, and sandals popular in Paramaribo.

Of course, he did not salute but instinctively came to attention, failing to achieve a heel click with the sandals but trying nonetheless. "Good morning, Sir!"

"At ease, Lone. Take a load off, have some coffee, and good morning to you, too." Ed waited while Lone took coffee from Inocente, looking very apprehensively at her girth, and seated himself beside Amos, who had unobtrusively been handed leftover breakfast hash and was shoveling it down his eager throat as quickly as he could. Despite the fact that this small house had seen comings and goings the likes of a train station this morning, Inocente had prepared more than enough food for everyone.

"Sir, we have communication from the States," said Lone. "It was encrypted and in Morse, of course, at this distance. Took a while to decode the whole thing. The Germans have invaded Russia."

"When?" *Damn fools must think they have the Brits whipped,* Ed thought to himself, surprised that Hitler would have betrayed his buddy Stalin in this way. There truly was no line these Krauts wouldn't cross. *I wonder if he ever read about what the Russian Winter did to Napoleon?* Ed thought, irritated.

"The estimate is day before yesterday. We even know they're calling it Operation Barbarossa."

"That would explain why the German Embassy is doing a good imitation of a kicked hornets' nest just now. Finish your coffee, Lone, take your time, and then go back and tell Captain Hodgins we are still a *go* this afternoon. Even if the Krauts decide not to try a bugout, it's our best chance to take away their toys and tricycles."

Lone grinned widely and ferociously. Then he sobered. "Hope we don't have to take out Oberst Kramer the hard way, Sir."

Ed gave him a hard look. "You have a problem with it if we do, Sergeant?"

"No, Sir!" Lone straightened. "I'll drop him in a second to keep one of us alive. But it would make me sad afterward. Sounds funny to say, considering his stinking job, but we've been talking to him a bit, and he's a decent sort."

Ed looked quickly at Amos, whose eyes revealed his distaste for such a concept. Amos stood quickly out of respect for military confidence, thanked Inocente for the food, and made his way back to George's store to await instructions.

Once he'd gone, Ed hunkered over the table confidentially, much as he had with Lone's captain when he had been setting this plan up.

"Actually, I knew Kramer in England, years ago, and that was my estimate, too, Sergeant—decent. We haven't let him know I'm around, you know that, right?"

"Yessir. I almost dropped that, once, but the captain caught me in time."

Ed chuckled. "He told me. Oh, and can you really kick Kramer's ass with a blade?"

"Usually, Sir. But he was in pretty bad shape when he got here. Might be close to a fair fight if he did some good PT for a year or so."

Ed considered. The sergeant deserved some support for his judgment; it was always smart to encourage a noncom.

"We know now, from eavesdropping for intelligence, when his men have been out on liberty, that he lost his wife and daughter to sickness some months ago, and that the Kraut command didn't let him go see them or even bury them. We know he went deep into the bottle after that, and he was deliberately scaring off the folks he was officially trying to catch. And risking his own ass to do it. He may *be* a decent man. Honestly, I sorta feel for the guy." He met the eyes of Lone, who nodded sympathetically.

Then Ed's tone turned abruptly serious. "But he's sober now and trying to get ashore with a really dangerous force. You be ready to *drop him*, Sergeant, decent man or not. Got that?" Ed's voice held the velvet-covered steel of command.

"Aye, aye, Sir!" Lone rose, nodded his thanks to Inocente, glancing again at her belly in amazement, and left.

⌛

At one o'clock, after a couple hours of puttering around and feeling anxious, Ed and Ysidro dashed for their bedrooms, grabbed bundles of weaponry and battle dress, and made their way out the door to the Chevy. Just before firing it up, Ed remembered something and popped back into the house. He strode right to Ysidro's tool chest and extracted a brace and bit. Once back in the Chevy, he keyed the ignition as Ysidro looked at the tools inquiringly, one eyebrow raised.

"Window maker."

Ysidro nodded.

As Ed drove, an unfortunate thought occurred to him: He had forgotten to ask whether the chandler's shed was wood or metal. It was, so far, his first foul-up of this battle, and hopefully it would be his last.

Lone and Hodgins had had farther to go, though they had a jeep. But the other Marines were already at the fig tree, sitting on bulging sea bags. They looked about as innocent in civilian clothing as tigers in a vegetable market.

Bolagi, his two other guards, the two engineers, and David and the three drivers, Otto included, sat on the bumpers or leaned on the sides of the truck that had brought them from the clinic. David had several securely tied burlap sacks with him, and he did not move away from them as all stood in greeting. Jacob and Amos strode up to join them just as Lone and Hodgins putted up in their jeep.

Ed gestured them close in about him. "Separate now and stand with your teams. Make sure you know who is in charge in each team. Tell me that. And tell me the weapons you have and how much ammunition."

Ysidro had brought four heavy bundles from the bed of the Chevy. "One to the captain," Ed directed, patting each to remind himself which held the shotguns and which held a Thompson and magazines, as he handed the bundle to Hodgins.

"One to the sergeant," Ed said, pointing to Lone as Ysidro handed over the bundle. "You keep that one; it's your favorite, Lady Tomasina."

Next, Ed pointed at the American engineers. "That one to the civilian volunteers."

Once the bundles had been handed out and he had taken his own, Ed said, "You all know how a two-man fire team works. But I'll remind you again, even you Marines, who should know this in your sleep. A two-man fire team is the smallest maneuvering unit possible. A four-man is a lot safer. But there just aren't enough of us, the places we may have to fight in are too small, with too-tight access. So, two-man teams."

As he spoke, he pulled grenades from their segmented cases of waxed cardboard, assuring himself that each had the pin crimped wide and bore a wrap of tape. He handed two to each Marine, dropped one in each of his own shirt pockets, buttoned those, and gave two to Ysidro.

Addressing Bolagi, Ed went on, "I didn't have enough of these to train you men how to use them, and they're hard to get. If someone is behind solid cover, like a steel wall, wait for someone with a grenade to throw it in before you put yourself at risk." All three nodded. Ed thought hard. Then he gave a grenade to each engineer. "You two are going to be security for the drivers and the blaster. You probably won't need anything but these shotguns, but you *do* both know how?" Both men nodded, and Evans turned and tapped the butt of a .45 like Ed's that rode in his hip pocket. Ed could see the outline of a couple of spare magazines in the other back pocket. When he looked to the other engineer, Williams, he saw the man pull aside his loose shirt to reveal a revolver holstered high for cross draw.

"Well and good. If our little sweets delivery decoy works, we may not have to fire a shot. Best if we don't." Jacob looked sick. Ed understood. But personnel choice was out of his hands on this one.

They went on with meticulous preparation before heading to the chandlery.

Behind the chandlery was a medium-sized warehouse. It held all of them, and the chandlery truck as well, backed up to a loading dock.

"Ysidro and me, and Sergeant Lone's team first," Ed instructed. "Only four of us can ride at one time and leave stuff to unload as mask. That puts four rifles, two Thompsons, and," he grinned, seeing what Lone was unwrapping, "one goddamned *sword* in the shed. Enough to take the ship by ourselves, and certainly enough to hold the vicinity if we have to."

All the Marines were changing into their combat utility uniforms, donning and double-knotting boots, putting on the billed caps that kept the sun out of a shooter's eyes. Ed looked to Hodgins. "No helmets?"

"Sir, I judged them to be marginally useful today. Sorry, Sir."

Ed shrugged and used the Marine litany. "Never say you're sorry if you think you're right! And you probably are. Damn things are useless against Mauser rounds under fifty yards, in any case."

Finally, they were uniformed, armed, loaded with safeties on, and ready to begin deployment. As they stood ready, distant, increasingly insistent drumbeats reminded all that this was Diwali day, the day on which to celebrate the triumph of good over evil.

Ed sauntered over to Lone, who had given his team's Thompson to the private first class who was his teammate, and eyed the silver-glinting cutlass slung and strapped across the sergeant's back for an over-the-shoulder draw. "Lone, you *know* you're a hopeless romantic, don't you?" Hodgins snorted laughter. The youngster ducked his head, blushing a bit. He wore his .45

and spare mags on the web belt at his waist and carried a lovingly polished Springfield, with the bandolier of ammo across his chest.

The shed was wood. The door was on the side facing away from the *Klein-Seyditz*. All was good so far.

They entered, moving as quickly as they could as the chandlery driver tapped the tarp cover of the truck bed to indicate a moment's unobserved grace. The dock smelled of grilling meat, beer, and wine over the prevailing taint of old fish. The shed smelled of linseed, tar, canvas, grease, and hardware. Ed's eyes went to a bare segment of wall on the side toward the freighter. Ed immediately set to it with the brace and bit to open a peephole, blowing chips out as he worked so as not to drop traces on the outside. When the bit's central guide broke through, he shifted to his bayonet tip, cutting an irregular little hole that would hopefully not look suspicious.

A face pressed to the hole yielded a clear view of the freighter and its vehicle gangplank. Bow toward shore, the *Klein-Seyditz* had its port side against the dock, mooring cables to immense cleats fore and aft. The vehicle gangplank was in position, its wheeled end on the dock to allow tidal movement. Her bridge house and superstructure were on her starboard gunwale edge, and just inboard the gangplank were the German military transports. Other deck cargo in that area had already been offloaded.

"Now, Amos," he said, turning to the boy who looked as if he had ants in his pants, obviously itching for a purpose, "please make another one of these that points back down the dock, so we can see what's coming out here." Amos eagerly took the tools and set to work.

Finally, when Otto was preparing to return to shore for the next trip, Ed addressed him. "Thank you. On the next trip, would you please bring water? There are big water cans on my truck back at your warehouse." Everyone was drenched. The Marines had canteens, but no one else did. Ed was ashamed—he and Ysidro should have known better. The boy nodded on his way out.

It was a long afternoon. The second trip brought more men to heat up the interior of the shed, and took longer to unload, as activity on the dock was steadily increasing the closer it got to nightfall. The drums had by now become a steady throb in the men's minds, feeling synchronized with their pounding hearts.

By the time the third load arrived, the crowds had peaked. The dock was covered with throngs of colorfully dressed families, many of them with lantern-bearing children. Several fishing boats held parties that obviously planned to spend the balmy evening on board. Many people drank happily and had set up pads and other seating to watch the anticipated fireworks after full dark.

"We're going to have witnesses. No help for it. But let's not have any civilian casualties, gentlemen. Aimed fire *only*. You men with the Tommy guns, keep your bursts short and control your muzzle climb, hear?"

Ysidro's reply of "*Si*" was amused. The Marines chorused "Aye, aye, Sir!" way too loudly. Ed scooted over to his peephole to check whether the voices had betrayed them.

Reassured, he glared at the quailing Marines, who had immediately realized their errors. "Sergeant Lone, what is the technical term for that sort of carelessness?"

Whispering, and trying hard not to grin, Lone said, "*Shit for brains*, Sir."

"Precisely. Keep it down to a dull roar, unless you want to charge riflemen who are behind steel bulkheads and with a height advantage of ten feet!"

The third load had been severely crowded. David had flatly refused to be separated from his prepared blasting materials. Remaining were Jacob, Amos, Otto, and the other two drivers. Astonishingly, Jacob debarked openly from the cab, clipboard in hand, and entered equally openly. No one gave him a second look on the dock.

Ed wondered where he had learned *that* trick.

⧗

As evening began stealing light from the sky, car lights shone at the shore end of the dock, revealing to Ysidro that the police at the shore end were mounting their jeeps, as they had been warned to do. Shortly after that, George's car pulled up on the side of the dock on the shore side of the gangplank—deliberate placement to avoid blocking the view from the shed. George emerged, linen jacket seeming to flare in the setting sun, and from the passenger side came Hannah, who approached the gangplank, basket in hand, and called, voice trembling only slightly, "Kucher! Unteroffizier Kucher!"

After a few repetitions, a blond head in a Wehrmacht forage cap appeared at the head of the gangplank, and there stood the motorcycle courier who had been such a rich source of information on his officer.

"Fraulein! Welcome! Come up!"

George strolled over beside Hannah. In very slow German, he made it known that he was taking his bakery girl home, but that she had wanted to bring him some pastries, as she had heard that he would have to work during the celebration.

"They are traditional Diwali sweets," Hannah called to him.

Kucher leaned his Mauser against the bulkhead and made his way down the gangplank, grinning happily.

From inside the shed, Ed watched as Kucher and Hannah spoke, just for a minute. She put her hand gently on his arm, appeared to say a warm goodbye, flashed him a knockout smile, and re-entered the car, waving to the young German as George backed the car into a turn and returned toward shore. Kucher pulled aside the covering cloth of the generous basket, sniffing ecstatically. With a satisfied smile, he turned and made his way back up the gangplank.

Ed could not help grinning. *Like father, like daughter,* he thought. *Both are talented actors.*

"Jacob," Ed said in a low voice over his shoulder to the man who stood anxiously behind him, "Hannah has performed her mission and retreated safely. Perfect work!"

Jacob's shoulders, which had tensed the moment he had heard Hannah's voice, slumped in relief. Where had Hannah learned such flirtatious behavior? Jacob shuddered at how naturally it had come to her.

"Now, we give it ten minutes, the doctor said, 'after ingestion,'" Ed said. "He also said the ipecac is in a solution with glycerin and sugar syrup. Just the thing to juice up all those fruit and jelly rolls, and the other goodies our Nazi friends took on board."

He glanced at his watch. "Let's just give them fifteen minutes, time to scarf down a couple of pastries apiece, and by then it will be dark and they can't see us coming." Still grinning ferociously at the genius of the plan and how nicely it was all coming together, Ed added, "If this works, we won't have to worry about killing any of them—just resisting when they *beg* us to kill them and put them out of their misery."

Laughter made the sweltering shed cooler, somehow. A sense of relief seemed to settle in, despite the fact that the hardest work was still before them.

Ten minutes passed in silence as Ed kept watch. "All right. Shotgun team, either side of the door, outside, keep the shotguns pointed down, along your legs so you just look like you're celebrating with everyone else, just leaning there after too much wine."

The engineers moved in obedience. "Wait," he said, hand up to stop them a moment, "I want you to hear the rest. Lone, you two go around the seaward end of this sweatbox, let your Tommy man lead up the gangplank, and take a prone position *before the top*, so you have cover, and prepare to deny them the deck. You follow with a ready grenade in hand. *Don't* pull the pin or untape it until you are ready to use it. Captain, your team to the shore end," he hooked his thumb, "again, rush at the same time as team Lone, on my voice command, the Tommy man prone at the top of the gangway. In your team, I see that's gonna be you. Your backup goes behind with a grenade."

Hodgins nodded affirmation.

"As soon as you wave a clear signal, I will come up with Sergeant Ysidro and all of my guardsmen, and we'll be prepared to push onto the deck and take shelter to cover your staggered advance," Ed barked. "Sergeant Lone, your team will be the first in that advance. Where you go is up to what we see and hear. After that, we'll just have to adapt to overcome. *Semper fi!*"

All the Marines whispered back, in chorus, "*Semper fi!*"

"Shotgun team," he addressed the engineers, "keep these civilians safe, and we will *try* to remember to call out when we are coming back. Jacob and David, you move on board only with the protection of at least one team. You drivers, a team will come to bring you on board to bring off the trucks. Amos!"

The young man was startled to attention, surprised to be called upon. "Yes, Colonel?"

"Do what you do best. You're on lookout. I want you to be my eyes and ears. You are a *ghost*, you got that? Keep your eyes peeled for Nazi scum."

"Yes, Sir!"

"Teams out to positions behind the shed. Now."

Ed emerged from the doorway, gesturing his group to stay inside, looked about, then popped back to his spy hole. There was no sign from the deck, no guards in sight. He re-emerged, went to Lone's end of the shed, then leaned around to peer and listen. Faintly, he caught the sound of desperate retching.

"Go! Go!" he commanded. The teams scampered forward, and Ed, standing against the seaward end of the shed, saw Captain Hodgins' wave of "clear" against the sky. "Ysidro. All out. Evans, Williams, I'm counting on you. See you later."

"'Luck, Colonel."

"God bless."

With that, the group rushed away from the shed to the gangway, Ed leading the way. As they approached, the sound of retching was unmistakable. *Nice work, Hannah,* he thought as he ran stealthily, flanked by the rest of his men. Bringing up the rear was Amos, running soundlessly and taking cover in the shadows, a mirage.

The goal was to control the hatch to the bridge and the galley behind it, as well as the main hold hatch toward the rear. Ed paused at the gangplank, peering around to ensure they were unseen and unheard. But all that could be seen were revelers in Diwali garb on the pier and the twinkling of thousands of lights from candles and lanterns. The steady beat of drums from points all over town were clashing with each other, drowning out Ed's words, as the Diwali celebration was reaching a fever pitch.

"Bolagi, your team to the deck there," he said, indicating with his hand, "one pointed in each direction."

This was all the direction they needed. They nodded, then sprinted like the dark shadows of rats in alleyways, along the bulkhead behind the bridge, their menacing rifles pointed forward and aft.

"Ysidro. You and your man stay here, inboard of the bulkhead, and prepare to deny the dock if a bunch of Krauts show up running."

"*Si*, Coronel," said Ysidro reluctantly, glaring at his patron and friend.

"I'm doing my damndest to get you home to those kids of yours," Ed said in response. "But I really don't want anyone crawling up our backsides. I know you can do it, *padre*."

Ysidro frowned but gave a slow nod.

"Captain, I will take my guard here. I'll get between those back trucks and command the bridge hatch. I want you to join us when we've settled. Sergeant Lone, you boys do the entry onto the bridge when you hear my rifle butt on the deck."

He was met with responses of "Aye, aye."

Lone's scuttle was straight across the open deck to the bridge. Ed could see him flick his head around the edge of the hatch; he saw the slung rifle and the .45 that led the way in. There was a guttural shriek. Lone's teammate leaped in after him. Then, a thump. Lone's head popped back out. His low voice called to Ed, "One Kraut sailor. We forgot rope, dammit."

"Just a second, Sergeant." Ed pulled his Bowie bayonet, slashed twice at one of the tarp lashings of the truck behind them, tossed the cut length of rope in Lone's direction, and thoughtfully mounted the bayonet on his Springfield, rather than sheathing it.

He turned to Hodgins, still beside him in shadow at the bottom of the gangplank. "Captain, the galley is the second hatch there," he directed, pointing. "Judging from the sounds I just heard, someone is in there, and he's probably in a bad way. But the galley on these things is small, with only room for the stove, supplies, and a little table with benches where four at a time can eat. Don't risk your lives to save a Kraut, hear me?"

"Aye, aye, Sir."

"Go."

And that was the end of an orderly advance. A Wehrmacht-uniformed figure lurched out of the galley hatch, Mauser waving wildly, and fired at Lone where he peered out of the bridge hatch. The round clanged off the hatch door and ricocheted away into the distance. Lone dropped back into shelter, even as Bolagi rose from his position almost at the man's feet, like a fluid shadow. His butt stroke dropped the German like a sack of rice. From the sodden *thump* of it, it sounded to Ed as though he had scored in the middle of the man's chest. The German's Mauser slammed onto the deck, muzzle first, and then cartwheeled away.

Ed ran back, cut another length of rope from the truck, and, summoning his guard with a shoulder pull, dived across the deck to where Bolagi crouched beside his gasping victim. He gave Bolagi the rope, then peered into the galley into which Hodgins' team had disappeared. Hodgins had a man pinned, but the fellow was spewing bile across the little table, convulsing madly and throwing the captain about as he spasmed from the violence of his nausea. The pastry basket and its surviving contents were scattered across the deck. Hodgins' accompanying private whipped a piece of rope from his belt, bent to tie the sick man's jerking wrists, and, with one foot, pinned the back of the poor fellow's knee to the bench. The young Marine looked up, saw Ed's stare, and replied, "Just followed your example, Sir."

"Good thinking, son," Ed said approvingly.

Ed hopped back out on deck, flattening out against the bulkhead. "Lone, Bolagi!" He whispered loudly. "Prisoners to the galley! Now!"

They made to move, but Ed's hand held them back for further direction. "Everyone out here on deck!"

The teams gathered around him.

"Okay, no passage the other side of the bridge house, no structures forward of it but the chain locker for the anchor. Lone, I want your team to get up there and see if anyone is hiding in the forward deck cargo or in the chain locker. Finish those checks before you come aft again. We need a secure rear."

Rapidly, as the two men began sprinting forward, Lone barked, "Aye, aye, Sir!" His feet seemed to keep time with the rapid patter of bongo drums.

Ed turned to Bolagi. His voice dropped lower. "We now have the interior of the ship, which includes an internal passageway that leads from the rear hold to the bridge house, past the engine room, the desalinator room, and two other smaller holds that open off the center passageway."

"Yes, Baas," said the guard whose dark skin in these shadows made his teeth appear to glow in the moonlight.

"Bolagi, your team goes into the bridge, that room there," Ed pointed. "Open the hatch to the passageway, *carefully*, and prepare to use rifle fire to hold them off."

"Okay, Baas." Bolagi's grin was an ivory gleam in his ebony face. He was enjoying the excitement of the evening.

Ed turned to Hodgins. "Captain, I'm inclined to wait until Lone rejoins us to move aft. Back there is an above-decks watch house and lashed deck cargo boxes. Too many possible fire lanes."

"Yes, Sir. Makes sense."

Then one round after another clanged off the bulkhead. All threw themselves prone, squirming to bring their muzzles to bear. The muzzle flashes were from the bow. Ed peered up the deck and saw an unsteady figure working a Mauser, half kneeling against a cargo pile, partially scattered. He'd been concealed in there, obviously, and even as Ed made the figure out, another lunged from the shadows, silver blade gleaming. Ed snapped, "Hold your fire!" and Lone whipped his sword out in a flash, bringing the edge down on the rifleman's trigger arm. Then he withdrew in the fashion of a saber man's whip. The Mauser clattered to the ground, and Lone stepped in and put his basket hilt into the German's face. At that moment, the German collapsed as Lone's teammate pounced on him out of the shadows along the starboard gunwale.

Ed did some mental arithmetic. That was one sailor and three troopers down. One trooper left. He sent a silent prayer of thanks to the heavens for the steady beating of the drums that had persisted throughout, a subtle battle cry urging them onward. Ed hoped that those drums, along with the fireworks that had erratically popped and fizzed since late afternoon all over Paramaribo, had masked the sounds of gunshot.

Lone and his teammate dragged their prey down the deck. The prisoner alternately retched weakly and whimpered.

"Sergeant," Ed called to him, "get a battle dressing on that man's arm. Good sword work. Was he hidden in the cargo?"

"I think so, Sir. We'd just cleared the chain locker and heard boxes falling behind us, so we split up and circled the piles."

Ed spoke loudly. "One left. Captain, get into the bridge and roll a grenade down that passageway to put our fugitive's head down. Then move to each forward hold and use another, putting Bolagi's team ahead of you down the passageway, to keep our fellow from taking you under fire. When we get to the outside hatch of the big hold back there, we'll chuck one in ourselves, but will *not* enter, so you can advance aft without us shooting your asses off, or vice versa. Clear?"

"Yes, Sir. Are we calling for surrender or just going for a kill?"

"Take surrender if it's offered, of course, but let's not lose anyone. We've come too close already. They *are* brave bastards, aren't they?"

The captain's emphatic nod was accompanied by Lone's muttered, "Oh, yeah."

Ed had his rifle trained aft, as did his guardsman. Lone's Tommy man took point, the submachine gun snugged against his hip, head up and scanning. They shuffled aft, spread across the deck between the railing and the bulkhead of the superstructure, then fanned out to separate themselves as they approached the hatch in the rear deck. The ship gonged as Hodgins' grenade went off inside her, and Ed bent to loosen the rear hatch that led down to the hold, kicked it clanging open, stepped back, and untaped and unpinned a grenade. Quickly, he dropped it in and circled, throwing the heavy hatch shut.

He waited five, maybe six seconds. The hatch popped open some inches with the pressure of the explosion, then closed again under its own weight.

Ed and Lone threw it open again, and Lone peered in over his rifle sights. A weak cry came up. Ed put a restraining hand on the sergeant's arm. "That is the sound of a German surrendering." A wide grin spread across Ed's face. "Kind of pleasant, isn't it?"

"Yessir!" Lone answered with his own grin.

In the end, Ed sent Lone back to the bridge to call off Hodgins' advance. Then, Lone's Tommy man and Ed's young guardsman had to go down to secure and carry forward a concussed and somewhat deaf German whose name, he moaned, was Kucher. Kucher was covered in vomit and drool, and was weeping inconsolably for some reason. *He'll be happy later,* Ed thought, *when he realizes he narrowly escaped becoming mincemeat.*

"Captain, please escort our drivers on board," Ed instructed Hodgins when they had all reconvened. "Remember to sound off to the engineers when you approach the shed. Evans and Williams, remember."

With an "Aye, aye, Sir!" they were gone.

"Lone, wake up that sailor. We need to get this thing going to scuttle it in a safe place."

"Yes, Sir," Lone whispered, grinning, and they too were gone.

Ed pulled his guardsmen with him through the use of hand gestures, and the two strolled over to Ysidro and his guardsman.

"Anyone seem concerned out there?"

"No, Coronel, many are setting off firecrackers on the dock. Like us."

His grin glistened in the reflected light from the shore, and his tone was happy. Any action where everyone was walking afterward was a good action.

Hodgins brought the drivers aboard, all moving quietly.

"Take the trucks. I see the Krauts unchained them for us. Anyone know how to run a motorcycle?"

Hodgins cleared his throat. "Uh, I do, Sir."

"Will wonders never cease," Ed chuckled and shook his head. "Take your teammate in the sidecar, with *my* Tommy, which I want *back*, Captain. Escort the trucks and trailers to the clinic. Have George find another driver for the cycle or hide it behind the clinic, and get your own tails back to your barracks. You still have liberty hours and a town full of tipsy girls."

Hodgins stroked the Thompson he held mock-covetously, looking sad, which elicited chuckles from all his Marines. Then he answered, "Aye, aye, Sir."

In a rumble of powerful engines, they were all gone in just minutes.

"Lone, you and these men," Ed said, gesturing to his guardsmen, "take all the Wehrmacht pukes to the shed." At this, every native English speaker snorted or chuckled. "Remember to call ahead to Evans and Williams, tie the *hell* out of the prisoners, and bring Jacob, David, David's explosives, and both engineers back here. Bolagi, follow Sergeant Lone's orders."

"Okay, Baas."

"Sir, just one little problem." Sergeant Lone was sincerely quiet. "That sailor has a concussion, I think, 'cause his pupils are different sizes, and he had some of those pastries, too. He is borderline unconscious, Sir."

"Can't be helped now. Send him off with the Wehrmacht," Ed said distractedly, realizing he now needed to steer this enormous ship away from the dock. He headed to the bridge and studied the controls. It was nothing he'd ever seen before. *Dammit!* He really didn't want to blow her at dock—it would likely take out ten percent of the dockage for this tiny country. Why hadn't this occurred to him earlier?

Jacob and David and the bag-bearing Marines and guards entered and proceeded to mill about, and Ed banished the armed men out to the deck, instructing them to check the holds for more ammo or interesting loot.

Jacob and David were moving and talking together, then were gone.

He addressed Lone. "You and I need to go to the ship captain's quarters to strip and bag everything, even if we have to use blankets. We're putting the man ashore and scuttling his ship. At least we can return his personals." Lone nodded in agreement.

Ed fidgeted and then remembered where their ship's intelligence had put Kramer's quarters. The two men went there and found a leather toiletries roll, a clothing folder similar to his own, a map case, and a small leather grip bag. Ed peered inside it and found a silver-framed photo of a tiny girl and a glowing young woman, along with documents written in German, and another frame containing two locks of reddish-blond hair behind glass. Under the bunk was a lockbox. He and Lone made bundles with blankets and toted them back to the bridge. He would have wanted the same courtesy.

Jacob and David were back, David laying fuses behind him that led into the internal passageway.

Jacob addressed Ed as if reading a list he had memorized. "Engine, propeller shaft glands, four sea cocks, and the keel of the ship where it comes up below the aft hold. We opened all the hatches so the ship won't swell like a big metal balloon."

"Great. Now the problem is turning on the engines and getting her away from this dock." Ed was sour and frustrated as he once again glared helplessly at the controls.

Jacob smiled, moved to the console, and moved a lever here and a switch there. Then, wordlessly, he darted back down the interior passage. Within a minute, the hull began to vibrate with engine sound. Jacob re-emerged, grinning.

"I spent weeks watching Captain Cervantes run one of these!" He flushed with pride.

Ed just gaped at the little accountant.

"Colonel Ed, do you have anyone who has ever run a ship?"

"No, actually." Ed hung his head and held his hands up in surrender.

"Then I must be the one to guide the *Klein-Seyditz* to her grave."

"Can you swim?"

Starkly, his fear showing, Jacob responded, "No." He gulped.

Ed turned and pulled a dusty life vest from the bulkhead where several of them hung—years-old decorations that probably no one had ever worn. He handed one to the little man. "Height of fashion, Jacob." Jacob produced a shaky smile.

"Lone, get that lifeboat back there into the water, get the outboard going, and stand by in her."

"Aye, aye, Sir!" His cutlass hilt gleamed a moment as Lone again sprinted away.

David, waiting patiently, made gestures and spoke slowly, in Dutch and Taki Taki. "This is a fuse that will burn approximately two minutes. This is a second fuse of the same length. At the end of the fuses is a radiating tree of detonation cord, which explodes along its entire length when a fuse reaches it. Light the fuse, run, jump, swim, and, less than two minutes later, all the charges go." The explanation took longer in the broken mélange of languages, but his meaning was clear.

"David, all you men, except Jacob, go to the dock and stand by the dock cables. Take all these bundles. Now."

Ed and Jacob were alone. Jacob trembled, minutely. Ed looked into his eyes. "Can you do this?"

Dark eyes, much like Sarah's in shade, looked hard at the colonel. "It is time to fight back, Colonel."

"Here is a box of matches. Light both fuses, then run to the starboard side, back behind the watch house." He pointed to avoid any misunderstandings. "Then jump as far out as you can." Jacob's eyes could not have been wider as he took in the immense height from the ship's deck to the surface of the water, and his overly rapid nods betrayed his fear and determination to see his mission through.

"Sergeant Lone and I will be there in the life boat when you jump," Ed continued, pointing. "Head her to the shallows over at the mouth of the river, and jump off well before she grounds, Jacob. You don't want her going off near you."

"I understand, Colonel. And if I should . . . tell Rebecca and Hannah and Amos I love them."

Amos! Where had that boy gone? Had he been found?

"I will, Sir," Ed reassured the man, too concerned about keeping Jacob on task. "And good luck."

⌛

On the north beach, the major fireworks began as Ed went to the bow, grasped the rope hanging there, and slid down, burning his hands just a bit, to the lifeboat Lone was keeping up against the bow of the *Klein-Seyditz*.

"You on the dock. Cast off the lines!" Ed made his voice boom, waving his hands grandly. "Sergeant, or Cox'n, or Dartagnan, whatever you are, head for the river yonder." He sat as the grinning Marine gunned the outboard and curved them away.

The *Klein-Seyditz*, slower to gain way, still moved smoothly after them.

"Hang off her stern, on the seaward side, Sergeant."

"Aye, aye, Sir." Lone curved the lifeboat about and arrowed back into the ordered position, throttling back to the big freighter's still-moderate speed as he matched her course.

The fireworks began as the boat gathered speed, the magnificent aerial display filling the sky on the other side of the dock, and Ed, genuinely enjoying them, was jolted to hear Lone's "Oh, shit!"

"What is it, Sarge?"

"All that rifle fire, Sir. We have a hole." Sure enough, there was a small spout of water just behind their bows. Ed stripped off his shirt, ramming it into the hole with the tip of his bayonet sheath, shedding his weapons belt to get the tool into play. Seawater splashed his holster and he cursed.

"Okay, keep us on course."

Ahead, Jacob's white-shirted form leaped off the starboard stern, legs flailing, and Lone, without waiting for orders, accelerated toward the splash.

But as they closed, it became apparent Jacob was having difficulty. The aged straps of his vest had simply parted as he hit the water, and Ed and Lone saw his one-handed grip slip off the bobbing vest as his head disappeared beneath the dark water in a spume of bubbles.

Ed stood, ready to dive in after Jacob, when he heard a splash behind him. He looked back and saw Amos, in wet clothes clinging to his long, lean form, swimming for all his might after his father.

Jacob was still thrashing close to the surface, but as his clutching hands interfered with his own retrieval, Amos poked his desperate father in the gut, turned him, and made great kicking efforts to surface both of them, his furious efforts helping them to at last gain some distance from the ship.

The water convulsed. There was a great throb and surge, and Ed realized he had heard the last heartbeat of the *Klein-Seyditz*. If they didn't move quickly, it would pull them all under with it. "Lone!" he called, then released his holster, letting the weapons fall to the floor of the boat before diving in after the Roseweig men. Within a few strokes, he and Amos reached each other, with Lone bringing the small boat up just behind. They broke the surface, and Ed climbed in. Amos clung to the edge of the boat and clambered in himself. The two younger men, with considerable effort, hauled Jacob aboard, where he promptly vomited seawater and began coughing convulsively.

Finally, they were all on board, gasping. No one had died, and Ed, rolling tiredly over a bench, said, "Sergeant, if you would, please, take us back to the dock so I can retreat several hundred miles inland? Thank you."

Against the few lights from the shore, the *Klein-Seyditz* could be seen, settled in the river's mud, listing to starboard, submerged to her gunwales on that side into the sea. She would not be going anywhere ever again.

The outboard sputtered to life, drums beat steadily, and fireworks crescendoed, echoed, and made brilliances in the sky.

CHAPTER 38

The president's palace was ablaze with light, and a band played softly within. The entryway was framed by torches that were tall enough to avoid igniting ladies' gowns but which, Sarah noted, emitted the unmistakable scent of citronella, as had the lanterns inside the front reception room. She had come to love this tiny South American country and think of it as home, but one of its few repugnant drawbacks was the mosquitoes, which took no holidays in Suriname, even after the rainy season had come to an end. They were few now but as bloodthirsty as ever.

She had accompanied George Butler tonight, Lijsbet having been kept up all night by Talia's wails and remaining home. Since arriving in Suriname with only one small bag of clothes brought from Amsterdam, Sarah had not purchased many clothes and had not found the need for many since she wore a uniform every day at the clinic. Only a few simple, utilitarian pieces to replace her old German rags were all she had invested in. But she had wanted to dress appropriately for such an occasion—especially one with such portent to their lives—and, yes, she had wanted to impress Ed Beltran but had been shy about admitting it. Fortunately, George had asked one of the employees at his store to assist Sarah in finding an appropriate dress, and he had given it to her as a gift. Its lovely jade green color had made it the most beautiful garment Sarah had ever seen. It was deeply satisfying to see how it swished against her skin, hugging her curves perfectly and contrasting pleasingly with her long, dark hair. In the mirror, after dressing earlier, Sarah had smiled at the prospect of Ed seeing her in the dress and felt sure she would stun him speechless.

Now, she wore it like a gorgeous suit of armor at this ball, surrounded as she was by Nazi soldiers and American Marines. Hodgins and Lone awaited them in the reception room, in full dress blues. The uniforms were perfectly appointed, and both wore pistols in white holsters, their swords slung. She was positively smug when she caught Lone's appreciative onceover as she and George approached, even though he had blinked and glanced away quickly when he'd realized how obvious he had been. The four exchanged pleasant hellos, all upholding perfectly innocent façades, as if their rag-tag team hadn't just that day overcome an entire unit of Nazis.

Then she watched as Lone's eye caught that of Colonel Beltran, who approached the party at the entrance. The men all exchanged equally crisp salutes in unison, like clockwork. Then Ed shook hands with George.

Sarah was impressed by the Marine turnout, considering the day's operation. There was only one notable exception, but she knew where Ysidro was. She looked back and forth from one to the next, smiling helloes at the men.

"You are all from the same mold, it seems. Very pretty," she joked. Hodgins blushed, and Lone grinned. Then Ed turned to look fully at her, and it became clear to her that, until that second, he had not recognized her. She had adequately stunned him, and she stood beaming as she watched him take in her entire person with his eyes.

"Sarah!" he said, then quickly corrected himself. "Ms. Lipinski! I... You... You are radiant tonight." He bowed respectfully at her and cleared his throat.

She dipped her head slightly. "Colonel Beltran, it's nice to see you. I trust you have... recovered, since the day's Diwali activities?"

They exchanged knowing smiles. For Sarah, the room may as well have been empty; she saw only Ed.

"Quite nicely, thank you! And you?" His face spread into a full grin.

"I, too, have had a wonderful day, thank you, Colonel! I come with happy news from Inocente."

Ed's jaw dropped. "She didn't?!"

Sarah nodded vigorously. "She did! Ysidro is with them now. But," she said, affecting a mock frown, "unfortunately, the doctor made one mistake."

Ed sobered. "A problem?"

"Just one tiny one. It seems that the happy couple has *three* daughters."

All five of them laughed heartily, but Ed's had him doubled over, tears in his eyes. "Poor Ysidro! Permanently outnumbered!" Once he had pulled himself together, he thought to ask, "And Inocente? She's okay?"

Sarah nodded again. "She's magnificent! She has amazed us all with her grace. She will be an excellent mother."

After exchanging a few jibes at Ysidro's expense with Lone and Hodgins, Ed straightened himself, nodded as an affirmation of the serious nature of the occasion, and turned his attention to George. "Mr. Butler, if you don't mind…"

George chuckled and pretended to cough in order to mask the humor he found in the situation before him—rough, indelicate Ed Beltran, in love. Now he *knew* he had seen everything. "Of course, be my guest."

Ed wordlessly held his left arm to Sarah, perhaps a bit more closely than decorum dictated, but she didn't mind in the least. Her purse bumped his arm awkwardly, and she giggled.

Ed turned his attention to Captain Hodgins and asked confidentially, "How does it look?"

Hodgins offered a polite smile. "Our ambassador, who I am told is called a representative, and his staff are milling about in a herd of diplomats in the Grand Ballroom. Our German friend is sticking pretty close to the wine bar, chatting up the president's middle daughter."

"Good recon, Captain." The two men exchanged salutes again, and Ed escorted Sarah into the room. George and the Marines looked on in wonderment, following behind without a word.

There was a receiving party of Surinamese government aides, but, of course, as this was an evening-long event, the president and his family were not on line, if they ever had been.

Ed shook hands, white gloves still on, and swept Sarah past the servant, whose intent of relieving guests of hats and weapons had been disappointed, into the interior of the palace.

"We are better armed going to this ball than we were going on a raiding party," Ed mused aloud, and Sarah smiled.

The "ambassador" from America wasn't technically an ambassador, just as Suriname wasn't actually a "country." But the Dutch government in exile was here, as were the Free French diplomatic mission and the German embassy, with relatively free movement in town for the Reich's diplomats; however, German citizens, including missionaries, had been interned since 1939.

All the diplomats, including the ones the others thought of as criminals, mingled amiably enough, fueled by fine liquor and champagne, plates of good food, and the chance to socialize.

The president, seeing the resplendent Marine cortège, homed in on them, despite the gaudy, iridescent sashes on the room's French peacocks. He approached them with enthusiasm, extended a glad hand to Ed's. "Colonel Beltran! How are you, Sir?"

"I'm well, Mr. President. Enjoying the Diwali festivities. Quite a show out there!" *If only you knew what a show it was,* Ed thought smugly. "You met Sarah earlier today, and I know you have met Captain Hodgins. This is Sergeant Lone, a fine noncommissioned officer of our Corps."

The president shook Lone's hand, bemused by the resplendent uniform with the broad gold stripes down the trouser legs, the silver hilt of the sergeant's cutlass, and his shining young face.

"Sergeant, you must meet my youngest daughter tonight. She is a great admirer of your Corps," the president said.

Lone looked startled.

"She is just fifteen and has been reading about the great battles of the World War; she has been reading aloud to me about your tremendous struggle at Belleau Wood."

Now, Lone looked seriously embarrassed. Sarah covered her mouth to hide her giggle.

"Sir, Colonel Beltran actually *fought* in that battle . . ."

"Yes, but you are so much closer to her age! Come with me. A moment, Gentlemen, and I will return." Unstoppable, the president swept the sergeant off toward a knot of giggling young ladies next to the buffet.

Hodgins grinned at Ed. "Don't think he understands about our sergeants, Sir."

Ed chuckled, and Sarah looked inquisitive. "I don't understand…"

"The Marine Corps couldn't exist without its sergeants. In other services, the rank of sergeant is just someone to give orders to a squad, under close supervision. In the Corps, a sergeant taking command of a company in combat is fairly common. We trust our sergeants a lot."

He thought a moment. "In fact, that one there," he said, gesturing to where the giggles had reformed with the splendid sergeant in a fluttering circle of confinement, "saved my life tonight. Twice."

Sarah just looked, astonished. Until this moment, she had not realized the extent of the scrapes these men had faced earlier.

"By the way, Hodgins," Ed said over his should in a low voice, "Lone has good small boat skills and edged weapons skills; he's an expert shot, as you know, and is ahead of the game on thinking and initiative. How's his education?"

Hodgins shrugged, regretfully. "Two years of high school. Joined us to avoid starvation. Reads all the time, but . . ."

"Shame. But you know, when they pinned bars on *me*, I hadn't any college at all. Had to do it while I was stationed in D.C. right after the war and by correspondence while I was detached. I'll write an old professor at Georgetown and see about correspondence. You okay with that?"

"Very much so, Sir!"

The president was returning. His face was anxious, and George Butler angled in and walked alongside him as he came, massive beside the president but with similar anxiety on his face. Ed knew exactly what had them anxious.

"No one killed," he assured them, hands up to halt the president's worry. "The *Klein-Seyditz* is at the bottom of the harbor. Out of your shipping lanes and away from your dock." All eyes turned to look at the president for a reaction.

The pudgy shoulders sagged with relief. So did the much bigger ones next to the president.

"By the way, you can trust the sergeant the way you would us," Ed added. "I need to have a talk with Oberst Kramer."

"He is there," the president said, distracted by relief and gesturing to the door into the next room. "Where he and my daughter have been talking and holding the *same* glasses of wine for the past hour and a half." The president looked simultaneously amused and apprehensive. "She has barely smiled since the fever took her husband three years ago. But a *German*?"

Ed and Hodgins shook their heads in solemn commiseration. Sarah was shocked at the mere thought but said nothing.

"Dr. Adelmann told me of your idea for the Germans. If you can do what you intend, getting them out of Suriname quickly, I would very much appreciate that," the president added. "I have enough confined Germans, and wouldn't want to add trained soldiers to the mix. What about their weapons?"

"At the outermost mine," Ed replied. "Their equipment has been off-loaded into locked storage in the mine compound, and their transport is going to come back to take them to Guyana. I kept some of their small arms out, so they can guard their own convoy, but they won't get those until we're over your border."

Sarah, though apprised of the basics of the day's events and the ultimate goal of the original plan, had given up trying to follow details. There was plenty of time to figure it out later.

The president nodded his approval. "Very good. You may use the meeting room where we met the last time. I'll put an aide at the door so you can have privacy. And I will come with you now to pry away my daughter."

"Good. Hodgins, go rescue the sergeant, and the room we are going to be in is down that corridor and three doors down on the left. Would you take Ms. Lipinski with you?" He held his arm out softly to Hodgins. "The three of you can find wine and snacks on the way."

Sarah was taken aback. "No!"

Ed looked down at her, startled. Hodgins and the president wore bland expressions, as if to say, "not my problem."

She was determined. "No, I am staying with you. This man, this…Kramer," she spat the word out as if it tasted badly, "has chased me as far as he is going to be allowed to. He and his *kameraden* hunted down and killed my husband, not to mention thousands of innocent people. I will face him with you."

"All right," Ed conceded, "but just don't get in the way of my right hand. If anything happens, move away quickly."

She nodded slowly and met his eyes with a smile.

⧗

Gunter was entranced. When he had entered the room earlier that night, he had thought this woman was Gerta.

This woman, Sandie, was a pale blonde, although Gerta's hair had been strawberry blonde. She was also taller than Gerta, and with eyes the blue of cornflowers, while Gerta's had been green.

Even so, it felt immediately as if they had known each other for years, although they had only gotten acquainted this evening.

Sandie looked beyond Gunter, which was not too hard for her, as she was nearly as tall as he, and frowned prettily. "Oh, here is Papa again. He has been *so* protective since I came back from Holland. And that is a *very* nice uniform the colonel is wearing. I've never seen him in uniform before."

Gunter turned, casually, then spun. *Beltran!* Gunter was visibly shaken to see the American Marine who was apparently a colonel now. What was he doing here? Gunter had never seen him in all the time he had been coming to the embassy.

Their ranks were equal, but Gunter realized that Beltran's was probably senior. Gunter initiated the salute as automatic courtesy. Beltran returned it crisply and smiled.

"Hello, Kramer. Oberst now, eh? Catching up to me."

"Well, as you know, Colonel, rank comes quickly in wartime." Gunter took note of the Colt .45 and sword on Beltran's uniform.

Sandie was looking back and forth at them, somewhat dumbfounded by their obvious acquaintance.

They were speaking English, and Gunter turned to Sandie, concerned lest he be giving offense. "You have English?"

She smiled and replied in crisp Oxford English, "A year of university there, Oberst."

Smiling, reassured that he had not been impolite to this delightful woman, Gunter turned back to Ed, and froze with shock to notice the beautiful woman in the green dress standing next to the colonel. She looked at Gunter as if she hated him. He felt a frisson of fear tingle his neck. She was clearly a Jew; her features reminded him of thousands of others whom he had put into captivity.

And from her expression, she clearly knew who he was.

Gunter nodded to her, face politely impassive. "And?"

"This is Sarah Lipinski," Ed turned to her, looking at her with such obvious pride and adoration that it made Gunter's stomach clench with memories of his old life.

He executed an automatic bow—ironic certainly, but not feeling as strange as he might have expected—but did not extend his hand, sensing it would not be welcome.

To his puzzlement, though her face remained intent, the beautiful woman extended her hand, palm down, in a courteous greeting. Gunter grasped it gently and briefly with thumb and two fingers, bowed again.

"I am honored."

At this, Sarah had to fight the urge to laugh aloud at the disingenuous comment.

"Kramer, we need to talk. Would you come with me for a bit?" Ed beckoned.

This could not be good—an American colonel that he knew had reappeared out of the blue, and the fool in the Reich had just broken a treaty and invaded an ally. This was bad timing.

"Of course, Colonel," Gunter replied regretfully, hesitant to leave Sandie, who had made him feel more alive in the last hour or so than he had felt in years, and whom he believed would think much less of him once her father had had a few words with her alone.

The president smiled, looking at his obviously irritated daughter, and offered a trade. "Ms. Lipinski, this is my daughter, Sandie, who is about your age. Perhaps you two would like to chat, while the menfolk talk?"

Sarah did not even hesitate. "No. I will be with the colonel during this talk."

Sandie brightened, took Gunter's left arm as the other woman had been taking the colonel's, and asked with determination, "Then, Papa, there is no reason to segregate the womenfolk, is there?"

The president, outmaneuvered, could only smile in acquiescence.

Ed was frustrated to have Sarah involved in this conversation, but it now seemed he didn't have any control over her. However, he couldn't help but admire her even more for her willingness to get in the thick of things. This was definitely the woman for him. No shrinking violet here. He would simply have to get used to the roller coaster of being out of control. He had already started to enjoy the ride.

As they strolled toward the meeting room, Kramer gestured to a German-uniformed noncom to join them. The man grasped a plate of food and a glass of wine in his huge left hand and saluted with his right, and both Kramer and Beltran returned the salute.

Ed did a bit of a double take at the man's size, which reminded him of a refrigerator.

"Colonel, Ms. Lipinski, Sandie, this is my oberfeldwebel, Ermenthaller." All nodded. Ermenthaller, not having two words of English, nonetheless followed his officer's introduction and nodded back amiably, his blocky face impassive. He wore the SS uniform (incongruously to German eyes) with Wehrmacht insignia and wore no sidearm except the SS ceremonial dagger.

"*Kom*, Ermenthaller," Gunter spoke to him in rapid-fire German, "this American colonel wants to talk to me, and perhaps you should know about something as soon as I do." He waved Ermenthaller to join the party, not permitting an objection.

Ermenthaller put his plate and glass down on the nearest table, and they were immediately pounced upon and borne away by a white-jacketed servant. With a regretful look, Ermenthaller joined Gunter as he made his way down the hall.

Two Marines in dress blues stood outside the entrance to the room, faces to the front. An administrative aide stood across the hall from them, hands folded in front of him, impassive as a piece of furniture.

Captain Hodgins and Sergeant Lone. And both wearing blade and pistol. *I didn't know Lone had a long blade,* Gunter thought. *This is a bad thing.*

Gunter halted abruptly in the hallway. Perforce, Sandie, who still held his arm, halted with him. "Sandie, perhaps you should help your father with the guests. This could take some time and may be very boring." *And dangerous,* he considered.

Her eyes searched his face, caressing even the great scar that marred one side of it. She reluctantly released his arm and stepped back, comprehending that this was an attempt to send her out of possible danger. She looked at Ed, then at the two Marines in blue uniforms, and her eyes widened. Then she stepped back to Gunter's side, regained her grip on his arm, and said decisively, "I am staying with you." Her look at the others was defiant.

Gunter thought at that moment that he might even be falling in love. *Gerta used to look at me like that.*

Apprehension twisted his gut, but he nodded acceptance. He marched forward, Sandie firmly on his arm. Hodgins and Lone came to attention and saluted their own colonel and the oberst; their salutes were returned, and Gunter peered pointedly at Lone's silver-hilted cutlass. Lone managed to blush somewhat guiltily while standing at attention.

"Hmmph. Much I have not known," Gunter said as he entered.

Hodgins shut the door, leaving the aide in the hallway, and Gunter noted how that man had moved to put his back to the center of the doorway, obviously there to prevent interruptions.

Then Hodgins and Lone, now inside, took positions of attention on either side of the doorway. Gunter suspected that if he wished to leave at this point, he would have to fight. He was only accompanied by one unarmed feldwebel, facing three armed men, one of whom could outfight him with a sword. He looked apologetically at Ermenthaller, sorry he had dragged the man into this.

"Captain, Sergeant, at ease!" Ed called. They shifted left feet out to a parade rest stance and put hands behind their backs, rigidly in place—the ceremonially correct response to the command.

"Oh, dammit, I mean *really* at ease. Sit down, relax. Ladies?" Ed pulled around a couple of the big easy chairs and offered them.

Soon all were seated in a broad circle of chairs, save Sarah, who chose to stand behind Ed's left shoulder, with her hand resting on it. He covered it with his right, briefly, and looked up to meet her eyes. He was pleased to feel her wrap her fingers around his briefly and squeeze. He returned his attention to Gunter. "Oberst, please reassure your sergeant, this is an informational meeting, not a fight. He looks like he's about to come out swinging."

Gunter relayed the information to Ermenthaller, feeling a tiny bit of his own apprehension ease with the colonel's statement. In German, he said, "Ermenthaller, relax. This American oberst is just going to tell us some information. I knew him in England in the last decade. He is known to be a good officer."

Beltran got to his point. "Oberst Kramer, you no longer have transport back to Germany, and you no longer have any weapons."

Sickness seized Gunter as he thought that he had been left behind. His eyebrows furrowed in confusion and fear.

"Your ship now resides at the bottom of Paramaribo Harbor," Ed continued.

After a moment to take in the information, Gunter spat, "You killed my boys!" He was on his feet explosively, clawing for his pistol. He moved so abruptly that none of the Americans had a chance to stand, and had their swords to contend with in any case. Ermenthaller was coming out of his own easy chair, but slowly, not understanding why his officer was suddenly enraged.

Sarah, standing alongside Ed's chair, seeing that this moment of confusion was the very moment she had waited a lifetime for, brought her gleaming Smith and Wesson out of her purse, whipping it in an overhead curve to bear on Gunter's chest. The sound of the hammer cocking into single-action position as she aimed was oddly loud in the roomful of velvet and leather. Everyone, including Ed and Gunter, froze.

Ed's expression told Gunter that he, too, had been completely caught off guard by her weapon. The cocked, heavy pistol was only feet away, and she could put six bullets in him in less than a second with that revolver. He could see the dull lead bullets in the cylinder, only the one behind the barrel being obscured.

Gunter's mind was reeling. Kucher had been on that ship. He was such a nice youngster. Gunter felt grief like a knife as he thought about the loss of the boy and the pain his family would experience upon learning of his death.

"Shut up. Sit down. You have killed your last victim, Nazi." Sarah was speaking clearly, in fluent German, her angry eyes locked on Gunter's. "You came here to take us for killing. You have a chance to live, but if you do not sit down, *I* will kill now. *Sitzen!*"

Ed looked up at her, loving admiration on his face. She was a constant surprise to him, which was not an easy feat.

Ermenthaller, too, was frozen, but his face showed instant comprehension.

"Every dog has one bite, eh, Oberst? Perhaps we *should* sit down?" Ed said. He looked at the other Marines, bent forward in their chairs in preparation for lunging, and then at Sandie's horrified face.

"Everyone, sit down," Ed instructed in his calmest, warmest voice. "Kramer, none of your boys was killed. A couple have real bad headaches, and one has a saber wound on one arm. They'll all heal fine."

Gunter dropped the hand that gripped the strap securing his holster flap and sagged back into his chair, gusting a great sigh of relief. Ermenthaller saw this and did the same.

Saber wound. Gunter twisted to give Lone a pointed look. Lone returned his look, put both hands up in an admitting shrug.

"Sarah, dear, would you put the pistol away, please? It's making people nervous." Across the circle, Hodgins grinned reflexively, and Lone chuckled. Ed and Sarah were already acting like an old married couple.

Sarah, eyes still intent on Gunter, elevated her muzzle, and, thumb on the hammer, pulled the trigger to lower it, uncocking the revolver, but let it hang alongside her, not putting it back in the purse. "If you please, I will keep it at the ready. I am not going to let these creatures kill another woman's husband."

Ed couldn't help but look up at her and smile with the implication of her words.

Sandie looked at the other woman with respect and a bit of pleading in her eyes. "Please, I realize you must have good reasons for what you feel, but I beg you, don't kill *this* one, if you can avoid it. I think *I* might want to keep *him*."

She spoke in Dutch, which Ermenthaller understood, and so Gunter's startled and hopeful look at the Dutch woman brought chuckles from every man in the room. Sandie's face flushed rosy.

"Oberst, do you even know *why* you're here?" Ed asked, sure that Kramer had been told nothing about the damning document the Reich was desperately seeking. "Hitler and his dirty band of criminals … do you have any idea why they sent you all the way to *Suriname* to find one lowly little Jewish family? Have you even thought about that?"

Gunter blinked, dumbfounded. He had no response. He didn't know. He had been so consumed by rage over the loss of his family, but now that he was here, in this extravagant home at the bottom of the world, none of it made any sense or felt at all like his life anymore.

"No," he replied honestly, looking down. "No, I do not." Then his eyes lifted to meet Ed's. "Do you?"

"I don't, but I have some idea," Ed answered him, meeting his eyes meaningfully. Sarah watched the men's exchange as if it were a game of tennis. "And I know that you have nothing waiting for you back home."

Gunter's brow furrowed in puzzlement. How could this American know this?

Ed fixed Gunter with his eyes. "We have listened to your men for a month now, drunk and sober," he grinned, "and even drugged and feverish."

Sarah had to turn her head to conceal her amusement at this. *Hannah, my love, you have saved us in more ways than you know.*

"We know, because your men know, that you lost your wife and daughter, and we know that the goddamned Reich didn't even let you go home to bury them."

Gunter's face crumpled into an expression of deep misery. His hands went to his face. Sarah watched, mystified. It seemed impossible, but her heart went out to this man who also had lost loved ones. Perhaps he could be reasoned with. Perhaps he was not entirely heartless after all.

"Your personal possessions are safe," Ed continued quietly, reassuringly, as Gunter composed himself. "So is your lockbox. Captain Krager's personal effects are already in his room at the Inn where he is staying. The *Klein-Seyditz* will never move again. She has been sunk, but she is shallow grounded. Krager's sailors can probably get some of their things, and he may be able to save some cargo."

The thought of his photo of Emma and Gerta at the bottom of the ocean made his stomach lurch, but he was as much a captive of the Reich as those poor souls he had sent off to Sobibor.

"This can only be a delay, Colonel. Sooner or later, the Surinamese must yield. We'll salvage our weapons, and we must do our jobs."

Ed smiled. "Your weapons weren't on board when the *Klein-Seyditz* went down. They aren't even in this country anymore." It was a very small white lie, but one worth telling. "And if *you* don't want to be, you don't have to be either."

Gunter jerked his head up. Somehow this American colonel who had arrived in the eleventh hour was still a few steps ahead of him.

"I have land in the next country over, Guyana," Ed went on, speaking carefully to maintain calm and maneuver the German oberst where he wanted him to go. "There is a need for convoy guards there and down into Brazil. Your contractor would add twenty percent for putting you up and feeding you between jobs. There aren't any women out there except two married ones, and you'd have to build your own housing and work to grow and raise food. However, it is hundreds of miles from any coast. It is *not* Suriname, where, if you left your service," he paused, treading carefully to avoid the word d*esert,* "you would be interned. Germans are not popular here, Oberst Kramer. Just think… You could be free. You could *live.*"

"How could we be guards without weapons?" Gunter's eyes gleamed with hope.

He was biting. Ed knew it was time to set the hook. He glanced at Sandie, and she was receptive enough to set it for him. She leaned over and put her hand on Gunter's arm, stark sympathy on her face. Gunter looked down at her hand, then covered it tentatively with his. It was their first touch, and both were obviously treasuring it. Ed kept his mouth shut until Gunter looked up again.

"We also know that the 'work' you have been doing for the Reich makes you sick. We know that you risked your life many times to warn people of raids. That is why, in the end, I decided to take the risks necessary to disarm you and offer you a chance at freedom." It would have been safer to lure you all into an ambush and kill you."

At this, Sarah felt compelled to speak up. "Don't you think, Oberst, that it would have been safer for all of us to lure you into an ambush and kill you? Colonel Beltran is offering you the opportunity, now, to live in peace. To let *us* live in peace. Surely, now, you too have something to live for?" She looked meaningfully at Sandie, who was still stroking Kramer's arm sympathetically.

"My men…" Gunter said, acutely aware that Ermenthaller watched him with laser focus. Ed was impressed to see a Nazi with such devotion to his troops.

"We know every damned one of your men would like to cut free and get out of the filthy business you've been doing," Ed said.

Gunter's head whipped around to Ermenthaller and began speaking in rapid-fire German. The NCO stiffened, then relaxed and nodded. Gunter continued, obviously explaining what was offered. Everyone held silence as they watched Ermenthaller's expression, seeming to warm to the prospect before them. He was hooked.

"How can we do this thing without weapons?" Gunter asked. "Does this contractor have arms?"

Ed finally relaxed for real. It was all over but the logistics. "*I* will be your contractor, Kramer. And I have *plenty* of weaponry to let you do nice, honest guard work."

Gunter finally broke into a smile. "And do they look like *our* weapons, Colonel?"

Hodgins and Lone chuckled. Sarah heaved the sigh of a lifetime's worth of relief.

Ed just smiled. He stood, walked over in front of Gunter, saluted, and extended his hand.

Gunter looked to Ermenthaller, who grunted, "*Gut!*" and nodded. Then he looked to Sandie, who smiled. He stood slowly, saluted, and firmly grasped the hand of freedom.

EPILOGUE

NOVEMBER 15, 1982
DIWALI, FESTIVAL OF LIGHTS
HOME OF THE BELTRANS
NIEUW NICKERIE, SURINAME

"**M**y love, you've outdone yourself," Ed sat back lazily in his chair, rubbing his belly with one hand and gesturing to the piles of empty plates before him with the other.

The extra tables and trays Sarah had placed in the dining room and living room to accommodate their eighteen guests now held the drippings that were all that remained of her pepper pot. It had been such a large pot of the savory stew, and with Yael, Lisjbet, and Louise all contributing dishes as well, she would not have imagined the party could eat all that food. But they had done so with gusto, even capping it all off with sweets in true Diwali fashion—Louise's *apfel kuchen* with a warm cream sauce, and plum tarts prepared by Hannah.

Hannah had actually rolled up her sleeves within minutes of arriving and, after exchanging tight hugs and tears of joy with her aunt, had begun baking, exclaiming, "It's Diwali! We must have pastries! Where is your rolling pin?"

Now, the dregs of Ed's special rum filled the tumblers that sat before each adult; they had officially emptied the Beltrans' stash, and the honey-colored liquid glowed in the candlelight. *I hate to see that go,* thought Sarah ruefully. Nonetheless, she was warmed by the chance to share it with those she loved most in the world. She scanned the table, hardly believing that she had Dr. Adelmann and Else; the Butlers and lovely Talia; Amos; Louise and Yael, both with their families; and Hannah, Rose, Josh, and Rachel, all in the same room. She struggled to remember the last time it had happened and realized it must have been the day they had arrived at Paramaribo Harbor on the *Bon Chance* more than forty years ago.

With regret, Sarah thought of Jacob and Rebecca, wishing that they had lived to see this day—Jacob had passed four years ago from a stroke, and Rebecca had died just last year, peacefully and in her sleep. The two would have been proud to see them all gathered around this table and to witness the legacy they had left behind. Sarah also sent a prayer up to Ezekiel, who should have been here to celebrate this joyous occasion with them.

"Auntie, are you okay?" asked Hannah, who had caught Sarah wiping a stray tear from the corner of her eye.

"Of course, yes!" said Sarah, dismissing her with her hand. "It's just, you know…"

"It's the day," Hannah finished. "I know. I feel it too. I was thinking about Papa and Mutter."

"So was I," Sarah said, reaching next to her to squeeze her niece's arm. Then she exhaled, took her tumbler of rum, and stood, catching Ed's eye. "Love, is it time, do you think?"

Ed, who had been in a bit of a stupor of digestion hopped up from his chair. "Damn, I almost forgot! Yeah, I'll get it."

He turned and left the room, and the chatter of their guests quieted as they realized that proceedings were about to begin. Ed re-entered the room in a moment, carrying a flat object wrapped in a soft blue blanket. He propped it up on the table and looked at his wife. "Take it away, my love!"

All eyes turned to watch Sarah, who beamed through eyes filled with joyful tears at the loved ones gathered around her, meeting each person's eyes one by one.

"Forgive me for such formality," Sarah said, and Amos met Louise's eye, chuckling. *How well they know me,* she thought.

"It honors and pleases Ed and me to have you all here in our home to spend this momentous day with us. Thank you all so much for being here. I don't have to tell you how important this day is in the story of all our lives, even those of us," here she paused to glance meaningfully at Louise, Rose, Rachel, and Josh, "who did not exist forty years ago."

She raised her glass. "Thanks to my dear Dr. Ben here, and to George and Lisjbet … without you, and without my dear niece and nephew, and to my Ed, our stories may have ended all those years ago." A single tear rolled down her cheek, and she hastily wiped it away. Ed rose, propping the flat object in his chair, and moved to stand beside her, fortifying her with a single hand placed gently on her back.

"Here, here," Amos said, raising his glass. Chuckles emitted from around the table, as it was obvious Amos was ready to down his rum, if only his auntie would wrap up her speech.

"In 1942, we lived on a knife's edge, my family and I," Sarah said, looking directly at Hannah. "For many months that year, we lived precariously balanced just on the edge of freedom, yet we wondered if we'd ever go over the edge, to finally live in peace. Until some brave men," at this Ed puffed up his chest and lifted his chin in mock self-satisfaction, "took it upon themselves to steal that freedom for us."

Ed gave Sarah's shoulder a squeeze, then maneuvered his way back to his chair to lift up the covered object and prop it vertically, once again, on the table.

"What is all this, Auntie?" Amos pressed. Even as a middle-aged man, her nephew was just as impatient and brash as ever.

"I'm getting there, Amos!" she laughed. "A few months ago, when Hannah and I first began to plan this Diwali gathering, to commemorate this important fortieth anniversary, I spoke to Ed of my wish to create a memorial, some symbol that will live on and honor all of you and that important day, long after we are all gone."

Ed nodded encouragingly.

"Of course, those of us who live here in Suriname have grown used to the familiar sight of the masts and broken deck of the *Klein-Seydtz* still visible in Paramaribo Harbor," Sarah continued. "But even the people who live in that city, who pass it every day, do not know the story—*our* story. It is *ours*. They do not know how a sunken Nazi ship could be the vehicle that delivered us to freedom. But it has."

Sarah looked at Ed and gave a slight nod, his cue to reveal the memorial. He nodded and delicately pulled the light-blue fabric up from the object he held, to reveal a painting. In the center foreground, a ship's mast rose from a quiet harbor. In the background, turbulent gray clouds parted to allow one ray of light to escape and shine upon the ship.

From the hush that had settled around the table rose Hannah's gasp.

"I call it 'Freedom's Edge,'" Sarah said quietly.

"Oh my," Hannah said. "Oh, Sarah…"

"You've bowled them over, my love," Ed said proudly. Applause rose from the table.

"*Prost!*" sang out George, and the others followed suit, raising their glasses and taking deep swigs of Ed's delicious rum.

"I want us all to sign it tonight," Sarah said, blushing from the praise and, perhaps, the warm liquor. "I want every one of us here tonight to memorialize this anniversary by adding your name. So that someday, your children, and their children, will know what we did, how we seized what was rightfully ours."

And with that, Sarah took the black pen that Ed offered her, and bent to scrawl her name.

THE END

ABOUT THE AUTHOR

Dr. Jagdish Goswami, or "Doctor G," as his colleagues know him, is a family physician, originally from India. He holds a Master of Public Health from the University of California at Berkeley.

Goswami was the Liaison Medical Officer for the British battleship *H.M.S. Fearless* when she docked in Guyana for commando jungle training in July of 1994. Fluent in English, Farsi, Hindi, Gujarati, Urdu, and Marathi, he was uniquely qualified to appreciate the linguistic richness of Guyana and Suriname, even receiving a commendation from the Lieutenant of the Royal Marines. He also served as a Hospital Liaison Medical Officer for the Pan American Health Organization's Polio Eradication Program while serving as a physician at St Joseph's Mercy Hospital in Guyana. Additionally, he worked in the Amazonian region of Rupununi in southern Guyana.

A historical tale told him by the local residents during the time he spent in Guyana provided him with the basic storyline for *Freedom's Edge*. Much of the color, complexity, and hair-raising adventure of inland travel in that area came from his own experiences. The sunken German transport (named *Klein Seyditz* in the book) is still visible in the harbor at Paramaribo.

Goswami's background in exotic places includes collaboration with fellow medical professionals in Yemen, Guyana, and the Sultanate of Oman. His travels have taken him to the Commonwealth of Independent States, Tajikistan, Kyrgyzstan, Uzbekistan, Kazakhstan, Turkmenistan, the United Kingdom, Germany, Israel, Canada, Guyana, Suriname, and the United Arab Emirates. He has done organizational emergency and medical needs planning for large public events and produced training materials for many audiences. In his first field assignment in his home country, he was stationed in a rural area where he had experience taking care of patients with tiger bites!

Now a United States citizen, Goswami has served as executive director for the Toiyabe Indian Health Project in Bishop, California; assistant professor at Samuel Merritt University; and instructor of both clinical medicine at the Touro University College of Osteopathic Medicine and Western medicine at the Acupuncture & Integrative Medicine College in Berkeley. He has worked among the indigenous Ameri-Indians in the Amazon on a social/economic/health project called "Hopeful Steps," a Guyana-based nonprofit organization, and created educational materials that were field tested and later adopted by the Guyanese Ministry of Health.

Currently, Goswami resides in California with his wife.

www.ingramcontent.com/pod-product-compliance
Lightning Source LLC
Chambersburg PA
CBHW020411260626
47156CB00007B/2324